Operation Trident Justice

the unedited debrief of Navy SEAL Karson Hunter

By:

Nathan Haston

Publication Information

Operation Trident Justice
the unedited debrief of Navy SEAL Karson Hunter

Copyright © 2019 by Nathan Haston

Created by Nathan Haston

Cover art © 2019 Haston Industries

All rights reserved. Printed in the U.S.A.

Library of Congress Cataloging-in-Publication Data is available.

ISBN 978-0-692-87779-1 (trade bdg.)

Typography by Nathan Haston

****

First Edition

For my uncles, my grandfathers, my ancestors and to those who have taken up the honor of serving our great nation. To my family past, present, and future, and to the God of the universe.

Peaceful Self Defense

In the year 2030, the world's leading governments began working on a system to disable all states from weapons, communications, defenses, security forces, commanding abilities, transportation; mainly disabling anything that gave a country power. Should a massive war erupt, this system of 'Peaceful Self Defense' would be enacted for the purpose of lives saved. The world has become so dangerous, that every nation either has, is developing, or desires weapons of mass destruction. The hope was to save lives and allow the allied United Nations to intervene to coax governments back on track.

In March of 2035, the United Nations headquarters was attacked by an unknown terrorist organization online. The virus cracked codes to built-in defense systems, activating them, killing people that came into its sights. The world's forces increased awareness and defenses, afraid of attacks by other terrorists, lone wolves, or even other nations. However, in the weeks after the assault, only death came up in the investigation. Nothing was taken. Nothing found. It was thought and confirmed to be a rogue attack; death for sport. An attack from nowhere by no one. It was placed on the back burner and defenses were toned down again. The perfect distraction.

Throughout 2035, numerous governments and countries disappeared off the face of the map. The term by U.S. intelligence agencies, Department of Defense, and Homeland Security: dark. Small governments. Mostly African and Middle Eastern nations, until finally, a banner rose over the rubble of the old. Becoming known as 'the Flag of Death,' every nation under its grasp had seen death on a genocide like scale. Nobody expected the events that were coming. With no one to target, no place to start, 'the Flag of Death' kept rising with no opposition. Now, nations could only wait it out, praying to their belief systems not to be destroyed, hoping that someone could find the source of the pandemic and crush it before more lives and nations are lost.

Aside

NATHAN HASTON

Nathan Haston is an American author, musician, actor, and director. Nathan adores his crafts and hopes you will join him in a new era of entertainment. Having trained with numerous agencies in emergency services as well as interactions with the United States Military, Nathan brings to you an understanding and respect of tactics and knowledge that keeps you on the edge of your seat. 'It's just plain cool.' What is normally pretend in the world of entertainment now becomes the raw truth. The world isn't easy. So we won't portray it as such!

Find Nathan's social media @nathanhaston or nathanhastoninquires@gmail.com

Operation Trident Justice

PROLOGUE - Special

Seriously, you guys do this before you deploy?

Yeah.

Every time?

After your first deployment, before your first time on this team... It's your first-time kid, just do it so I can get some food you twit!

This is so dumb. Hello. I-I... Uh... Humph. Yo! Man, do I really have to do this?

Yeah.

This is so stupid.

Hunter, do it, or you're on the bench. It's an essential item to be on the team.

Ugh, yawn! Hi. My name is 'I don't care! I kick ass and get paid. End of transmission.

SEAL PUP! DO IT RIGHT. PUT SOME THOUGHT INTO IT. I KNOW THAT'S HARD FOR A DUMB HIGH SCHOOL DROP OUT LIKE YOU BUT DO IT. OR ELSE!

Hey, dude! Don't scream in my damn ear, twat! Now it won't stop rigging. Dude, I don't even know what to say... I just want to go home and pass out before this deployment. OW! Alright, I'm recording!

Hello, my name is Kadin Karson Hunter. You can call me Karson. This recording is in case I'm killed in action on deployment or something. We make one after boot camp and it goes in our file. I guess it's... I don't really know why, except that we all have to do it for our records. Okay. My nickname, the name my family gave to me when I joined is Serval. Apparently, I'm small. Smaller than any other Special Forces warrior in the United States military, and I guess other men. *I* like to say it's my boyish charm! Servals are small. I'm fast, and agile. Servals are fast and agile. And I always land on my feet. I fell off of the rappelling station in boot camp and dropped like a ton of rocks. Two hundred and seventeen pounds with my seventy pounds of gear. I landed on my feet doe! Hurt like hell, but I landed on my feet! Like a serval!

Anyways, I've attained the rank of Petty Officer First Class in the United States Navy by way of rigorous work, even though I'm still a SEAL candidate, never finished BUDs. Prodigy, I guess. It's kinda weird, anyways... Hours upon hours of range time achieving above excellent scores in weapons of all sorts, becoming one of the best shooters in the military. Day after day in the gym to condition me to all kinds of rigorous tasks that could be sprung on me. Miles and miles in the water for the water missions. I love the water! Jump after jump for parachuting-HALO (High Altitude, Low Opening), HAHO (High Altitude High Opening), LALO (Low Altitude, Low Opening) jumps for air insertion. I've run so many miles for ground infiltration. That's the one thing I hated and still hate. All the running… Never ends. Run. Run. Run! I've learned how to fly aircraft should that need arise.   Let's see, what else can I bore you with? Martial arts are fun for me, having learned from a young boy to the deadly tactics by the SEALs, I'm a force to be reckoned with. I can kill you so many different, creative ways, especially with my ka-bar. That's my knife. Let's move on to something else.

I am a Special Forces operative for the Navy SEALs, called the United States Navy SEALs High Profile Threat Neutralizing Force. That's a pretty long-ass name, so we give it a long ass acronym to try and shorten up the long-ass name. USNSHPTNF. Basically, SEAL Team Six does not exist, HPTNF is the real SEAL Team Six, but for your sake, my job is operator in a sub-section of SEAL Team Six. We deal with everything. Insertion, hostage rescue, threat neutralizing, etc. Any threat to homeland and world security, we deploy to protect America and the world.

Integrating into this elite group of men. Indeed I've joined a family. I guess I've found myself here. They aren't just my friends or teammates. They are my brothers. And for some reason, they've taken a liking to me. Except when I pull stunts like at the beginning of this…

THUD

Ow! Shut the hell up!

THUD

Ow!   I've never heard face to face, but I've overheard a conversation accidentally while waiting for my Commanding Officer to give me my new assignments. Had I not exceeded in my abilities as an operator, I'd have been on just another SEAL Team. Don't get me wrong; that is a high honor right there, and I respect all my brothers from any branch. But I wanted to be the best. To make a huge difference. They say that there is a "spark" in me that they haven't seen but in a few operators. That's why I was fast-tracked to my position. Above excellent performance and a drive to be the best in the nation, and perhaps the world. My team and I have gained the attention of our government leaders, especially the President of the United States. My leaders see me too! SEALs have been in the spotlight for civilians recently.

My team has received deployment after deployment because of our skills to provide effective and major history-shaping results. The deployments I've been on have been to Europe to investigate a major event. My performance has gained me some of the attention that the team receives which is barely any in the first place. Mostly a 'good job' from the other guys at the bar or at a buddy's house telling stories! All of this attention on me, I am the best weapon these people, my country has ever created. I don't want the praise. That is not why I joined. I joined to serve my nation. However, the praise makes me want to be the best that much more. I need to be the best! I need to be the best I can be for my team. To keep them safe. It's not about my making it back home; it's about helping my brothers to see their families again. Like I said, I have many talents; weapons, tactics, medicine, aviation, swimming… I can cross countries, I can talk and act, blend and evade, hide and attack, become and forget, appear and disappear. I can love and hate, I can build and destroy, I can… I can… Uh, well, you get the point.

I'm not saying I'm invincible. I'm still a man. I'm still human. I make mistakes. I've missed my target, I've been caught, I've been hit, I've been sad, happy, pissed, screwed. I've been everything an average person is. I learn quickly, and I have common sense. If I mess up, I'm punished severely-

Hooyah to that, bro! Ain't we all!?

And then I never make the mistake again. I am normal. I'm trying to say; I've put blood, sweat, and no tears to get to where I am. Let that be a lesson to you whoever watches and listens to these dumb recordings when we send them to God knows where. If you work hard, you can achieve what others say you can't. You can become the person you want to be. Hard work pays off! Maybe then, you wouldn't be behind the desk listening to these.

Now, I'm going to probably face all of these challenges and utilize them in real-life situations. Evil is brewing off in the distance that the United States feels it can't stop on its own, nor stop if it becomes what it shouldn't. I may fail. My flight response versus my fight response may kick in; I may die. Who cares? Not like I have anything to live for anyway. Fresh out of high school. I dropped out to avoid the shame of what happened. My parent's hate me for who I am and who I've become, and now, at nearly twenty years old, I am a Petty Officer First Class in a warrior group that is just as elite as me. Even though I can do all of this, I don't want to. I wish I had a normal life. I wish I could stay with the one I love, the one who made me feel special like I did before. Oh well. Who am I kidding? This is the calling I was put on this earf to do! People need killing! No other place I'd rather spend my life! This is my life, hooyah!

Everyone else calls me unique, so I guess the thing I believe is true. From the beginning, I knew I was special. It looks like I'll have to show how special I am in my Special Forces atmosphere and career. Who knows where my life will take me. You, listening to this, will just have to follow along and find out! My first deployment with Special Forces. I call it Cataclysm. Let's do this!

FIRST MILITARY FILE RECORDING-KADIN KARSON HUNTER, PETTY OFFICER FIRST CLASS, UNITED STATES NAVY HPTNF

Hunter, out.

****

Karson took his headphones out laughing as the he boarded the plane to England.

Bye America! Hope to see you soon!

****

Cataclysm

"Ladies and Gentleman! Please, if you would so kindly, take a seat. Let us begin!" Secretary-General Jun-seo Ch'ŏn stood and requested of everybody. Representatives from every United Nation leisurely moved to their seats.

Down seventy-three floors in the lobby at the security desk as well as throughout the newly designed, one hundred ninety-three story United Nations' headquarters, one floor for every nation, UN Soldiers kept solid guard of the world leadership building.

"What are they talking about today, mate?" Corporal Tayler, an Australian Soldier, asked as Corporal McKinney of Scotland checked in another diplomat.

"There ye are, sir. Have a great day." He turned in his spinning chair and looked at his friend resting atop of a file cabinet. "Maybe one United Government. Probably the Middle East again to be honest. You know they united under one flag. Created a United Middle East, they did."

"Seriously? It sounds like the end times are near." Tayler said, a fake shudder ravaging his body.

Laughing, McKinney threw a squishy ball back and forth. "Yeah, no kidding. Looks like the Bible may have been correct. Maybe it's a bunch of hogwash. Who knows? Wup, hold that thought. My computer just glitched out a wee bit."

"Let me see!" The Soldier stepped closer to the monitor. "Let's go down to the security center and check it out, aye? Tayler asked opening the door and walking around in front of the desk, giving McKinney puppy eyes.

He held Tayler's gaze for as long as he could with a straight face then broke smiling. "Alright. Alright, dude, damn!" He said, cuffing his friend atop his helmet. "You're good at that. Got a special 'fwend' at home, aye?" He chuckled. "Hey, Danny?" The Scotsman called, standing from his chair and grabbing his rifle.

A security guard turned around from the fountain. "Yes?" He said, prowling over to the desk.

"Quit pissing in the water and come monitor the desk, would you? We have something to check out." McKinney said, hopping over the front of the checkpoint to grab his rifle, leaping over again only to wipe out. "OW!" He shouted, gaining the attention from some passersby.

The guard ignored the shenanigans hoping to make something of himself. Tayler on the other hand was rolling on the ground laughing. "As you wish!" The guard walked around the desk, put in his code to get through the door and took the Soldiers' post.

"Can we stop and get something to eat when we get back, mate?"

"Holy boobs, dude! Look at that girl!" McKinney slammed the back of his hand into Tayler's vest.

"Where? Oh, wow! Dude, she's one to make me crack a fat!"

"What?" He laughed. "What does that mean, Tayler?"

Tayler gave the most hilarious, innocent face. "Oh... you don't say that? Means hard-on. Erection... Ya know?"

"Oh! You Aussi's are weird, man!"

"You don't say that?" They slithered behind the indoor trees to gain a better advantage for spying on the unsuspecting female sex. "No!" Corporal Tayler breathed.

"Oh look! That's her boyfriend!" McKinney cooed.

The Soldiers watched on as the two embraced in a kiss.

"Aw, noosh!"

"Noosh? Dude, English." Grabbing Tayler's face and squeezing it, shaking his head back and forth, he said: "Do you speaky the engly?"

"Means cute! What say you we go and break them up?"

McKinney bounced on the balls of his feet. "And maybe get a piece of that tail? She'd be a great lay!"

"Bloody oath, mate! Bloody oath."

Corporal McKinney rolled his eyes as the Soldiers started to walk over to the couple.

"Who gets the girl, mate?"

"Threesome? We're close enough, eh?" McKinney said matter of factly.

Tayler thought about it for a second. "I guess that's true. Deal!"

"HELP! SOMEBODY HELP US! THEY'RE SHOOTING US!" Screams pelted the soldier's ears before they could reach the lovebirds.

Both Soldiers stopped, Tayler drawing his pistol and McKinney raising his automatic weapon removing his safety, finger on the trigger, swiveling, trying to identify the threat. Both moved to cover under the marble wall taking a side and looking around the lobby area.

"Report of shots fired. Tayler, use your rifle man! We're not in CQC!"

"Mate! It feels like close-quarters combat! The weapon systems are activating, we're stuck here." Tayler called back to McKinney switching from his secondary to primary weapon.

"What? Where? HOW?" McKinney looked around like a bobblehead.

Corporal Tayler pointed to the ceiling. "The ceiling guns!"

"Let's get back to the-"

Again the Soldiers were stopped in their tracks, this time as the weapon systems opened fire on civilians. The two sprinted back towards their command post and dove into the fountain as the couple from earlier was impaled by flaming lead as well as the desk security guard who was unaware of any danger.

"OF COURSE HE DOESN'T SEE ANY THREAT!" McKinney shouted. "USELESS WAKNER!" The two listened as people died instantly around them. Not much sooner as it had started, the death streak stopped. The Soldiers were shaking, afraid to move.

"What just happened!?" McKinney screamed.

"Shhh! Maybe it was when your computer malfunctioned, now shush! Listen…" The fire alarm started going off.

"People are going to be filling the lobby any moment! We have to warn them, or they'll be target practice, Tayler!"

"We have not a strategic possibility that we survive this, man… We have to stay put. Maybe we can shoot a couple of guns?"

More people, unaware of the massacre that had just taken place started filing down into the lobby. As they did, the ceiling guns yet again found their marks, terror in the greatest capacity set in and unleashed.

Corporal Taylor stood and screamed for the people to run back upstairs, and as he did, a bullet connected to his head. He fell face-forward over the railing of the fountain, and McKinney pulled him down into the fountain as a bullet impacted right where he had been before. "Tayler? TAYLER!" He shook the young Australian man to no avail.

He stood and shot at a weapon system that turned faster than any man-made machine should possibly turn, and was pelted with a barrage of bullets and had to duck back down to survive.

"AHHH!" Tayler shouted, scaring the snot out of McKinney who dyed the fountain yellow.

"You just pissed!" Tayler laughed, somehow finding a way to be joyful in this situation!

"I THOUGHT YOU WERE DEAD, MAN! DON'T DO THAT TO ME! HOW CAN YOU LAUGH RIGHT NOW, YOU PSYCHO?" He started hitting Tayler, who laughed a little harder, fending off the blows.

"Helmet." Tayler patted his. "Hurt like hell, though, mate. You definitely don't want to get shot."

"We have to find a way up to the representatives." McKinney put his head back in the fight. "And don't tell anyone I pissed my pants, bro. I'll kill you myself."

"You cried a little too, mate. Did you miss me?"

"No, I'd have had that lassie all to myself then, man." McKinney turned. "The representatives."

"That's on the seventy-third floor, bro. How do we get up there with all this happening?"

"All troops, the building is under attack. Multiple civilian casualties. Shots fired. Contact local police and EMS. Scramble Defense Forces. Alert all. Our nation, our world, it's under attack!" The Soldiers dropped back down, looking around for somewhere to go. "The buildings weapon systems have gone on the fritz. All need to duck and cover, protect anyone and everyone you can. Do not come downstairs. Safeguard the representatives at all costs. Take them up."

"I'm staying right here, man!" Tayler said, giving up.

"Same. There's nothing we can do. Except... try shooting the guns?"

"I already tried that!"

"It's worth another shot!" The Soldiers stayed flat under the railing of the fountain and fired at robotic, man-made death machines, trying to break free and lay aid upstairs.

****

"Right. Today, we are going to be discussing the issues regarding the Middle East. While I am not too worried about the United Middle East, I am concerned about terrorist activities within the world. The flag of this nation represents the pirate flags of the past. History shows that pirates follow no rules. No laws. They do not discriminate in killing. This United Middle East, we have no contact. Nations include Saudi Arabia, Iraq, Iran, Yemen, Oman, Egypt, Sudan, Eritrea, Somalia, United Arab Emirates, Turkmenistan, Afghanistan, Pakistan, Uzbekistan, and Kazakhstan. I'm sure there are others. A group of nations like this means they have more nuclear weapons in different areas. A plethora of radical beliefs leads us to believe that they are uniting their militaries, as well as with the major flow of western radicals from allied nations to the Middle East, we fear that this threat could far outnumber our coalition forces. Along the lines of military power brings about control of all resources traded with the rest of the world. They can decide at a moment's notice, if they don't like something, to sanction the world. They become the most powerful nation, rather than Russia, or the U.S., or England."

"Mr. Secretary-General, I'm sure some good can come about to it as well!" The Indian representative spoke up.

"Yeah. I agree. Maybe less war comes about. Better cultural diversity means a learning experience for people, and along the lines of learning, better educational abilities. Maybe the ones in support of the UN and allied world outnumbers the radical. We shouldn't jump to harsh accusations without establishing contact. We could attack a peaceful force by mistake." The Argentinian spoke.

"I would like to say that-"

"I should have stipulated; these are all speculations." Ch'ŏn interrupted the Wales representative.

"Precisely. You say we do not have relations with this nation? No contact?" Wales started.

"Correct." Ch'ŏn nodded.

"Well, other than waiting for it to become another North Korea, we should send UN ambassadors into the nation's capital with UN soldiers for protection, and peacefully begin talks with the vast new united superpower. What is it called?" Wales completed his thought, looking at his friend from England who agreed.

"Again, we do not know." Ch'ŏn was becoming irritated.

"Well, let's find out!" England hit the desk. "We're wasting time with these meetings. We need to get a handle of this. This could be a chance for peace."

"Everybody slow down." The Secretary General finally raised his voice, his anger getting the better of him.

"Where is the capital?" South Africa asked.

"I would assume it would be in Saudi Arabia. This was the richest nation to begin with. Possibly still is the most prosperous region now." The American spoke up, his hand raised.

"Then let's start finding out and sending people there!" The Russian representative added in.

The doors at the back of the room opened, and a UN Colonel entered, flanked by two armed Soldiers.

"Colonel, may I ask why you are here?" Ch'ŏn asked as the rest of the room turned their attention to the additional heavily armed troops standing in the hallway.

"I need all of you to exit this room immediately, follow these Soldiers, and head up to the roof of this structure, where a helicopter will be waiting to take you out of this area of the area."

"What is the meaning of all of this?" The Canadian representative stood. Frightened faces followed suit.

"We are all not safe up here. It is time just to do as you are told for once, and exit the building."

A Black Hawk helicopter flew by the window. As it did, a missile fired from above at the chopper caused the pilot to take drastic action, the door gunner opening fire. The Pilot failed to act on time and the explosion hit the door, killed the gunner and sent bullets flying into the building hitting multiple people. The chopper lost control and tried to turn, but as it did, another missile hit the tail and spun the helicopter, impaling the gasoline line and rotors into the room turning the room from a beautiful bright yellow to a dark red as people ran and were struck by high-speed metal rods.

"Everyone, move now!" The Colonel shouted, diving from the room. "Rooftop compromised. Send them to the basement!" He yelled into his radio.

Screams filled the air, and no one could hear any instructions being shouted. The first wave of people made it to the elevators as troops held the doors open. These elevators were granted access to the heavily protected basement. As the doors began to close, the people inside saw the gun systems in the ceiling drop down and start firing upon the unarmed and armed people on the seventy-third floor. The troops began to open fire on the systems, but they were overrun with barrage after barrage of bullets, and soon, every air breather was snuffed out. The forty who made it to the elevators were crying, screaming, calling loved ones and colleagues. The elevators, however, halted on the tenth floor and opened to a wall of UN uniformed Soldiers. Everyone breathed somewhat relieved now as they started filing out of the elevators towards their safekeeping.

These representatives, however, were face to face with the first glimpse of an invisibly hidden enemy. The UN Soldiers raised their weapons revealing their true intentions. The unarmed innocence stood like deer in headlights, some pleading, begging for their lives. Some of the more pitiful tried to run.

And the bullets flew, loud, fast, hot, and sharp as they ripped through, pushing lives from the planet, killing everyone from the elevators. The troops began walking through the building, killing everyone, taking no mercy and no hostages. A terrorist attack like no other. With the UN systems in disarray, information hacked, viruses hitting vital systems and fighting into other nations' databanks, as well as the death of the entire

General Assembly, a never before seen assault was ready to be launched in Europe, and eventually, the world itself.

A large dark man stood in front of the entire wave of enemy troops and stooped down to the last living soul in the building and smiled as he drew his long, thick, knife and put the blade to his victim's throat and mounted her like she was an item. Once his satisfaction was reached and his victim writhed beneath him, he drew the blade along her skin, eventually severing her head from her body. Everyone laughed and chanted, amused by the brutality this new threat offered and the promises and rewards they would receive once this new crusade was accomplished. The man stood and walked from the horrible scene, placing his blade back and looked out the window as simultaneous attacks ravaged England. A phone was handed to him, and he hissed his words into the phone, giving his report.

"Supreme Leader. The spark has ignited."

****

CHAPTER 0 - The Art of Deception

"So, everyone is going, Commander?"

"Yes, Sailor. Everyone goes. I know you're new here, but when the world is in trouble, we are the first to go." Commander Sanders dozed.

"No, I understand that I just didn't think for something so little as a building to be attacked is a reason for Navy SEALs to go. We have more important things to do, do we not? Saving the world? Are all the teams going?"

"This could be 'world saving.'" He mocked the young SEAL. "We have actionable intel that this is more severe of an attack than it has been let on to be. We need more intel. So they chose the best for the job. We don't know exactly what happened, so that's why the president chose us. The other teams are engaged elsewhere. So, we're here to help the US know what happened. Along with the world, the only US troops going are Team Three; that's us ya know?"

"I'm new, not stupid!" The newbie said.

"Team Six is in the area too. Try not to make us look bad, Karson. I want my free ticket into the elites." Sanders stated.

"Oh! Team Six sounds so cool!" Karson said!

"Yeah... You'll have to wait a few years SEAL pup. Probably 'til you grow which is never, so shut up and just do as you're told. And... Try not to shoot us in the back."

"Do or die!" Karson whispered.

"Thirty seconds, gentlemen." The British Osprey pilot called back. "We'll be landing you on the ground. Work your way up. Intel reports minor resistance if any is left. The majority of the fighting should be completed. Find survivors. Kill the enemy should they be there. Try and find one to capture, and watch out for the internal building security systems."

"Why England?" Karson piped up, unable to stay quiet, looking outside at all the sights.

"Huh?" Sanders jerked out of his daze.

"I like England. Never been. And it's cool, but why a British pilot?"

"Why a British Pilot? Because the attack happened on British soil. My country. You are only here at Her Majesty's request for a second opinion of the incidents. Our jurisdiction. You are helping us."

"Pfft. We follow our own orders." Karson shifted in his seat.

"Hooyah!" The SEAL on Karson's left poked his head around the restraints. His name was Erickson.

"Who gave the first opinion on the attack investigation?" Commander Sanders stood up, readying for the upcoming day's events.

"French Foreign Legion. Working hand in hand with Her Majesty's military. Wanted a group of all nationals, not one nation's troops. Now it's our turn." The British Soldier at the back ramp said.

"Ten seconds." The pilot looked back at the security force.

"Hunter. Up." Commander Sanders said.

"Whu- Oh, yeah!" Karson rose, kneading his boots into the ground, unable to stifle his excitement.

"Awe… is SEAL Pup nervous?" Chief Owens busted Karson's balls.

"No, sir! Not at all! Excited more like it. Ready to do some good! Hooyah?"

Owens smiled. "Well, let's go then." The ramp opened; the Osprey landed. The SEALs were out. However, there was no building. Just a fence, blocking a road into the city.

The SEALs instantly were uneasy. "What?" Karson asked, looking up at Erickson, head cockeyed.

Chief Owens shouted above all the noise. "Hey! We don't see a building. We are American Forces. We do not like to be ball tapped like this. Tell us the plan! Now!"

"Relax, mate. You take a van in. Too dangerous to fly right now with the enemy scoured through the city. Country by the reports. As you approach the building, you will drop underground into a parking garage and work your way up into the building. You're here to analyze everything you see and uncover anything we missed. Find a motive. Why is the Middle East so quiet? Why the UN Council?" The Soldier at the ramp lifted off into the sky as the turbines spun up, leading the Osprey into another mission.

Karson looked at the other SEALs as Chief Owens and Commander Sanders spoke to each other. "Men, mount up in that van. We'll be right there." Owens said over Sander's shoulder. Sanders walked a few paces away and radioed to Navy Command.

Karson got in first only to be pulled out onto the ground. "Hey! The hell man?" Karson scrambled to his feet puffing out his chest.

"Awe, look how cute you look!" He pinched Karson's cheeks. "You're smaller than us, my man. You sit in the middle." Erickson smiled, hopping in the van and scooting over to the right side window, patting the seat next to him. "Your turn."

"I don't like the middle, man." Karson defiantly crossed his arms and looked at his teammate behind him. "You take it."

"I don't think so." The two hundred and thirty pounds of muscle African American Navy SEAL grabbed Karson by his vest strap and belt and hoisted him in the van. "You're barely a Navy SEAL, Pup. You don't make orders."

"Ya know..." He readjusted his pants. "Just because I'm not freakishly large like most of you and maintain an average body size, you're gonna be sorry one of these days for lifting me up like that."

"Maybe when... Ha. Sorry. If you're a higher rank, but for now..." He smacked Karson on the helmet. "I think I'll continue to mess with you!"

Erickson laughed.

Chief Owens and Commander Sanders closed the doors behind them as they climbed into the van with the driver and his teammate entering in the front.

"Ha! He's in the shotgun with a shotgun!" Erickson chuckled.

"So amusing." Karson rolled his eyes.

"Team, listen up," Owens said without turning around. "Erickson and Walt, I want you to open your windows and have your guns at the ready. Any sign of trouble, you end the threat. We operate here on the assumption that we kill, or be killed. Understand?"

"Aye, sir."

"I've got our ten," Walter said.

"If hell comes to pass, SEAL Pup, you have our six. I read up on your file. You have the best shot out of this entire van. Don't let us down."

"You have me, sir!" Karson said, spinning around, his rump right in Erickson's face, who in turn, smacked it as hard as he could, flopping Karson into the trunk space. "Ow." He muttered as he sat up to roaring laughter.

"Alright, I needed that but all hands on the ready. I doubt we have any trouble, but if we do, you know what to do. We're a team whose got each others' backs. Any questions?"

All SEALs shook their heads no.

"Good. Here we go. Driver, we're ready to move."

"Good on ya, mate!" He said.

The ride into the city was even less suspenseful than the spontaneous speech, but it did give Karson the chance to see just how much devastation had been inflicted to England.

"We haven't had a devastating event on our homeland since World War two, friends. It's pretty disheartening."

Buildings were smoldering like the towers from September 11th. People slinked through the street, bloody bodies searching for their loved ones. Soldiers and police on foot, horseback or in vehicles patrolled the streets with martial law authority. What stuck out to Karson were the long black bags that lay throughout the street and people with different colored tags on their bodies, some moaning, some laying still with people tending to their wounds. Some were bleeding out and screaming for help, only to be ignored as their last breaths were taken.

"What are those bags in the street and why aren't people helping those people?" Karson whispered.

Walt looked back. "Those are body bags, man. And those tags on their bodies? Those are triage markers. England's is similar to ours. Green means priority three, which means they can be helped later because they are practically unharmed. Yellow is priority two meaning they can wait a little longer, but they have some wounds that need tending to. Red is priority one, meaning they need immediate attention, and black means dead or are beyond help."

"That means they are going to be sentenced to death if no one helps them."

"It means, they are already dead. There is no helping them, Karson. That's the reason it's black."

"This isn't fair, man. These people were innocent and yet they were slaughtered in their streets. It's a load of bologna."

"Hey, I feel ya. But we have a job to do. Don't let your emotions in it."

"There is the building, straight ahead." The driver said as the van started to descend below the street.

"Why is this parking garage still able to be accessed?" Sanders asked the driver.

"We have that same question. Must have been how they got in and exited."

"Must have." Sanders agreed.

The SEALs exited the van and immediately saw the extremity that foreshadowed what ay still come. A possible aftershock. Entering the building, the SEALs passed carnage, broken glass, and bomb scraps, just like in the street. Alarms were still going off, but no one was around to heed their warning.

"You know what I've noticed about war?" Karson crouched with his brothers behind him. He put his corner shot weapon around the wall. The corner shot lets a Soldier stay behind cover while the tip of the gun rotates so he can see what enemy lies in wait and take them out without any danger to his well-being. "Clear. I've noticed in war that noise is one of the major aspects. You have gunshots, screams, agony, and that piercing fire alarm. This is pretty awesome when you have people to shoot at. But no one is here!"

"I like your eagerness to protect the stars and stripes but have patience, SEAL Pup. You'll see your fill of this soon enough. You'll have plenty of 'wet' missions to come. This one just happens to be dry. Maybe that is a good thing." Owens tapped his shoulder to move around the corner.

"I'm not saying I want to kill people; I just want to do well. Earn my title. Blood or not, I just want to make this all stop. These are innocent people." He motioned to the corpses on the floor. "Were…" He trailed off.

"I thought you were crazy for this work?" Erickson asked as they stopped at another corner.

"I am… Within the bounds of protecting the United States. Not killing the innocent. Freeze!" Karson shouted at six heavily armed men.

"Lower your weapon, kid. Captain Richardson, SEAL Team Six. Identify yourself?"

"SEAL Pup, sir." Karson bounced on his heels.

"What the kid is saying… Chief Owens, Team Three. Pleasure, sir."

"Yeah, nice. I-" Richardson started to speak when he was interrupted.

BANG

BANG

Nonstop machine-gun fire pelted the walls around the Americans, striking Sanders to the armor plates covering his neck and spine.

"Ahh, God! I'm hit!" He said as he hit the ground gasping for air.

"CONTACT!" Richardson shouted, pointing behind a now crouched Karson who had already folded his body so he could aim behind him, his feet facing Richardson, his weapon facing the soon to be dead then

POP

POP

POP

Four enemies. Three simultaneously fired bullets. Karson looked up at Richardson and smiled. "What?"

Richardson looked at Karson's smoking gun.

"Kid, you're on me!" He patted the young SEAL who stifled a roar of success!

Take that ass kisSanders.

Karson stole a glance at Sanders, who stood wide-mouthed. "He didn't even finish BUDs, sir! How can he be-"

"Don't care. He's on me. Let's go. Owens, you take the right half of the building, we have left. Head to the roof, we'll meet you there, unless otherwise engaged. Stay in contact, ready if something changes. Channel nine. Gather any intel you can so we don't have to come back here."

"Aye, sir. Hunter…" Owens said to the star-struck young SEAL Candidate.

"He's on my watch now. Go." Richardson ordered Team Three, spinning Karson around by his shoulders. "Stay in the present, kid."

"Sorry!" Karson tried to recover himself, wiping the 'drool' off his facial expression.

"He's my SEAL, **Dick**son." Sanders pipped in.

Salty much? Karson thought. *Not my fault I'm better than you!*

"Excuse me?" Richardson turned and thrust himself into the sore loser's face. "I believe you meant Captain Richardson and forgot that I outrank you… By a whole lot. Now piss off and do your job. You're not going to make it on Team six, Daniel. Stop trying. Let the younger generation have a chance. We serve America, not ourselves. Go." Richardson pointed to his already maneuvering team.

"He's still got so much to learn!" Sanders called after them. "You're gonna get him killed, or worse, your entire team!"

"I'll teach it to him!" Richardson kept walking.

Karson followed the Team Six SEALs as they formed up facing the way they would be traveling.

"Hunter, you're the only one with the corner shot rifle, surprisingly. Hand it to me." Richardson caught up.

"Respectfully, Captain, as much as I want to follow your orders, I'm gonna keep my weapon on me. You're all more trained than I am anyways, to be determined, and so I'm gonna stick with my gear loadout."

"Give the Captain your weapon, kid." A voice behind him spoke.

Karson twisted around as a large hand lunged for his weapon and Karson wrapped the larger SEALs arm around his back. "Don't touch me, man," Karson said in his ear.

The others raised their weapons, shocked that anyone would act the way he was. When just given the opportunity of a lifetime.

"I'm gonna shoot you, SEAL Pup! Stand down!" Another SEAL barked.

"What is your name?" Karson asked him.

"Viper." He spat. "Release my brother! NOW!"

"Alright, everybody stand down. Relax, we're all brothers. I've been around Karson before." Richardson looked at Karson approvingly.

"DUCK, SIR!" Karson shouted, throwing the SEAL he held into an oncoming enemy combatant, then running his knife through the stunned man's throat.

"Team, let's move." Richardson hung back and pulled Karson to him. "Try and capture an enemy next time." He instructed.

"Why?"

"Because we need information. This situation, it's all very strange. Nothing like this has happened on this magnitude. We need to know why, and if it's isolated or something else." Richardson responded. "You ask too many questions."

"Aye, sir." Karson nodded. "Sorry about that, I just want to stand out... Won't disrespect you again, sir."

"Don't ever apologize, son. SEAL Team Six is about adapting and innovating. Keep it up, though, do make sure you follow my orders. I've been doing this a lot longer than you, son. I watched you in BUDs. I'm impressed with your ability then and now."

"Thanks." Karson smiled. "Uh, sorry. Thank you, **sir.**" He followed Richardson into a cafeteria. Tables all around.

The SEALs spread out, staggering throughout the room. Rather than stay in a single file line like SWAT members providing a range of targets, the SEALs were trained to create harder targets to hit, allowing for someone to take out an enemy before allied death. The team was nearly through the room when Karson ran straight into Richardson.

"The hell, man?" Karson said stopping.

"Team, halt!" A laser danced around Karson's helmet. Richardson lunged, grabbed the young candidate, and spun him around a pillar as a bullet smacked into the exposed pillar Karson had been blocking a moment before. "SNIPER!" Richardson called!

"Anyone have eyes?" Viper said through his mics as his teammates took cover around the atrium.

"Hunter... Corner shot. Find the target." Richardson said as he scanned the second floor. No response. "Hunter?" Richardson looked behind him where the smaller man should have been, but he wasn't. He looked up the stairs directly across from the pillar and saw a boot disappearing over the crest of the final step. Karson spun around a corner and fired shot after timed shot at the sniper to back him off of the opening to the first floor. He maneuvered around rubble and bodies, closing the distance to his prey. The sniper turned and aimed at Karson who used his gun like a sword and knocked the barrel away, spun his rifle behind him, struck the enemy's shoulders around and jumped onto the shooter's back. Karson wrapped his arms around the man's neck, struggling. The man slammed Karson around, knocking Karson's head against a wall, Karson's helmet taking most of the strike, but his brain still taking a blow. Luckily, Richardson was on Karson and the enemy fast before the sniper could break free of Karson's lessened grip. He pulled both Karson and enemy to the floor. Karson untangle himself from around him and drove his pistol into the back of the man's head.

"English?" Richardson shouted. Karson started looking around and walked away. The man rolled over and looked up at Richardson. "Oh, you think this is funny?" Richardson bent down and started pelting the man with punches.

"Can I try?" Karson padded over with a chair from the adjacent café.

Richardson looked over his shoulder. "Excuse me?"

"I-I have an idea about getting him to talk," Karson said, standing now beside Richardson and in front of the detained.

"Yeah? How's that." Richardson asked flatly, anger starting to get the best of him. "You know what, no. Forget what I said about getting him to talk."

Karson stepped in between the SEAL and combatant. "Let me try."

Richardson looked at the enemy who had now been thrown into the chair by the other SEALs, one detaining him with wire ties to the chair. "What if he-"

"Gives me a Cuban Necktie? I can hold my own, sir. I believe I have shown you that." Karson pressed.

"Oh, you have far more to prove, my boy, but I would be lying if I said I was not impressed." He grabbed Karson's right shoulder. "Alright. Get to it."

"He won't talk if you're all here. I think you should continue on. I'll catch up!"

"Alright... I just don't see why we can't shoot his kneecaps out."

"He'd faint, sir. Too much pain. That would be in opposition to our objective. Plus, this isn't Hollywood. We can't do the same old thing over and over and over again, people would get bored. The reader of this story would be expecting us to torture him. We can torture others later. For now, I have to get him to talk. Sir, we're wasting time arguing. Enemies might be coming. Let me try my idea. I'll have the information in ten minutes at most, or I'll give this guy a Cuban necktie."

"Ten minutes," Richardson said. "Team, let's go."

"Aye, sir." Karson smiled and waved as his team shuttled by. *My team. SEAL Team Six. Finally!*

"All alone? What, are you going to torture me, little boy? Why'd they give you a gun? You look like a sixteen-year-old!"

"You like that about me don't you?" Karson circled him like a shark.

"My nation has trained me into a high pain tolerance. Your petty laws won't allow you to reach anywhere near the required atrocities to get me to sing. Your art of torture is obsolete."

"Oh... No papi! I'm going to give you the time of your life, sir! Do you know the last time I got laid?"

The man's eyes got wide. He looked Karson up and down. "You're bluffing."

Karson grabbed his crotch, noticeably showing through his pants now. "Does it look like I'm bluffing?" He whispered, his breath now tickling the man's ears. Surprisingly to Karson, he leaned into him. He stank, like blood and sweat. And surprisingly, shit. Karson stifled a gag.

"In the open?" The man whispered back, licking his lips.

"I came from that way, my team is going that way. We have time." Karson unzipped his pants. "But, you have to do some things for me as well. See, I want sex, but I also want a promotion. Don't we all? I'm sure we can both benefit here… me of course more, but you as well. You get to live, and an orgasm!"

The soldier squinted his eyes. "What you want?"

Karson gaged inwardly. *Disgusting, nasty, smelly man. The least you could do if you want to court another man, person in general, is be hygienic! Sheesh!* Karson moved closer to the soldier, and walked around him, rubbing against him like a cat, then rubbing his shoulders. "You like that?" Karson asked.

"Oh, yeah! But I'd like it more if you massaged something else." He whispered. "Maybe, untie me? Let me tie you."

"Well, if you're a good daddy, maybe I will! Maybe I won't!" Karson slid his hands over his prisoner's chest, rolling his eyes. "Who do you work for?"

"Like I will tell you that. Get on with this, gay boy!" The soldier's head snapped to the side, a handprint forming on the side of his cheek.

"Wrong answer, papi! If you want your reward, you're going to have to do better than that. Tell me what you call yourselves. You said your nation a moment ago. You're Japanese. Do you mean Japan? You speak English very, very well."

"It's not my place to say… Hey, where are you going?"

Karson was nearly to the door. "I'm not in the mood anymore, Jap. You have to motivate my whore self otherwise I lose interest." Karson flipped him off and exited the room. "See you in the burning pits of Hell!"

"WAIT! Hey, man! Okay! I'll tell you!" Nothing. "I TELL YOU! COME BACK!" The Japanese soldier called into the empty hallway.

Karson poked his head around the corner. "Your service name. Now."

"How do I know you're gonna make your promise?" He squirmed in his seat, uncomfortably tented, trying to break free to meet his natural desire to release.

"You'll get your head blown off, I promise!" Karson slithered over to him.

"My head? You're gonna kill me! Like I said!" He scoffed.

"No! Are you stupid?" Karson walked over to him. "Your dick head!"

"Really?" He affirmed. "You promise? You're American. You have rules. Loyalty. I need your word."

"Yes." Karson lied through his teeth. "Yes, you have my word I'll blow your dick head."

"We call ourselves the Nation of Death. 'Death Nation.' We don't know everything as individual mercenaries, however, we plan to take the world. They plan to take over the world. We are all hired muscle. Our payment; being alive. We are tired of the way the world runs. These nations of individual laws. Some thriving while others do not. Why do some nations get to rule most of the world? Have so much power? With Death Nation, we have no laws. Only do."

"How do you do it?"

"Look, kid! I know what you're trying. That's all I'm going to tell you."

Karson reached down and started unbuckling his pants. "Look, I know I said last time I got laid... but... oh it's kinda embarrassing. You'll laugh at me."

The man's eyes were locked on Karson's middle waist. "Tell me."

"I-I'm... still a virgin. But I know you want to so just tell me what I want, and we can get on with this! Okay? How do you do it?"

The Japanese man tried to resist, but Karson rolled his eyes and buckled up.

"We hit the capital where the nation's ability to function stands. We kill all of the possible chances for the country to revive itself. Leadership, deleted or taken information, codes, operations. We hit the country everywhere at once. We kill as many people as we can to halt the advance of the enemy; sorry, your allied troops. We convert them through our camps. Those who turn, we welcome; those who don't, die.

Remember the unknown launch into space. You confirmed it was destroyed in orbit. It was. That was the unconverted troops. We launched them into space, then jettisoned them into the vacuum. Plain and simple."

"Why so dramatic?"

"It made a statement didn't it? With a nation thrown into turmoil, we can easily establish a powerhouse. It's like the Europeans did in the colonization days. We are colonizing the world for ourselves. It started in the Middle East. That, of course, was easy. Our leader united the Middle East under one flag. However, they report to the leadership. Once the Middle East fell, we moved onto Asia, which was somewhat easy, where I was welcomed. We moved into Europe, striking the source of all allied power, the UN. With the UN down, we are easily more maneuverable. Troop gain, take the world's nation's headquarters. Cause fear. Now, as we speak, the rest of the plan is taking place. China, Russia, United States, all of world will soon fall! That is proving hard. Like me. Now get on with it. You will never win, might as well join us, and be my slave. I promise, I'll take care of you! I'm only mostly evil." He licked his lips again.

You know, I read eyes when I interrogate. You're being truthful! Good for you! "Of course, sir! Of course. You earned it!" Karson smiled and unzipped the man, dropping to his knees, the man's head leaned back and

BANG

The man's head snapped forward, his mouth fell open in an inaudible scream as blood sprayed like piss from his mutilated cock. "Argh! What the hell!"

"I told you you'd get your head blown off! And now you have! Karson holstered his pistol. Have a beautiful day bleeding out!" Karson turned and walked towards the hallway where his team disappeared to.

"HALT!" A voice called to him.

Karson spun around, eyes wide. Bullets flew at the young SEAL as he fired back and bolted around a pillar, eight feet from the hallway. The advance of troops was too powerful, but Karson had to keep moving if he had any chance of survival. His gun ready, he took a deep breath and pushed around the pillar firing as he stepped across the gap, pinning the enemy down until he could reload behind another pillar.

"Two magazines left. I have to do this." He loaded his second to last mag in the rifle and did the same maneuver, making it to the hallway and sprinting into the dark. Karson ran and ran, calling for his team.

"Captain, Captain!" Karson called. Footsteps followed him as he broke free into another clearing. Two SEALs appeared and pulled Karson into a room.

"SHUT UP!" They hissed.

"I'm compromised!" He around the frame and fired into two soldiers. "I have information. We need to get out of here. I need to relay to command."

"Bull! You totally raped that man you freak. Why is this monster on our team?" They looked at Richardson who was looking at maps of the building. "Yeah, we stayed behind and watched, you queer."

"It's called the art of deception, dude! I had you all fooled that I was a raging fangirl when I just wanted on your team. I tricked him into thinking he could have me when I stole the information from him! I knew that he'd either speak from desire, or speak to avoid me! Or I would have just killed him, and caught up. I had to try something!"

"We can talk about this later." Richardson shot a Death Nation soldier as he poked his head into the room. "Out the windows. Go. Run into the woods."

"WAIT!" Karson called. He ran over to the window and aimed out. One-shot. Two shots. "Sniper. I saw a flash. You guys need to be more vigilant. I thought you were SEALs."

"Excuse me?" One SEAL rounded on Karson. "You're not even a month out of training, and you're mouthing off?

"Man, get out the window." Karson ran his mouth back. "To the woods." Karson moved back to the stairs. "I will follow." As Karson arrived at the stairs, the gay Death Nation soldier appeared and slammed his rifle into Karson's stomach. Even with the vest, it took the wind out of him, but as with all SEALs, when a brother is in danger, they react. Richardson and another SEAL both shot and killed the soldier and assisted Karson in securing the staircase. Karson too fired down the stairs cracking the helmets of the enemy and sending them to whatever higher power awaited them. The SEALs turned and bolted out of the windows and tore across the dusk strewn, snow-covered ground into the dense woods that lay behind the building.

"We're not out of the woods yet, gentlemen. Literally. Keep your heads on the swivel. Don't get caught sleeping." Richardson said. "There should be a ski lodge up over that ridge; we can ride the ski lift up if it still works. There will be a construction site. Hopefully a car or something will be there. Otherwise, we'll have to hike out of this hell hole!"

"Leaf has six." The SEAL behind Karson said.

"Shadow has sides."

"May I take point with you, Captain?" Karson asked politely.

"You need to learn your place, SEAL Pup." The commander of the squad said.

"Wing… He's okay. At my side, kid." Captain Richardson said.

"Man, seriously!" Commander Wing said.

"Hey, Commander, we are recruiting… and teaching. He's shown he can hold his own. Give him a chance, men. Just because the situation is a little more action-packed than just picking from a wall of accreditations, just looking at this young SEAL work is enough to allow him a leadership position. If any of you have a problem, come to me directly on base, or take it up with higher command. For now, we do as I say. I'm the Captain."

"Aye, sir." Karson barked. *Ha ha! Seal reference!*

"Suck up!" Wing said, though he understood the Captain's idea.

Karson stuck his tongue out, only to receive a cuff over his ear. "We're not in high school, kid. I just stuck my neck out for you. Grow up and prove me right."

"Yes, sir, sorry, sir, right away, sir!" Karson spluttered. He stared ahead as they walked through the dimming world and saw the shadows of a pillar with wires attached at the top. "That looks like a lift, sir. I think two should go check the ridge out, ensure there are no scouts."

"I agree." Richardson started. "Wing-"

"Of course you agree, sir." Wing thumbed his nose. "Shadow, with me."

"Aye, Commander." Shadow crunched his way up to stand beside Wing as they disappeared into the dark.

"Sir, that is suicide. We aren't prepared for this type of battle."

"You should always prepare for an invasion…" Karson stated.

"Unless your intel is sound enough to say, you'll be operating in a non-combatant area…

"That just became combatant. These men are SEALs, son. They know how to function in dire circumstances. As should you."

"Honestly, sir… Right now, I'm not sure I can operate in the winter environment."

"Then if you have a problem with this, maybe you should resign when you return to America. Until then, do your job. Find work."

Karson stared into the darkness, listening on the other's conversation.

"Man, this sucks… That kid is brand new, and already he is being treated like royalty. Just because you shoot well doesn't mean you deserve the title SEAL Team Six."

"Wing, I agree, but we should focus on this mission. I doubt your job is in danger." Shadow rounded a pillar, vectoring his area of engagement.

"You never know, dude… Besides, I really don't want to get killed right now. I have three kids and another on the way. This is stupid."

"We're okay, man… Nothing-" Shadow's voice cut off, and he and Wing were laid in a pool of blood together, alone, and in silence. Their bodies already starting to harden, two bullets, one in each of their brain, not even seeing the threat laying right in front of them. As their souls departed, their bodies lay oozing red into the pure white snow, quiet and lonely.

Karson couldn't take any more of their statements and blocked them out. "Why are you Richardson, when everyone else has a code name?" Karson asked in a whisper. He turned his Corner Shot monitor on to read thermal signatures. "SEAL Team Six has code names do they not?"

"I just didn't want one. I have nobody to protect. Forty-five years old, nearing the end of my career, no wife, no children, no family. I was orphaned when I was five… I don't know who my family is if they even existed. I'm the perfect warrior. I don't need a cover."

Karson nodded. "I lost their signatures, sir… And they haven't spoken in minutes." He said. Richardson and the two remaining SEALs moved into the darkness, maneuvering based off of Karson's orders.

"No sign." Richardson relayed.

"Ditto," Leaf said.

Karson rounded a corner, sighting a hue of red right in front of him. "Contact. Everybody drop."

He heard crunching from behind him and to his side. "What do you see, Pup?"

Karson honed in on his target and fired the shot, the hue instantly starting to cool, turning from bright orange and red to darker as the cold started taking over the body. In watching the body cool, Karson could have sworn he saw a heatwave lift from the body and disappear into the sky, but wasn't sure. *Weird...* "Target down. Move up. I see purple signatures..." Karson advanced first and tripped over the bodies of his downed colleagues. Richardson was on top of them in moments.

"GOD-" He kicked the ground. "WHY?" He shouted. He reached down feeling for a pulse as Karson took in the sights of blood and brain matter.

That's... My fault. And it's going to haunt me. He thought as he moved and checked the enemy's body. "Same uniform, sir... Death Nation." He ripped the flag off the right arm and searched for more clues.

"Aye... Leaf go and turn this on at that hut over there. Be extremely careful, Pup you go too. I'm going to relay this to command and-" Bullets pelted the ground in front of him as Leaf ran to the structure and Karson and Richardson hoisted the bodies of their downed brothers onto their shoulders, Karson firing his pistol in the dark as German commands were shouted at the SEALs.

"NO MAN LEFT BEHIND!" Karson shouted as he and Richardson took off towards the structure. The carts started to move as they entered and locked the door behind them. Karson made to the side of the door, ready to strike anybody who came through as the others prepared themselves for a fight. From the sounds of the shots and commands, the force was smaller, but more would now be coming to this location. Lights entered through the glass paneling of the door and it wiggled as the men tried the knob, finally prying it open. The GIGN uniformed man with the strange flag also on his shoulder spotted Karson as soon as he entered and dropped Karson to his knees faster than Karson could react.

"Damn." He said as a fist clocked him aside the jaw bone.

"Vhere are your overs?" The man slurred.

"'Scuse me?" Karson lisped. "I don't sveak your vanguage..." Karson taunted, receiving another slam to the other side of his face.

The man was not amused with Karson, however, before Karson could mock again, the man took a bullet to the vest and Karson took his chance to draw his weapon. From a crouched position, he fired into the man's throat, knocking him out into the snow, as the others tried to enter, dying with their leader.

"Nice!" Karson said, loading his downed friends onto the lift as more lights were appearing in the distance. Don't see why we're fighting the English or Germans. We were allies a year ago. Humph. Anyways, Captain, I think we should-"

"Hush, SEAL Pup... Leaf, Pup, make sure you lay on the lift. Fire at anyone who sees you. This is a suicide mission, but if we succeed, it'll be a pretty boss story!"

"You don't take orders or requests well, do you, sir?" Leaf piped up for once, finally impressed by how the team operated.

"Why should I? I'm the Captain..."

All three chuckled.

Karson nodded and hopped onto the ski car and felt himself fly higher and higher into the dark, cold night air. Before he'd loaded up, he had grabbed another strange flag patch from the man's uniform and examined it as he rode to his escape from England.

****

Elding's Promise

"My fellow Americans, and the world. Today... Today is a changing tide in U.S. involvement in the world. As you know by news broadcasts, there is a new and emerging threat looming outside of our borders. When I ran for president, I wanted to run on honesty. Be a new species of president, one that is transparent in every situation to the extent that I can be. We currently have measures in place to protect our interests here in the homeland and abroad, as well as ensure the safety of American citizens throughout the nation and the world. However, I would be lying if I said that we had this situation under control. What little information we have on this threat, gathered by operatives involved in the first attacks from this new enemy, I cannot divulge at this time, as we are trying collect information for ourselves. However, I will be giving some instructions out as to ways that you can help in our endeavor to once again achieve a peaceful planet to live on."

The president glanced down to see where he was, as the prompter scrolled too fast. "War is a human monster, but a natural cycle. Man has been fighting wars with man since the biblical times, the first war between the brothers Cain and Able, all the way up to this. What I can tell you is that the United States will never fall to foreign influences. The morals and principles of this nation will remain high, and the people of all identities who protect this great land show a dominant force to be challenged. The American resolve will hold. I want everyone to channel their inner patriot. Our military is strong, but we could always use the extra help. Enlistment is fast-tracked, and your training begins three days after you enlist. Enlistment papers are being sent in the mail. Please fill them out and take them to your nearest recruiting station or mail them there if you feel called. Now, there are going to be a few changes in the way the nation is run. Numerous threats have been stated against our country. I am taking a lesson from some other countries in allowing the military to show their presence in the streets. State National Guard units will be out and about throughout the states to show extra support for the police and other emergency services. This is just a precaution. Martial law is not being implemented. We are forever and always a free nation."

Elding continued. "Finally, to address the rumors. There have already been fatalities in this fight, American and otherwise. And yes, Middle Eastern nations have united under one flag. England has been invaded, but we have troops stationed there, and yes, other countries have fallen that we have not been able to regain contact. I am declaring war, approved by a bipartisan congress, on this dark day to ensure that this issue does not get out of hand. Australia, Canada, other European Nations and Russia have all already joined me in the declaration of war, as well as Mexico and other South American Nations debating on joining or not, we all agree this cannot stand. The Headquarters of the United Nations was attacked today. Thousands perished in the slaughter. September 11th was a new era's Pearl Harbor, and it is no different now; the UN attack today is this era's September 11th, and just like the world responded to our aid when our nation was attacked, we too shall answer right now, March 13th, 2035 in support of our friends and family suffering from this ordeal. What we went through on 9/11 in the few hours and few days, people all over the world are feeling now and feel for their entire lives. Yeah, the scars are still there. Missing our loved ones is still there, but we have healed. It's time to bring that relief to others around the world. Presidents Bush, Obama, Trump, and three Presidents before me have all spoken with me on what they believe is a correct plan of action, as well as instruction from my advisors. I've listened to all, and have made my own decisions based on what I feel brings the best possibility of success. The terrorist way is to instill fear in our hearts. But even with our flag flying at half-staff, our resolute power still shows through our thirteen bars and fifty stars.

Bloodshed does not scare us. Terrorists, not only just foreign but from every corner, every walk of life, every nationality, even Americans with no establishment, you have attacked us before and will attack us again, but I ask you… Are you willing to deal with the overwhelming defiance and revenge and retaliation the United States, as well as our allies, have to throw back at you? We will get down and dirty to fight for our freedom, even if it means we have to spill our own blood like those all the way back to the Revolutionary war did to ensure our freedom! Our freedom is bought with blood. We are no stranger to this reality. We defy any threat to us. And I declare war on you. Just like with World Wars I and II, we will intervene again to bring this new threat to an end. Whether or not you call this World War III, it's time for the entire planet to get involved. This risk will not go away unless we make it and we will make it die."

President Elding took a sip of water. "Now. I want to turn my attention to the enemies of the Allied world, all. Like Europe, the Soviet Union, and the United States did in World War II when Hitler threatened to invade Czechoslovakia, I too warn you. Listen carefully. Maybe clean out your crusty ears and pay attention. It may take a lot for you to understand this, so I'll try to speak slowly. This is a battle you will never win. This world has faced an enemy far worse than you in our history, with World War I and II, and this one will be no different in ousting you from our world history. We will track you down. We will demolish your structure. We will find your leadership and end them. No mercy. We aren't just attacking terrorists or the enemy forces God knows you call yourselves. We're hunting you. We will indiscriminately identify terrorists and nations who harbor them as hostile and will make no warning of our strikes against you. You are killing people of age, adulthood, and childhood. This disgusting, cowardly, barbaric act will not stand in our new world order. We have a way of living; you're not welcome to it. I can tell you the allied world is mobilizing. We are deploying our resources in halting your advance. We are coming for you either way. You decide if you want it quick and painless, or long, drawn-out and excruciating. You have four hours to surrender. Four hours.

Let this be a warning to you, son! Satan himself does not scare us! You have provoked the wrong country. You've poked the wrong President. You have threatened my nation and you have threatened everything that this nation stands for. You are the incarnation of evil. Let me make this clear to you. Your days are numbered if you refuse. You have killed one too many Americans. You killed one too many when you killed men, woman, and children of any nationality. Like all before you, I will unleash the full might of the United States against you. You hide behind cameras. You hide behind the bodies of the victims you kill. You combat noncombatants. You kill unarmed men, woman, and children. And you call yourselves warriors. You say you are doing the right thing, but a key element of the to doing the right thing is that no one should be forced to do what you want, peace is a cornerstone, freedom of thought and religion are paramount, compete with each other in doing good, thou shall not kill another human and yet you do every day. I implore you, face the force you wish to destroy. Face my military on the front lines. If you want to test our resolve, come out and play! I tell you boys, I'm not afraid. My Soldiers, Marines, Airmen, Coast Guardsmen, Sailors, and the troops you don't even know exist have more confidence, more bravery; they do not fear more than any of you cowards. Even the resolve of the American people, from the baby that was just conceived, to the grandparent that just passed away, from young to old, sea to shining sea, and anywhere in the world, American citizens have more courage in their pinky toenail than you have in your entire ranks. Stop fighting by killing those that cannot defend themselves. I promise you that will not inhibit, nor destroy our resolve. Come out. Stop hiding in your holes and show your face serpent. You have a limited amount of time to surrender, **four hours**, before we you one of the things you want. I know you like to kill yourselves. I promise you, we'll deliver that for you. And I promise your war is your end. We're easy to find.

To the world, this is not a war on religion, rather a war on extremism. Foreign or domestic threats beware, this same message applies to any who turn from humanity and threaten the United States of America or any ally. This message is for those nations who are enemies of freedom. The land of the free, home of the brave, nations alike, and anyone who stands with us will liberate, and create one world. One World of different ideals and thought. United, but separate. We'll have disagreements, we'll have skirmishes, but we will not forget the mindset we all are born with. That we are all brothers and sisters in the human mind. United we stand, divided we fall.

Elding paused for a long time to let the speech so far settle in.

"To my friends. Nations have fallen."

But this nation of ours will stand tall above any and all who fall and the ashes of our enemy as they smolder before us will be stamped out and thrown to the winds never again to rejuvenate. We will help build another world. But before we do that, we must stand and fight for what is right. Freedom. Let's get to work! To my service people, I offer you this one order now. No matter how much of a joke our enemy is, they are trained to kill you and anyone with whom you side yourself. They are a robust and formidable, well-trained, and highly advanced threat. Watch yourselves out there, and give them hell. To those here at home, I promise you, we will be at peace once more. May God bless you, this government, this world, and may God bless, The United States of America!" President

Elding saluted and turned and walked away from the camera deeper into The White House.

The servicemen all around the world looked at each other and roared in triumph. "YOU HEARD OUR COMMANDER AND CHIEF! LET'S FIND OUR WORK!"

****

Explosive Departure

CRUNCH

CRUNCH

CRUNCH

Could these guys be any louder? Karson followed behind the others. Distant lights of a construction lot pierced through the dark haze in the night. The moon reflected off the cold snow and the crystals glistened.

"I love the snow, guys!" Karson tried to make conversation.

"Shhh." Richardson lifted his hand. You hear that?"

Karson listened. It sounded like an advancing army of Sparta pounding their spears against their shields.

"Construction machines?"

SILENCE

Karson woke moments later, feet away from where he stood. He felt like he had just taken the beating of a lifetime. He was buried under snow and couldn't tell which way was up. He let spit slither from his lips. *And of course I'm upside down so it goes in my nose.* He sneezed. He wriggled is body around and popped his head out of the snow like a polar bear mother does when she leaves her hibernation den with her cubs. No threats were present and Karson's eyes locked onto the massive scorched crater and blood-stained snow.

"CAPTAIN RICHARDSON- Oof!" Karson felt the force of a baseball bat pelt his stomach and rolled backwards into the crater, again winding up under snow. "Son of a monkey's nut! He pulled his P226 from his leg holster and rolled onto his stomach. "Where did that come from?"

Movement from behind. Karson spun onto his back and fired a shot, knocking Richardson back onto his ass and he slid down into the crater gasping.

"Sir! I'm so sorry! I should have-"

"Save it. I'd have shot you in the face, we're good."

Karson stared at the SEAL captain, terrified.

"Quit looking at me kid, this will be over quick. We're fine. Four targets ahead in the construction site from what I can tell. They were standing around a fire; they've spread out. I'd assume under those four hazes of light. We're going to run for it... Well, you are. There is a vehicle in the site. I'm going to pick off our enemy. Run at a diagonal and I'll pick the targets off. Here." He unstrapped his vest. "Around your head, run in that diagonal. It'll be quick."

"Sir, I-"

"You're Team Six now. No crying 'bout it. Here." He helped him put it around his face and positioned himself the correct way towards the vehicle. "RUN!"

Karson leaped up and-

"You're running the wrong-" Shots erupted and Richardson took his chance. He crawled over the lip and picked his targets.

Karson felt the impacts of three shots to his back as he kept running continuously off balance. Right before he lost his footing and fell onto his face, however, he ran smack into a tree, knocking him on his back.

Dazed, he listed and waited for the death shot. *Hey, there's no sound! Except the sound of footsteps!* He scrambled to get the vest off, like a person stuck in a turtle neck sweater. Laughter met his ears, and he relaxed slightly as hands pulled him into a hug!

"We did it my boy! Hooyah! And all because you made an ass of yourself! I feel like leaving you like that! Come on, let's get to that car!"

****

The Oval Office

"Mr. President?"

"Yes?" President Elding looked up from his desk. "Ah, Secretary Jones, we have a tough task ahead of us my friend. But we can accomplish anything, would you agree?"

"Mr. President, our CIA wet team and SEAL Team operatives have found information that I'm certain you need to be informed of." Secretary Jones handed the President a massive book. "I've highlighted the relevant sections, but you'll probably want to read all of it tonight."

"Wet team?" Elding flipped through the pages.

"The operatives are sent with the intention to draw blood."

"And blood is wet. I see. What information?" Elding stood and put on his suit coat.

"Situation room in ten minutes, but I will brief you on one thing. This war will not be ended with your little warning. These people have already proven themselves far stronger than any force we've ever had before." The Secretary stated.

"We'll see about this. How did we go about obtaining this information? I was never informed of a 'wet' operation."

"A young Navy SEAL did some impressive acting I've been told and also interrogated a captured enemy soldier. They call him SEAL Pup. They say he's a prodigy. That's all I know."

"Hmmm... SEAL Pup... Nice to know! I look forward to meeting him. That is if anyone survives this God-forsaken war."

"Luckily, sir, he's alive and in the Situation Room with his Captain. He wants to promote him, but to do so at the pace he desires, he needs a bit more power than the rank of a captain." The Secretary turned and walked away.

Elding nodded. "Oh, Jones? I want our Tomb Guards and other forces armed at all times. I know on 9/11 most of our fighter jets were not armed and resorted to an order that if they need, kamikaze into a highjacked aircraft. We will not make that same mistake. I want everybody armed. Air Force, our Tomb Guards... Every single service person." Elding walked with his secretary to the Situation Room.

"Will do, sir. Will do." Jones smiled, opening the door once they reached the Situation Room.

A young boy stood up faster than anyone and held his arm at a salute. His pristine white Naval uniform devoid of any decorations. A far more decorated Sailor smacked the boy and whispered at him, his face dropping from excitement to fear and embarrassment.

The decorated Sailor spoke. "Mr. President, Captain Richardson, USNSHPTNF."

The President looked at his Secretary.

"SEAL Team Six, sir. I'll fill you in on the acronym later."

He nodded. "And, is this your son?" He smiled. Richardson laughed. The boy even more embarrassed.

"Petty Officer First Class Karson Hunter, Mr. President." Karson whispered. Richardson elbowed him in the ribs.

Elding looked on, shocked. "Well, Petty Officer. This nation owes you a great service. Or should I say, Lieutenant. Congratulation's, son. Your Captain has great faith in you, as do I. Please, sit."

Karson's puffed up his chest beaming, looking at Richardson who gave the slyest wink, then kicked Karson under the table to focus.

"Sorry, I'm late. Mr. President." A Navy Admiral entered the room.

"Admiral Thompson. I've just promoted our young Navy SEAL here to Lieutenant."

"Dammit! I missed it." He looked at Karson. "Congratulations, son. You earned it. I'm sure we can expect more greatness from you in the near future!"

Karson beamed more, but kept his composure.

"Obviously, he still has some to learn, but he's exceptional!" Richardson said to Thompson who laughed. Karson slumped slightly.

"Gentlemen, fill me in on what you've learned. Please." Elding interrupted, crossing his hands on the table. The Sailors nodded and began their debrief.

****

CHAPTER 1 - Nation 1

Six months after Karson's first mission and President Riley Elding's issued warning to "Death Nation." September, 2035. Petty Officer First Class Kadin Karson Hunter, after a dire need for leadership, fast-tracked from SEAL Team three to SEAL Team Six. Rank: Lieutenant on orders of Captain Andrew Heath Richardson and President Riley Chase Elding in filling open position of Commander Lot Zavier "Wing" Boone.

MISSION LOG:

- **0107 HOURS: UNITED STATES NAVY SEAL TEAM SIX OPERATOR; KADIN KARSON HUNTER (SERVAL) BY UNIQUE ASSIGNMENT OF THE UNITED STATES NAVY ADMIRAL STACY CRAIG THOMPSON AND BY DECREE OF THE PRESIDENT OF THE UNITED STATES OF AMERICA RILEY CHASE ELDING LANDS AT U.S. ARMY FORWARD OPERATING BASE KODIAK. LOCATION DEPLOYED: FINLAND. STATUS: NEUTRAL MILITARY ZONE. DEPLOYMENT TWO: RUSSIAN FEDERATION. STATUS: DARK. UTILIZE EXTREME CAUTION.**
  {SEVEN MINUTES BEHIND SCHEDULE.}
- **0300 HOURS: LIEUTENANT HUNTER BRIEFED BY JSOC (JOINT SPECIAL OPERATIONS COMMAND.)**
- **0530 HOURS: INTRODUCTIONS BEFORE MISSION BRIEFING.**
- **0601 HOURS: LIEUTENANT HUNTER BEGINS MILITARY MISSION BRIEFING FOR U.S. ARMY RANGERS FOR JOINT SPECIAL OPERATIONS TASK FORCE OPERATIVES' MISSION TO COME.**
  JSOC PRESENTATION.
  {ONE MINUTE BEHIND SCHEDULE.}

"Multiple nations, as you have already known, have gone dark; victims of the "riches" the new enemy alliance has claimed it can offer for any and all who come to their side. Those that have not risen this image here, their united flag, have been or are currently conquered by force and raising the flag against the will of the nation."

Karson hit next on his remote for the slideshow and aimed a red laser at the Russian Federation. "Russia, thought to be very powerful and undefeatable thanks to multiple events in history like Napoleon's raid as well as the Second World War, is now a strong example of how our unknown enemy operates. We can only assume that the Russian government has lost its control of the region and that the enemy leadership has gained control. We know this, to reiterate, because Russia has proven a formidable opponent to this alliance, and Russian phone calls and intercepted intelligence were obtained by the United States before, like other nations, Russia disappeared off the face of the planet. No contact, no media coverage, it's like the government vanished. We do not know exactly who the alliance follows, one man, or a group of leaders, nor how robust and powerful its fighting force is; but let us just say if you can drop Russia, you become the most feared threat to The United States. I've dealt with this opponent, and they know how to fight, let me tell ya. When we arrive, Russian informants should inform us on what is going on within the country, unless they are dead. We haven't been on great terms with Russia lately even before this crisis, so we'll be careful. However, they must really need our help if they even considered asking for U.S. intervention in the first place. Gentlemen, this enemy is allied with various nations that don't care if they kill Americans. 'The Big Satan' is its target and if they can nab Americans, it makes their extremist esteem skyrocket and causes the world to lose faith. Do not die on this mission, but it's pretty likely some, if not all of us will. These enemies include the countries who went dark six months ago: North Korea, figures," Karson scoffed, "United Mexico, having taken over the entire Central American landscape within two months. Iraq, Iran, Afghanistan and Pakistan. Burma, South American nations of Colombia, Brazil, etcetera. African tribes and nations. Even South Africa is struggling to stay allied with us. The Middle East have all taken up arms against Israel. It's only a matter of time before it goes dark. All of these nations under the enemy alliance want to take down the peaceful earth as we know it. Some would say, they may have already done it. You get the point."

Karson took a sip of water and continued, now sizing up his men and pacing the room, a college lecture hall-like space, with risen steps and Soldiers at desks, with Finnish Soldiers armed to the teeth standing around the room as well. "The United States and allies, as you well know, do not negotiate with terrorists, or any enemy for that matter. Even neutral Finland doesn't put up with that crap." Karson nodded at his colleagues from the foreign nation. "Enemy troops in each region have started strategic maneuvers. So, to meet this threat, The United States has decided to make a stealthy, very decisive strike with some of the help of our still Allied Nations. Canada. England. France. Spain. Portugal. Poland. Australia is trying to stay out of the war, but they have sworn that should the time come, they will too take up arms for the Allied cause. There is, of course, nothing wrong with trying to protect your men," Karson ignored the arrogant disapproval from the U.S. Troops in the room, "but President Elding is attempting to change the Prime Minister's mind. We need all the help we can get." Hunter placed his hands on the table and furrowed his brow.

"We are heavily outnumbered. Our mission is to

a) scout and obtain as much information as possible, finding out who is causing this and how they're so effective. We need this information before a war on these extremists is deployed by the United Nations." The Lieutenant continued. "We are the precursor to World War III. If we fail, then the war of all wars, tried so very hard by the United Nations to avoid, will erupt.

b) Our mission begins in Russia. However, we will all be seeing combat in many countries in the months to come, gentlemen, maybe not together, but guaranteed you're going to be fighting. A lot.

Now, it seems that Russia is falling into revolutionary war to try to fend off its attackers, while also charging a civil war by those extremists in the nation who welcome the change. Loyal Russian allies are heavily engaged with the enemy and other Russians in some parts of the nation as we have heard, but it's impossible to decipher who's who on that field. Death Nation soldiers look like this, most of the time. Here too is the flag."

Karson pointed at the screen.

"That said,

c) our rules of engagement.

While we are undercover, no shots. You listen to my orders. As soon as I say fire at will or we are being overrun, or something goes wrong like the death of myself or another Soldier, then you smoke every last bad guy until your dying breath. Let me put it this way as well, if you are given or deem it necessary to fire at will, you shoot indiscriminately. Anyone with a gun, or anyone with a uniform like this, you destroy. We shoot first, ask for forgiveness and ask our questions and clean up later. I say all that because we keep moving. Our mission never slows down. Clear?"

Heads slowly nodded as information sank into the brains of highly trained Soldiers.

"This mission is code-named Operation Helping Hand. Any questions?" Lieutenant Hunter asked.

"Sir, what is the itinerary of this mission? I know the basics of it, but can you go into detail or is this a play it by ear mission?"

"Name?"

"Sergeant Jared McCollum, sir."

"Sergeant, we are heading to Russia. Moscow to be exact. Once there, you are partly correct that this will be a play it by ear mission, however, the mission style is similar. Limited rules of engagement with intel-gathering by scout team. We act as if we are local. What's interesting is that from what we can see, there is tight control over the nations that are conquered. However, the large countries still operate as if they were normal. At least in the beginning. We land, we go to the hotel, and we spy. The Kremlin is in sight, so we will utilize equipment from the CIA to gather information as well. That's pretty much all we got so far. We need to know this, though, even with limited rules of engagement, we aren't the start of the ground war. That may come after us, but for now, unless prompted, do not fire a shot, and ensure that they are suppressed if we do. We will be dressed as civilians, and are flying over on a passenger jetliner. Helpful, sir?" Karson pressed the Sergeant.

"Hooah, sir." He replied, writing in his journal.

"Good. Then let's get assigned and move out. This is too much talking, not enough working. Study this well; we don't want taxis or other attention drawn to us. I'm sure you're not all fluent in Russian as I am?" He paused. "Didn't think so. From the airport, dressed as civilians, we will meet at the Baltschug Kempinski Hotel there in Moscow, where we will survey the land, go over last-minute plans for the mission, sleep, and then begin. We are all arriving on different flights, and arriving at different times. I'll be on this first flight with Sergeant McCollum. Here is your passport." Karson tossed it to the burly man whose hair, like his eyes, were brown as mud. "Love the beard by the way."

"Thanks."

"You will be known as Vladimir Patelly. My name is Nicolai Sarpskey. We are on the 0830 flight from here, to Moscow. Also, before I continue, these countries are nuclear powers, so if we can find the codes and locations, that would be a plus. If we have the nukes, then maybe we can save lives, especially on the home front. Anyways, raise your hand when I call your name, I studied you, but I've got a lot going on in my head right now. Corporal David Blarney, you and Private Chris Davis are going to be on the 0945 flight to Moscow. Here are your passports." Karson passed their passports up to where they were sitting. "Blarney, you are Alexei Bogdan, and Davis, you are Vsevolod Anatoly. We are all going to arrive at a Finish airport together in the van outside. From there, we part ways until we rendezvous at the hotel suite. Head straight for the Baltschug Kempinski Hotel. The room is on the fifth floor, king's suite 508. Don't mosey around. It's a full out war over there, even if there is no combat seen in the streets where we are. Death Nation rules here, even if the nation hasn't fallen yet. We risk traveling public. We could be shot down or halted if they cut transportation off. People are dying, and we are easily able to be those people. Any further questions?"

"No sir." The Rangers chorused.

"Good. Then let's move out. And work on your Russian. You may need it."

The men walked into their locker room and grabbed their equipment. The blond-headed Davis stared at Karson as Blarney, the ginger, placed a Bible over his heart and prayed. Karson had already packed his clothing. He had plenty of civilian clothes, as well as a black combat uniform with his battle gear, should the need arise. It was all battle-tested, ready for use in combat. "Battle check your equipment gentlemen, just to be on the safe side. You need civilian clothing, and anything dark. I'm sure as Rangers you have some sort of black uniforms. I have left my other uniforms and equipment back at my command post, you'd be better to leave yours here. Less weight and chance to be exposed. Don't take what you don't need, men. Leave all identifying materials, i.e. dog t's, licenses, U.S. flags and patches… I know it sucks to take off our flag, but we don't need unexpected nor unwanted attention." Karson called to his Soldiers.

Karson's battle gear consisted of his light infiltration kit in civilian clothing, with slight modifications in clothing, with a coat to conceal his MP5. All weapons, of course, were suppressed to maintain stealth and invisibility. The Rangers would carry similar gear: MP5, M9 pistol, and knife, minus Karson's favorite back up the XDs. They finished loading their weapons, packing their gear, and headed out to the car. Once at the airport, they went through a security checkpoint held by American Soldiers to get through without question. Karson and Sergeant McCollum soon boarded the Boeing 757 to Moscow.

As the plane took off and reached cruising altitude for the hour and a half long flight, a Russian air waitress started making her rounds to ensure, like her job description stated, that all passengers were comfortable and well taken care of. She stumbled slightly as the plane turned towards Moscow, but quickly regained her composure. Stopping at the Americans, she asked what they would like to drink in English. McCollum started to answer, but Karson replied for him in Russian. The Russian woman smiled at him, relieved to be speaking her fluent tongue with another 'Russian citizen.'

"Здравствуйте, мадам! {Zdravstvuyte, madam!} (Hello, Madame!)" Karson started. "Как проходит твой день? {Kak prokhodit tvoy den'?} (How is your day going?)"

"Занятый! Все, что я могу получить вы и ваш друг? {Zanyatyy! Vse, chto ya mogu poluchit' vy i vash drug?} (Busy! Anything I can get you and your friend?)" The air waitress asked.

"Да, пожалуйста. {Da, pozhaluysta.} (Yes, please.)" Turning to his friend, he asked quietly so she wouldn't hear his English, but still in a Russian accent to be certain: "vat do you vant?"

"Beer," Jared replied.

"Any food?"

"Oh, um… Yeah… What do they have?" He asked hungrily licking his lips and holding his rumbling belly.

"Не могли бы вы сказать мне, какие основные блюда можно готовить? {Ne mogli by vy skazat' mne, kakiye osnovnyye blyuda mozhno gotovit'?} (Could you tell me what main dishes you can prepare?)" Karson returned conversing with the waitress.

"Вы двое выглядят, как вы бы насладиться Кулебяка... {Vy dvoye vyglyadyat, kak vy by nasladit'sya Kulebyaka ...} (You two look like you could enjoy a Coulibiac…)" She pointed out.

"Не могли бы вы сообщить мне о том, что это такое? {Ne mogli by vy soobshchit' mne o tom, chto eto takoye?} (Could you inform me on what that is?)"

"Кулебяка является лосось с рисом, яйца вкрутую, грибы и укроп. Kulebyaka yavlyayetsya losos's risom, yaytsa vkrutuyu, griby i ukrop.} (Coulibiac is salmon on rice, hard boiled eggs, mushrooms, and dill.)"

"Звучит вкусно! Две из них, а также пиво, и что морс... {Zvuchit vkusno! Dve iz nikh, a takzhe pivo, i chto Mors ...} (Sounds delicious! Two of those, as well as a beer, and that Mors…)"

"Да, морс. Отлично! Я вернусь! {Da, mors. Otlichno! YA vernus'!} (Yes, mors. Perfect! I shall return!)" She smiled and hurried away to begin preparations.

"Спасибо! {Spasibo!} (Thank you!)" Karson called after her.

"What did you get us?" Jared asked eagerly.

"Coulibiac, which is salmon on rice, hard boiled eggs, mushrooms, and dill, and got you a beer and myself a Mors."

"What is a Mors?" He laughed at the word. "Sounds like it's disgusting!"

"Tastes like cranberries only it's made out of the Russian fox berries or bilberries. It's thicker and has little alcohol in it. I'd suggest you not drink too much, man. We have work to do, but do as you like. I don't really care as long as you can deliver."

"Yeah, yeah! Whatever! I've done more missions than you have!" Jared smacked Karson's leg.

Karson rolled his eyes. "Highly doubt that but if you say so!" He smiled as a small laugh escaped him. He turned and smiled as the waitress returned with their meals and after thanks and your welcomes, the men started eating, loving the Russian cuisine! After eating their dinner and with an hour left in the flight, Karson relaxed as best he could and kicked his seat back slightly and shut his eyes, falling into an uneasy sleep, but one his body needed desperately. Being a commanding officer even at his lower rank was kind of like being Vice President. Just as much work as the Captain/President, with less praise and attention.

****

After arriving in Moscow, Karson and Jared set off for the hotel. Karson had a map of Moscow and all the objectives that he and his team needed to accomplish. He decided to walk alone so he could get a good view of the city. He sent Jared to the hotel to wait for him and the rest of the team. "When I knock, I'll knock three times, then say… uhh… hmm…"

"Skull? It's one of our insignias. Sorry, sir." Jared corrected himself as Karson looked up from the ground at him.

"Say it in Russian. It is череп. (Cherep.)" Karson said.

Karson walked away. He walked towards Red Square and the Kremlin, but before he could reach it, a man jumped out screaming, "Дайте мне все деньги в вашем распоряжении. СЕЙЧАС! {Dayte mne vse den'gi v vashem rasporyazhenii. SEYCHAS!} (Give me all the money in your possession. NOW!)"

These missions never can go smoothly, can they? Always a guy in need for his family or something like that. Dammit! Karson turned slowly, raising his hand up as he faced the man, and noticing that he had a Desert Eagle trained on Karson's face. *Of course a Desert Eagle, the loudest gun you could possibly choose, man. Great!* Karson calmly replied to the man, "Сэр, я не было денег. Почему бы вам не замедлить это вниз и- {Ser, ya ne bylo deneg. Pochemu by vam ne zamedlit' eto vniz i-} (Sir, I do not have any money. Why don't you slow this down and-)"

"ЗАТКНИСЬ! Вы, кажется, достаточно богатых, то, что с вашей рубашке и галстуке, хороший и смокинге обуви. Теперь, дай мне денег. {ZATKNIS'! Vy, kazhetsya, dostatochno bogatykh, to, chto s vashey rubashke i galstuke, khoroshiy i smokinge obuvi. Teper', day mne deneg.} (SHUT UP! You seem wealthy enough, what with your shirt and nice tie, and tux shoes. Now, give me the money.)"

"Мне жаль, сэр, но вы делаете большую ошибку. {Mne zhal', ser, no vy delayete bol'shuyu oshibku.} (I'm sorry sir, but you're making a big mistake.)" Karson starting walking slowly in a circle, positioning himself with the enemy's back against the wall.

He continued talking to the man, finding the prime spot. "У вас есть выбор. Один ведет к долгой жизни. Другие концы быстро, с задницы на местах, приятель. {U vas yest' vybor. Odin vedet k dolgoy zhizni. Drugiye kontsy bystro, s zadnitsy na mestakh, priyatel'.} (You have a choice. One leads to a long life. The other ends quickly, with your ass on the ground, mate.)

The man laughed, looking up at the sky, then lunged for Karson, Karson blocked the man's hand, grabbed the enemy gun and shot it into the man's shoulder. What Karson didn't see, though, were the militarized civilian rebels that had walked into view across the road behind him. They started running at him as he looked over his shoulder, screaming, drawing their weapons. As Russia was in civil war, Karson could get away by firing his weapons in this situation. He put on a ski mask while running to conceal his identity, and turned around shooting the Desert Eagle from the man he had wounded, acting like another loyal citizen as he jumped onto a dumpster, and climbed a ladder to the roof of some building. D.E. rounds ricocheted off the side of the building from the double threat, but Karson kept running starting to see red now that rounds were being fired at him. *Why can things never go as I want them to? I mean really.* The pursuers were on the roof in seconds and fired again at Karson.

Karson dove behind a structure on the roof and waited. As one man came around the corner after splitting off from his partner, Karson grabbed his gun, and shoved the man over the side of the roof, flinching as the man hit the pavement with a sickening thud. The other armed rebel came running around the corner towards the scream and started shooting, but Karson shot the gun out of the man's hand, eliminating the threat as he blew off his fingers, and slid behind him, pulling the rebel knife from his boot and driving it into his calf.

With both threats neutralized, Karson fled the scene towards the hotel, making sure to stay out of sight of the other armed threats that had flooded into the area. A helicopter flew towards Karson's location and hovered near him. Karson split from cover and dove down an air condition shoot right as the chopper turned its sights to check the area Karson had been a moment before. On the street, Karson blended into the crowd, lifting his hat over his ears to be less noticeable. He headed for the hotel, having to make do with the intelligence he'd gathered from the ground. He arrived at the hotel, and walked straight through the lobby, into an elevator, and pressed

⑤

The doors opened at the fifth floor, and Karson turned right, taking in the layout of the hallway, and listening for sounds on the other sides of the doorways, hearing televisions and speech but muffled so he couldn't make out what anyone was saying.

If I speak low, no one will know!

Once at the room, Karson knocked three times and said the entrance code. Jared opened the door.

"Skull seems too obvious, man." Karson teased the Ranger's insignia. "It's a sissy's symbol... You need something better-"

"Like a seal?" He looked at Karson, arms crossed, his face sideways.

"Hey, man! Don't underestimate the power of a seal. Just listen to them bark, makes your body boom like a blast wave!" Karson winked and laid out his pistol in case he needed it, and told Jared to get some sleep for their upcoming mission while he planned whilst awaiting his other Soldiers. He looked at his watch.

Anytime now, fellas! Karson thought. *This war isn't less of a war, even if it hasn't 'started' yet!*

****

CHAPTER 2 - Da D

Two and a half hours passed, when there was a knock at the door. Karson grabbed his P226 and walked over to the door with it at his side. He looked out the peephole in the door and saw David and Chris. To be safe, he cracked the door weapon facing out the crack to ensure they were truly standing there on their own free will. Karson had heard the stories of how Soldiers had been on a mission, looked out the door, saw their friends' faces, and opened the door, only to be killed on the spot because their friends had been decapitated, and their heads were held up to trick the Americans.

Once Karson was satisfied, he opened the door and ushered them inside quickly, then looked up and down the hall to make sure no one was following them. "Okay guys, we have a busy time coming up," Lieutenant

Hunter whispered so as not to wake up Jared. "I want you guys to go to sleep right now, like Jared, and unpack later. That's what I'm going to do. We need our strength and our wits about us for the mission ahead. I'll brief you later."

"What if someone breaks through the door? Who's going to be sentry?" Chris asked worriedly.

"We're in Moscow, Russia. This enemy has a country to take control over that is many, many times larger than any they've taken before. They have their hands busy, and they know the United States has no clue what is going down." Karson looked at Chris, who still wasn't convinced. "I have already taken care of the door. I placed a charge on the door. Laser connection disabled by a code. If that laser connection is broken by anything other than that code, kaboom! Anyone at that door will die. We are safe in here; it blows outward. We'll wake up and combat anybody left, and disappear into the building or the night. But, that precaution is not needed. This scenario will not happen. Now get into bed. I'll wake you at 0110 hours. At 0230, our mission briefing begins and 0315, our mission begins. Understood?"

"Hooah," both Rangers said in unison.

"Good. Rangers lead the way!"

****

At 0100 hours, Karson got up to take a shower; 0110, each Soldier, washed, woken up, and ready in civilian clothes. 0230, Karson started his briefing, however before he could even begin his presentation, three shots went off down the hallway from the Americans' room. Karson's eyes widened, and he pulled his P226 from his holster and headed to the door to investigate.

Sleepy people were opening doors and looking outside and shouting down the hallway. Karson thought about opening the door, but that could reveal his position...and nationality. Luckily the two skirmishing men fell into his area of sight. They were both bloodied and shouting. Karson couldn't pick up what they were saying through the muffled door.

"Team, be ready..." He kept watching through the peephole.

"Yes, sir!" Blarney said behind Karson.

Karson's men were standing on either side of the door. Karson's hand rested on the doorknob. He looked to his man on the right closest to the area where the door opened.

"You ready?" Karson asked him, eluding to the fact that he'd face whatever danger lay outside that door first.

"Hooah!" He said.

"I'll be right behind you!" Karson watched for another minute or so and heard more footsteps. Russian hotel security intervened, throwing the men into the walls and cuffing their hands. One tried to fight and received a club blow to the face, splitting his face open. Blood ran down and pooled on the ground as the men were carried away.

"It's over. You know what I find strange?"

The fact that you put a black man to go out first." Blarney spoke up.

"What? No!" Blarney scoffed at Karson's defense!

"Look, man, iss' cool."

"No, listen, man. I could care less your color! You ever study war?"

"Yeah... basic..."

"So that's a no. In the Vietnam War, there was a group of Soldiers all African American. They called them 'the Bloods,' and they were some of the most instrumental troops in the entire combat history of America. If anything, you were there because you were the most competent for the job."

The men relaxed and returned to where they had been sitting during the briefing.

"As I was saying before I was wrongly accused..."

"I was joking man..."

"Even in wartime, the way a city runs or the way a country runs still stays somewhat the same. I mean, we're in a luxury hotel room, and there are security guards to keep that feeling of luxury relaxation, even though it's a war zone right outside the doors to the building..."

"Strange, sir!"

"Very odd." Karson agreed. "Anyways, back to the briefing. Where was I? Actually, that skirmish out there helps. I need access to the roof, however, when I arrived here, I realized that there were people on the roof. Snipers. Only, they wore the same uniforms those security guards wore. So, we'll be dealing with a hotel security force rather than trained, heavily armed enemy soldiers. I need a way up there. I will be gathering a lay of the land, trying to find the best way out of this hell hole. Watching both day and night. Our mission is to locate and save the Russian President. No clue where he is. But as he's seen firsthand the impact of this enemy, we need his intelligence. That is where Chris comes in. Chris, I need you up here as well. The Kremlin is within our sightline from this location. At least from the roof. When Osama Bin Laden was located, the CIA sent a team to listen to his conversations; only there was no way to get near him. They invented a laser beam that can pick up vibrations on the window and make out what the men inside the compound were saying."

"How do you know all of this" Chris asked.

"I study. Military culture, the news..." Karson smiled. "Anyways, here you go. A 'this day and age' version of that laser. It has been twenty-three years. We've upgraded. It's invisible, so you don't have to worry about being caught. Once the laser lands on the window, it will pick up the words. Once we find the information we need, we'll head to the HVI and extract him."

"How do you know that is where the information will be relayed from?"

"I don't. If worse comes to worst- Actually, no. Better idea. I still need access to the roof, but I have something that may make this better. Hold on just a second." Karson moved to his pack against the wall and took out a briefcase. "I brought this drone along developed by Haston Industries and DARPA. You guys familiar with the DragnFLI?"

"No." The Rangers leaned back in their chairs.

"Right. Rangers, not SEALs." Karson winked.

"Hey, man. Not cool!"

"Just messing. The DragnFLI is a helicopter-like aircraft that moves exactly as a dragonfly does, except that if a person moved at full speed in an airplane, they would suffer whiplash so severe they'd die. Haston Industries made it possible. This plane moves like a dragonfly, meaning it can dodge and weave, and then take off like a rocket. It can fly backward, operate weapon systems far superior to any other aircraft known to man. It's an overall, fantastic piece of human machinery. This is the DragnDrone. The DD."

"Ha! He's gonna get the da Dee!" The Rangers laughed.

"Anyways, the Da Dee" Karson laughed "is the exact thing I just described, significantly smaller to resemble an insect. I will load this with two darts; one with a microphone, the other will look like a stinger. The microphone will have an anesthetic, like a mosquito. You know the needles we have when we get shots? Painless correct? Can't even feel them. This microphone won't be felt, but to ensure it isn't, we will sting the man on the opposite side of the neck to divert his attention away."

"What man, sir? I'm starting to think you SEALs are whacko."

"Oh, we are. Intelligence shows a significant amount of people entering and exiting the Kremlin every day. The Kremlin holds an important part of Russia's power. Functioning powers that is. We'll just have to wait until someone rolls up that looks like they are important, tag them, and just hope that they are a higher-up."

"Why not just use the laser."

"It will only hit one part of the building. The entire building functions above and below ground." Maybe this will save us some time. Instead of years trying to find the Al Qaeda leader, we could find our target in moments.

"Why not just put the bug on his person."

"Too big. A microphone is a risk enough, let alone a bug crawling around on his back."

"Alright. The roof. How do we get up there?"

"Stairs?" Karson asked.

"Too risky. You saw those men out there, sir..."

"We could use the rope..."

"That may work, except for the people looking out the window..."

Karson stood pondering. "Chris, go unlatch the window. Have you guys ever seen Spetsnaz climb a building?" They shook their heads no. "God, why are you so unprepared. Here," he pulled up a video online to show the rangers what came next for them. "they use each other as a ladder. David, Chris is going to be on your shoulders first. You'll hoist him to the next window. Then, the rest of us will follow. When you have a Soldier on your shoulders, hoist him up, climb up the next Soldier, and get to the roof. The last of you will reach up and climb the legs, and up onto the shoulders, and hoist up to the roof. I will go last and climb all of you to the top."

"Why don't you have to hoist anyone?"

"Number one, I outrank and lead all of you. Second, you're all stronger than I am. We'll drop a rope and repel back into the room when we're done."

"This is going to suck isn't it?"

"Probably. Let's go! One pistol each. Suppressed. Don't get caught." Karson grabbed the case with the DragonDrone in it and waited as his team made a human ladder hanging outside of the hotel. Karson moved to hang out the window and grabbed onto David.

"Aye, watch the ass, man!"

"Well, it sticks out pretty far, gotta grab onto something!" Karson moved to his shoulders; he stood, and Karson kicked off and up onto the next Ranger. He was about to climb onto the top when a gust of wind and a roar of helicopter rotors thundered over the roof. A spotlight shown onto the roof, barely missing the human ladder.

"Nobody move!" Karson called down as the helicopter started to hover over the Americans. As quickly as it appeared, it disappeared out over the city, shining its lights over the Kremlin. Karson looked up and over the lip to the roof and found that no snipers were on the roof; they were filing down the stairs as Death Nation soldiers moved to patrol the roof. "Something's happening. Everybody up. Weapons ready."

Karson climbed over and when his team too made it over, scurried over to the roof lip nearest the Kremlin and looked through binoculars. "Motorcade. We go now! Cover me!" Karson hurried to grab the drone as the sun started to rise over the horizon.

"Sir, we need to hurry. We'll lose our night advantage soon!"

Karson readied the drone and turned it on. He turned on the battery in the controller, checked the video camera, and threw the drone. However, it nosedived towards the street. Karson frantically tried to gain a connection between the drone and the controller. Finally, the link hit and the drone flew off towards the motorcade. "That was close. How are we looking?"

"Safe for now. About three minutes until the sun is up."

"I always forget how early the sun comes up in some places. Okay, the cars are pulling up. I'm flying over the gate. Stinger is ready. The microphone is ready." The cars rolled to a stop and the men started to exit the cars. "Chris, I need you to video the people exiting the cars. My binoculars hold the camera. Now."

"Aye, sir." Chris moved to do as he was instructed.

Karson flew over to the third vehicle in the line. "Normally, important people are in the third car!" He whispered to himself. As he spoke, a car door opened and out stepped-

"The Prime Minister!? Jackpot! Yup, he's getting stung!" Karson maneuvered the drone to strike, and dive-bombed. He stung the Prime Minister twice on both sides of the neck. The mic stuck as the minister scratched at the stinger side. Karson flew the drone back and landed on the roof. "Deploy the rope. Drop back down!"

"Aye, sir!" Karson packed the drone up and moved to where the Rangers were already dropping back into the room. The sun was up over the horizon now, and the enemy troops were looking around, getting closer and closer to Karson's location. *Not good, not good, not good!* Karson handed Chris the drone as he descended, and Karson dropped over the lip. He took the rope as Chris entered and strapped it to his side and dropped as a soldier walked past. Karson grabbed onto a ledge with a loud thud. The people inside could be heard gasping. *Drop again Hunter!* Karson dropped four more times, reaching the floor that his room was on as the window above started to open. *That's a far jump!*

Just then, though, David stuck his head out. "I got ya!" Karson didn't wait and leaped, grasping David's hand and was pulled in right as people looked down. The window closed, Karson panted, but stuck his thumb up.

"Success!"

"Now what do we do, sir?" Chris asked, handing Karson his drone back.

"Now, we wait and listen!"

****

The U.S Soldiers woke up to find Lieutenant Hunter listening to the Russians inside the Kremlin.

"Anything yet, sir?" Blarney yawned, staying under the warmth of the blankets.

"Not yet. Flip on the news would ya?"

"Yes, sir, but I doubt we learn anything. It's all on replay."

"I know, it's to drown out the noise and any chance that we're being listened to."

"Hooah!" Blarney said, reaching for the remote.

"Sir, what's it saying?" Chris asked, eyes still closed.

"Shush! I've got something."

"SIR!" McCollum shouted out of nowhere, bounding over. Their first lead.

"SHHH!" Karson smacked his comrade and walked over to the window. Looking outside, gunfire ricocheted off the walls beside their window!

"They're shooting at us!" McCollum had followed Karson.

"No, they are not!" Karson said, raising his hand for silence. "Come here."

"No!"

"Okay, dude! You are more experienced than I am, and older, and you're sissying out. Get over here. You guys always just look to blow people up, but you have to pay attention. Okay. So-"

"Why aren't the police doing anything?" Blarney also was beside Karson.

"They don't know who to follow. They are still loyal to Russia, but they don't want to die, nor want their family to be killed. Nazi's in World War II for example. Some went along to not be executed themselves. These people are torn on who to follow."

"So why are we-?"

"LISTEN! Just listen, alright? Look. See the soldiers in that ally? Those are loyalist soldiers. They still believe in mother Russia. The police who follow them are welcomed, but the police who turn will die. Hopefully, nobody will know we are here because I'm not sure how the Russians will react to the fact that Americans are helping to keep Russia alive. However, see the soldiers in the black? Those are enemy troops."

Suddenly, an enemy vehicle with a fifty caliber weapon had driven to the other end of the ally and opened fire.

"Wow. God, those screams. See. They are the enemy. They just kill for fun. For sport. It's horrible! We have to stop them. Those are the men at the Kremlin. So, yeah, they may be Russian, but they've turned their Russian citizenship into money, and death. They don't deserve to live, so no backward glances or hesitation. Those are the men we are only allowed to kill?"

"Yes, sir."

"Also, you guys should know, there was an attack in Poland yesterday. Six men killed hundreds of people. Gruesomely. Poland will fall soon. We have to catch these demons and fast. Hooah?"

"How do these guys do it?" McCollum looked at Karson.

"Let's discuss our next objective. Just found out where the President is. Prime Minister is working for Death Nation. When I was in England at the UN, I learned through impossible means that the enemy captures and converts people to work for them to take a nation. He stated he'll be heading back to the cabin. In the laws of war, a leader of a country at war who is part of the United Nations must always be permitted to check in with the United Nations. If captured, they must still have contact and be well treated. Not tied up in some guy's basement. The President is dark. We are targeting the Russian President's residence. When I listened to President Obama and Putin's meeting during Obama's presidency in a viral video a while ago, I remember him saying "welcome to the cabin, my home.' We need to enter his house, capture the President, get him out and gather any intel from his house and him. If you see something, take it. If it's important, we'll find out when we return and ship it to intelligence. We will head up to his house from here. There are vehicles on the East side parking lot. We're going to take one. See here on this map? There is forest cover nearby his house. We will stash the vehicle in the woods, and travel the mile to the house. An electric fence surrounds the home. Once there, we will disable the electric fence and make our way to the security checkpoint on the grounds and disable the security of the premises. After that, we will infiltrate the house and grab the Intel first. We are going to have to kill for this objective, so silenced, lethal weapons only. After obtaining Intel, we will head to the president's master bedroom and capture the High Valued Individual, who is Kuznetsov. Once the HVI is secured, we'll make a run for the vehicle. Clear?"

****

CHAPTER 3 - Ganzorig

Meanwhile, in Poland

"Sir, the bombs are in place. Ready on your go." General Wajidali Hatyara said to his superior.

"Fine job, Wajidali. If this goes as planned, you will be highly rewarded."

"Thank you, Supreme Leader Ateso. Your precision and vision live up to your name. I pray this pleases you."

"I'm sure it will. Go on with the next phase. I await your company at my palace."

"Long life, sir!"

"Indeed. Long life."

Hatyara closed his phone. "You. Zip it up. You will expose us before we begin."

A soldier for Hatyara obeyed the order to cover his red uniform.

"Okay, my children. Prep those and let's head up topside." Hatyara watched his men type in their codes and press the arm button. When they all confirmed their weapons were armed and the bombs were ready, Hatyara led them out of the maintenance hole, into the waves and waves of a sea of people. As they walked with the crowd, awaiting the long sought after moment to take as many lives as they could, the small group of soldiers noticed four police officers moving down the stairs towards them. The men tried not to be seen, but the officers had already taken an interest in the men security footage had captured of their entrance. One of Hatyara's men started to get jittery and slithered his hands through his jacket, revealing the black metallic sheen of a weapon. The officers noticed his nervousness and decided to confront Hatyara's gang. They drew their weapons. The police sergeant stepped forward.

"You men need to come with us." He addressed the six extremists in front of him. "Remove your hands from your jacket, or you will be shot. Do it now."

"And why is that, officer?" Hatyara responded, calmly raising his hands for his men to relax.

"We have reason to believe you have tampered with the subway system." The police sergeant was noticeably shaking.

Hatyara laughed and sized the officers up, noticing their weapons and uniforms. He relayed his commands in his native tongue: "उन्हें बर्बाद। गले में निहित ऊपर निशाना लगाओ।." [Unhen barbaad. gale mein nihit oopar nishaana lagao.] (Hindi: Waste them. Aim above the vests into the throat.)

The six men raised their weapons and fired on the police officers. Not one officer fired a round. The scene broke out like any other terror scene from past attacks. Naturally, people started screaming, sending panic into the crowd. Hatyara's men sprinted up the stairs, knocking terrified people out of the way. They stationed themselves at the top of the stairs.

"Do it now!" Hatyara ordered, "Before police reinforcements arrive." He shot at unarmed civilians coming up the stairs. "Many people must die for us to be noticed! Today is the day our king will surface. Today, we must show world who we are! Are you filming this?"

"Yes, Hatyara. We will be sought." The soldier on Hatyara's right had a camera in his tan hands.

"Good." Hatyara and the men deployed the remote signal. Sixteen bombs went off simultaneously, incinerating hundreds of men, women, and children, as well as caving in the tunnels, flattening the fully loaded subway cars coming through for rush-hour. The subway entrance caved.

"Alright. Onto phase two. We-"

"Sir, the police are coming. We must be moving." Hatyara's man on his left spoke.

"I was speaking, man!" He pointed through a hole in a building. "Do you see that?"

"Sir, we really should-" Hatyara shot the cameraman in the forehead.

"Pick up that camera. Do you see that?" After a pause... "I asked a question. I expect an answer, or you'll wind up like our example here. DO YOU SEE THAT?"

"Yes... sir." The man on his left replaced the cameraman and Hatyara's other soldier took position left.

"This is the bank of Poland. Gold is through that hole. It's heavy, take as much as you can muster. We give it to Supreme Leader when we get back."

"The police-" The new cameraman started.

"We will handle the cops. For now, get in."

The tunnel destroyers nodded to each other and slithered through the hole in the back of the bank of Poland. Expecting heavy resistance, the men raised their weapons as they entered a vaulted area.

"Hatyara, how are we to get in? It is locked." The black man holding the camera asked, his yellow infected eyes glimmering in the dim light.

"I know."

"Sir?" Hatyara's Indian comrade now spoke up.

"I have help on inside."

"Who?" The Austrian man asked.

"Hatyara? You?" A voice from ahead called out.

"Where are you, Ganzorig?" Hatyara called into the dark, smoky corridor.

"At the door."

The men rounded the corner and revealed a Mongolian man holding a card, sliding it when he saw Hatyara. The two men embraced.

"Ganzorig, your name gives way to you. You certainly showed courage today. Let's get out of here. Here, explosives, fire those at the back wall. Men, grab the gold-"

A blast ripped through the Austrian soldier, and he cascaded into the bars of the vault. Had he not been killed by the high caliber bullet, the electric shock of the bank bars guarding the gold certainly did. He looked as fried as a person who had burned alive in a car fire. Hatyara found the source of the shot and returned fire, eliminating the bank guard. "Continue with the mission."

Ganzorig turned to Hatyara; "you have five minutes to be in and out. I'll see you soon! Be safe. Long-life!"

"Long life," Hatyara replied, and turned to inspect Ganzorig's job on the wall. "Parfait! Men, three minutes, grab the gold and let's go."

"What we need this for, sir?" The camera man's Nigerian voice spoke.

"Besides the obvious appeal, even as extremists, we must have money. Grab and go!" He pushed the Indian into action.

Hatyara blew the wall when the three minutes were up and stepped out in the streets of Poland. The extremists sprinted through the city, loose to rampage, shooting into hordes of people. Up the road, the men noticed police vehicles racing towards them and ducked down an alley. One police car had honed in on the extremists and followed down the driveway and raced up on them. It hit the slow-paced Indian soldier, as Hatyara dove to the side and shot at the car, killing the driver, and his downed man to silence him. "RUN! If you are captured, you spill. I kill you so don't get caught." He shouted to his final soldier.

They ran out into the street, running in front of cars and buses. Hatyara chose a car to take, killed the driver, running the vehicle into a pole. Hatyara ran up and threw the man's body into the street, and drove as fast as he could to get out of the city.

"What separates us from any other group is that we are not afraid to do the damage it takes to win a war. We have no rules to follow. Nothing to keep us from actually doing damage. We kill everyone, indiscriminately. Unlike the sissies who have gone before, we demolish humanity; we rampage, and we kill gruesomely. Good work. We will be rewarded well for this day."

"Money and women, sir!" The Nigerian smiled into the camera.

"Oh, you'll get as many women as you want my friend! We just need to get past this security checkpoint. Post our video to our channel. And send out our cryptic message. Recruit the masses, my man!"

The men drove up to a military checkpoint on the road to the airport. The government had decided to set up checkpoints in case of terrorist attacks. They failed to stop Hatyara's plan. The Soldiers sauntered up to the car. Noticing the three men in the car. One Soldier was radioing to his command center.

"Evening, sir. Can I have identification? Each of you?" He looked in the vehicle suspiciously.

"Why do we need to do that? We just want to get to airport." The passenger said over Hatyara's orders. "This nation obviously can't protect itself."

Hatyara merely smiled. "Isn't this against the law of Poland? A free nation? We just want to pass."

"Identification now, sir." The Polish Soldier shifted, anxious to get on with his job.

"Hey, what is your buddy doing?" Hatyara asked.

The young soldier looked to his comrade. Hatyara pulled out his weapon. He shot the Soldier to the side of his neck. As the Soldier crumpled, Hatyara killed the other Soldier and drove through the blockade. Hatyara failed to notice the third Soldier, and as he drove by the Humvee, the third Soldier shot, hitting the Nigerian in the passenger seat through his eye, spewing eye juice all over Hatyara. He looked at Hatyara as his life ebbed.

"Quit looking at me like that!" He shot the man in the other eye. Hatyara raced to the airport and screeched to a halt by the plane. He ran up the stairs to the aircraft. Hatyara locked the door into place on the plane. "Go!" He yelled into the cockpit. As many Soldiers ran onto the tarmac and fired at the plane, its landing gear left the field, and Hatyara was airborne.

This world will feel the worst war it ever has been dealt before. This war has already begun. You will all die. You will all die. And we will have long life.

****

CHAPTER 4 - It's International

"How are we going to take a vehicle from under their nose, sir?" Private Davis asked.

"Glad you asked! Pack up your gear and turn that radio on. I need one of you to come with me; the rest of you, ready the gear, you're gonna carry all of it out to the vehicle and load it up on my order. Understood?"

"Hooah!" They all said, turning to complete their 'chores.'

"Good. Have weapons ready, but out of sight. If an enemy appears, take him out."

"Him? Sir, we have to remain gender-neutral nowadays…"

"I understand your concern. Anywhere else I might agree. But do you honestly think Russians are going to be gender-neutral? Also, you think a woman fights these fights? Number one: anyone who is gender-neutral knows the importance of life, and nothing against women, but they are above war. Honestly, you think they have time to fight?"

"You should meet my wife, sir… Absolute devil." Sergeant McCollum smiled.

Karson and Corporal Blarney headed out of the room and down the stairs. As they rounded a corner once off the stairs, Karson nearly blew the entire mission. The hotel had a square courtyard surrounded by windows. In the darker exterior and lighter interior, Karson saw his reflection in the window leading outside and raised his weapon to neutralize the threat. Blarney stepped in and pushed it down right as Karson's finger hit the trigger.

"Just us, sir. But we'd better get out of sight." He said before the SEAL fired a shot.

Karson regained his escaped breath, calming. "Agreed. Sorry 'bout that."

"I probably would have done the same thing had I seen it first." He patted the Sailor on the back.

The two Americans turned right and headed through the kitchen and staff area towards the back of the building where the cars had been parked. Reaching the door to the staff and delivery parking lot, Karson halted his friend. We need a window to see outside and what we are facing on the other side of this door. There's no one working in here right now, but just in case someone enters, be ready for that."

"There's a window, sir!"

"Great. Stay put." Karson scurried over and hopped up onto a counter, and peeked through the window.

One, two, three, four, five… Guard checkpoint times two… At least one sniper top. Black van. Other vehicles.

Karson headed over to Blarney. "Alright, dude. Five people, two guards, armed. Sniper on the roof. Vehicles around. We need to disable the vehicles before we leave. I'm not sure if the five people are armed. We'll decide that in the moment. As soon as we exit, I will take the sniper; then we'll duck down beside the dumpster. Get to that point; we'll talk there, hooyah?"

"Hooah!"

"Good. Go!" Karson opened the door, aimed his pistol up and shot the sniper through the head. He crumpled backward onto the roof. *That could not have gone any smoother! Hunter, you da bomb!* Karson dropped behind the dumpster. "Hope there's no one else up there." Karson looked around the dumpster. *They are offloading supplies. Civilians.* "The five I said are just employees. The security guards then. Can you fire from this distance?"

"Duh, sir. We can shoot just as well as you, man!"

"Okay, okay! Just wanted to be sure. I'll take right. You take left." Karson moved to the right side of the dumpster. When Blarney gave the thumbs up, Karson counted down. "There, two, one..." Two simultaneous suppressed shots ended two lives. "Nice shot, dude!"

"You as well!"

I know! "Alright." Karson grabbed his radio. "Team, make your way down the stairs. When you reach the bottom of the stairs, turn right and head through the kitchen and staff area, out the door, past the dumpster and you'll see a van in the middle of a parking lot!"

"Hooah, sir!" The Sergeant's voice responded.

"Okay, man. Drop under the other vehicles and cut as many things as you can and move onto the next-"

Shouts echoed around the parking lot.

What are they saying? Enemies in the area. "Team, quickly hurry up! Blarney, get cutting. I will cover." *I guess there were more snipers on the roof.*

"Sir, we are at the bottom of the stairs." Chris echoed in Karson's ear.

"Hurry," Karson said. The civilians had exited the area. Karson and Blarney were alone.

"Team, stop at the door." Karson ordered.

"Sir? Shouldn't we get out of here as quick as possible?" Jared asked, wanting to help with the fight.

"They'll shoot up the van if we leave," Karson said, looking around for the enemy. Karson looked up and saw more and more. Suddenly, Karson heard a step behind him. Felt a bullet whiz past him. And heard a groan.

The men on top shouted.

"Team, let's get out of here! Quick!" Jared said as Karson kept sighting targets.

Karson's team ran out as bullets started to fly, and tossed him his MP5. Karson started picking off targets, yet the sound seemed to grow instead of decrease. Man after man took up position, firing down.

"Team, they have the high ground. Load the van, and drive. I'll draw their fire!"

"Sir, you'll die!" David shouted.

"Won't. I'll run through the front of the building and enter the van at the front. You'll drive off." Karson said. "Is that van loaded?"

"Yes, sir." The Rangers shouted from the side of the van.

"Good, mount up." Karson fired another shot, this time the sniper fell to the ground with a sickening thud of bone-shattering on concrete.

The Rangers obeyed, and mounted the van, firing their weapons as well. Karson looked, and as he did, a bullet hit at his feet, and he fell to the ground.

"Sir?!" The Rangers started to exit.

"No! I'm all right, no harm. Drive! Go!" Karson shouted, standing and ran out from what little cover he had, drew their fire, and jumped back behind the dumpster just as the van exited the parking lot. *Okay, Hunter! Just don't get shot! Yeah... It's like dodging rain! Run as fast as you can! Go!*

Karson bolted from cover and ran into the kitchen, through the staff area, knocking people out of his way, past the stairwell, through hallway after hallway, not looking back, not seeing if an enemy was nearby. He ran through the lobby and burst out into the street. The black van was just pulling up, a Ranger opened the door, and Karson hopped in. "Drive! Fast!" Karson lay winded in the vehicle, holding his belly. It bobbed up and down as a Ranger handed him some water. Karson sipped the water, then turned to his side and wretched in the car from running faster than he'd ever run from the fear of the possible demise of his life. Then he laughed. "How's that for teamwork?!"

"Hooah, sir!" Jared said from the driver's seat.

"That is disgusting, sir!" Chris gagged.

"It is a four-hour drive, Rangers, the palace is. Soo… Entertain yourselves somehow. I'm going to eat this sandwich I grabbed from the kitchen." Karson unwrapped a baguette of a sandwich and his knife. He cut it into equal slices and handed each Ranger a bit. "It's not much, but it's enough!"

"Thanks, sir!" David said from the passenger seat.

"Teamwork." Jared swerved to avoid people in the crosswalk.

The Soldiers checked their equipment one last time as they headed out of the city, munching happily on the snack. Driving up the road, Karson kept checking to see if they were being followed, but everyone was turning in as curfew approached, and every time someone would pull up on the van, they would soon turn off again. "Good cut job on the vehicles, Blarney!"

"Thanks, sir!"

"Didn't even see you!" Karson continued.

"I'm sly as that raccoon in that video game!"

"Ah! I loved that game!"

Soon, not a soul was left on the road, and Karson ordered the lights of the vehicle off as curfew came and passed.

"Night Vision." Karson's response to one of the Soldiers complaining about not being able to see?

"I'm a Special Forces Soldier, I swear!"

"You're also human and a stupid one at that." Karson retorted. His normal sassy way.

Two hours into the ride, the men started to get antsy.

Chris stared out the window. "Dude, this is creepy. Look at this fog!"

"Let's just hope that no one sees us!" David looked back at the two behind him.

"Yeah… That reminds me. Keep on the lookout for checkpoints. It's possible that the enemy has settled in already. I have an idea. Karson ruffled through his rucksack and pulled out the drone. "Mm… Here we go! Alright. Which of you knows how to fly a-"

"SIR! Headlights!"

Karson turned and poked his head to the front. "Off the road. Now!"

"Sir? Where do I go! There is no-"

"Just do it!" Karson grabbed the steering wheel, and the van dropped down into a ditch, flipping thrice. As the van came to a halt, the men were holding their heads. "SHUT THE ENGINE OFF!"

"Well, that was a dumb move..." The driver groaned.

Karson ignored him and scurried out of the van and up the hill, going prone as a vehicle came into view, slowly traveling up the road as if searching for something. It came to a halt up the road. Three men and a dog hopped out of the vehicle; the gunner stayed topside.

"I could have sworn I heard something!" A British voice came to Karson's ears.

"Yeah? Vell, ve hat better hurdy dis up. Boss wants us back to roadblock now!" A Russian accent responded to him.

"Yeah, yeah, mate. Just a second." The men hurried down the hill. Karson slithered over the top of the ditch.

"Men, I've got four targets that-"

"WHAT WAS THAT FOR, LIEUTENANT?" Just then, the dog started to bark, and the gunner turned his attention towards the sound.

"Nobody. Move!" Karson whispered. Staccato.

The enemy came running. "Over here! I told you!"

"Silenced weapons..." Karson said.

Karson rolled down the hill like a kid would and into the tall grass at the bottom, his weapon pointed up. The enemy rushed past him, surprisingly silent. *Why can't they be my teammates?* Karson rolled on his back and sat up, but a growl sounded behind him. Not taking his aim off of the men running towards the van, Karson pulled the pin on his grenade, shoved it behind him and then tossed it into the brush ahead of him, next to the men. The dog started barking and darted after it towards the men. The people turned around and saw the commando sitting up. They aimed and shouted. Karson fired his first silenced shot, when suddenly a massive explosion ripped through the trees, shredding the two other men.

"Men! Grab your gear, and disappear into the trees." Karson turned his gun up and saw a man coming down. He shot him, then too disappeared into the trees. Two minutes later, more vehicles approached, and men raced down into the ditch, investigating.

"ALRIGHT! WE'VE GOT PEOPLE AFTER CURFEW. TRAINED IN TACTICS. SPLIT UP. YOUR SQUAD, HEAD THROUGH THE WOODS. MINE, WILL TRACK DOWN THE ROAD. YOU, STAY AND SEE IF YOU CAN RADIO BACK UP AND CHECK OUR DEADS' TRUCK, EH."

Canadian.

"AS YOU COMMAND! LONG LIFE!"

AMERICAN. Karson flinched.

"LONG LIFE!" Everyone repeated.

Multiple nationalities. Karson didn't take his eyes off the American.

The troops started disappearing. Karson and his team watched through the trees on the other side of the road as only one man was left in the area at the enemy vehicle. "Take him."

"Yes, sir." Jared fired a shot into the man's chest, and the team raced through the trees into the truck.

Karson grabbed the coughing, brown-haired, scrawny soldier. "Where is the checkpoint?"

The man was terrified. "Up the road, but you can't pass it... You're gonna get caught and- "

Karson smacked him in the mouth like a father his teen son and lifted him up by the collar. "We're gonna kill all of your friends, dude. Don't put it past us. Is there another way we can go? Seriously, help me out. I need to preserve my ammo, but have no problem pumping your friends and actually, yourself full of lead. TELL ME!" Karson punched him in the face.

"There is a small pass... It goes around a lake, and then hits the main road again a half-mile up the road from the checkpoint!" The enemy spit blood. "Please, I have a family."

"Should have thought of that before you betrayed our nation. Thanks for that. I'm not going to kill you... yet."

The man spit more blood and looked up at the SEAL terrified. "Please..." He whispered.

"Men, mount the truck." Karson threw the man up into it. "You're coming with us. We could use you. And I promise you'll be rewarded for your help if you follow through."

"I want immunity." Karson turned from his seated position.

"You have no say. I decide what goes on here my man. If you had a say, there would be no need for me-" Suddenly, the truck took a hard right turn, knocking the enemy soldier from the vehicle, and sending Karson over the edge, holding on, and running alongside the dirt. A tree was coming up.

"SIR! STOP THE TRUCK-"

"NO! KEEP DRIVING!" Karson turned his head, to see the man standing up and running away. Karson swung himself up into the bed of the truck, got on the .50 caliber machine gun, and as the truck took a turn, fired a bullet. Karson couldn't see if the bullet had connected or not.

"Did you kill him, sir?" Jared asked.

"We'll see... It depends on if we have company here in a few moments. I honestly have no clue."

"Let's go back..."

"No, no... Keep on the mission. Our hope is that we can get there in time. HEY! A LITTLE WARNING NEXT TIME AND MAYBE THIS WOULDN'T GO DOWN? YOU HEAR ME? INCOMPETENT! NOW WE'RE FLYING BLIND MAN! WE ARE COMPLETELY FLYING BLIND!"

"Relax, Lieutenant! We are going to make it." David called back.

"We better, or your ass is grass."

Karson stayed on the .50 caliber machine gun as the men continued around the lake. Karson looked into the water, totally amazed at how the stars would reflect in the mirror-like liquid. As if nothing was wrong in the universe. *If only I could live out there. In the great unknown. Nothing wrong. Nothing to worry about. Nothing to fight. Maybe, just maybe I could have the life I want... Except aliens.*

"Lieutenant, there is a road ahead." The driver said.

"Kill the lights." Karson swung the gun around, and as they turned onto the road, the men could see the lights of the military checkpoint down the road. "Crap..." Karson breathed. "Just coast, dude. No sounds." Just then, though, the truck backfired. A spotlight came on and shined up and down the road. Vehicles roared to life and headed in the direction of the Americans. "Man! Just once I'd like it if we could just do something easy... For once? Please? FLOOR THIS TRUCK! GO, GO, GO!"

The truck picked up speed as the Rangers started to pull away from their enemy. As they came around another bend in the road, Karson spotted some lights in the sky and heard the distant thundering of a chopper, as well as real thunder. *Maybe a storm can help hide us.* "STOP THE TRUCK!" Karson changed his orders.

The truck skidded to a halt.

"OUT! OUT! INTO THE FIELD! Go stealth, and follow me!"

"Why? What's wrong, sir?" Chris hesitantly jumped out of the truck.

"Grab your gear. Just do as I say."

With that, Karson and his team jumped out of the truck and slid down the slope into the field that ran alongside the roadway. As the Americans started hiking through the field with night vision goggles on, they scanned for enemy soldiers. The chopper was getting closer, and the sky was starting to spit its rain. Not thirty seconds late, Karson stopped dead in his tracks, turned to his left, and dropped to his knee, unlatching the safety on his MP5. The team did the same. Karson scanned his area whispered through the mic, "five-foot mobiles, AK-47's, heavily armored, and I see rockets. Three German Sheppard dogs. Let's not take them out. They'll be rendezvousing with someone, so better not draw attention to us. We'll let them pass."

"Yes, sir," David whispered in response as he was the closest Soldier to Karson. His breathing was picking up.

"Calm yourself, Soldier." Karson laid a comforting arm on his comrade. "We're going to be just fine if we work together. That is what is keeping me from running to safety. I always wondered why people would not flee from a fight. Now I know. Because the price that would cost on our Nation would be more than if we just stay and fight."

"Aye, sir, I'm just cold, though..." David countered.

Karson only grunted. "Sure."

"SHHH!" Chris growled through the comlinks.

Karson noticed now how close the enemy was to him. "Don't shoot. Just let them pass."

The enemy troops walked so close to Karson that he could have licked the enemy boot. The dogs didn't even notice them, as they were a yard away. Karson, after the soldiers had passed, looked behind to see where they were, then breathed, "Stay right behind me, and do exactly as I'd do, hooyah?"

Karson then crawled noiselessly through the brush for about three yards, staying quiet by moving his body slowly, and leopard-like, laying his hands down softly, along with his body. His team wasn't as soft. Finally, Karson stood up and continued sneaking north towards his waypoint, a point he would pick as a goal to reach, before scanning the area for new threats and new locations to hide.

"Sir, that chopper is coming back." Jared whisper-screamed.

Karson had been so focused on his ground surroundings that he hadn't heard it coming, but he dropped fast, rolling under some brush.

"Aye."

The spotlight slowly slid over the Soldiers and SEAL. Karson watched in horror as the spotlight stopped and returned to the American Special Forces operators. Karson's thumb instantly removed the safety from his weapon, and he readied his M203 grenade launcher. If he had to, Karson would blow the bird right out of the sky. Immediately, the door opened, and a rope dropped down on Karson's position. Karson knew they'd been discovered. Bullets flew, but Karson flipped over onto his back and fired the grenade launcher inside the helicopter, killing the crew, and the helicopter started spinning out of control.

"RUN!" Hunter yelled, grabbing his closest member pushing him along. Enemy vehicles were heading through the field towards the Americans, and Karson could see their dogs racing fast ahead of the enemy forces, barking their heads off, desperate to sink their teeth into dirty American flesh, killing at the first possible chance. The chopper hit the ground and exploded, taking out a wave of opposition. The team sprinted to some trees on the edge of the field, and ducked into the shadows, moving among the trees to a river.

"Boat! Team, fill the canoe, and we'll paddle the rest of the way. It'll be faster than walking."

****

CHAPTER 5 - American Betrayal

"And this is how you frogmen trained?" Chris asked.

"Yeah. In the Pacific. We had waves. This is just an extra-long canoe trip for me! Nothing too complicated about it! Except you pricks aren't helping me paddle."

"There is only one ore, sir." McCollum pointedly stated.

"Chris, you take over. It's your turn."

"What?"

An hour later, the team arrived behind a fence that crossed into the water.

"Okay, guys. Soo… We are three hours over our schedule. We are going to have to move a wee bit faster than we had anticipated. This operation must be done before sunrise, and we have to be on the road to meet up with the Spetsnaz by the sun," Karson whispered through his comlink. "If not, its mission aborted and the president is as good as dead, especially after blowing up that helicopter *if he's not already dead*." At that, he turned and started jogging to the President's house.

Within moments, the team had made it to the electric fence that surrounded the house and Karson hooked up a battery with jumper cables on it to block the charge. He wire cut the fence and broke through. A guard turned, but Chris shot him in the head. He shivered. Karson noticed this as odd. Ranger comforted Ranger, but Karson had the strange sensation he enjoyed the kill… *That wasn't dislike. That was orgasmic.*

The enemy soldier stiffened and fell to the ground, blood splattering the leaves, and pumping from the wound.

"Quickly, hide that body," Karson whispered moving to the guard tower climbing the ladder. He pounded on the wooden door. It opened, and an AK-47 barrel came pointing out. He grabbed it and pulled the weapon owner through the door, and the soldier plummeted, snapping his neck as he hit the ground. As Karson jumped up into the tower, he pulled out his P226 and shot the three other guards through the heart. He tapped into the security system and watched the video feed. He discovered enemy dragging the president by chains to the master bedroom, Veniamin Kuznetsov successor of President Vladimir Putin, thought strong and the face of Russia was barely conscious at the excessive force that he had taken during his interrogations. Karson informed his team to move up to the house. "I'll be right there."

Karson turned and started to drop down when a barely audible tone came from the computer. Karson stopped, looked at the computer, and rose up to check it out. He pulled up an email.

Karson's eyes widened as he read the document.

> WITH THE HELP OF –RE- AND THE EXCESSIVE
> TROOP GAIN, RUSSIA HAS FALLEN TO OUR
> CONTROL.   PRESIDENT KUZNETSOV IS NO
> LONGER NEEDED. WE ARE JUST INTERING DE
> ALLIED LIFE INITIATIVE.

"Team, are you at the house?" Karson asked as he dropped down to the ground. He hid the enemy who fell, took his weapon, and moved up to the house.

"Hooah, sir. Ready when you are." The Sergeant acknowledged.

Karson hurried up and crouched beside his men at the entrance to the mansion. "Okay team, this is it. Private Davis and Sergeant McCollum, I want you to clear out the basement, and floor one, gaining as much Intel as you can. Kill all enemy combatants. No mistakes, gentlemen, or it is our hides on POTUS's chopping block. Corporal Davis and I will clear out floors two and three, with the president on three. We will extract him, and meet you at the cellar door to escape out the back. I want the back of the electric fence cut so we can go straight out. After that, we'll loop around and escape in whatever vehicle you two find. Jared, you and Chris should have it running when I come with President Kuznetsov. Do you understand, have it pointing out the gate so that we can make it out quick. Chris, you are driving as soon as my feet leave the ground and the door is closed. Hooyah?"

"Yes, sir."

With that, the team made entry into the lobby of the mansion and headed to their respective floors of operation. Enemy soldiers knew the team of Americans were there and opened fire from upstairs, having the element of surprise and the advantage of the high ground. Karson was pinned down in the vast lobby of the mansion.

"Chris, Jared, GO! We'll cover you! Go clear the Basement and work your way up! Have that fence open and car running." Then Karson broke from cover, firing at the enemy. There were an infinite amount mercenaries staring down and firing fully automatic, armor-piercing rounds at the team of U.S. Soldiers. Karson dove, rolled, and fired a magazine into multiple people, killing only zero and wounding only zero. "David, fire into their faces or something. Maybe that will stop them. They all have body armor on and are firing armor-piercing rounds. That will crack body armor, and we'll be torn to shreds if were hit!" Karson was on the other side, hiding in the room opposite of David, nearest the stairs. "If you can draw their fire, I'll head up the stairs and kill them. Shoot their faces and try to stay in cover as best as you can."

"Yes, sir!" David whipped around the corner and shot and killed one mercenary, as they turned their fire from pinning Karson to pinning David. Karson sprinted up the stairs, dove to the floor and shot into the hoard of mercenaries at face height. David was right behind him and was also shooting. The men in front of Karson and David fell, and soon the people behind them fell. After all foes had been eliminated, Karson and David reloaded and started to move to the next flight of stairs, when the door behind Karson slammed open, knocking him onto his belly. David pulled his knife, and slit the first mercenary's throat, but didn't react to the second. David was stabbed in his shoulder, the next to his stomach.

Karson rolled over and shouted to get the enemy's attention as he watched his comrade slump to the floor. "NO!"

Thinking his comrade was dead, Karson fired three shots into the exposed neck of his enemy. He jumped up and ran to David. "Soldier, are you okay?" To Karson's surprise, David was sitting up.

"Yes, just patch me up, sir, and let's keep going."

"You can't go like this!"

"Just patch me up, sir. We have a job to do."

"Aye, but… carefully." Karson patched him up and handed him a downed mercenary's gun. This will crack them like eggs. Hopefully! Good thing you had armor. He'd have gutted you."

****

Meanwhile, down in the basement, unaware of the events transpiring above dirt, Chris and Jared were having a tough time killing the heavily armored juggernaut mercenaries that were attacking them, also, trying desperately to make it down the stairs and to cover.

"Dude, we should have brought our armor-piercing rounds. This is crazy. I've only killed one guy." Jared was saying.

"Grenades?"

"NO! THAT WILL BLOW OUT THE SUPPORT BEAMS. WE'LL BE BURIED ALIVE!" The men took to screaming as the explosions of gunfire were starting to become excruciatingly loud. "WELL, MAYBE WE'RE GOING TO HAVE TO DO SOMETHING! THIS IS INSANE!"

"CONCUSSION GRENADE!"

"I JUST SAID-"

"OKAY!"

Chris threw a concussion grenade into the crowd of enemy troops and watched them skirt the stairs and trip down to the ground.

"Dude, we're gonna have to take a chance."

"What?" The Americans had their guns raised, ready to fight some more, as the basement got quiet.

"We have to kill them, and take the chance that the roof caves. Use the grenade launcher, or, wait! Look here." Chris pried off the rest of a box lid from a storage container and found four RPG-7s waiting to be used.

"'Aight! Let's kill us some 'Kill Seekers'!" Jared cheered. Jared grabbed an RPG. As he stood up to shoot, however, Chris hit Jared in the head with his crowbar and shoved it through an unarmored part of the vest and Jared's skin on his back, twisting it to Jared's sickening screams, and the squelching of his flesh as it was torn apart. Yanking it out, Jared fell to the floor, rolled, and said, "What the fu-" as Chris kicked him in the face. Chris loaded an armor-piercing round into his D.E. chamber and shot through Jared's vest into his stomach.

Chris stood up laughing, and picked Jared up, tossing him over the edge of the railing deeper into the basement of the building. The basement was a square room, with a pit in the middle that dropped fifteen feet to concrete, where the Russian President and his guards would practice martial arts, military tactics and weapon practicing. Chris then, after watching his 'friend' plummet, turned to the mercenary commander.

"Thought you'd changed your mind." He said shaking the traitor's hand

"You kidding? Treason sounds like so much fun! Hatyara has a billion in gold in his possession. You think I'm going to let that slide past for an assassination order on the Russian President and a few U.S. Special Forces? Uhh... no."

The heavy troops smiled.

"Here's the SEAL's stupid plan." Chris said, heading back the way he came.

****

CHAPTER 6 - Arlington

Having patched David up, he and Karson proceeded to the next floor. Reaching the top floor, both Karson and David heard a loud scream through their open frequency earphones. Karson and David both grabbed their ears in pain as the crack reached them. "Chris, Jared, are you okay? Bravo, respond!"

THUD

STATIC

"Sir, we have to keep going and get to President Kuznetsov before they kill him. Chris and Jared are Rangers, U.S. Soldiers; they can handle themselves, sir."

"Even Navy SEALs need to call '911' sometimes. So go-" Karson was interrupted by an enemy soldier in heavy armor hurtling up the stairs behind them. Karson fired eleven shots into his mask, but no bullets pierced the Kryron.

"Crap. Kryron!" Karson shouted.

"Sir?"

"It's aluminum alloy and nanotubes. Can take multiple .50 caliber rounds. MOVE!" Karson and David dodged behind the enemy as he opened fire. Drawing an armor-piercing pistol from a dead soldier, he shot three bullets into the mask, one finally piercing the plates, killing the man. Four more followed suit.

"David, we can't fire ammo like that anymore," Karson said while reloading his gun, diving behind a pillar. "We'll run out of bullets before we can kill one more."

"What about grenades?"

"That won't work. I don't have any. They fell out trying to escape that field. Plus, I didn't want to jeopardize the President anyways."

"Sir, luckily I disobeyed the rules of engagement for this one time. I grabbed two!" David chuckled as bullets ricocheted their covered position.

"You little prick-" Karson ducked back as a shot splattered pillar shrapnel into his face and open mouth. "Gah!" He groaned wiping concrete and metal from his tongue. "Okay... Okay, throw one."

David nodded, an evil Special Forces smile on his lips, and threw a grenade into the advancing 'tanks' of men. Two tried to run to the rail of the stairs, but when the frag blew up, they were thrown over and dropped three floors, and with all their armor, they fell like a ton of rocks and were too injured to get back up. The others, because of shrapnel and the blast wave, had imploded organs, and lay dying on the floor. Karson and David ran past them towards the stairs to the room in which the President of the former Russian Federation was being held, tortured, and interrogated.

Before he could get up the stairs, however, Karson took a round to the back and fell onto the first step. David pulled him up. "Sir, you okay?"

"Finish the mission!" Karson spluttered, taking deep breaths as he found his feet and lifted himself up the stairs to outside a door. Using the thermal imaging mode on his goggles, Karson confirmed President Kuznetsov was inside the room, tied to a chair. Switching back to normal mode, Karson turned to David. "David, get ready to breach." Karson planted the explosive on the door and said, "Weapons tight. Pick your targets, careful not to hit Kuznetsov."

BANG

Everything slowed down in Karson's eyes, peering through his goggles as he and David entered the room and shot their weapons. Ten enemy soldiers were guarding the true leader of the Russian Federation, and they fell by the American rounds.

Confirming each kill, David, guarding the door; Karson rushed over to the President's aid.

Karson spoke to the Russian President in his native tongue. "Господин Президент," {Gospodin Prezident,} (Mr. President,) as he was talking, Karson, medically trained, quickly did a field check over the President to ensure he was safe, and fit to travel without first aid. "Мы Соединенные Штаты Спецназ здесь, чтобы получить вас отсюда, сэр." {My Soyedinennyye Shtaty Spetsnaz zdes', chtoby poluchit' vas otsyuda, ser.} (We are United States Special Forces here to get you out of here, sir.) The Russian President knew English; U.S. intelligence had explained, but to calm him and get as much information as possible that could make this extraction run smoother, Karson deemed worth the thought process. "Каков наилучший выход из вашего дома отсюда, господин президент?" {Kakov nailuchshiy vykhod iz vashego doma otsyuda, gospodin prezident?} (What is the best way out of your house from here, Mr. President?)

"Крыша." {Krysha.} (The roof.) He started coughing, his condition deteriorating fast.

"David! Throw me a bottle of water."

David fiddled around in his bag, producing a bottle, and tossed it to Karson.

"Здесь, сэр. Выпей немного воды. Мы вытащим тебя отсюда" {Zdes', ser. Vypey nemnogo vody. My vytashchim tebya otsyuda.} (Here, sir. Drink some water. We'll get you out of here.)

President Kuznetsov did so gratefully and allowed himself to be helped.

"Lieutenant! They are coming, sir!"

Karson pulled the chair the President was tied to around a corner and aimed back around as David came to Karson's side for cover as well.

"No, David, hide behind the desk to flank them."

David took cover under the desk as much as he could as the kidnappers filed into the room.

The only voice that Karson heard. Chris's scared and screaming voice. "Sir, wait for me," Chris said, emerging from the doorway. Footsteps followed him. "You're not going to leave me behind ar... Ugh!"

Karson drew his P226 and fired right into the traitorous American Soldier's stomach four shots. He then turned, cut Kuznetsov free, and pushed David and the President towards the door to the roof as tanks of men came rushing towards the Americans, not shooting as they too needed the President alive just a little longer. Karson and David hooked into the railing on the roof and repelled down to the cellar. The men appeared over the edge, and Karson and David shot them as their heads poked over the side. They took off towards the fence where Jared was lying right beside.

****

Having been unconscious for ten minutes, Jared knew he was running out of time before his team leader would be coming down to the fence to rush away with the Russian President. He crawled up the stairs from the very bottom of the basement to the stairs leading outside and dug deep into his Soldier spirit to propel himself farther and farther towards the fence, the one chance for his body to be buried in Arlington. He stood up outside and wobbled as his vision came in and out. He pushed his way across the yard to the fence. He had no battery or jumper cables to stop the wire from being fully charged, so he had to take the voltage. Pulling out his utility knife, he began to cut. He put the knife onto the wire and felt one hundred thousand volts come rushing through his body, knocking him to the ground. He lay panting as a guard came rushing towards him. Jared stood, trying to cut again, as the guard spun him around, pushed him into the fence, sending volts through Jared and himself. As he put the knife to Jared's throat, Jared pushed the knife aside, cutting the fence as he and the man fell to the ground. The man stood, and stabbed Jared in the arm, Jared looking up towards the house to see Lieutenant Hunter repelling down the building followed by angry enemy combatants, and drifted towards a white light...

****

Karson hit the ground having seen Jared in trouble. As David hit the ground, he passed over Kuznetsov who was complaining about how he could easily move on his own.

"David, take the President and head to that jeep. Start it and have the back open. I'm right behind you." Karson turned and sprinted for Jared.

Jared heard a gunshot and felt blood spray onto his face, and felt himself being scooped up into his Lieutenant's stronger than anticipated arms. Karson ran, putting Jared over his shoulder like a firefighter carries a victim from a burning, collapsing building. Jared woke up with a start and looked at Karson's back, now drenched in blood.

"That's my blood! Ugh... Sir?" Jared said moaning.

"Jared, take the P226 from my holster and shoot as I run. Hang in there buddy; we'll get you out of here and to a medic." Jared channeled more of his warrior might and reached for the gun and grabbed it, and fired over Karson's shoulder as they all ran towards the jeep. Jared missed every shot, but Karson knew it would give him purpose for hanging onto life until they could get some first aid for him. Karson reached the jeep, and opened the back hatch door, laid Jared in, and climbed in after him, closing the main door, but lifting the glass lift gate to shoot out. "DAVID, DRIVE!" Karson equipped the armor-piercing AK he had taken and fired into the crowd of enemy men, mowing them down. When the jeep turned around a corner, Karson turned to his dying friend.

"HQ, this is Retriever One, squad leader. We are heading to the primary landing zone. Have our bird at the LZ; we're coming in hot with the HVI and one wounded, and we're running low on ammo. Best have your Soldiers shooting as we come to them. Enemies are in pursuit. Heavily armored, and pissed."

"President. Is he dead?" HQ responded. A female's voice.

Hey, I was wrong! Women are fighting in this country! "Since this is pertinent to future missions as well as this one, I can neither confirm nor deny his death."

"Where are we taking you?"

"Again, as this is pertinent now, I can't tell you where I'm going. I can only tell you from where I came."

"Sir, why did you kill Chris? He was on *our* side. He was coming to help us!" David interrupted.

"No, he wasn't! That loud scream and thud; that was Jared. A man, one, never leaves another brother behind, and too, doesn't instigate the killing. My only regret is not getting to properly kill that traitor."

"HOW DO YOU KN-" David had started to yell but was cut off.

Karson grabbed his pistol and David around his throat and pushed the gun hard against his temple, bending his head sideways. "I JUST DO, DAVID! DO NOT QUESTION ME RIGHT NOW, OR I SWEAR I WILL SHOOT YOU TOO! MAYBE YOU'RE IN ON IT WITH CHRIS?" Karson bellowed, pushing the gun harder into his temple, growling.

"NO! NO, SIR, I AM NOT! I'LL FOLLOW YOUR ORDERS. I AM LOYAL TO THE UNITED STATES! WHAT ARE MY ORDERS?"

"JUST DRIVE THIS FREAKING JEEP TO THE LZ!" Karson shouted over David's worried voice.

"Yes, sir... R-right away." David whispered, shocked, and scared for his life. He'd never had a weapon at his head, especially by a commanding officer. He thought: *shouldn't have pissed off a Navy SEAL Lieutenant.*

Kuznetsov merely chuckled.

"You okay, sir?"

"Да." {Da.} (Yes).

"Okay. Can you hold this here, while I help my friend?"

"Da. I can shoot too."

Karson took Jared's pistol. "Here. Don't shoot me."

"I shoot well then you, American."

"Better than me? On another day, I'd challenge you to a duel, sir," Karson gave a tense chuckle, still worrying about his friend's and his own life, "but I'm afraid these aren't the circumstances to do it. Pleasure to meet you, though. Thanks for helping." They shook hands.

"Yes."

****

Eight and a half miles away sat the LZ. However, thousands of enemy troops were looking for the Americans all over Russia. The odds of getting out alive, *are slim.* Karson admitted.

Karson sat down and pulled his legs up into his chest, having finished his work on Jared as best as he could, and decided to say a prayer for whatever it was worth. *Father in Heaven, God, please protect me and my men, Sir. God, though I kill people, please forgive me. I know they are Your children, but You do say, child, you may defend yourself if necessary. God, please let me be doing the right thing. And God, please heal my Soldier. Forgive me for my ways, and for not talking more. I serve for you. Amen.*

"David, are we being followed?" Asked Karson as he checked on his downed comrade.

"Umm... No, sir. I don't believe so."

"Believing is not enough. I need 'for certain' data."

"No, dude! We're not."

Karson muttered under his breath. "When we make it out of here, I'm putting you in your place." Karson pulled the laptop he had brought along, and looked at his arm. He placed his wrist against the laptop and relayed all the information from the computer he had touched earlier in the guard tower.

"Vat is dat?" Kuznetsov asked.

"Sometimes I forget to gather intel... My wrist has a small data vacuum and takes information from any electronic that I touch. There's a sentence that I noticed pops up all of the time. 'We are just intering de allied life initiative.' I don't know what it means. Entering is spelled with an I."

"Hmmm... you believe it is message?"

"Do. Not sure what it is yet. But I'm going to find out."

KCHSHHH

Karson's head dropped as glass shattered all over the vehicle and a massive hole sharply protruded from the side. Suddenly, the jeep spun hard to the right, flipping over itself twice, and skidding to a halt on its wheels again. *Wow, that's luck! Thank God!* A bright light burst through the windows now, and Karson thought for sure he was dead. As the ringing in his ears subsided, he could hear David screaming for orders, and Kuznetsov shaking Karson to arouse him.

"DON'T JUST SIT HERE! DRIVE!" Bullets punctured the hull of the jeep. Karson leaped out of his skin. He and Kuznetsov hit the deck, blood pooling on the floor of the vehicle as it drooled from his head. Karson grabbed his AK-47. *This won't do anything, but might as well try.* "Stay down Mister President. I THOUGHT AS A SPECIAL FORCES SOLDIER, YOU COULD TELL IF WE WERE BEING FOLLOWED!" Karson shouted at David.

"WELL, IT'S DARK, SIR!" David took off into the night, and to Karson's horror, so too did the enemy troop transports.

Karson turned and aimed out of the shattered glass now, and fired into the driver of the military truck behind him and killed him. However, as that vehicle skidded off into the trees, another took its place, and another, until a Stryker came out of the dark and smoke, pushing other trucks out of the way like a tin can. It started gaining on the fleeing Jeep, easily.

Well... That'll leave a way bigger hole.

****

CHAPTER 7 - Iunctus

"China falls today." Hatyara turned to look out the window of his helicopter.

"We are two minutes from Zhongnanhai, General."

"Good. How are our forces doing?" Pistol in hand, Hatyara chambered a round, pulled the magazine, and added one more bullet.

"Many dead, sir. But the missile strikes in the major cities and at military strongholds places Chinese troops in hysteria, and with significant loss."

"Navy? Air force?"

"We have no worries with their naval might. Building those new islands out in the sea brings the ships close together. Easy to strike down with the Thanatos-class ship. In addition, we destroy many ships. We have captured five ships. Two aircraft carriers, three destroyers."

"And land-based air forces?"

"We have a jamming signal over the entirety of China. Radar remains ineffective. In addition, our troops have jets in the air. No one is getting anywhere near us."

"Except that." The pilot pointed at the choppers radar. "That's a fast-moving aircraft."

"I want it destroyed."

"We don't know what it is. And this chopper can't combat a fighter jet, sir."

"Then drop down over the streets."

"That leaves us vulnerable-"

"DO AS I SAY." He pointed the pistol at the pilot's head.

"As you wish, sir." The pilot lowered the chopper below the line of the cityscape, still heading to the government headquarters of China. Hatyara opened the door and readied a stinger missile. "How far out is it?"

"Five seconds, General."

"One. Two. Three." Hatyara fired the missile ahead of the chopper. As the enemy fighter jet approached the helicopter, the missile locked onto its target and took a near ninety-degree angle up, and connected to the wing of the plane, rendering it disabled. As the pilot ejected, Hatyara pulled on the throttle and launched the chopper upwards. The Chinese pilot plummeted and was struck in half by the helicopter rotors. The helicopter, damaged, trudged along and finally landed at the Zhongnanhai compound and Hatyara disembarked with his escort of armed commandos. "Kill them all. I want the President for myself."

"Yes, sir!" The commandos spread out as Hatyara's security detail took care of the minuscule security force tasked with guarding the building.

"This is going far easier than I had hoped! This is my new palace!"

Hatyara walked through the front door looking around at all the decor this Chinese president adored to have as his. An old emperor's musket, Chinese swords, defeated Samurai armor, dragon paintings. Lots of purples. *Hmmf!*

The distance of gunshots and screams as men and women were slaughtered both by Hatyara's and Chinese forces; Hatyara couldn't stifle his pleasure at the devastation he'd caused in so many different locations of the world. The tremendous amount of dead, the impeccable decisiveness of taking leadership from so many people. *My life. My life is amazing.*

"*Hatyara... We have the Chinese President in our custody. Waiting for you, sir.*"

"Perfect. I'll be right there." He said into his radio as he drew the sword of the great Emperor Qin Shi Huang, the first Emperor of China, a battle-hardened man. Hatyara pulled a cloth from his side pocket and slid it down the blade of the sword, coating it in a greenish transparent liquid. "It's time for China."

He walked away from the wall of weapons and up the stairs to the President's bedroom. Interesting. Being in a bedroom and not a bunker during a war. Wife must have wanted her clothes. And sure enough, three men were holding the woman down about to have their way when Hatyara stopped them.

"Stop that. Leave us."

"But... Sir..."

"I'll be okay in here on my own. There are plenty of women in China for you to do that with. You'll have more tail to come. Get out." The Chinese President was bound and teary-eyed. Hatyara looked at him with a menacing smile as everyone left the room. "Alright, Mr. President. Let's talk about your nation. You are going to die in about two minutes. Your wife is going to feel my rod and then join you. You must know you've already lost. Give me your Iunctus access."

"I don't know what you're talking about."

Hatyara slammed the weapon through the man's genital area, sending immense pain through the Chinese President's body. "Every nation in this world not designated as terrorist or psychologically insane is given an Iunctus account. In this account, you are given nuclear strategy, targets, and warnings. Not to mention locations of Allied fleets and aircraft, ground troops and whatnot. There is more, but you already know this. I want this. Don't play coy with me. I already have said accounts from multiple nations. I want them all. To have them all builds a stronger nation for me, and a blinder world for the rest of you. Give it to me now, or I'll rape your wife while you're watching." He moved towards the woman and yanked up her dress, revealing a most decorative, opium smelling- "You have the woman of this nation smoke opium through their coochie? Give me the account."

"It is written down on my desktop. You mus' know I already am logged in-"

"Thanks!" Hatyara beheaded the man in one stroke of the blade, turned to the computer, ensured he didn't kill the man too early, and then turned back to the woman of whom he would deface after enjoying the woman against her will. *Feminists would be ashamed and flabbergasted of me. Or probably wouldn't have ever told about this. Time for the world to really know what happens in war!*

****

CHAPTER 8 - Unconscious

8 .5Miles Later

... There is no way we are going to get out of this alive.

Karson still fired out the back of the jeep. "I'm running out of bullets! I need-OOF!"

The bumpy road and the winding turns continued to knock Karson's aim off the prize. He tried breathe control to steady his aim, but momentum continued to win. He opted for his own perfected technique and shoved his foot into the right side of the vehicle and his shoulder into the left, and pushed down on the lip of the liftgate to keep his rifle steady and tried desperately to fire under the tiny hatch that safely kept the driver. *Not gonna work, Karse. Think boy, think!*

As they rounded the corner and sped towards the landing zone to the helicopter that would fly them to safety, the Stryker took a chance on the wide-open road and hit the jeep like a Police PIT maneuver. Flipping on its side, knocking its occupants around, the vehicle slid towards the helicopter. When it came to a stop, the Stryker was spinning around, its gun turning around towards the jeep. "David, get the President! Get to the helicopter!" Karson had to get the President to safety, even before his dying comrade because that was the objective and the priority of life.

As his team ran towards the chopper, Karson fired shots into the eye of the machine gun so the occupants could not find a way to lock onto their targets. Instead, the gunner fired in random directions, trying to hit his enemies. As the Navy Lieutenant staggered to the chopper with Jared the Stryker started moving towards the men; one enemy soldier had decided to mount the devastating machine gun for manual use rather than the use of automatic fire. Karson ordered the chopper into the air. Karson took off sprinting after it. It was air born and Karson, even with the pain, threw Jared into the air. David ran to the ramp and nearly fell out, but caught Jared. He looked back into the chopper to see that President Kuznetsov had a hold of his pant leg, and was helping to pull the dangling Soldiers back up into safety. David now understood the meaning of "Super Kuznetsov." Karson ran under the helicopter and down an incline of rocks towards the river that lay beyond the landing zone. The Stryker couldn't help but follow. The driver now insisted on killing the people who had invaded the country from out of nowhere, outperformed the men of Death Nation, and outsmarted every other military force in the country and the people who had taken President Veniamin Kuznetsov, the only man that could possibly stand in the way of overthrowing the country, from the extremely well hidden, well-guarded compound. Karson was nearly in the water when the rocks shifted, knocking the SEAL off balance.

"Woah!" He fell sideways and walloped his head on the rocks. Karson rolled onto his back, his world spinning, to see the Stryker right on top of him. Karson lifted his legs and felt them hit metal. The Stryker kept moving, revving his engine, and pushing Karson farther from safety.

Karson felt the water close over his head as the Stryker kept pushing him into the water. There was no way for Karson to escape. The Stryker would crush him if he lowered his legs or if he tried to swim. Karson was going to drown. He tried swimming anyways, but as he propelled forward, the Stryker propelled forward too. Karson could see through the water a man coming around the Stryker and waded into the water.

David looked down at the Stryker and knew Karson must be in trouble. He grabbed a sniper rifle and tried aiming, but was too shaky. He fired, but the round bounced off the Stryker's armor. The gunner turned his gun and shot in the air.

Karson started to fall asleep, from lack of oxygen. He kept feeling bubbles escape his body as each rock that hit him blew more air out. He struggled to stay calm and keep his eyes open.

As David kept desperately firing, Kuznetsov stood up and pulled him off the rifle. David stood up to fight back, and pulled his pistol. "If you kill my friend, I'll-"

"Shut up American. He saved my life. I repay favor."

David kept the pistol aimed at the Russian President's head as Kuznetsov first took out the gunner, then the man in the water. Next, he found the cockpit of the vehicle, aimed at the glass that allowed the driver to look out from the metal vehicle and took aim. He fired, and with the thermal scope saw a heat signature. Kuznetsov honed in on the driver as the man realized what was happening, and Kuznetsov sliced a bullet through his head.

Karson felt the weight of the Stryker stop pushing on him as hard as it was and weakly pushed away from it, right as he blacked out, unconscious.

David saw the Sailor surface back up and ordered the chopper down.

When Kuznetsov felt he was low enough, he jumped into the river.

Kuznetsov felt the water's sharp fangs swarm around him, but he persisted and swam to Karson. He pulled him over his body and swam to the bank. He started pushing on Karson's chest. The squad from inside the back of the Stryker, however, had new plans. They had jumped out of the Stryker and ran around towards Kuznetsov and Karson. One kicked Kuznetsov in the face, knocking him off of reviving Karson and grabbed Kuznetsov around the neck. The others turned towards Karson. David fired as best as he could, but the chopper took off again and fired at the enemy soldiers, pinning them down momentarily.

"Lieutenant Hunter! Head to the secondary landing site! Half a click north of you!" David called.

"You better be there, ramp down, with those soldiers shooting whoever is following us!" Karson said coming to.

"Yes, sir! Just run down the hill!"

Karson turned, looking for President Kuznetsov, but he was still struggling. The man still had a hold on the President's neck, and they rolled into the water, disappearing under. Karson rushed over, looking up to David dropping a loaded AK-47 down to him. Karson grabbed it and splashed into the water, looking for bubbles; ripples. As he aimed his gun down into the water, looking for any sign, a hand-launched out of the water and grabbed the gun barrel. Karson's first instinct was to shoot, but instead, he fell back, and a man dressed in black soared out of the water, picking up the weapon and pointed it at Karson's head. The helicopter above was too busy keeping the others pinned.

"Americans! I'll have to report this." As the man relieved the weapon of its safety, Karson braced himself for the inevitable. "Goodbye, American scum! Ha!" The man started laughing, and as Karson looked away he heard a

THUD

and heard blood splash into the water. He looked up to see President Kuznetsov dropping a bloodied rock into the water as he rolled the body into the current, watching it flow down the rapids and disappearing over a small waterfall. As Karson took his hands, he relayed the plan. The two started springing towards the new landing zone, looking back to ensure that the men were pinned, but the helicopter was flying over the men.

"RUN!" Karson heard David's nearly drowned out voice. Bullets pelted the trees around the two men, and they ran even faster. As they zig-zagged between trees, suddenly, they felt the ground give out beneath them, and both men toppled down an inclined hill, disappearing into tall grasses. The enemy was right upon them, and as Karson started to stand to fight, Kuznetsov grabbed him and kept him down.

Kuznetsov pulled Karson close and spoke into his comlink. "Act like you have us and are flying away."

"I only take orders from Lieutenant-"

"Do as he says, David. Tell the pilots. There is no way out."

The chopper turned its doors backward to the approaching enemy force and fired its weapons as its back door opened. The men used the wind to move to another position. The chopper stayed for ten seconds, then rose into the sky and disappeared.

The enemy started cursing and shooting randomly into the brush. Dogs were barking, and the men walked through the brush, hoping to find something to kill. A man broke off from his patrol group and headed towards the two men. Karson felt his blade unsheathe, as Kuznetsov moved in front of Karson. The man came over, unzipped his trousers, and out flopped the biggest excuse for a man Karson had ever seen. Instead of a penis, this woman had a tool that allowed her to stand and urinate. No matter, the woman had seen the men and started to scream as President Kuznetsov lunged up, grabbed her face, jabbed the knife into her throat, and disappeared right back down into the brush, without anyone seeing him.

"Nice move, sir."

"I too vas Spetsnaz. I train vell!"

"What happened under the water?"

"He try to twist off my head. I act dead. Then he come up to you. I smash head vith rock."

"Well thank you, sir, I-"

"Shh. They are leaving. Call helicopter back."

"David, come back now and launch rockets into the tree line that we came through. We are in the middle of the field; we will hurry over to you."

"Yes, sir. On our way."

Karson and Kuznetsov waited two minutes until the thundering of a helicopter came to their ears. "Sir, bird incoming."

"I hear it, stupid. Get ready."

The chopper came in low and fast, barely skimming over the grass, it launched missiles into the tree line and as it approached the trees, lifted off, turning on its side, coming back around and hovering down, weapons blazing.

"THAT'S TIGHT, SIR!"

"RUSSIAN PILOTS! BEST THERE IS!"

Karson and the president raced over to the ramp and climbed on board, the chopper lifting off, and the ramp closing.

Inside the helicopter, David was working on resuscitating Jared.

President Kuznetsov turned to Karson and shook his hand.

"Sir?"

"Thank you for vork, rescuing me! Vhile that vill never happen again, and you can never tell anyone I said dis, I am forever in your debt. 'Sank you."

"Just following orders, sir!"

Kuznetsov nodded, walking over and sitting down on a chair, a Russian Soldier heading to his side, not to leave it again. Karson chuckled inwardly as the chopper lowered itself above the water to disable the enemy Stryker so it could not be used again. One rocket was all that it took, but two were used to be safe.

"Hey! Americans! Where to go?"

"The U.S.S. John C. Stannis will see us, pilot. Off the coast of Storfjorden in the Barents Sea. Can you make it there? Coordinates of 75°39'39.41" N and 22°08'06.52 E.

"We need fuel." The copilot told his passengers.

"No, no fuel! We need to get to the ship, right now!"

"We need fuel, and we need to let President off." The pilot affirmed.

"No, the President comes with us!"

The man beside the President raised his gun.

"No, Americans, I stay in Russia. My people need me. I must also find family." Pausing, President Kuznetsov stared at the poised, and ready to strike American Lieutenant. "You have no negotiating power here."

"Respectfully, my country needs to speak with you, sir. We need to know what this terror probe was used for, and if this is a terrorist cell or a real enemy. We need your information."

"I vill speak to vorld leaders vhen possible time arises. For now, I have job for do."

On this chopper with too many risks, Karson knew all arguments were useless. He truly did not have any negotiating powers. And in order to keep relations as much as possible, he could not overpower the crew. All he could do was wait to land, fuel, rearm, and head to the ship.

****

"Lieutenant Hunter. Ve are refueled, sir." A Russian helicopter crewman found Hunter.

"Good. Let's get out of here."

"One problem. Ve cannot fly in storm. Storm coming. Ve fly tomorrow."

"That won't work! NOW!"

"You have no authority here. We fly tomorrow. Sleep."

Karson however, could not sleep on a foreign base. In the middle of a war-torn, dark country. The president had left four hours earlier, heaven only knows where he could be, and Karson had had no contact with his country. Jared was taken to a medical ward, but sadly, Karson had received news that he'd been dead for hours. Chris had betrayed the United States, David was suffering from post-traumatic stress, and Karson had some strong words for his commanding officers if he were ever to make it out of Russia. All he could do was turn in and try and rest before tomorrow.

****

CHAPTER 9 - The Base

The lights were out on the Russian base, and Karson had managed to find a comfortable corner to curl up in and waste the night away. Dosing in and out of alertness, Karson just could not release himself to the pleasures of sleep. Instead, he had this horrid feeling that something was going to go wrong; like someone was there, someone knew he was there, someone knew that attacking this base on this night at this remote facility at this moment in time, this random act could stop a war from even beginning, and spell a victory for the entire enemy force of Death Nation.

I can hear my heart beating, and I can hear my lungs working as I breathe. I can hear my blood flowing through my veins. It's as if... this base is too quiet. Something's wrong. Where are the night patrols? The sounds of airships, the military turbo trucks. The clock that chimed at every hour...

Karson rifled through his bag and pulled his pistol and night vision goggles, strapped the pistol to his waist and put the night vision on his head. He then stood from his spot, hoisted his bag onto his back, and went on his own patrol. If anything, this would give him something to pass the time.

Nothing is going on; nothing is going on... Everything is fine, Karse. You are safe.

Walking down the hallways at night, in Russia, at a military base never known about until now, was kind of creepy but Karson had his head on the swivel. Nothing seemed to be going wrong; until he heard the noise.

A sound that could send chills down your back in the middle of the night, the sound that you are definitely not alone, the sound that lay just outside of your view in the shadows, lurking there, ready to pounce on you at a moment's notice. Karson started to walk faster, away from the noise of imminent death. Karson turned down another hallway, weapon equipped now.

This place is just playing tricks on me. There are no demons, no ghosts. Nothing is going on...

"AHHHHHHHHHHHHHHHHHHHHHHHHHHHHHHHHHHHHH HHHHHHHH!"

The sound was muffled, but Karson knew it distinctly. The sound of men being tortured to death. Karson darted off, lighting speed, but silent as a lioness approaching her prey. The sound was gaining, and as Karson reached it, the door creaked open, and a hunched back, camouflage-covered doctor came hobbling out, carrying an arm, with a sleeve that looked much like that of one of the Russian Soldiers that guarded this place.

Karson gasped. The man turned around in a mass of skin and bones and let out the most horrendous sound that carried through the deserted halls. Karson turned, firing a shot at the man, and as he turned, from out of the darkness appeared a six-legged, ant looking creature, ready to devour Karson, teeth bared, mouth open, and-

Karson jolted awake, pistol swinging around and around. "What was tha- "

Suddenly, the wall to Karson's right exploded, sending Karson flying to the left, burying him in rubble. Not enough to crush him, and as he moved, trying to get out, a hole opened, and Karson could tell instantly that this explosion was the only thing keeping him alive right now. Seven armed men, one carrying a severed head, walked through the blast hole. The attack alarms started going off, and Karson knew that he would have to escape here and make it to the ship on his own. He had to find David, and fast.

These mofos mean business.

When they passed, Karson waited three minutes, until he was sure they were gone, to dig himself out. Even still, he had his pistol aimed, as he pulled his bag out of the rubble, and suited up in his vest, helmet, and pulled his MP5 out of the bag. He hoisted it onto his back and scurried through the hole.

"David? David, can you hear me? Come in!"

Nothing was audible over the communications channels. *Okay, okay. Karson, what would you do if you were David? Try and find my Lieutenant, but also a way of escape, just to make him proud. But that's me. Navy SEAL training, and I'm a kiss ass... Maybe... Just try it. Hanger.* Karson climbed a ladder on the side of the armory building, to find where the jet hanger was.

"There you are; due east. Alright. Here I come." Karson said as he slid back down the ladder. "David, you better be there." Karson moved around the building, ducking behind some cars, checking the surrounding area, before he could make his move around the perimeter of the buildings to make it to the hanger. *So far so... Wait.* Karson zoomed in with his night vision and could see some soldiers surrounding a man. From the looks of him, he was the one giving the orders for this operation.

Do I get him or do I let him go? Karson looked from him to the hanger. *He is in front of the hanger. It couldn't hurt to listen in...* Karson decided to make his way to the boxes that lay behind the troops. But as he made his way in front of the buildings, the door opened and out stepped three soldiers. Karson dove under a car, causing some dust and noise. The men, hearing the sound, swung their rifles in Karson's direction and fired. Every enemy invading soldier ran towards the ruckus.

"What was that!?"

"I don't know. Check it out."

"WHAT IS GOING ON HERE?" Karson peaked out to see the man he assumed was the leader yelling at his soldiers.

"W-we heard a noise, sir. We thought it came from here..."

"And you don't know what it is?" The man shook his head. As he did so, the leader pulled out his skinning knife, and ran the man through, severing his neck from his body. The headless man fell, crumpling into a bloody mess in front of Karson. Karson gasped, gagged, not only because he thought the body in front of him was alive and could spot him but realized what had happened and life pumping fluid from a foreign body was now on him. *gasp *gag* Blech!*

"I- Did you hear that?" The man's feet turned towards the vehicle and stepped slowly towards it, the man unholstering his weapon. "We can have no loose ends, gentleman. If this operation gets out, then Hatyara will have all of our heads, or worse, the supreme leader may pay us a visit. That would be UNSATISFYING!" The man dropped, aiming his weapon under the vehicle, but no one was there.

Karson sat panting silently behind the wheel.

"Humph. As I was saying..." The man stood up, and Karson slithered under the vehicle again as more foot mobiles came towards him. "This operation needs to move smoothly. We have reason to believe the forces that took the former President are on this base. Find them. Gain information, then silence them. Nothing can get out to the world."

"Nothing to be reported, sir." A soldier came up to the leader. "All quiet; all forces eliminated. Bodies heading towards the incinerator. We're changing into their uniforms now."

"Good. I assume-"

"GET YOUR HANDS OFF OF ME! AS SOON AS I GET LOOSE, I'LL KILL YO' SORRY ASS, JUST YOU WAIT AND- AHH!"

David!

"And what do we have here?"

David spit into the man's face. In return, the man gave a powerful punch into his solar plexus. This man was thick and surely could lift Karson and David up with both hands over his head.

"An American? Ahh, this is too good. You don't travel alone. Where is your team? Or better yet, where is our 'President'?" The man spat the word President at David.

"Go to hell!" David spat back.

"Gladly! I hear the parties there are flaming!" The man laughed. "First, though, I must raise Hell on earth. Enforce that people believe that death is a better alternative than life. Being able to give the gift of mortality is what Death Nation stands for. Sure, we like to bang people, hang with people, experience the way the world is, and the riches, but killing others so we can have more room to enjoy sounds good too! Don't worry; you're in good hands. I'll make your death long, and painful! You'll feel the full service of my calling. So too will every nation we are moving on next, and so too will your President, and your family, and your friends, and your team. As we speak, our forces are moving, internally in every government, through cyber networks, and in physical forces. It won't be long until we strike again, and when we do, thousands will die! It'll make your September eleventh seem like a hay day! The funny thing is, you'll be able to give no warning! I'm gonna kill you right here and right now!"

"I beg to differ." The leader's head snapped up to see Karson, holding a struggling soldier by the head, his shotgun aimed at the leader. Karson pulled the trigger, sending the leader flying into the wall. Karson snapped the man's neck, pulled his pistol and shot the seven other men paralyzed by shock, releasing David. Karson tossed the rifle to him. Get to the hanger. I've got to get-"

A bullet whizzed past Karson's head.

Karson turned towards the leader and shot him in the chest. He lay back, his red uniform now scarlet. Karson walked up to him and grabbed his chin. "Who is your leader and where is this attack coming?"

"The Supreme Ruler will be victorious; you'll never see it coming."

"Wrong answer. David rush to the hanger and secure transport." Karson pulled out his medical gloves. "I'll meet you there after I get Jared."

"Sir, we must go now!"

"WE NEVER LEAVE A MAN BEHIND. NOW GO!"

"Sir."

"Ahaha! You can't even lead your team without it falling apart. Worthless American scum. You'll die like every other per-"

"Tell me," Karson growled.

"Never." He replied flatly.

Karson drove his finger into the man's eye socket. "Who is your leader?"

"Ungh… ahh… haa…" The man started spasming from the pain.

"TELL ME!" Karson shouted, twisting his finger.

"Achkkkkkk!"

Karson pierced the man's brain with his finger and kicked the man in the face, knocking his body over. "BURN IN HELL!"

Karson turned and made his way to the medical ward, shooting people as he went. Entering the infirmary, he found Jared's lifeless body guarded by an unarmed doctor. "OUT!"

The man raised his hands and nodded spastically.

As the man ran out of the room, Karson changed his mind. "On second thought…" Karson pulled his pistol and shot the man through the back of the head. Karson hoisted Jared over his shoulders, and fireman carried Jared out of the room, past the lifeless body of the enemy doctor,

-I killed him 'cause he may cause more torture

and rushed towards the jet turning onto the runway. Enemy vehicles were converging on the jet as Karson made it. He threw Jared up to David, who tucked him into the cockpit with him, and Karson grabbed onto the handholds.

"This jet is extremely thin…"

"Size matter, sir?"

"No… not at all! I'm a firm believer in it's not the waves of the sea but the motion of the ocean… Just… wow, it's small! Must be why it's so stealthy! Anyways, PUNCH IT!"

David did as he was told, and the engines roared to fiery life as Karson's body started to turn horizontal to the plane, parallel to the ground, as the G-Forces started taking hold of his body. Karson had to work fast, and he pulled himself into the cockpit, one handhold at a time, pressing the close cockpit button as the jet lifted off. The plane started pressurizing, as anti-aircraft fire rocked the aircraft as it climbed higher and higher-

BANG

"We're hit, sir!"

Karson looked back, then at his instruments. "Just engine two, minor hit!"

"Can you fly us to the ship?"

"Yeah! I had a few lessons in aviation." Karson said.

"Great! A few lessons. We're gonna die. We're gonna end up like you, Jared." He told the lifeless body next to him. "Yeah… Just like you, buddy."

"Oh, shut up. We're not gonna die. I've got this. I was a pilot before SEAL."

David grunted.

"Just watch the radar, dick head!"

"It's clear," David replied.

Reaching an altitude of fifty thousand feet, the men could finally relax as they left the Russian airspace and entered international waters.

"David?"

"Yeah?"

"You ever sit at night at your house, and lay in bed looking out the window, looking at the lovely colors of the evening, the sun setting, the birds chirping, and just feel so at peace? Pure bliss. Man, this is it. It's so peaceful up here, no war, no death; not a single sound. No other souls up here, the ground miles below, it's just so peaceful. I used to sit on my roof on the fourth of July and look out over the ocean, listen to the bird's chirp, then silence as a giant, earth, and organ-rumbling sound of fireworks shattered the cool, crisp night air, and watch their colors mix with the sunset. You ever do that? Just sit out, meditate and relax in the evening air, or wonder, is there any way we can ever be peaceful again? Any way that we could be like the sunset or night sky, just so quiet and peaceful, just ourselves? You ever think of that? Feel that way?"

The pause made this conversation feel so much more to Karson than just a talk. It felt like they were actually living the moment Karson had envisioned.

"No. I'm not a pansy; I don't go and sit around nor wish the wars away. I'm not a softy. I am a warrior. What you just said, what you preached about, that's just weakness."

"Wow. Way to kill a moment. And here I thought you were human enough to relate too. We're nearing the ship. Keep an eye out for. What was that?" A flash launched in front of Karson as he lowered his altitude and speed.

"Sir! Two enemy AAMs! Fast approaching."

"John C. Stennis, this is Lieutenant Karson Hunter, of the United States Navy, approaching on you port side in stolen enemy aircraft, disengage, I repeat disengage. Abort missiles, abort missiles! Repeat, this is a U.S. taken enemy aircraft." Karson disengaged his autopilot and released flares and dodged the missiles. The first missile hit the flare and exploded. As the second shell whipped around, two more were launched.

"Two more, approaching fast. That one behind us... Sir, it's about to- AHHHHHHHHH!"

Karson lifted the nose of the aircraft, cutting speed completely, and as the missile flew under the plane, Karson dropped the nose, firing his machine gun, exploding the shell, and turning his wings right, dodging the first, and flipping the plane over on the second. Flying upside down, Karson launched two heat-seeking missiles. "USS John C. Stennis, this is Lieutenant Kadin Karson Hunter of the United States Navy, flying a hijacked enemy fighter jet attempting to make contact with you. Repeat, friendly aircraft in your airspace. Abort your attack."

"Commence attack, Commence attack." The aircraft chanted at Karson.

"Sir, the plane is locking onto the Stennis." David's voice shook.

"NO!" Karson frantically looked for a way to disengage the lock, but the attack was set.

"Commence attack, commence attack." The plane now had a mind of its own. The John C. Stennis launched seven more Anti-Aircraft Missiles.

"Sir? Orders?" David shouted.

"Grab Jared. Eject." Karson shouted back.

Karson pulled his eject button, launching him into the air. David pulled his, forgetting to grab Jared, the body launched into the air. Having a heavier seat, the two fell faster than Jared's body.

"DAVID GRAB HIM!" But as David fell away, he missed his chance. Karson instead was up and reached out his hands and grabbed his fallen comrade's hand, flipping Karson and the seat over and over and over. Karson pulled Jared close to him, strapping him into the Velcro, and pulled the parachute. He watched as the plane took a nose dive, and exploded as seven missiles hit it all at once. The light was brighter than the sun, and Karson had to look away. Finally, aiming for the ship, Karson and David both landed onboard with Jared. Laying him down, Karson looked up to see Master at Arms rushing, fully armed towards the intruders, weapons raised.

"WHO ARE YOU!" They shouted. "HANDS UP. HANDS! NOW!"

"My name is Karson. I am a Navy SEAL." A rifle hit Karson in the stomach, knocking him back on his knees. "HEY! Stand down!"

"Nonsense. We have no record of you." He replied.

"BECAUSE I'M A SEAL!"

"Give me your name."

"Serval," Karson replied.

"Real name." The MA raised his weapon.

"NO!" Karson said.

The Master at Arms fired a shot past Karson out over the water. Karson grabbed his ear.

"Lieutenant Kadin Karson Hunter, United States Navy-"

"You could easily be a spy."

"Do I have an accent rookie?" Karson was getting pissed.

"No… You could be faking-" He had no argument.

"Take me to the Admiral of the Fleet," Karson ordered.

"You don't give the orders-"

"He will clear my name." As the men hesitated… "Fine. Phone him and say you have Karson Hunter on board.

"Bridge, this is intercepting team." The Master at Arms spoke into his radio.

"Go ahead." A woman's voice replied.

"Radio the Admiral and tell him we have Karson Hunter on board. Ask him for order to shoot or capture."

"Aye, aye. John C. Stennis, USS Elding."

"Aye, USS Stennis." A voice Karson knew all too well.

"We have Karson Hunter onboard our ship. Requesting orders. Capture or kill."

"RELEASE! ALLY! HE'S A LIEUTENANT! NAVY LIEUTENANT. FRIENDLY! I'LL BE RIGHT THERE." Admiral Thompson responded.

"We're taking you to the brig until we can get this sorted out." The Master at Arms still didn't trust Karson.

"Fine. But first you need to feed David and me. Jared, he deserves a place in Arlington. Take care of him, or it's you that I'm gonna punt overboard." Karson threatened, not leaving his friend until the man nodded.

"Follow us." He said.

David and Karson followed the armed escort, got cleaned up and fed, as they awaited the Admiral. Once he arrived, he and Karson shook hands, hugged, and set everything straight. He shook David's hand, offered his condolences, and led them to the bridge of the Stennis.

Once outside of the bridge, Karson said goodbye to his Ranger friend. "Sorry for threatening you... The stress and everything."

David grabbed his high five and pulled Karson into a hug. "I understand. Brothers?"

"And you're the one who called me weak. Always brothers. Always. If we survive this war, we'll need to meet up! Beers. On me?"

"Sure thing! You'll have my record. You'll find me. As long as you remember me."

"I could never forget you, my friend!" The two saluted each other, and David walked away to receive his next assignment, to accompany Jared back to the States.

"You salute other branches?"

"We all serve the same thing. He is my brother, just like all protectors of our country."

"Very impressive, Serval." The Admiral patted Karson on his back as he guided him through the bridge doors.

"Thanks, Admiral Thompson."

On the bridge, Karson spoke of the imminent attack, the man named Hatyara, and how there is a supreme leader. He also spoke of the cyber and physical attacks, as well as the assault on the base and how they needed President Kuznetsov. He also explained how the whole Russia mission had gone down. Also, he gave the computer to the hackers, and all information he'd taken physically and by his wrist data vacuum.

"We have his last name… But not his first?" Admiral Thompson asked.

"If I had his first name, I could find him." An analyst spoke up.

"Exactly, now something of primary importance is this email I discovered. More, I intercepted it. I don't know what this message means. Here, I'll pull it up."

Everyone read the message.

'WITH THE HELP OF –RE- AND THE EXCESSIVE TROOP GAIN,
RUSSIA HAS FALLEN TO OUR CONTROL.
PRESIDENT KUZNETSOV IS NO LONGER NEEDED.
WE ARE JUST INTERING DE ALLIED LIFE INITIATIVE.'

"This is more than we could have asked you for, Lieutenant. Great job in Russia. My sincerest apologies to the Soldier, Sergeant Jared McCollum."

"He… He did his job, sir, and he was one of the greatest teammates I could have ever asked for. He did a lot in his wounded state and saved my life multiple times. He's one I'll have to thank up there when my time comes."

"Yeah. We all will, definitely. Let's take a moment of silence."

The moment, however, was shattered by a shriek.

"I have him! Wajidali Hatyara." An analyst spoke up.

"How you figure that out?" Karson rushed over.

"I looked at the words that made no sense in the message. 'We are just intering de allied life initiative.' I typed in Hatyara and discovered seven people with that last name, and I put the sentence in a cross-reference. W A J I D A L I. Hatyara. Wajidali Hatyara. It means Obsessed Killer."

"Holy fish sticks!" Karson said. "She deserves a promotion."

"So do you. Commander." Admiral Thompson stated.

"Excuse me?" Karson said, starting to smile.

"I promote you up from Lieutenant to Commander." Admiral Thompson saluted and so too did the rest of the crew.

"Thank you so much, sir. All of you. I promise you, I will not fail you and if I do, if there is still breath in my body, I will fight harder for you."

"We're right there with you, sir!" They responded.

"Serval, time to go. We have a briefing."

"Aye, sir." Karson followed the admiral into the next room.

"Alright. We still have work to do. The time for celebrating and grieving will come later, but for now, we need you again. No R and R for this period."

"That is fine, sir. Duty calls. It's my job!"

"You're right. At least you'll have some Navy SEALs to duke it out with. Your next mission is in China. Captain Victor Paul is on the ground, picking up some leads on people to watch. As you have more knowledge of what is going on than any other military personnel in the world right now, you are to meet up with him there and execute the mission. On his order. You are there as a secondary, but it is still his operation. I know how the leadership goes, you all want the lead. But it is his. You understand? You still need a break kid. Don't try and take over; it's his mission, and he knows more about China than you. You've been in Russia too long my friend. He is very excited to work with you again. You guys became pretty good friends at BUDs right?"

"Oh, yes, sir, we became best friends. This mission is going to go smoothly, sir. I won't be taking over. Are my SEALs here going with me?"

"Nope. You, and just you, leave tomorrow at 0600 hours. Captain Richardson awaits your return after your mission, he currently is on assignment in Poland, working with Polish Special Forces to clear up an incident at the train station. Another SEAL team is at that second terrorist attack site, trying to work out some details. You'll be back later. Anyways, for now, you best get some rest."

Karson saluted his Admiral. "As you command, sir. I'll go say goodbye to Jared, then turn in for the night."

"That would be great." The Admiral of the Fleet saluted back. "Again, great job! I expect the same if not better on his next op."

"You got it!"

Karson smiled and made his way through the ship to the infirmary, where an autopsy on Jared determined the voltage he had taken, then the beating in the jeep progressed his body to death faster, but there would have been no possible way to revive him. Had he received medical attention after the blow to the back of his head, he still would have died, and with the continued abuse, certain death was solidified. His vigil was cut short as Karson's friend and mentor called. Karson made his way to a rack and took the call. Captain Richardson had some news and encouraging words for Karson's next operation. Then, much to Karson's dire need, he turned in for the night, having uneasy dreams to curse his rest.

Something about this next op seems off…

****

CHAPTER 10 - Basic

"Harris! 3, 1, 4, 2!"

POP

POP

POP

POP

"Harney! 4, 2, 3, 1!"

POP

POP

POP

POP

"NO!"

Karson stood watching as the Sailors before him fired on the flight deck of the carrier into targets 1-4.

"Don't worry about packing your things. You're staying right on this ship. You call that marksmanship? How did you make it out of boot camp?"

Karson remembered last month, graduating from Naval Station Great Lakes by Lake Michigan. *It wasn't that hard to pass. It was kinda like high school, and gym, only with more on the line.* Karson finally felt free. His parents never appreciated the way Karson lived. High School never gave Karson anything but drama and bullying. It was time for something greater, and so he left his Texas High School and headed North for Navy training. Two weeks after graduating, he was assigned as a fighter pilot to the U.S.S. Gerald R. Ford. F-22 Raptor squadron. Mainly because Karson was already a pilot. One thing his father had given him. Additionally, the Navy had cleaned house, reassessing seasoned pilots with new curriculum that many couldn't pass. Meaning, just the right place, at just the right time with many, many jobs to fill. Karson, however, felt that there was still just one more thing missing from his life that needed to be accomplished.

"If you think you're gonna kick me out, keep me from being a SEAL, you're dead wrong."

"I think I'm right. If you can't pass this small task like firing your weapon, you're not ready for that kill or be killed world out there. And in my opinion, if you can't pass the first time, you need not return. Just look at the 2016 presidential election! Pretty hard to get the job after you didn't get it the first time. There is no *making* a SEAL, ladies. SEALs are born. NEXT!"

I agree with that. Karson nodded his head.

"What you nodding at, Hunter?"

"Your last statement, sir!"

"1, 1, 3, 1." The SEAL Chief shouted not giving any cares today, tired of cocky young Sailors. Karson scrambled ahead of the three others ahead of him, struggling with his pistol.

That's impossible. If it is shot, the target retracts and drops down.

POP

POP

POP

POP

Karson closed his eyes, bared his teeth, shrugged his head down and to the right, and waited to be scolded. *THAT WAS IMPOSSIBLE, SIR! I DEMAND A DO-OVER!*

"Head up, Hunter!" A friend behind him whispered, confident.

Is that admiration I hear? Karson looked behind himself, shyly. "What are you so sure about-"

"Unbelievable. You shot the first target twice before it could retract, hit the third one, and struck the first target again right before it dropped down. Humph. Fine shooting. I was automatically disqualifying you… but just found my star Sailor."

"Thank you, sir." Karson holstered his weapon, beat red!

"See you in BUD/s. NEXT!"

****

"IF YOU CAN'T KEEP THIS FUCKIN TELEPHONE POLE ABOVE YOUR FUCKIN HEADS, YOU'LL BE RUNNIN PT ALL DAY LONG. THE LITTLE KID RIGHT HERE HAS HIS ARMS UP, THE REST OF YOU CAN'T BE WEAKER THAN HIM, SURELY!"

"It's heavy, sir!"

"ARE YOU KIDDING ME?" Karson shouted. "WE'RE A TEAM! MIND OVER MATTER! HELP ME!"

The weight suddenly intensified on Karson and he had no choice but to drop the log, however, he held it all the way down, sending a massive slash across both of his hands.

"Gah!" He shook his hands sending blood flying everywhere.

"All of you drop."

Karson grimaced as he clenched his fists to start his punishment.

"Not you, Hunter. Let me see your hands."

"All due respect, sir, but I'd rather pay my punishment with my team."

"YOUR HANDS. NOW."

Karson presented his hands. "I promise you, sir, I can manage until night."

"That's bad. Blood is pooling. Run down to the water, put your hands in, then visit the doc." He addressed the entire group. "AFTER, WE'LL ALL BE RUNNING BECAUSE OF YOUR WEAKNESS. Get moving, Hunter."

"Aye, sir!" Karson ran to the waterfront and slipped his hands in, moaning at the intense pain that in the same moment subsided because of the Pacific salt. He ran back up the beach, had his hands patched, and took off to catch up with the group.

The medic and another DI stared after him. "That kid... He's got something about him. He's getting his ass kicked, and he still manages to keep going. To be honest, I thought he'd have been one of the first to drop out."

"That's the same kid they said shot one target three times before it fell. It's why he's here. Doc, if you ask me, that kid has found something here he hasn't had in his life. Whether it's a comradery, a passion for something... I don't know, maybe he gets off at being yelled at; I haven't figured it out yet. But I can tell you; I think we have a SEAL that is going to do great things very, very soon."

"You think he'll get fast tracked." The medic asked heading to his truck to catch up to the injured candidate.

"The skills he has? Yeah. I do. And we need it. Hell is rising out there, my friend. The demonic side of human nature."

"My question to you is, do you think he'll measure up to the rest of the guys here? The world out there? He's kinda a small guy. Very young. Barely 19?"

"He's got leadership ability. He can get into the heads of his team and make them want to make it work. He has intelligence, something many of these guys lack when they come in. He's strategic. And he's not weak. Not soft. He just has a different body. But that's why SEALs prosper. Because they have a team. If they are weak in one aspect, it is made up in the team. And he's pretty much a team of his own. Leader. Shooter. Medic. Pilot. Intelligence..."

"What about if he's on his own for real, though? You can't do it all on your own."

"He'll adapt. He'll adapt."

Karson overtook the group within sixty seconds and moved up to his spot in the row closest to a significant drop off to his right, fifth in line from front to back. His hands throbbed and oozed, his muscles hurt, his head ached, but he felt more alive than he'd ever felt before. At home. In his element. Like he had a purpose, a purpose to help others. Soaking in the ocean had rejuvenated him, and this nighttime run was a chance to think over his day, his life, his future. The **-SEAL wannabes** chanted in response to their **Drill Instructors** as they ran, each trying to win a spot in the world's most elite. Knowing full well just how many dropped out from start to finish.

Superman is the man of steel

-Superman is the man of steel

He ain't no match for a Navy SEAL

-He ain't no match for a Navy SEAL

Chief and him got into a fight

-Chief and him got into a fight

Knocked his head with kryptonite

-Knocked his head with kryptonite

Superman is no more

-Superman is no more

Crushed his head to the floor

-Crushed his head to the floor

Ready, Halt!

-Hooyah!

The medic got out of his truck. "Alright, gentlemen. Hit the showers, hit the rack. Sleep. We're up bright and early tomorrow. Weapons, and tactics. Hunter. A word."

Everybody cleared the road and headed inside the barracks to shower and sleep. Karson ran up to a Drill Instructor.

Panting, he answered. "Aye, Drill Instructor." He looked up into the massive SEALs eyes.

"Don't breathe your nasty breath on me. Drop!"

"Aye, sir, sorry, sir." Karson stifled a laugh. "One, sir. Two, sir. Three, sir-"

"You have heart kid. For laughing, give me fifty. Tomorrow I want you at the front of the line. Up early, out the door, at the range first. Your weapons and tactics scores are the highest I have ever seen in the history of the Navy. Very impressive. I DIDN'T SAY STOP!"

"Sorry, sir!" Karson groaned from the pain in his body and hands but kept going. "Thirty-one, sir. Thirty-two, sir-"

"START OVER!"

"Aye, sir! One, sir. Two, sir. Three, sir. Four, sir. Five, sir. Six-"

"That said, I will be watching you hard tomorrow. SEAL Team leaders from every team will as well. You'll be in the first range closet to the Team leaders. You want to be there. Make a great impression. No one else will be as accurate as you. Under this pressure especially, they will not. That's not what we're looking for. We want to get the job done. It's rare to get the job done well. You must thrive under the pressure. The ones that thrive under pressure and get the job done and get it done well are the special Special Forces. Team Six. If you get all of the teams' leaders to want you, you place for a SEAL Team Six selection. Immediately, while everybody else has to be selected. Don't let me down."

"I won't, sir." Karson looked up exhausted.

"Get to bed. Now!"

"Aye, sir." He panted.

Karson limped inside and got into the shower, forgetting to take off his clothes for a moment.

"Best get those clean, Hunter. DI's will have you for dinner if you mess this place up."

"Thanks, man!"

"I'd personally love to see them chew you out." The candidate continued.

"I'm sure you would. An attractive guy like me getting-" Karson gagged as the candidate slammed his hand into Karson's throat. "What! I was just joking, man! But this kinda proves my point... I'm ass naked and you're pressing up against me." Karson tried pushing against him.

"You're not attractive. You don't belong here, trust me. You're weak. Measly. You're not SEAL material. What good do you think you'll be able to do here?"

Karson laughed. *Ugly huh? Not what I've been told! This from the guy who's a nasty red faced fat headed gross-*

"Hey, man! Let him go! Leave him alone." The candidate, Karson's friend, who admired his shooting on the ship spoke up.

Karson didn't want his friend to be a target. "Slink, I've got it man."

"It's time he learned what happens when someone impersonates a Navy SEAL, Slink."

"Well, you're not exactly SEAL material either. Let me go. I'm your teammate. Teammates fight against the enemy, not each other."

The candidate reeled back.

If you hit me, you'll go down.

"You better watch yourself. You won't make it too much longer, and when you fail, I'll be the first one to bust your balls."

"I certainly plan on it!" Karson rubbed his throat. "Thanks for sticking up for me, Slink!" Karson fist bumped his friend. "Night fellas."

****

"We'll start at one hundred and fifty meters."

"Wait! Move Hunter's back to five hundred meters."

"You need to train them to shoot that far, Drill Instructor."

"Yes, you do. Move Hunter's to five hundred meters."

"The heck, sir," Karson muttered.

"You've got this." He replied.

"Aren't you not supposed to take favorites?"

"You're not my favorite. I really don't like you at all. Drop."

Karson rolled his eyes at the incredibly obvious lie but did as he was told.

"When you get up, shoot two into the heart, one in the head between the eyes. You have three seconds." The Drill instructor said.

"Three shots, three seconds, sir. Two more than I need."

"Put your money where your mouth is. UP! FIRE!"

Karson launched himself up pulling his M4 Assault rifle with him. He readied it while taking a breath and fired.

POP

POP

POP

When the gun smoke cleared, Karson glanced up at the SEAL Team leaders smiling. One handed binoculars to another. "DAYUM, KID!"

The Drill Instructor came over to Karson. "Tighten up your grouping Hunter. Even more."

Karson looked at him. "You mean like this?" Without looking away, he fired thirteen shots. "Just seeing where I could shoot, sir. If you go look closer, you'll notice they are all killing shots."

"LOOK AT THAT!" A chorus sounded behind him.

The drill instructor smiled. "Nice. But you just earned yourself some punishment. Drop."

"Aye, sir!" Karson's voice dropped. *Don't be too much of a smartass. They can all easily change their minds.*

Karson finished his fifty pushups, mouthed 'sorry' to the DI who in return nodded forgiveness. Karson continued to prove himself.

"Great shooting, Tex!"

"Funny you say that. He's actually from Texas!"

Karson nodded.

With each new exercise, the leaders followed. Karson recalled when he was hooked up stark naked on a treadmill how racing horses go through the same training to weed out the weak. The machine would be turned up for humans to eight miles per hour for one mile, then ten miles per hour for the final half mile. With anatomy flying every direction, everyone kept their eyes high. The exercise was meant to see what the basic, animalistic like man could do. It didn't matter what each man had, all the mattered was the second purpose of the exercise, comradery of the Teams. Third, to keep as cool as possible for the test.

Karson blinked, and found himself in the next scenario. *Come With Me Now* playing through his head as he kicked in the door. He shot the first three targets in the last part of the live-fire exercise when suddenly he could taste the dirt of the ground. The air knocked from him; he rolled over to see Charlie, his roommate, above him.

"Oops…" He raised the weapon to Karson's face. "Every once in a while, there is an accident on the range…" Karson grabbed the rifle and used it to stand himself up.

The rest of the team entered the building as the bullet slammed into the ground right between Karson's legs.

"Woah! What happened here?" A drill instructor looked over the railing. "He aim thAT WEAPON AT YOU?" The DI's voice rose in volume. He started walking to the ladder, not taking his eye off of Charlie. "THAT WOULD BE UNACCEPTBLE, CANDIDATE!"

Now is my chance… "No, sir… I-I was about to hit the civilian. All good."

"Drop down, candidate. Or you'll drop permanently." The DI said to Karson. "BOTH OF YOU!"

"You ever point that weapon at me again; I will kill you myself." Karson glared at Charlie, slammed his elbow into his face and pushed him against the wall. "I promise you, next time-"

"You won't have a chance." He glared.

"Yeah." Karson put his knee where the man's gonads were. "Twenty-seven-year-old failure. You pick on the new guys for your second to last chance to be a SEAL. A wise man once told me… If you can't pass the first time, you're not SEAL material. This training hasn't been easy for me either, but one part of a SEAL is to adapt to put yourself in control. I have. You need to drop yourself. You'll never make it."

The sailor raised his weapon again. The drill instructors and SEAL Team leaders dropped down into the pit to intervene, but Karson was faster. He used his own weapon as a sword and smacked Charlie's rifle barrel to the side as a round went off striking a candidate in the vest, knocking him to the ground.

"Wait." Karson's drill instructor intercepted his colleague about to shoot Charlie. "Watch what he does."

"What if Karson gets killed or had the round hit the candidate in the head?" The weapon wielding SEAL DI didn't lower his pistol.

"This is no different than an engagement with an enemy."

"Sir, he's not trained-" The DI argued, his finger slipping to the trigger.

"He knows more than you think. Don't shoot."

Karson spun and slammed his right elbow into Charlie's face, spun back around and wrapped the strap of his M4 around Charlie's neck. Charlie took his opportunity to place the rifle to Karson's stomach and fire. Karson gasped, but swatted the rifle away, taking the round to the vest. It stopped the death, but the round pierced through, the hot metal searing his belly skin.

"Hold your fire. He'll take that mistake and make it an advantage."

Karson could feel the acid rising in his throat, finally spilling his breakfast all over Charlie's face. Charlie, distracted, slipped away from Karson and tried cleaning his eyes. Karson wiped his mouth, eyes wide, swallowing back the second wave and removed his magazine from his weapon, and slammed it into the side of Charlie's face, knocking him to the ground, then kicked him hard in the nose, slamming his nose flat, and knocking him into oblivion.

"Traitor." Karson's voice cracked.

"Medic!" The drill instructors called.

"Hunter, you'll be in my quarters tonight. Take a warm shower, have a good night of rest."

"All due respect, sir… My team is more important."

"I know. But, you've taken quite the beating and I have things planned. I want you to in that room. It's an order."

"Okay, sir." Karson sighed, about to wretch again from the horrible flavor in his mouth!

The instructor walked over to the candidate who also got shot. He was sitting up dazed. "You're in Master Chief Rodgers quarters."

The candidate nodded.

"Good job uncovering this traitor." Slink said to Karson.

"Yeah... He had it coming, man."

"Why didn't you turn him in?" Skink asked as Karson was summoned away.

"Everyone deserves a chance..." Karson followed his DI to his quarters for the night. Karson's first idea was to take a shower. He turned on the water but didn't get in.

"I knew he was a no-good slob. He's wasting water, Andrew."

"Just wait."

Karson removed his clothes and checked himself over. His body had taken beating after beating, cut after cut, but it was holding up. And the massive bruise and burn on his belly sent pride in Karson. *My first combat injury!* "Your body will always push and give more than you thought!" He said to himself, remembering a high school theatre coach's words.

The DI's still watched through the camera. "I don't want to watch a grown man get naked and clean himself. Why are we doing this?"

"To see if he has the behaviors of a SEAL." Andrew answered. "Craig we-"

"How?" Craig asked. "Seriously, how does this narrow it down?"

"Well, think about it. If he does everything thrifty and quickly, he's left his civilian life. If he does it slowly, then he isn't broken yet."

Karson let the steamroll through the bathroom, relieved himself, and did a light exercise in the heat to keep up with the rigors he'd continue to face in the future. Finally, he entered and let the water flow over him, but he didn't hesitate. He washed thoroughly, then exited, putting on his clothes, and shutting off the water. He walked out of the room and sat at the desk, pulled out his journal and wrote about the day he'd had. When he finished that, he said his nightly prayer, and got in bed, after finally getting to brush his teeth with premium toothpaste. *If I use anything luxurious, it will be on my teeth.*

"Just like that. Knows nothing about us watching him, has the pinnacle of luxury, and he follows orders to a T. No television, no masturbation, no phone calls or video games or internet... He's a 'born' SEAL. Not an 'I'm a born SEAL but have to be shown'. He actually lives it."

"He took a long shower."

"He was remaking a similar scenario that his teammates were during the exact same hour. He was keeping up with his training, while also maintaining his hygiene."

"Whatever you say, Captain. But, whatever you see in this kid, he's just that. A kid. Wake him an hour before the others. He still has much to prove to me. And unless I sign off on it, not even the President could get this kid fast tracked."

"As you wish, Chief."

****

The next day, Karson woke to find a replacement candidate for Charlie. He was lean and mean, tall but firm.

"Woah! Damn! You look like Goliath." Karson said, testing the waters as he moved back into his barracks.

"You look like David." The candidate smiled and laughed.

"Thank God you have a sense of humor!" Karson wiped his brow. "Phew! My name is Karson."

"Karson, pleased to meet you." The two shook hands. "Victor Paul. I just want to warn you now... I'm all business. I've dreamed of this my whole life. So, if I come across as overbearing and power-hungry, it's partly true. Don't take it personally."

Karson nodded. "Believe me, we're one and the same." *But, you'll have to get in line behind me, bro.*

"So I heard that there's a race today?"

"Yeah. A kinda break midway through. I don't know. Everything is a test here though. So, I'm going to leave you in the dust."

"Like hell you are!"

Karson smiled as they started towards the door to head to the rendezvous point. "Hey. What do you do in the Navy?"

"I'm an MP on the U.S.S. Ford."

"Seriously? I'm a pilot on the Ford! How'd we never meet?"

"Cause you're a pilot. You're the smart one! I'm the one that stays below deck."

"Karson. Victor. You've been fast tracked. Your scores are off the charts good. You graduate Thursday with class 2301. The reason; you're to be deployed within a week under SEAL Teams 2 and 3. Karson, you'll go to Europe. Victor, you'll go to Asia. You'll finish training together for the final four days you're here. Even though you graduate, you're still not SEALs until you prove to the teams you've got what it takes. I know you do. Show them. Go clean up. It's time to go. Karson, Drill Instructor Richardson wanted me to tell you something. He was deployed late last night. He said, 'Six is watching.'"

"What about the simulated pain exercise? I want to see this one squeal like a pig." Karson asked, trying to cover the fact that he was almost about to explode with excitement.

"Yeah right. See my body? You think I squeal-"

"HEY! The beating you took yesterday is enough of a simulator. You maintained your effectiveness and turned your mistake into an advantage by spewing chunks over that guy. Victor already took it. Like he said, he doesn't squeal. He's a tank."

****

DEPLOY

The rocking of a ship, Karson always felt, relaxed him. As if the sea, beyond the thick, reinforced hull of a Navy Destroyer, was a mother rocking her baby to sleep.

At 0600 hours, Karson opened his eyes from his dream but still lay on his rack, dozing in and out. At 0700 hours, it was time to arise and begin this day of work. His flight left at 0800, so for now, he could shower, dress, and pack his gear. Heading to the armory, the Master at Arms saluted the higher ranking officer, to whom Karson saluted back, and allowed Karson entry. Inside, Karson thought about his briefing and grabbed all that was needed. Light insertion gear package. Checking and loading his weapon in the weapon clearing station, a metal cone shaped bowl like fixture mounted to the wall that when loading and unloading a weapon, will catch accidental discharges, or jammed rounds if they fired on their own. When all was ready, Karson made his way up to the flight deck, where he was flown over to an aircraft carrier and loaded up on a single engine prop plane, so as to avoid any detection. Reaching one hundred and fifty miles per hour, the drop zone was two hours away, so Karson studied his maps and rechecked his gear. The time flew by almost as fast as the plane. At twenty-seven thousand feet, Karson put his parachute on and said thank you to the pilot who offered up a fist-bump. SEALs frequently enter behind enemy lines at night with a team, but as the enemy territory was too hot, Karson had to infiltrate and ruck to his team alone. In the day time. Luckily, they were overtop the middle of a Chinese forest.

"Go get'em, Commander Hunter!" The pilot shouted back.

Karson winked and dove out of the plane at fifteen thousand five hundred feet, doing some flips to get his blood pumping. At Karson's weight and height of the jump, a fifteen thousand, five hundred foot drop would take sixty-seven point one seven seconds to hit the ground. Two hundred and thirty feet per second. *I can watch the world for a few seconds!* Plummeting thousands of feet, the world looked blurry, however, bright at the same time. Karson could see the curvature of the earth, see the endless wilderness as well as the forests of humanity with rivers of roadways.

Peaceful, the rushing wind. Being airborne. Like a bird. *No wonder birds fly all the time. This is amazing!* When he reached nine hundred feet, he deployed the chute by pulling on the line. But nothing happened and Karson looked up to see nothing happening. No canopy. He pulled again. *Jammed!* Nothing popped out, and Karson continued to fall. His HUD showed the loss of altitude.

2,000 FT-DEPLOY

1,500 FT-DEPLOY

1,250 FT-DEPLOY

1,100 FT-DEPLOY IMMEDIATELY

1,000 FT-DEPLOY IMMEDIATELY

Karson was falling without his primary chute. He kept pulling and pulling, but it wouldn't come out.

"Dammit!" Karson fumbled for the secondary chute. Nothing. There was no second chute. Only this one. The parachute pack was old; military spending wasn't so hot these days, and so any new equipment was held back until the old had been expended. That means Karson was subject to what the old equipment's mind had in store for him. Instead of being able to pull a secondary chute, Karson had to make the primary chute work. Karson pulled the pack off of his body and checked his HUD again.

950 FT-DEPLOY IMMEDIATELY

"Crud!" Karson opened the pack, and wiggled the chute out of the bag. With one hand, Karson placed the parachute pack on his back again.

900 FT-DEPLOY IMMEDIATELY

Karson let go, but the chute still didn't deploy. He shook the chute, desperately trying to get it to release. Instead of fear, though, Karson felt anger. *If I die, it's gonna be in a fight, not some dumb, hard splat into the ground.* "OPEN!" Karson thought back to his boot camp days and to the songs they'd chant. *C130 going down the strip. SEAL Team Six gonna take a little trip. Stand up buckle up shuffle to the door. Jump right out and shout hoo-yah! If my chute don't open wide, I have another one by my side! If my reserve don't blossom round, I'll be the first one on the ground! Lo, right- left lefty, right lea eft lo, right left lefty-right left.* "OPEN! OPEN CHUTE OPEN!"

850 FT-DEPLOY CHUTE IMMEDIATELY

800 FT-TOO LOW_DEPLOY CHUTE IMMEDIATELY

750 FT-TOO LOW_DEPLOY CHUTE IMMEDIATELY

Karson's HUD was flashing, and alert tones were going off, trying desperately to slow the rate of falling. At maximum velocity, Karson weighing one hundred and fifty-seven pounds normally, plus his light gear load of ten pounds, plus the parachute weighing in at twenty-five pounds, equals a whopping one hundred and ninety-two pounds plummeting to earth. Karson's HUD was flashing **124 mph.** At that speed, Karson would hit the ground at six hundred pounds, or a quarter ton of impact force. When your body hits the ground, injury comes from the sudden stop; the g-forces you take. It takes sixteen G's, and eighty pounds of energy averagely to kill a human. Karson would die seven and a half times over if he hit the ground.

Finally, though, at one hundred feet, the parachute took. Karson felt the turbulence and felt himself slowing down, though the ground below him still rose drastically fast. Still slowing, the trees reached Karson quickly, and he covered his face as his body pelted each tree branch as he fell slower and slower, coming to a halt as one tree branch smashed between Karson's legs, giving him the hardest ball tap he'd ever received. Harder even than his cousin a year ago playing a prank for his social media sites.

Ouchy! His voice rose in pitch like a little boy. Groaning a breathy moan, Karson took some deep breaths, his body racing with adrenalin; he had to slow his heart down. "Oooouuucccchhh." Karson's hand slid down to his balls, cupping them sympathetically, and lifted himself, relieving the pressure from his nuts.

He raised his knife and cut himself free. Having had a great view and now looking at his global positioning device, he discovered he had landed fifteen miles from his rendezvous with the SEALs. Fifteen miles more of hostile, unwelcoming, deadly enemy territory, with little body armor, just covering the back of his body, his MP5, his P226 pistol, and a knife. He had planned to meet up and gear up with the SEAL team and broke one of his top rules. 'Always prepare like you're invading somewhere.' Now, that was no longer an option. He was going to have to march through swamp and forest to the campsite, behind tense enemy lines, in a place he was unfamiliar with. Worse still, no one was going to know where he was. So help was out of the question, and in Death Nation, a sworn enemy to any American, especially military, death for Karson would be certain; horrifically torturous, painful, and drawn out. But certain. No chance of survival.

Karson, calming down, lowered himself painfully to the ground, cut and bruised, his balls very tender and sore from the blow he had received from the tree.

'Welcome to China, bitch!' The branches waved.

After a few minutes of steadying himself on the ground, Karson started hiking east towards safety. It was just crossing the ten o'clock mark, Karson a little beyond his scheduled time to meet the men, his schedule would continue to be late. But, as Karson had a reputation, late was Karson's on time.

In other words, from people Karson worked with before, 'he is always late.'

Hiking through the dark forest was tense. Karson had his weapon raised at every sound and continuously looked over his shoulder, ensuring that he was not being followed or stalked by an animal. It would also be incredibly easy for Karson to get turned around, as everything looked the same. So to ensure he was heading the right way, he followed his compos, his HUD, and would always pick a target to walk to, just to ensure he'd make it to his desired goal in time. It would take five hours to reach his rendezvous, so his desired time to arrive would be 1500 hours.

At around noon thirty, the young SEAL met a clearly traveled forest road in a large clearing, with fields all around. The next tree line was barely visible through the fog from the moist forest, virgin to the touch of the sunlight, and the distance across. It was cloudy out, and so the gray of the fog and sky were playing tricks on Karson. Following the road to the point in which he had to go would be stupid, and could lead to suicide if an armed squad found him but, since there was no tree line for cover, and all that surrounded him was the field like clearing, Karson had no choice. He started jogging across the open fields towards the other tree line at an angle, so he was following the road, but also making some ground on the trees.

Thinking out loud as he jogged, "when I make it to the trees, I can follow the roadway more quickly and-"

The sound of an engine, a massive engine at that, made Karson slow to a walk, looking around.

Drop!

But Karson stood upright. The ground started to shake. Karson looked around more frantically. The ground was vibrating more viciously now, and the engine noise was growing louder and louder in his ears. Then, he saw it. Two heavily armored troop transports were driving over the hill down the road somewhat behind Karson, straight towards him. Dropping down, hoping not to be seen in the short grass beside the road, Karson made a straight line towards the trees. The vehicles stopped, and people stepped out. Words reached Karson's ears, clearly pointing in his direction. The two vehicles turned into the grass, and slowly headed in Karson's direction. Knowing he'd have no chance, he stood up and fired a shot as he made a mad dash towards the trees. Cover blown. They acquired him in their sights.

BANG

BANG

The shots exploded feet from Karson, and he could feel the dirt ram into his body and felt his feet stumble. *That will slice through my armor like butter!* He kept moving towards the trees, firing around his waist with his MP5. Karson really had no way to fight back; all he carried was a rifle and a pistol. Running faster and faster, Karson dare not look back. His training said 'make it to the safety of the trees and disappear into darkness.' He could feel the ground shaking again, and heard the engines roaring as the trucks bounced over the uneven ground.

"Why is it always an armored vehicle!?" Karson shouted. He ran in a zigzag so as not to be an easy target to hit. The first truck nearly had Karson, but it hit the muddy land and slowed to a grinding halt, to which the gunner responded by firing sporadically in Karson's direction.

Less of a threat! Can't aim. Other vehicle a threat!

The other transport turned around and made it back up onto the road, and sped around the curve to catch up to Karson. As it did, it turned back into the field to try and cut Karson off from the trees. It was at least a football field away, and closing the gap fast. The first truck gunner, still firing sporadically, must have lost control of the massive gun. A round hit the second truck's driver, causing the vehicle to swerve, as the passenger grabbed the wheel. Steadying the truck, the gunner fired at the first, killing him instantly. Turning its attention back to the enemy stranger, the enemy personnel floored it again to try to shoot or crush Karson.

Karson took advantage of the seconds of confusion and ran harder and harder. He had about thirty feet to go, when

BANG

The gunner bullet hit the ground right in front of Karson, knocking dirt into his face, and knocking him onto his rear end. Sitting up, he could see the enemy nearing, and he rolled over, his ears ringing, and started crawling to the trees. The vehicle stopped and opened its back to let the crew of troops out of the back to go and confirm the kill. Karson kept crawling until the debris cleared and he had to run again.

Twenty feet, Karson. It's twenty feet. You can close that in five seconds and GO!

Sprinting, a barrage of bullets met him. The troops gave chase shooting at him, and the truck gunner shot the trees trying to knock them down on top of Karson. Karson made it to the trees but kept running. These Chinese soldiers wouldn't give up without a fight. They took off after him into the forest. Karson kept running, ducking as rounds pelted the trees around him and tried to blend in. He rounded a bend in a trail and slid under the bushes, pulling brush over him to hide his location. Luckily there were no canines that Karson could hear.

Yet.

The young SEAL waited until the enemies passed him, then, his head clearing and the ringing subsiding, he could hear waters somewhere behind him. Keeping himself flat, he slithered backward, towards the sound, until he found a dip in the ground, and slipped silently into the water, where, as a Navy SEAL, he was pretty comfortable. Water, like this morning on the ship, brought comfort to Karson. This offered both an easy way to travel closer towards his team, and also kept his scent off the trail in case enemy dogs came. Also, if humans came around, Karson could duck under and swim farther downstream before resurfacing.

As the sun started to dip below the trees, Karson began to tire from swimming and the events of the day. But he continued towards his rendezvous, which seemed to get farther and farther away, rather than closer. Flowing water gave way gradually to a roar ahead of Karson's floating body. He listened more intently.

"Waterfall." He muttered. He was so close that he could see the water dropping down. He was about to go over. He started corkscrewing towards the bank. Safety was a branch pull away, and as he reached it, he grabbed on tight, stopping his progress towards the waterfall. He took a moment to appreciate the sweet power of what Mother Nature had to offer, then tore his gaze from the beautiful sight and tried pulling his way up. As he reached the top, pulling himself over the lip, he was face to face with an enemy soldier. Karson's eyes grew wide, and he lunged for his pistol.

However, when a Navy SEAL is surprised, he is prone to victory even in the face of all odds. He is always on guard. When a Navy SEAL is caught off guard, his chances of winning drop from 100% success rate to 60%. Karson was caught off guard. As the SEALs say, 'he caught me sleeping.' 'Sleeping' could mean death for an operator.

Karson-

****

CHAPTER 11 - Panda!

"Team leader?" A static voice relayed through the birdsong filled forest as the troops scanned the area ahead of them for signs of movement from their fleeing prey. The leader pulled his radio from his belt and raised it to his lips.

"Team Leader." The Chinese Commander responded into his radio.

"General Hatyara has intelligence of an enemy entering your local. Prop plane?"

"We heard one earlier. We have been investigating. Was about to radio to you."

"That plane is carrying U.S. personnel. Probably one man. More people possible in de area."

The Chinese soldier smiled. "I will end his life very, very slowly."

"If you can take him alive, do it. But he is not to escape. Kill him very soon. Long life."

The Chinese soldier looked to the right out the window as they drove over the hilly road. "STOP!" He shouted. The vehicles rolled to a stop. The team leader hopped out. "Did any of you see tree disappear?" He asked. He grabbed his radio. "I believe I have found enemy. Will engage. I want you all to walk through grass, and two trucks drive through brush as well." Immediately, the trucks sped through the grass. As quickly as they dropped into the field, a bullet was fired, striking the driver beside the team leader. "FIRE AT WILL!" A young man stood and ran in front of the soldiers, and the team leader took off after him.

The vehicles split apart; one firing at the intruder, the other racing to the road to intercept him. When the enemy disappeared into the trees, the team leader grew even more enraged. "RELEASE THE DOGS!"

Unfortunately, the man eluded the team leader, and he walked around the forest path, following the river. "I guarantee you, he slipped into the water. This waterfall here, however, gives us a chance-"

"Waterfall." The team leader heard a young, American voice right below him. He motioned to his team to stay quiet. The Chinese soldier finally found his target through the trees, making his way to the vines that would bring him up, right in front of him.

The man paused to catch his breath, then pulled himself up the lip of the bank.

Shame I'm going to kill dis elusive creature. He could be used for Death. But orders are orders.

As he reached the top, pulling himself over the lip, the Navy SEAL stood right before the Chinese soldiers. His eyes grew wide, and he lunged for his pistol.

"Hello," the soldier said slamming his foot into the gun.

****

-Karson didn't get the chance to utilize his weapon, as the soldier in front of him slammed his foot to Karson's hand, pinning his weapon in its holster. As the soldier raised his weapon, the butt of the gun immediately found its way to Karson's forehead, and, blacking out slightly, Karson could feel the force of a foot kicking him over the lip of the river bed and felt gravity pull him towards the water. Time slowed as the men came over the lip and aimed their guns, then blurred as water covered Karson's eyes. Bullets pelted the water around Karson, who, coming too, started flailing, tossing over and over as the water picked up towards the waterfall. Swimming in a corkscrew again, Karson desperately tried making it to the side of the waterfall to climb down, but to no avail.

"Give me a break!" He shouted towards the heavens, firing from underwater to hit a target. His weapon was useless wet.

Karson grabbed onto the massive rock that protruded over the waterfall and hauled himself up on it, looking over at the far drop beneath him. As he stood completely, the Chinese who hit him fired a shot.

A force the power of a baseball bat slammed into his body armor protecting his spine. Rock gave way to air. Falling head over heels into the water, then over into the air, Karson prayed that no rocks were under as he hit the water below, knocking all the air out of him, and knocking him into oblivion. His body sunk straight down to the depths of the river, the current sweeping him along the underwater floor, pelting him with rocks and logs. His lungs now a water balloon, everything in his vision was white, except for a black dot, ever-increasing. *This must be me passing over to the fire…*

****

Voices filled Karson's dreams, as the roar of the river faded away. He felt comfort and woke in a room like that of a palace. Servants stood by, with leaf fans waving and grapes held in front of his face. Karson gladly ate his fill, his mouth dry and stomach rumbling. He felt airy and free below his belt, strangely. Sliding, his junk felt like they were on a cloud. Standing up from the soft, silk covered bed, he felt his balls dangle and looked down, to find that he wore only a leaf to cover his bits.

Where am I? Wait! His head snapped up. "Am I dead!?" He looked around at everyone.

Nobody answered Karson except with, "Feast, master! Feast!"

Karson was led to a table where many, many morsels of food like cow, pig, bird, potatoes, corn, and fruit; all the food Karson had ever seen.

WHERE AM I!? Can I stay here?

Karson turned and walked through the room towards the door and entered a large marble hallway.

Maybe this is the palace I saw before I deployed in that movie on the Middle East?

Racing through and up the stairs to the uppermost floor, he opened a door and looked out into a massive city, with people in the markets, people bowing down towards the palace, and towards a giant statue that Karson assumed was him.

Turning back in, he heard a window break and saw a fully armed man dive in and stop. Karson ducked behind a pole and looked around the corner, a wave of hatred hitting his body. The man who crashed in turned down a hallway and disappeared. Karson raced towards the other direction as suddenly gunfire erupted and mens' voices shouted through the halls.

His eyes burst open. Karson jolted awake, finding himself in a tent. The sun cast a sunrise sort of feel through the tent, and Karson heard voices again from outside. He reached for his pistol with no clothes on, and was laying on top of his blankets, completely open for anyone to gaze upon his damn sexy body!

"Perverts." He cursed under his breath. *I'm gonna slay all of you!*

He rolled off of the cot, and slowly stalked towards the flap at the entrance of the tent, not sure what he'd find beyond it. Suddenly, a shadow was cast over it, and the flaps to the tent were drawn back, showing Karson in his pouncing position. Karson attacked. Striking hard and fast without seeing who he was about to kill. He grabbed the enemy's hand and twisted him around wrapping arms around his nemesis's neck, about to kill him and use him as a shield, when he heard the well-known, soothing, milky deep, friendly voice.

"Karson! Stop! I'm *cough* on your *harder gagging cough* side!" Victor gasped.

Karson released him at once. "Victor!?" Karson said confused, his head tilting to the side like a puppy, walking in a circle, rubbing his eyes and covering them from the sun. "Man, I almost killed you!"

Victor spun around rubbing his throat and smiling. "Wow, look at that slim nineteen-year-old, sexy body." He laughed. He pulled Karson into a hug. "Like the prank I pulled? You certainly firmed up since BUD/S!

"Wow, dude, I didn't realize you liked me like that!" Karson laughed, breaking the hug, and staring at Victor.

"It's not like I haven't seen it before. Remember? We were in boot camp together? You always were so proud of your body, always eager to take your clothes off." He play winked at Karson and licked his lips.

"I didn't realize you fancied checking me out!" Karson laughed harder.

"Mmm!" Victor kept teasing. Taking it even farther, he gave Karse a love tap. Only this love tap wasn't as loving as was meant to be, because Karson dropped, holding his balls yet again.

"Ball tap!? Really!?" Karson moaned.

"Want another?" Victor advanced again. Both hands ready to smack.

"Shut up and get me some clothes ya freak. And tell me what happened. How long was I gone?" Karson's belly rumbled as he shakily stood, his nuts still throbbing from the harder than expected strike to his exposed organs.

"Awwwe! Someone's tummy is rumbling." Victor turned to leave.

Karson's belly growled, and he looked down and up and licked his lips. "Can I have something to eat, please?"

"We kinda have to ration, ya know," Victor said, sternly.

Karson's face fell, and he held his belly as it growled again. "Yeah, I know. I-I... I'm just so hungry..."

Victory laughed hysterically. "I'm kidding, man! You're an honored, high metabolism guest! I'll get you something quick! Just don't eat all my food!"

"Oh thank God!" Karson breathed.

Victor got Karson some clothes and food and led Karson to an arms depot to replenish his gear.

"Here, take whatever you need. You lost pretty much everything else you had come in with.

"How do you have all of this stuff?"

"This was an enemy camp we took. We found all of this after we removed the bodies."

"What happened to me!?" Karson asked, stuffing his face.

"You got beat pretty bad, Karse. That guy hit you, you got shot, then were dragged along by the river. We killed the enemy patrol and threw their bodies into the river to wash downstream, taking their gear and radios. I got my guys listening now trying to find out where our HVI is. Don't know who or where."

"Hatyara."

"Huh?"

"The guy's name, I think is Hatyara. Or at least one of them is. There may be more. That's what I got from Russia."

"So that's where they shipped you off too, huh?" Victor smiled. Immediately behind enemy lines."

Karson nodded.

"Nice! Great work, we've heard Hatyara a couple of times. We thought it was a weird word they said. Now we know different. We thought you were dead, by the way. You're a tough cookie, little guy!" Victor ruffled Karson's hair.

"A little rifle butt and puny rifle round can't kill me, bud. Takes a lot more to kill this SEAL, hooyah?"

"Hooyah!"

"What's been up with you?"

"NO! What's been up with you?"

The two SEALs caught up on their lives after BUD/S. Karson learned Victor entered the Navy at twenty-five to be a SEAL after service with the Marine Corps. Karson had to remind Victor he was far too young for him, teasingly, and relayed that he was a bullied high school dropout who joined the Navy and learned that rather than being artistically gifted, he was also a skilled warrior. He was smart enough to be a pilot and fell in love with the idea of being a Navy SEAL. He also stated after he was deployed to England that he was drafted into SEAL Team Six.

"You're Six?" Victor screamed.

"Shhh! Dude, seriously! Yeah, Team Six."

"Man, I'd kill for that job! I thought they kicked you outta Three and that I'd take out on."

"It's the same as any other team, just more dangerous, I guess."

"Still, that'd be so cool! I was deployed to Columbia for an imminent attack against the U.S. I got commander when two SEALs left the team and ranked up to Captain before heading through Africa to here, a month in beautiful China!"

"You've been here for a month? How've you stayed undetected?"

"As you always said, Karse... Gear up for the invasion."

"Oh, you mean plan like you're invading a country?"

"That is literally what I just said, ya dumb."

"Yeah. My head took a rifle butt, you know, that you failed to stop? It took me a second to realize what you were saying, dick head."

Victor punched Karson's arms. "Just messin'!"

Once Karson was cleaned up and full, Victor told his team to come meet the new addition to his team.

"Men, this is my best friend and BUDs brother. Petty Officer?"

"It's Serval." Karson smiled and laughed.

"I know your name, bro... Are you a Petty Officer?"

"Oh... Commander..." Karson stifled another laugh. "Serval."

"Nice, dude! Rock on! Commander Serval. You will treat him as you treat me, with respect, and as I'm sure you'll soon find out, he is the nicest guy in the world, so he'll treat you the same and have your backs like we all have each other's. We're all SEALs. We all, no matter the branch or rank, serve the same country."

"Nice to meet you, Commander!"

Karson nodded.

The team talked and bonded, Karson telling the story of a guy in BUDs training before to Victor arrived who made a huge spectacle of himself. "Let me tell you how insane Charlie was." The dude shoved an alcohol soaked tampon up his ass, climbed the rock wall... and then it hit him. He passed out and he frickin' fell!" Everyone burst out laughing. "And... And when he woke up..." Karson couldn't breathe remembering the awesome sight he'd been pleased to witness. "When he woke up, the drill instructor was like, you okay, candidate? And he was like mamana homana mehagna! The dude knocked a screw loose. Never recovered. Always a problem. Wonder what happened to him? Maybe I knocked the screw back in when I socked him. One can only hope!"

"I remember the time when you stopped a drug deal in BUDs..." One of Victor's SEALs tapped his buddy.

The buddy gave a confused look. He stared at his friend, eyes looking up in though. "Oh, yeah... We were walking along the last night we had training and heard these screams. We snuck into the barracks and saw these guys strip a man using his balls as a speed bag. Then it got gross, a lot of cream... but what got us was the beating this guy took. These guys tried to cut him up. We intervened, dodged the knife attacks... They never told us, but that night might have been my first kill. The Master at Arms found out later on, and an investigation found like, forty pounds of cocaine in the barracks. We ultimately were thrown in the brig for the night until the inquiry was over. Found out it was a cult. Freaky stuff man!" The SEAL finished.

"Seriously?" Karson asked.

"Yeah... My rise to the SEALs is a weird story, man... Almost unbelievable!"

"That is insane!" Victor laughed to ease the intense weight in the air.

"Talk about ghost stories," Karson added.

"Alright, gentlemen. It's time to get moving for the day. Ten minutes; grab your gear and meet back here."

"Aye, sir!" The men moved to do as they were told.

"What's the mission?" Karson asked.

"Yup, you weren't here... We're meeting up with a Chinese allied force, and clearing a village. HVI may be there."

"Hatyara?" Karson bounced in his seat.

"Woah, slow down! Yeah, we believe he's here."

"Oh yeah!" Karson fisted the air then ran to get his things. Victor smiled after his friend and went to get his own.

In the woods, Karson could tell the men all trusted and respected Victor and each other. Karson felt at ease back with SEALs rather than anyone else. Not that others weren't okay, but SEALs all had the same training and mindsets.

Victor stopped, raised his hand and mouthed, "New orders, stand by." He was listening to orders from command.

"Clear. Viking squad will go! Be advised, Commander Serval is alive and well, standing right next to me, pretty as a peach."

Karson smiled. "You're a freak!" He mouthed.

"Clear. Serval will stay with us."

Karson nodded. "Awesome!"

"Team, we have our mission. From the information we've relayed to HQ and the patching of their radios as well as from intelligence from back home, we've learned a few things. One, Commander, your Intel is accurate. His name is Hatyara. Two, we've got word he's in China, checking on the progress. Just arrived. We're gonna snag him before he can escape. Alive is the first option we have. If things get hairy, though, we will execute him. Capture kill mission. This reminds me; did you guys read up on the Bin Laden mission years ago in 2011?"

"Sort of..." Was the team's conclusion.

"I have."

"I know you have, Commander. Anyways, whatever. This is similar. Catch him if we can. Kill him if he has the slightest chance of escape. Command will alert us when complete. We are going to meet Chinese Special Forces in a clearing three clicks east of here."

"He the gingerbread man?" Karson smiled. The Sailors stared at him. "He said 'catch him if we could... I thought it was funny. Obviously wasn't." Karson up his hands up.

The SEALs acknowledged the mission briefing and readied up.

Funny moment has passed away.

"**Chinese.** CPLASF. China People Liberation Army Special Forces. One of the many special forces of this country. They will have eight members: their commander, assistant commander, a sniper, a machine-gunner for support, a bomber, and two assault troops. Questions?"

"Chinese? Another group of people who don't like us." Victor's second in command spoke up.

"I know. Hopefully, we get along. If not, you'll know what to do."

"Yeah. Kill them. I don't want to, but will." Karson said.

"Yeah. Guys, look! A Panda!" Victor whispered to his team. "No one scare it or hurt it. Let's watch it! This is cool!"

Karson was in awe of the creature lumbering by. Karson wanted to be a zoologist long ago and knew a lot about animals, even this secluded, barely studied animal. This would be a way to study up more on the creature.

The panda gave very little notice to the strange-looking men, having never seen them before, it at first stopped and stared at the moderately armed Sailors, but then went along on its way, eating bamboo as it went. Karson watched as it curled the leaves to make bamboo leaf cigars and loved watching its powerful jaws chew its meal to feed! As it continued on its way, the SEALs followed him, Karson noticing now that it was indeed a 'he.' As they came to a stream, the panda made a sharp turn, heading up the path, saying goodbye to the SEALs. Their mission lay beyond the Panda's territory, which ended, it seemed, at the stream. As the creature disappeared into the brush, the team of armed Americans hopped the creek and continued on their way, unhindered.

"Wasn't that incredible!?" Karson bounced up to Victor, standing in front of him.

"Karson, for real? It's an animal. Not the ninth wonder of the world." Victor pushed past him.

"I know, but it's cute!" Karson looked back to see his new friends rolling their eyes.

"Yeah… Okay… Anyways-"

"SHHH!" Karson interrupted Victor.

"Excuse me?" Victor turned on Karson. He'd always outranked Karson and didn't like it when a subordinate questioned his authority.

"SHHHH! Can you hear that?" Karson asked, hand up in a halt position, head turned left, looking into the brush.

"Hear what?" A SEAL asked, readying his weapon.

Karson listened and listened, but nothing came from the trees.

"Let's keep moving." Victor turned and as his team did, gave Karson a rough kick.

"Ouch! Sorry, I could have sworn-" Karson stopped speaking as he heard gunfire back from the way they had come and a terrified shriek that only an animal could make.

"THE PANDA!" Karson turned and hauled ass back the way he'd come.

"KARSON! WHERE ARE YOU GOING!?" Victor shouted. "WE NEED TO STAY UNDETECTED!"

Karson ignored his superior and kept running, each stride taking him closer and closer to the sounds. As Karson jumped over the stream farther up from where they'd crossed, he found the panda running, desperately trying to escape the area as Chinese soldiers kept firing their weapons at the scared creature. Karson felt rage soar up from his toes to his head. He removed the suppressor from his rifle and fired a whole magazine, downing seven men. Eight other heads popped up, aiming at the Navy SEAL.

Karson's eyes widened. *Bad idea! That is what it means when you see red!*

Karson spun around a large tree as bullets pelted the bark. He watched as the panda escaped into the woods and felt relief for the animal. He reinstalled his suppressor and dropped under the plants as the enemy soldiers came up to his location.

The men looked around but couldn't see the Navy SEAL beneath them. Karson took aim at the furthest man away from him and fired. As his body dropped, the soldiers turned their gazes, giving Karson the chance to raise up, drive his knife into the temples of the first two men, and shooting the other five with a single, well-placed pistol shot right between their eyes. As they dropped, Karson reequipped his rifle and vectored his area as his team arrived.

Ensuring no one was left, Victor came up, spun Karson around and slammed him into a tree.

"What the fuck, dude!" Karson growled at Victor's face.

"Me what the fuck? You what the fuck! What was that! Are you trying to get us all killed? They could have been a larger force. They could have radioed for backup. Maybe they did! You could have died. All for a panda! They could have ended the war right here before it even starts! AND FOR A PANDA!"

"One, they didn't end the war before it started, it's already begun. And two, yeah a panda. They are endangered and helpless, and if you think for even a moment I'm gonna let a couple of inhuman people get away with murder-"

"IT'S AN ANIMAL!" Victor shouted, punching the tree beside Karson's face.

"WITH A SOUL!" Karson shouted back.

"Karson, this is not a joke. We may be best friends. Your squad may run differently, and that is fine. But out here, if you're on my mission, you do what I say, WHEN I SAY IT! If you can't do that, then you're out. You can go back, and we'll take it from here."

"I'm staying," Karson said through his bared teeth.

"One more stunt, Karson."

"Enforce it, dick head."

Victor gave a warning glance to the stubborn young SEAL as Karson pushed Victor off of him. "If this gets to our superiors, you could lose your job, Karson."

"STOP USING MY NAME!" Karson shouted. "IT'S A SECURITY BREACH!"

Victor grabbed Karson by his vest. "One more word. One more, Karse... give me a reason." Victor tapped Karson in the mouth.

Yup, there it is. Just like my abusive father.

Karson held Victor's gaze, dangerously calm. *This is an argument you can't win, dude. I'll take your squad from you. Happily.*

Stalking past Victor and the other men in complete shock, the Americans continued to trek through the dense Zhangjiajie National Forest Park, heading up a mountain, as silent as possible. A usual three-mile walk would take an hour. The SEALs covered a mile in an hour. Many enemy squads were patrolling the area after hearing gunfire and learning now that enemy forces were in Death Nation controlled territory. Enemy or rebellious forces that is.

As the SEALs were sneaking around another patrol, Karson, still furious from earlier, wasn't being as careful and felt a stick crack under his feet.

"Ahh damn," Karson whispered.

Victor smacked Karson's helmet. "Screw you."

"I'm gonna throw down on you if you hit me again." Karson hissed.

The enemy patrol spun around and aimed towards the SEALs.

"No one moves!" Victor said.

"Herro?" One enemy asked.

The SEALs chuckled. One enemy fired a shot, hitting one SEAL in the arm, knocking him back in the underbrush with a crash.

Blood splattered onto Karson's face, taking him off guard, and the SEAL shouted in pain and shock, the underbrush where he fell was moving, revealing the intruders' location. More shots were fired. Karson took a hit to his helmet and was knocked backward as a bullet impacted his chest. His helmet and Kevlar had stopped the death part of being shot, but the full impact felt as if the bullet had gone through. The pain was intense, and thinking he was shot, Karson felt around on his body, panicking. "Ha! Haelp! I'm hit!" Karson whimpered. He ripped his glove of and slipped his hands into his vest and found the bullet nearly did go through, the hot metal searing his skin. Karson pushed the bullet out and caught it, putting it in his pocket. Finding nothing, he looked around to see his friends, totally taken by surprise.

Sixty percent chance of success here. Karson had more plans in the future than dying in China.

"GRENADE! FRAG OUT!" Karson deployed a fragmentation grenade, and it exploded behind the enemy force, taking a line out. Giving the SEALs a split second of control, Karson, Victor, and another SEAL stood and unleashed the power of their assault rifles as Karson threw another grenade. Exploding in the middle of a group, the enemy forces retreated into the forest. Karson fired into the trees, picking off a few, but not all of them.

"They know we're here now," Karson said.

"Not who we are, though, so let's get out of here, so they don't find out." Turning to the downed SEAL, Victor stuck his hand out. "Stand up; you can still fight. Just a flesh wound. Medic, patch him and let's be going." Turning to Karson, "Nice work. That is two mistakes you've dragged us into. What's next, Commander?"

"Jerk."

Angered, but only because Victor was right, Karson questioned if this trip was cursed.

Taking up the rear of the SEAL patrol, Karson was left alone with his thoughts for the rest of the half mile trek to the clearing rendezvous.

Finally, they arrived, exhausted as their adrenalin subsided in the clearing and waited for the Chinese. The distant thundering of a helicopter had the SEALs scurrying for cover as the aircraft landed in the clearing. Karson aimed at the dismounting men.

Victor walked slowly and cautiously out.

"Herro, prease. I am Commander Jing Sang Wu. You are?"

"A United States Navy SEAL Captain. It looks like we'll be working together."

"You rook correctry. Tank you. In copter prease." The Navy SEALs looked at the leader but did not move. "Oh. I'm sorry… How to do da Engerish? Tis hard for us…"

"No. They just don't take orders from anyone except me, sir. Excuse me. You heard him, team, mount-"

As the team was entering the Chinese helicopter, a force the size of a comedy club audience broke through the trees, killing one Chinese friendly Soldier. Karson grabbed him as he fell and dragged him into the chopper.

"GET US OUT OF HERE!" He screamed.

As the last man hopped up into the chopper, the pilots punched the throttle forward, and the chopper rose quickly into the sky, dodging anti-aircraft rockets. Karson almost fell out as he made his way to his seat as the ramp slowly closed, escaping death by a helping hand, and finally strapped in as the chopper flipped and turned dodging the rockets as it gained speed, finally settling into a routine flight pattern as it headed for the mission zone, waiting for a confirmation on the location of the man the joint special operations team was after.

****

CHAPTER 12 - Sorry

"We've found Hatyara. He at virrage just norf o'here, high up in mountain virrage!" A Chinese Soldier relayed the information to the American 'guests.' "We heading der now to engage forces. We wirr drop you'r off at de rock warr correc?"

"Yes, please." Karson piped up.

"Capture him dead or arrive, yes?"

"Yes, sir," Victor said to the Chinese commander. "But-"

"But arrive is betta!" Karson chipped in, cutting off his superior. Everyone on the American side of the chopper burst out laughing. Victor gave Karson the coldest death glare ever, and Karson snickered to himself.

So I'm being bad today. Big woof! Loosen your tights, Victor. I'm a button pusher!"

"We try to catch him arrive!" The Chinese commander didn't understand what was happening, why the Americans suddenly had his accent, and why they were laughing, so, in the spirits of alliance, he went on his way, smiling, believing that they were all friends. In any other circumstance, maybe this principal could have been true, but the United States, and certainly Karson, didn't trust anyone, anywhere, for any reason at this moment in history.

"My team, listen up. We, for some reason from our bosses, are ordered to jump from this chopper and squirrel suit our way onto the ledges behind this village. Once on the rock ledge, using our climb assists, we are going to work our way up the rock formation, over the lip and in through the back of the village. This will allow us to flank the enemy encampment. Once all opposition is defeated, or if we arrive stealthfully, we will rendezvous with the Chinese and begin looking for the war criminal, Hatyara. Hopefully, then, we will gain information, and stop the war before it begins. The fall of Death Nation could be at our fingertips; we just have to catch this guy. ALIVE! Hooyah? To search the structures, two man teams. That'll split us up to cover more ground alongside the Chinese. We're team players, so treat them with the utmost respect. But, keep your wits about you. We're Americans. Not very liked around the world. Remember that. Any questions?" Victor prepared his team.

"Sounds good. Let's do this." He red haired SEAL looked up at his leader.

The team chattered as they pulled their squirrel suits from their bags and clothed themselves. So as not to alert the enemy encampment, the team would be jumping from a half mile away, and soaring in, deploying chutes to slow their impact onto the wall, then immediately cutting their chutes loose.

"We are approaching drop zone!" The Chinese commander said.

Victor stood. "Alright men, ready up!"

The Navy members' final check went smoothly, and the green light appeared. The back of the chopper lowered and out jumped eight U.S. Navy SEALs, heading to hit a target high in the mountains of China. What could go wrong?

"Karson?" Victor whispered beside his ear.

"Don't use my name!"

Victor sighed. "Sorry. About earlier…"

"Okay," Karson said, readying his chute.

"Don't you want to say something to me?"

"Yeah." Karson stood face to face with Victor now. "Don't ever touch me again. You're not my father!" Victor's eyes opened wide, knowing full well what Karson was talking about. "Yeah, he hit me too. I'm not sorry for saving da panda's life. And we're not friends. As soon as the mission is over, I'm done. I'm leaving."

Victor's face dropped but he nodded, salty. Victor moved back to his duties. *That really hurt.*

****

CHAPTER 13 - Bunny Ranch

The lines were especially long over Memorial Day weekend. LAX was especially slammed with vacationers streaming into the sunshine state; internationals entering and exiting the nation. Specifically today, the United States welcomed in the world's most dangerous man alive. The plane dropped two hundred and fifty pounds as the six foot eight inch dark complected Ugandan man disembarked the aircraft. Four men flanked him.

"Gentleman, welcome to our final obstacle. Not so tough from the looks of it."

"Sir, all the same, we should get you out of here, and out of sight of-"

"You there. Do not move." A Transportation Security Administration officer intercepted the five men. "You've been selected for random screening. This way please."

"I have just arrived here, sir. Why do you need to see me now?"

"Let me repeat myself, sir. Take some more of my time from the others. You have been selected to be screened. Now. This way."

"Do as he says. We are right here, Supreme Leader Ateso."

"Do not say my name!" He turned and grabbed the man's shirt.

"Sir! I do not have time for this, and I don't want to arrest you. The faster you oblige, the faster you will be on your way."

"I am coming." Ojore followed the TSA officer over to the side and gave over control of his luggage. The officer opened the case and found money, passports, and clothing.

"What are all of these documents for?" The officer was now suspicious. "Hmm?"

One of Ojore's men stepped forward and held up a paper. "My friend here is the Sultan of Saudi Arabia. We are here on a diplomatic mission. We wish to be left to our day's agenda."

"Why do we not have a prior arrangement for your arrival?"

"I am a Saudi Arabian king. I do not need to give you warning of my arrival. I may go where I please in the free world. Also, I do not wish to have a crowd. I wish to speak to your manager. I will have your job!"

"No, no, sir. There is no need. You're free to go!" The TSA officer walked away, clearly swamped from the day's travelers.

"Thank you," Ojore said, zipping up his case and walking out to be greeted by another one of his followers with a vehicle. This man, an American.

"Supreme Leader. Your stay is an honor." He said, pulling out of the airport. "Long life."

"I hate your country," Ojore said.

"I do as well. We have plenty of opportunities to destroy it later."

"Honestly, how do you people live here? You have Presidents and elections where people allow people to do what they wish. You have a massive debt, now past twenty-five trillion dollars from a woman in office. Why was a woman in office, you didn't like the way your country was in

2020? If it were a man, you would not have these issues if he were strong leader like me. And, all these freaks wishing to schtup the same gender and/or lose gender in the first place. I don't understand. Obviously, immigration is a problem. I'm here!"

"It's called freedom apparently, sir. Most people here just want the chance to make money and live the way they want without a government. This is how you won me over, sir. This is how you can win others." The driver closed the slide between his seat and the back.

"Yes, I know." His phone rang. "General Hatyara, have you arrived at your location?"

"Yes, Supreme Leader. I am landing at village now, heading to meeting place, so forces know who they serve."

"And the SEAL we have recently learned about? How does one man take a base?"

"We lost contact with the team assigned to killing him and found their bodies four miles downriver from where they radioed contact. They were all shot. There is a SEAL Team here, sir. Not just one person. They could pose a problem for just the same reason. A base of Russian troops was taken by half of our men, a large number, and one man killed and escaped them." Hatyara stepped off of the helicopter and walked through the entrance into the side of the mountain. The temperature instantly dropped to a chilly jacket climate.

"Then you best be careful, General. I have predicted there will be one man who can turn the tides of this excursion against our favor. Prophecy, or just a dream, I do not know. But from our reports, it seems I have been correct."

"You as well, Supreme Leader, stay safe. And all the more reason that I should be with you now. Not here, in this place, but by your side to serve and protect you, sir. Our mission is far too important to be thwarted."

"I need you in China, Hatyara. I have U.S. under control. Finish there, then head to the next country. I will meet you soon."

Hatyara sighed. "Yes, Supreme Leader. Rally the troops, give them their assignment, and be done. Set the pawns in motion. Then go home, sir. Long life, sir."

"And then you will rule at my side. Long life, Hatyara. See you soon." He closed the phone after Hatyara returned the so long. "Las

Vegas. Bunny Ranch. Then, Washington." Ojore laid his seat back for the long ride to pleasure, and death.

****

CHAPTER 14 - Ooooohhhhh

Karson could feel the wind blowing over his face and heard it whizzing over his helmet, and ensured that his gloves, fitted with gecko-like attachments, made it easier to grip into the rock when climbing. If a rock came loose, his glove could efficiently suction to the rock face long enough for Karson's HUD to find the next suitable place to put his hand, thus, saving his life; a technology he'd not had while in Basic, a feat that could have made his climbing score a hundred instead of ninety. His window of safety, though, was only about three seconds so the repositioning would have to take place extremely quick.

TEN SECONDS FROM IMPACT

Karson's HUD relayed information in flashes.

"Captain, ten seconds," Karson shouted through his microphone.

"Ten seconds heard; team brace for impact," Victor yelled back over the wind.

Karson counted the time down. "Five, four, three-"

"Deploy chutes." Another voice was heard.

Karson saw the mountain wall and fired his chute, the chute deploying beautifully and slowing him down just enough to where the jolt he felt from hitting the wall wasn't enough to kill him, though, it was a landing he'd be feeling tomorrow morning when he woke up. *That is if I get to sleep tonight...*

"Alright, team. Slow and steady. Silent. The village is one hundred feet above us."

UGH! SO FAR! Karson complained internally. The gloves kept them to the wall. Didn't help them climb.

Victor, as if he heard Karson, looked over to him. "Pretty far, huh?"

Karson nodded. Still a little sore from earlier.

"Hey, race you to the top." Victor tried to lighten both of their moods.

"You are on, big time!" Karson took the peace offering. Victor was truly his best friend. They had been through thick and thin together. All they both wanted to do was make it home, alive, to be with their loved ones. In stressful situations, of course, they were going to lash at each other. Part of the job.

Karson stuck his fist out, and Victor bumped it.

Karson took off up the rock face, Victor close behind, covering the distance to the top at breakneck speed.

"You're gonna have to buy me a lot of beers when we get home, Serval."

Karson kept racing up, looking down from far ahead of Victor. Keeping his voice down, he radioed to his friend. "I think I'll just hang out here, more than half way up! Watch you and your men struggle. Maybe I'll drop down, and do the stretch again, at how slow you're all going, thinking of all the nice 'cold ones' I'm gonna have back at the bar in Coronado we always loved to go to. Remember that, Vicky?"

Victor flipped Karson the bird from below, looking up. "I'm just taking my time, knowing you'll tire and then I'll pass you. Don't worry, though; I'll definitely be sure to kick your-" Something flashed in Victor's eyes, about twenty feet above Karson's head. "Karson? What's over your head?"

"Wah?" Karson looked up, straight up into the barrel of a censored machine gun, spinning up.

"Oh, no!" Karson pulled off and jumped back in a flip, dropping away from the rock face. Victor stuck his hand out and grabbed Karson's, pulling both men off the face of the mountain, but not far enough. Both Karson and Victor had a suction grip onto the mountain, they slowed, and as bullets fired past their heads, both dropped under a ledge.

The first shots barely missed the SEALs. Suddenly, as more machine guns started spinning up, bullets pelted two SEALs, knocking them in agony off of the rocks, sending them plummeting at least a thousand feet to their deaths.

"NOOO! MEN DOWN!" Victor shouted, looking down. "Karson, we have to take out those turrets!" Victor turned his head to look at Karson.

Karson glared out at Victor.

"No, I thought we should just look at them." Karson looked down at where SEALs had fallen. *Please don't get shot, bro.* He thought to himself.

As Victor started a retort, Karson launched himself up the rock face like a mountain goat, darting from the first ledge to an even smaller one, twenty feet up, where the three SEALs were trying to stay out of the way of bullets. Karson's glove was suctioned in but his weight was starting to pull the seal away. Karson eyed another ledge with a rock sticking out, allowing for hand holds. Karson jumped and grabbed hold, barely missing bullets, -

TINK

"Fuck!"

- well, one ricocheting off his helmet knocking him down three feet. Finally, after pounding up the rock face, Karson hung seven feet away from the first turret. He reached into his bag and pulled out a C4 sticky explosive.

"Take cover!" Karson called below.

"Team, take cover. Explosives!" Victor called up, steadying himself under the ledge far below.

Karson launched the sticky explosive up towards the first one and missed, immediately clicking the button.

BOOM

The force of the explosion almost knocked the SEALs off the cliff, but disabled the first turret, and damaged the second and third. Karson climbed higher now, taking better aim, and threw two more explosives up onto the other turrets. Dropping back down as his smoke cover faded, Karson pushed the button again, engaging the explosives. Again, the explosion, now bigger that the last, nearly knocked everyone off the wall.

Yaaaaaaaaaaaaaassssssssssss!

"Think that was explosive enough, Serval? Are you trying to kill us!?"

"That wasn't even that much! I'd have used more if you guys weren't such pussies, Victor! Gawd! Just get up here!"

Karson sprung up the cliff face. The way was now clear *thanks to me and only me of course,* and the SEAL team propelled themselves up the rest of the rock face and over the rock ledge, now in sight of the village.

As Karson pulled himself over, machine-gun fire pelted the ground around him, and he dove into the cover of the trees that surrounded the village. The team did the same as they too met the same force.

Karson led the way around the trees and into the village where Victor made his way to the front, nodding at Karson.

"Spread out around the village, and with suppressed weapons, shoot the enemy."

"Aye, sir." A low voice replied.

Karson turned and disappeared into the brush, taking up a stalking position that resembled that of a lioness showing his true skill as an American operative.

"In position." Victor's voice came over Karson's ear piece.

"Dido," Karson responded.

"Team?" Victor focused on the lesser talented SEALs.

"I'm in." The first SEAL said.

"Same." The second whispered.

"Got eyes." Said the third.

"Team. Light 'em up."

The Navy SEALs fired their weapons at clearly positioned targets and dropped them like flies.

"Commander Wu, are you in?"

"Yesh, we are waitink for jou!"

"Our way was compromised. We are surrounding the village. We are moving into phase two, search and capture. We're breaking into two man teams and sweeping houses."

"We wirr do da same. Rendezvous in teen minutes."

"Aye, sir."

Karson met up with the third SEAL to talk.

"Name's Wasp." He stuck his hand out.

"Wasp. Nice! Ya know mine."

"Victor told us all about you. You really are kinda small to be a SEAL…"

"Oh, really! That's cool. And yeah. That's why they call me Serval. I can hold my own, man, trust me." Now Karson was embarrassed and wanted to know exactly what his friend had said. But for now, he had a mission, and they were approaching the first door.

"We know! We've seen and heard stories!" Wasp nodded.

Karson and Wasp took up position on either side of the door. Karson grabbed the doorknob and turned it, entering slowly. The sun barely came through the bamboo chute house, but they could still see, so night vision stayed off. The small shack was empty except for an older woman sewing red camouflage clothing in a corner, chained, and not taking her eyes off of the intruders. As the house was cleared, Wasp walked over and unbound her legs and helped her to a stool, where he gave her some water. She gave no sign of smile or relief, just worry and fear, but as Karson and Wasp left, her eyes followed the American's and a tear rolled down her cheek.

"This enemy works fast, dude," Karson whispered.

"Yeah. That's a good reminder of why we do what we do, eh?"

"Hooyah to that, brother," Karson said.

The men approached the next house. Karson looked around to see the other forces, Chinese and Americans hitting the other houses, only hearing gunfire randomly as small pockets were hit. "What's the other teammates' names?"

"The rest of the team: the red head is of course "Gingie," and the fat one is 'Ox' and Captain Paul is Pharo. He's the boss. Feel special. We're not on first name basis with him…"

"Yeah, I know he is the boss." Karson smiled. "That is an awesome name."

"Yeah. You got 'Serval'." He smirked. "Still a cool name. What do you mean by, 'you know he is'?"

Karson smiled wider as he and Wasp positioned themselves at the next door. "In BUD/s our less than a week together, he likes to think he took me under his wing, thinking I was at a disadvantage. He-"

"He quickly found out you weren't! You're kind of *in*famous in the SEALs, Serval. I emphasize *in* cause it's a good and a bad thing. Bad to enemies, but you took the spot we all want."

Karson chuckled a little. "Yeah, but I still was kind of nervous, so he helped me find my confidence. Bad start in life. I helped him become calmer, instead of gun hoe. But he... In every team session, he was the leader, though. He took command of everything. Not a bad thing, we crushed the bad guys, but he took control of everything. I always disobeyed where I thought was right. I wanted to lead at times."

"And that is why you stood out." Wasp nodded. "Too scared too. Wanted a spot on some team so I did as I was told."

"It did more bad on me than good most of the time. I always was in trouble. But the Drill Instructor was the SEAL Team Six team leader. He liked what I was doing. Couldn't allow anyone out of line, though."

"You were in line most of the time, yeah?"

"Hell yeah. It's why I'm here and not in an office somewhere, flunked out of SEAL school."

"Hooyah!"

They could hear movement inside and the loading of weapons.

"Section clear," Pharo said over the radio.

"Ox and I are clear." A new voice said. *Gingie? Humph. Sounds like a leprechaun.*

"Pharo, we need you over here, now," Wasp whispered.

"All of you. We need support." Karson added.

Karson looked at Wasp to make sure it was okay he spoke. Wasp nodded. Karson then looked back to see his brothers running over.

"Multiple enemies inside," Wasp whispered.

"Alright. Anyone have flashbangs?" Pharo asked.

Karson pulled one. Victor pulled another. Everyone else shook heads.

"Do they know my rule?" Karson asked, smiling.

"No. The 'always prepare' speech? No." Victor said.

"You have to teach 'em that, Captain Paul!" Karson winked.

Victor took Karson's flash, and as Karson opened the door, he threw them in.

BANG

BANG

Two simultaneous explosions.

"Team, ent- Argh!"

"CAPTAIN!" Karson yelled.

Victor was hit in the chest by a shotgun blast, ripping through the wall. Karson swung his gun and fired into the hut as Victor rolled down the steps onto the ground.

"Ox, Gingie, make entry with Wasp. I have Pharo." Karson said, taking command as he jumped down the steps as the others entered, and as a few enemies made their way from around the back of the hut. Karson took up support position over Victor, checking his pulse as he fired his weapon, hitting the advancing forces as they came into sight. Victor was coughing, attempting to stand, but Karson held him down.

"Sir, two more, stay down." Karson fired two rounds into the first, "One left!" and three into the last one. Then, lowering his weapon, he helped Victor to his feet and checked his body.

"Team, no harm. Vest." Captain Paul said. "Karson, I'm all right." He whispered, pushing the SEAL away.

"I'm just making sure, sir."

"Karson, seriously." He placed his hands on Karson's shoulders. "Hey. I'm fine!"

Karson looked up, Karson's blue piercing eyes fixed intently on Victor's brown eyes. He said sternly, "You have no medic anymore. I am trained in medicine. Just a second more..." Karson spun him around, searching for blood. "You're all good."

"I told you! You are so stubborn!"

"I was just making sure my best friend is alright, Vic! You're more than that. You're my closest brother. You're my real family, even more than the SEALs! I can't lose another friend like I did-"

"Okay, okay. None of that mushy gushy stuff in combat!"

"Yes, sir." Karson looked down for a second, embarrassed. "Sorry, man."

Rounds were still being fired in the house as the Chinese team came over and rushed past the SEALs outside and entered. Karson and

Victor stayed out, keeping over-watch for about two minutes until the joint force came out.

"THAT WAS AWESOME!" Ox high-fived the Chinese machine gunner as they walked outside.

"No sign of Hatyara." The Chinese commander said.

"That's odd. We've searched everywhere. Did you all check the barn?"

"No." Wasp said from the back, last to walk out of the hut.

"Didn't know there was one, honestly!" Ox muttered.

Karson started bouncing up and down!

"What are you so cheery about?"

"It's another mission!" Karson said, barely containing himself.

"What is wrong with this SEAL?" Gingie laughed.

"He's always been like this. Like a dog. Doesn't take much to excite him, especially if it is a challenge or the possibility of a challenge." Victor looked at Karson. Still bouncing up and down, looking at him, and waiting for orders to go!

"I'm a Serval, remember?" Karson said like a pouting child, but still moving in excitement.

Victor's eyes flashed in amusement. "Les' go! Come on!"

Karson skipped into position. He looked at the others. "Sorry, sometimes I can't contain myself. Who knows what we'll find in there!" He gave a small, cheeky and white, toothy smile.

The others chuckled as Victor pointed out the direction. "That way. Second take lead. Let's go!"

Wasp took the lead as Victor's second in command.

The joint force ducked around the corners, checking for enemies as they made their way to the barn. They entered and found a small resistance force, but they dropped their weapons as they were outnumbered by four. The men were restrained and questioned as the Chinese looked for secret passages.

Karson was interrogating a small boy from the village, but he refused to talk. Instead of talking with his mouth, he was speaking with his eyes. Karson watched as the kid kept looking over at the massive pile of hay behind him. Karson turned and smiled back at the kid. "Thanks!"

The boy's eyes widened as Karson gave the boy his compos, then turned and made his way over towards it. The man next to the boy started to scream, and jumped up, snapping the boy's neck, and rushed towards Karson. Karson turned as the man forcefully launched into the air and side kicked Karson into the hay, but was shot dead before he could land and instill more harm by the Chinese commander standing up on the second level of the barn. Karson swam his way out of the hay, with the help of the Chinese medic.

"Are you orkay?"

Karson nodded. "Thanks. That boy kept looking at the hay and down low. Think we can move it?" He asked.

"Sure!" He summoned his teammates.

Karson walked over to the boy, but he was indeed dead. *That is disgusting and a shame. I'm so sorry.* Death Nation didn't discriminate on age. If you were in, you were in, and any betrayal was rewarded with death. Karson picked up his compos.

The men in the room started pulling the hay and throwing it on the other side of the barn, but the hay kept falling and falling, seemingly having no end in sight.

"Karson? Are you sure about this?" Victor asked him, quietly. "Maybe the intel was wrong. Maybe he isn't here, and this was just a village that the enemy took."

"Possible, but that would be unusual, doe. This area is so isolated that this lone group wouldn't just take it for no reason. They have to be hiding something here. If it's not Hatyara, then it is something important, and I want it. Maybe it's both. And it is under this pile."

"I know you really want to nail this guy but what if you're wrong and-"

"Right there!" Karson pointed and dropped to his knees and grabbed a circular handle.

The rest of the people brushed off the hay, finally revealing a small wooden door that would have gone unnoticed if the boy hadn't given it away.

Karson looked up at Victor. "See! Wonder what's down here." Karson started to lift it, but the Chinese commander pushed Karson off with his boot.

"We take over command now, Americans. Do what we say, and no one gets hurt."

"Excuse me!?" Victor stepped forward. "Don't ever tough my SEALs again."

"Let them go first. Something's not right about this anyways. If they want to be heroes, then let them be heroes!" Karson glared.

Hesitantly, Victor slid his pistol fully back into his holster and stepped off the door, looking at Karson.

The Chinese opened the door themselves. Karson looked inside from where he was standing, confirming his superstitions. The dark, dank hole did, in fact, hold a secret that he spotted instantly in the *gothic structure? Wow. Interesting architecture for China.* Karson felt he heard a distant '**ooooohhhhh**' coming from deep from the catacombs.

The Chinese insisted on going first. Karson tried to object, at least warn them but was shut down by the big bad Chinese leader who felt he had something to prove.

"We know what to do. We go first."

"Your funeral," Karson muttered.

"Excuse me?" The foreign leader pushed Karson back.

Karson lifted his hands. "You want to go first? You can go first."

"Tanks. As if we neetet your permission." The commander turned to his men and ordered them down. Karson stepped back as the first man jumped in, and blood splattered up where he stood a moment before as a loud cracking sound like that of a machine gun on a Black Hawk erupted. The man had met with a mounted sentry gun with a barely visible laser, and as soon as the man jumped down, he was ripped in half by the high caliber machine gun.

The commander glared down at the hole where his bomber had gone to his death and threw the two dead bodies in. Nothing happened. Then he threw the three remaining hostages in and watched as they met the same fate.

"YOU KNEW ABOUT DIS!" The commander turned on Karson, who had his pistol in his hand.

"And I tried to warn you. I can disable it. If you'll let me, oh great and mighty Wu!" Karson mock worshiped the man.

"I should kill you now." The Chinese leader drew his knife.

"Ha, mmm, ehh, yeah. You won't get very far. The SEALs had their fingers on the triggers of their guns. "See, we may argue from time to time, but we are all brothers on the American side, and we don't let anything happen to each other, so rather than fight, let's work together like we've been doing. It's worked."

"Fine. Make it quick." Wu said.

"As you wish!" Karson said perkily.

"You're really going to piss him off, Karse," Victor whispered in his ear.

"Kinda the plan, Victo!" Karson smiled like a puppy with his tongue out!

Victor rolled his eyes as Karson pulled two smoke grenades from his leg pocket. He dropped them down into the hole. The machine gun started firing desperately, but only in a straight line, so Karson hung down, keeping his legs out of the line of fire and dropped low on the side of the wall in the smoke. H switched his eyeware to thermal imaging. He sighted a control room at the end of the hall. Karson launched another smoke grenade and made his way towards the chamber. The door was propped open, so he thought about a grenade, then thought of a more fun option. He positioned himself under the hanging gun and jumped up, flipped his legs onto the ceiling and twisted the weapon to fire through the window of the underground control room, painting the room a gorgeous splotchy red to light up the darkness! The rest of the force dropped down on Victor's orders and made their way through the smoke too. The sentry gun did not fire another bullet.

Karson was patted on the back by a proud Victor, and Karson walked up to the Chinese commander, looking at the dead people at the entrance. "This could have been avoided. It is your fault. You need to leave one of your men here in the control room and shoot anyone that jumps down. Use the gun on the wall."

"Isn't gun, braked? You bent it out of place."

"It can't be fired automatically, but manually. It will give us cover." Karson responded.

Hesitantly, the commander gave in. "Orkay." He told his medic to stay put in the control room to keep overwatch as the rest of the allied Special Forces team made their way deeper into the labyrinth.

As they continued to move, the Navy SEALs were starting to get antsy. Karson turned to his leader. "Sir, this isn't right. They are probably amassing somewhere deeper. And is it just me or is that eerie sound getting louder? Sounds like a KKK meeting or something. A choir of demons."

"It's not just you. I hear it too." Ox said. "Gingie pointed it out to me."

"I Agree." Victor looked at Wasp who nodded too.

All of a sudden, the lights went off. "NVG's on, team," Captain Paul ordered in a whisper. The SEALs put on their night vision. The Chinese had one pair and their commander, the coward, of course put them on.

"Have your team follow ours?" Karson requested to the Chinese. "We can see better than your team."

"Thanks for concern, American, but we go first. Our land, our mission."

"Suit yourself," Karson said flatly. "You're just gonna die faster."

The Chinese glared at Karson as they passed.

Karson flattened himself against the wall as the Chinese filed past; squishing the already small bodied SEAL Pup. If he was smaller than his team and squished, his friends would be even more pressed against the wall by the ignorant Chinese men.

They aren't going to be too happy about that I betcha! Karson smiled, picturing his fuming friends cursing the Chinese under their breath.

Captain Paul went next. "Screw them! Their 'kung pow' funeral." He smiled. Karson followed attempting to stifle his outburst of laughter, only emitting a small giggle instead, gaining glares from his all too masculine team.

"What?" He whispered. "A guy can't giggle?"

"Team, press tight together." Captain Paul said into his com.

As the joint force continued down the tunnels into the catacombs, the men heard crunching sounds and felt what seemed like twigs snapping under their feet. Everyone looked down, lifting their feet to see what the source was.

Karson flinched as did his team as skulls and bones lay beneath.

"That explains the smell!" Gingie said.

"Skeletons. And bodies. These people are insane, man!"

"This is just dandy," Ox wrathfully said. "I can't wait to kill these animals!"

"SHHHH! Listen!" The American Captain said.

They heard voices and saw lights ahead. They stopped to plan.

"We 'aw coming to openin'. We wirr attack at first sight." The Chinese commander said, rather loudly.

The SEALs stopped moving and breathing as the voices ahead silenced.

Karson shared a glance with Wasp. Both of their eyes bulging, removing the safeties of their weapons.

The voice started speaking again, forgetting the intrusive sound quickly.

"Don't you think we should survey and see what's going on?" Commander Hunter called around his leader.

"No, we wirr kirr arr opposition."

"We may be in your jurisdiction in this country, using your help," Karson's Captain spoke up, "and this may be your mission to lead, but we have our orders to view and gather Intel first, as well as trying to take Hatyara alive. That's what we will do. Once we have done that, then we will let you do or kill whatever and whoever you want.

Except a panda.

"Do you understand me? If you don't like it, tough. We have plenty of bullets to spare for you, too. Understood?"

"Do you even know who you're talking to American?"

"I said is that understood?" The SEAL Captain stood face to face with the Chinese with his hand on his sidearm. Karson smiled at Victor's ferocity, staying behind him though as an added barrier, ready to pounce if Victor gave the word.

Finally, Commander Wu nodded slowly, patting Victor roughly on the shoulder. He smiled. "What eva you say, Amedican."

He and his team made their way into the clearing and up the rocky slope, to take up overwatch positions.

"That was creepy. Almost threatening. Sir, we should cross streams." Karson said.

"Yeah, team, moving forward, keep eyes on the Chinese 'friendly' force as they may not be friendly anymore. Anything makes you uncomfortable, shoot first, and ask questions later. Our mission, gather Intel, capture Hatyara, and stay alive. Our lives are all that matter. No one else's. Clear?"

They all nodded.

"Take up positions over the clearing. When we fire, we will cross streams to kill more enemy. Half take right, half take left depending on your line of site. We have no tracer rounds, flash suppression, and suppressors, so we should be firing from the dark like specters."

"Sir." Ox whispered.

The SEALs made their way, too, up the rocky slope, positioning themselves so they could watch the enemy force below them searching for Hatyara, but also 'babysitting' the 'friendly' Chinese force.

As the allies took up their positions, the enemy soldiers took up positions also. They stood in line as a man walked down the line, decorated in a dark red, Death Nation military suit.

The sea of red uniformed enemy soldiers started speaking, shouting that is, the name of the man.

"HATYARA! HATYARA! HATYARA!"

"Team, be advised. General Hatyara confirmed. Target in sight. This ritual should be coming to an end soon. Hold fire." Victor spoke through his comlink.

Karson started to squirm. Seeing the man responsible for this downfall of the earth, the man who killed for no reason, and the man whom Karson could easily kill with one well-positioned shot right between his eyes through his brain. It would be so easy for Karson. So smooth, like an NBA basketball celebrity shooting a free throw, or a professional quarterback tossing the ball to his teammate; Karson could end this guy's life in a split second.

Victor laid a hand on Karson's shoulder.

"Wow, he's a sight to see," Karson said to Victor, shaking.

"Focus, Karson."

"I could kill him in an instant, Victor. The threat would be over."

"You and I know we need to capture him alive to end this. You know the objective. The mission. It's your call. Kill him; you'll be reprimanded. Catch him; you'll be a pivotal part of ending the war sooner rather than later."

"Aye. I know. And I know he has leaders above him... But I want him. Sorry, sir. My head is in. I have lock on target if needed."

"Good. Keep on him."

"Aye."

"Team, be ready to strike. If the chance arises-"

The Chinese commander stood up and aimed at the General, shouting in his native tongue.

"No!" Karson shouted. He turned and fired three suppressed shots and killed the Chinese Soldier. The Soldier had managed to get a shot off, but it pierced the brain of the man in front of Hatyara, not the ruthless General who now knew to run.

Shame. Oh, and there you go. Now we have to chase you.

The enemy soldiers instantly dove on top of their leader to protect him as the Chinese fired on them and also turned on the U.S. The SEALs were now caught on two fronts. The enemy and the enemy. The Chinese and Death Nation.

Yeah, lots of diplomatic talks to come later, Karse! GET OUTTA HERE!

It was every team for themselves. The five SEALs fired back at both enemies. Karson and Victor focused on the Chinese, pinning them down as the other four shot at Hatyara's men.

"Hit, Hatyara. Kill him before he escapes!" Karson relayed calmly to Wasp.

"Aye, Commander!"

"We have to get out of here, Serval," Victor called pushing his men back into the tunnels they had come from, he grabbed Karson's vest and pulled him away from the enemy blood bath. Victor threw frags and flashbangs into the masses, then turned tail and ran into the tunnel for their lives as the explosions rocked the clearing and the tunnels.

BANG

BOOM

They rushed back towards the entrance, dirt, and then crunching bones.

This is not where I'm going to be buried. Not down here! Not in this country!

As Karson was thinking his thoughts, Wasp in front of him tripped and fell, knocking Karson and Gingie down. The bones poked into Karson and the stench was nearly unbearable. The enemy forces on both sides were now after the SEALs.

"Serval, get up! Let's go! We have to get out of here!" Ox called.

Victor ran back and helped Gingie up as Wasp helped Karson up. Karson took the lead in front of Wasp, making his way back towards the entrance. The Chinese Medic who had stayed behind, having no clue of the chaos that had ensued just watched. Waiting for his teammates, *probably afraid to join us.*

Karson stopped and shouted at him. "Come-on! We have to go!" *Not your fault your team failed.*

The Chinese soldier helped the Sailors up. Wasp hoisted Karson up. As Wasp was lifted, the Chinese Soldier was shot in the head, dropping like a rock, Wasp slamming onto the side of the hole. Karson dove back and grabbed his hand. He started hoisting him up. Wasp's mouth opened and his voice came out in agony!

"Get me up! Hurry!" As if someone was punching raw meat, Karson heard bullets connect into Wasp's body, and watched his face twist in pain.

****

CHAPTER 15 - SA 321

Karson hoisted Wasp the rest of the way up as Victor and Ox fired down into the hole at the pursuers. Karson rolled Wasp onto his stomach to find bullet holes riddling through his lower half. He'd possibly never walk normal again.

"Karson, I need a grenade!" Victor shouted firing down into the hole. The Chinese enemies were now playing whack a mole. Sticking their heads out. Only Victor, instead of smacking them, blew their brains out. FUN!

Karson tossed it to Victor.

"Thanks." He said.

"Wasp, I'm going to carry you." Karson turned back to his patient.

"Just leave me behind. Find Hatyara." Wasp said, wincing at the pain.

"Dude, don't tempt me! You know we don't leave men behind. Especially brothers! You're more valuable than a scum bag like Hatyara." Karson lied through his teeth.

"FRAG OUT!" Vic said when he had a brief pause from firing at targets.

"Come on. Up you go!" As Karson hoisted Wasp onto his shoulder, the grenade Victor had thrown blew off the door to the catacombs below. Karson carried Wasp out of the barn. The Chinese helicopter was landing in the clearing, and the Chinese Soldiers stepped off to support.

"Pharo?" Karson called behind him.

"They don't know. We're all right." Victor ran up and grabbed Wasp's other side, speeding the hobbling duo along.

Karson trusted Victor's words and made his way onto the chopper, helping Wasp into a seat. "Sit tight. We'll be at medical attention soon."

"Thank you, Serval." Wasp shook his hand.

"Don't mention it!" Karson returned the shake, then turned and looked out the door, weapon up ready to fire.

POP

WHIZZ

"Oof!" Karson jolted back into the chopper as more shots filled the cabin and the SEALs returned fire. Finally, it stopped.

Victor was at Karson's side in a second. "You okay, bud? Karse. Open your eyes."

"Don't say my name!" Karson growled, opening his eyes.

"Don't scare me like that and I won't." Victor held out his hand.

"Sorry, sir. He caught me sleeping. I owe you one of the loads of beers you owe me; I'll make it up to you. Get me back in."

"Nope. You're done. Rest. Sit and just enjoy the flight."

"Hell nah! I'll rest when I'm dead! Patch me up, I'm still combat effective, I'm a SEAL for damn sake! I'll push through the pain. Fix me later."

"Serval... I can't let you die. If you die, you messed up. If captured, kill as many of them as you can before you die."

"I taught you that. You forgot that if you're shot, you were caught sleeping."

"You already said that."

"Oh..."

"Where are our soldiers?" The Chinese pilot asked.

Karson was about to speak up when Victor took over. "Dead. They were ambushed as we were making our way out. We tried to go back, but they blew the entrance to the tunnel, leaving themselves trapped inside. We're terribly sorry for your loss, but we need to get out of here. They are coming. The enemy force, more massive than we had planned so get us outta-"

Victor was interrupted by a Death Nation soldier jumping into the chopper. Victor had his pistol in the man's face and kicked him out off the back of the ramp.

"WAIT!" Karson shouted, lunging and grabbing the man, pulling him back in the chopper but leaning out himself, the only thing stopping him from death was the Death Nation soldier's grip on Karson's arm.

Everyone stopped, gun pushed in the back of the man's head.

"Pull him back up!" Victor said, low in his throat, tense at the situation.

Karson stared up into the soldier's eyes.

After a second of frozen time, the soldier hoisted Karson into the chopper and was tackled by the other SEALs.

"Stop! Let him up!" Karson said, standing.

"Hatyara's in a chopper. He's about to take off. SA 321 Super Frelon variant." The soldier relayed. "You only alive because you save me."

Karson's eyes widened. "That kind of chopper is used to transport and attack people. It will totally outperform us if we're not careful."

"Why should we believe you?" Wasp shouted.

"Where's he going?" Karson asked.

"Don't know, but you need to stop him." The foreigner said.

"You betray him?" Karson asked.

"Yeah but he's not trying to catch me. He's trying to hunt me. Trying to kill me. You need to kill him. He is a major player in this war!"

"We need to leave, Serval!" Victor said. He turned to the pilot.

Karson looked for the chopper. "There's Hatyara! We can still get him!" Karson said.

"We go!" The Chinese leader said. "That will blow us away."

"Karson, we have wounded, we need to leave. Get us out of here!" Victor overruled Karson's order.

"NO! WE ARE GOING TO GET HIM! HE'S RIGHT HERE! WE CAN CRIPPLE THE ENEMY HERE AND NOW!"

Karson opened the other door as the helicopter turned back towards the enemy. "You hang out the left, I'll take the right!" Karson grabbed a sniper rifle from one of the soldiers in the chopper and gave it to the Death Nation soldier.

"Hey! No, he doesn't get a gun!" Victor said.

"Shoot him if he turns, Vic. Don't have time for this!" Karson took aim out of the door, as Hatyara's helicopter started lifting off the ground. It fired warning shots as it hovered around, taking aim on the smaller Chinese chopper. Karson fired shots, aiming for the cockpit, striking the glass, but only scratching it. He hit the same spot again, puncturing it, but not going through.

"DAMN!" Karson yelled. "You have to hit the glass at least three times!" Karson took aim again. However, the chopper rounded on the allied rotor copter and fired. Karson dodged right. However, the Death Nation soldier took a direct hit to the back of the head and dropped out of the chopper.

"Well, he killed you alright!"

Karson glared at Wasp.

Wasp shrugged and grimaced. "What?"

The enemy helicopter took to the air, turning on its enemy like a hornet attacking someone innocent just walking by.

"Go around the mountain!" Victor told the pilots. "Serval, you need to shoot that pilot."

"WHAT DO YOU THINK I'M TRYING TO DO?" Karson shouted aiming again, firing. A missile flew past the helicopter. "Vic, we're going to get shot down. I can't hit it!"

"Try! Keep working!" Victor said, looking back up to the cockpit, struggling with his backpack. "Can you spin around and shoot?" He called to the pilots. "Team put on your-"

Karson took aim one final time but knew his time in the air was about to end. The enemy chopper spun its guns and fired both bullets and missiles at the allied helicopter. "BRACE YOURSELVES!" Karson grabbed onto the handle of the door, and hoped to God he wouldn't fall out as-

BOOM

A blast wave, stronger than Karson had ever felt jolted the chopper and his body. The helicopter started spinning out of control. Karson was thrown from the helicopter, but still managed to hang on with one hand. The helicopter was hit in the prop and was going down, at least one thousand feet to the ground. Karson only had a few seconds to react. He pulled his pistol, and dropped his magazine of bullets, and replaced it with a tracking magazine. The one bullet in the chamber would fire, allowing the tracking bullet into the chamber. Karson fired down to chamber the tracking device, then took aim, and aimed at Hatyara's helicopter from where the devastating explosion had come from. Karson's world spun around and around, the chopper each time getting that much farther and farther away. Hatyara's chopper came into view and disappeared a third time, and as he came around on the fourth, Karson fired. However, Hatyara's chopper flew straight at the disabled Chinese chopper, and slammed its wheels into the side of Karson's helicopter and pushed it out over the lip of the mountain.

The chopper dipped over the lip of the ridge and continued to fall. Karson and the rest of the crew were sucked out into the air and were freefalling to their deaths. Karson screamed, clawing at the air in a feeble attempt to try to slow down as the trees below came ever closer. He tried making himself bigger, like a parachute of clothes, but that, of course, didn't help.

"I DON'T WANT TO DIE! PLEASE, GOD! PLEASE!"

Karson had no way to survive. He looked around and saw parachutes above him, slowly floating down, but Karson still fell at terminal velocity. Suddenly, however, Karson felt a firm grip pull him back against what felt like a tree. Victor hooked Karson into him.

"Relax, Karse," Victor said, too calmly.

Karson screamed as the world came closer and closer to ending, the ground rising quickly up.

"VICTOR? WHAT THE HECK? I HAVE TO TELL YOU SOMETHING!"

"NOT NOW!"

Suddenly the ground shot under Karson, and the wind blew through his hair and looking over, he saw that Victor had thrown on his squirrel suit. He deployed the reserve chute and glided gracefully down to the ground. As they hit, Karson heard a massive explosion a mile off to the west, the sound of the apparently downed Chinese helicopter. Karson looked up as the sound of his parachuting friends took his attention. Wasp landed first, crumpling in a fit of cursing as his legs gave out, and Gingie and Ox with the two pilots. The other crew had fallen off the ramp in the disaster.

"Everyone okay?" Victor asked. "Wasp?"

"Yeah. Fine. I need help, though." He said, laying on the ground, his voice soaked in excruciating pain.

"We'll help you. Pilots?"

The pilots nodded. "Fine!"

"What did you want to tell me, Serval?" Victor helped Karson up from the ground.

"WHAT ARE WE GOING TO DO NOW!? I MEAN WE HAVE NO RIDE, NO CONTACT; WE'RE STUCK IN ENEMY TERRITORY, AND THOSE GUYS UP THERE ARE COMING FOR US. WHEN THEY FIND WE'RE NOT DEAD, THEY ARE GOING TO KILL US!" Gingie started panicking.

"Well, they are certainly going to find us with you freaking out and shouting like that," Victor said sternly.

"Whatever. Gingie is right!" Ox joined the distraught SEAL. "This is just great! We're lost, and we lost Hatyara AGAIN!" He kicked a tree. "This is bad man. This is really bad."

"Not necessarily, dude. We are taught never to give up, and I didn't!" Karson said, his body and voice shaking.

"You almost died, Cat and screamed like your name suggestions. Like a puss. If anyone should be the one heeding your advice, it's you." He said.

"I'm freaking out right now too, but I have a job to do. I can be me after the war. I can cry, panic when this is all over. Right now, I'm a warrior, with a job, and someone who is more powerful than anyone else. For now, I am death. For now, I am pushing my emotions down, and getting stuff done and holy fuck that is a giant-ass bug! Kill it! KILL IT!"

Victor rolled his eyes and stomped on the bug. "Never much liked bugs. Only thing that scared you at basic."

"Anyways, what was I talking about? Yeah. As I was saying, as we were going down, while you sissies panicked, I shot his helicopter with a tracking bullet. It is going to relay his position with my tablet."

"We heard you screaming as you fell!"

"Well, how would you feel-"

"That is sick!" Victor perked up. "How does the tracker work?"

"It plays a game of 'Marco Polo' with a satellite, and that satellite tracks its position. The bullet lodged in the hull says Marco, and the satellite says Polo, relaying it to my device. That is… um… Let's see if it stuck. Hmmm…"

Wasp started shivering.

Karson looked at the captain who in return, smiled. "Great job, Karson."

Karson looked at Wasp. "We need to get out of here. He's in bad shape. Shock."

Victor nodded. "Ox, you're the strongest. Help him through the jungle. Let's start moving. Enemies are going to be surrounding this area so we cannot let off a distress beacon at this time. We need to travel into the woods to the south. A few clicks away from here, I'll relay information to Command, and we'll be out of here in no time. We'll be okay as long as we stay stealthy."

As the SEALs headed into the forest away from the crash site with the Chinese pilots, enemy troops did, in fact, find the crash site, and finding bodies, were convinced that the 'infidel' were dead. They went on their merry way, without a clue that their worst nightmares were heading to safety.

Karson kept an eye on his tracking bullet for an hour as they made it to their extraction point where a Para Rescue team of the U.S. Air Force had deployed with a SWCC team as support to pick up the stranded American Sailors. Racing over the water, Karson lied down on the floor, taking a quick nap. The only team he trusted other than his own to sleep around were the highly skilled and trained SWCC teams of the United States Navy. They would and did get the SEALs back to Victor's camp, where they packed up and headed out to more open water on the river where a Chinook helicopter lowered cables to lift the SOC-R boats out of the water, and lowered a rope ladder down into the boats. Three total were around the area with two Apache helicopters for support. Karson was the second to last to go up the rope ladder, following Ox and Gingie. Wasp was hoisted like a person rescued by the Coast Guard from the ocean. On board the chopper, the medics got to work on Wasp, and Karson was put in contact with his commanding officers, and he relayed what information he could to them as he headed back to the USS Zumwalt where he would transfer to the USS Elding to regroup with his SEAL Team Six team, under Captain Richardson's command; Karson's 'immediate' family.

"Hatyara got away, sir. I did manage to get a track on him, but I have reason to believe it did not stick."

"Mission failed then, Serval. We needed that information."

"I know. I thought it-"

The device in Karson's hand flashed once, as a little tan dot shown heading out of Chinese airspace towards the country of-

"Pakistan! They just entered Pakistan!"

"Nice work, Serval! We need the codes to track it!" Thompson ordered. "ASAP."

"Aye, sir. Just hack my device. It should be in the database of supplies I took: Tablet sixty-five. seal.19314.kksh@usnavyspecialops.mil. Password: serValKat#335119314 with a capital V in serval and capital K for Kat."

"Okay. It's asking a secondary code." Richardson said.

"That would be on your end. That's all I've got. It's probably part of a firewall to ensure it's you hacking and not an enemy country or something like that. Speaking of which, I don't think any of these guys here heard me, but you'll need to change my password and email."

"We'll have that done by the time you get here. This is truly great work. Safe flight. We'll see you when you get here. Out." Thompson ended the transmission.

"Out." Karson turned to Victor. "Thanks."

"No, thank you. Without you, we'd probably not have found him in the first place."

"Yeah. I'm pretty brilliant." Karson smiled and turned.

"I'm sorry you have to leave when you get on the ship," Victor said, Karson turning back to him. "It was fun to work with you again... Friends still?"

"Yeah. I'm going to miss you my **best** friend. Get through the war. You have some alcohol to buy me." Karson winked.

"It's not goodbye yet. We have a long flight ahead of us."

"I'm gonna sleep! I have this odd feeling that for some reason, I'm probably heading to the place I've dreaded going to, and have luckily avoided so far in my career." Karson groaned.

"Where's that?"

"Towards the Middle East. I want to see the culture, but it's not safe. At all."

"Yuck! Remember when President Obama said the U.S. were not going to send troops back in?"

"I wasn't alive yet... But I read that."

"Yeah. Looks like he was wrong."

"Hopefully I'll just get Hatyara. I always thought that each time we defeat a threat, a worse one is born. Now it's Death Nation, adopting every enemy tactic dating back to the wars of the beginning of time and then some. It has no rules. If I'm lucky, the only country I'll be deployed to is Pakistan."

"What did you want to tell me?"

"Oh. Yeah…"

****

CHAPTER 16 - Dead End

Four Months later in Pakistan; 1700 hours:

The sun was starting to descend in the sky, dipping down behind the mountains in the distance of the scattered tree covered desert of the Pakistani landscape. The United States had deployed the Operators of SEAL Team Six, Captain Richardson's group of elite Sailors to Pakistan four months ago in the search for the war criminal, Hatyara. Having lost trace of Hatyara as he disappeared in Pakistan, the SEALs patrolled the vast area that his trail was known to go dark. The remaining Allied Nations of England, France, Spain, Portugal, Belgium, Australia, Canada, and The United States of America had formally declared war on Death Nation and had begun small campaigns against pockets of Death Nation as a distraction as the SEAL team attempted to find the leader. Finland even decided to join in.

At dusk, the SEALs were wrapping up on patrols. Having been on the hunt in the country for months now; and with the element of stealth and surprise gone, the SEALs had discontinued their nightly raids and search missions, knowing that any movement would be harder to find in the night. Now they just patrolled with the hopes that command would give them Intel. With the days turning into weeks without new information, the team knew that soon, they would be pulled from Pakistan, the war on Death Nation would intensify, and that they would be either sent in to fight as infantry on high valued missions or retasked on stealth missions elsewhere.

For now, Karson was slightly leaned back and reclined in the passenger seat of the U.S. Navy Humvee, alone with his thoughts. It had been a long day of patrols, clearing missions, and small skirmishes, as with all days, consisting of a small pocket of terrorists spilling over from the wars in Afghanistan and Iraq. The skirmishes went along the lines of scouting the small SEAL team, and as they cleared a house, set up an ambush which was the same tactic that ended the Vietnam War for the United States fifty years ago on April 30, 1975. Generally, one of the SEALs would notice that the people in the street were staying back and would alert the team of a possible ambush. The SEALs would exit through the side doors of the building or house they were clearing, head up onto a roof, and as the terrorist would get impatient and rush the house, the SEALs would have the element of surprise and the high ground of a building and fire on the enemy squad. Ambushing the ambushers.

After the bulk were killed, the SEALs would head into the street in a diamond formation, Captain Richardson at the point, Hunter and Smith at the secondary points, and the other two SEALs covering the sides and back, each SEAL, though, played a pivotal point with his head on the swivel to keep the enemy at bay. Any man they could capture, two today, were placed in the trunk of the Humvee until they could be transported back to the small Pakistani military base that Pakistan had loaned to the U.S. for interrogation. Once interrogated, the enemy combatant was handed over to the authorities of the country, where God only knows what happened to them then.

On rare occasion, a skirmish would break out where the U.S. Military would have to fight the Pakistani Military, or Police, where rogue soldiers and officers thought it better to join the enemy alliance than to truly fight for right. Money, woman, the promise of better friends and family, or the mere thought that it would be cool to kill Americans.

When are these people going to learn that one, we are not the 'infidel.' All the United States wants to do is give the world what we have. Freedom. Democracy. Better life. I don't understand extremism. In the U.S., people don't die all the time. People don't rise in status by maiming each other. We coexist. I wish radical people would do the same. Instead of fighting with the police, maybe we could get along and make ends meet.

****

"This is a special news alert!"

A blonde haired woman popped up on CNN. New and improved, the beautiful young woman captured America's attention as the first news anchor to be unbiased when telling a story.

"The United States and Pakistan, two nations trying to seek peace in a time where peace seems to have vanished, have attacked each other yet again. Some would say the two countries act as if they were young siblings fighting over whose turn it is to play Xbox, yet these fights are deadlier. The Army says that thirteen of its Soldiers are dead, with seventeen other people injured, while Pakistani counts are reported to be much greater. It all started when police stopped a routine patrol for straying too far out of the agreed patrol route, a strategy U.S. Army General Westbay says was necessary to maintain peace. Obviously, he was wrong today. The U.S. Army's posture was deemed a threat, and that is when police opened fire, and when reinforcements from the Pakistani defense force were mobilized. Overall, we've seen these skirmishes popping up more and more frequently in the nation as U.S. Forces continue to operate in the sovereign nation. President Elding is expected to speak about his foreign policy and military intervention in the coming days."

****

CHAPTER 17 - Poverty isn't a thing, it's just how people live here

Karson was looking out the window at the Pakistani landscape and villages, pondering how these people live out their days. His heart was heavy. *My country is so blessed, but these people are suffering.* The American world, even for the crapshoot that it had become is still so much different than these people living in poverty, with a constant threat of its own government coming into their neighborhoods killing men, women, and children. *Children. Something I'll never understand.*

The Humvee turned down a road passing a town, or more like a favela. Tin roofs and cardboard walls… The small huts barely able to fit a small family of mom, dad, and offspring, let alone the large families these people had. Grandma and pa, aunts and uncles, cousins, and other relatives. Another strange sight were the heaps of clothes where people would go out into the streets and take their day's clothes from the marketplace. Dirty, ragged, used up and donated. These people would barter and beg for American waste, unwanted American clothes tattered and torn, but the only things these foreigners could get. But what stuck out to Karson the most were the heaps of trash cluttering the streets where people walked, and children played soccer… with the junk in the road. The soccer balls were made from plastic bags and rubber bands the kids had sifted from the mounds of debris that lined the area. As the SEALs drove past, the natives and children would stop their game, look, and wave and smile, as if nothing were wrong. But deep in their eyes, the people who could resist the call to extremism, the SEALs knew these people wanted to be rescued, wanted help, wanted to be out of their third world nation. These people wanted to either have a better, more urban, more developed city, country, life, or they would rather move to the west. Karson looked away.

"If we come back, sir, we are bringing them a soccer ball."

Karson turned and looked at his family, the small team he knew and loved. Five men including himself. Karson's Captain was driving. The Commander sat in the passenger seat, and three other SEALs accompanied them; the gunner, medic, and sniper. Karson's role was rifleman as well as secondary commander on this mission, but of course, his role could switch if circumstances out of the team's control were to befall them! Richardson's role was primarily commanding the team, leading them and strategically placing the SEALs or giving them objectives to complete. He too was trained as a rifleman.

The medic and sniper had the unique assigned job of finding and pointing out targets for the gunner in a firefight/combat mission, as well as potential threats coming up in the road, like improvised explosive devices, enemy vehicles, and other threats that might have gone unnoticed. They used computes in the seats in front of them. Karson's commander merely placed his hand on Karson's shoulder, squeezed and shook him a little smiling, not taking his eyes off the road.

"Hopefully if we come back this way or whatever way we go, we will have done a lot more for them than giving them a day's worth of entertainment." The medic behind Richardson said, so soft spoken.

"Hooyah to that, man!" The gunner shouted down.

"We need gas. Everyone, when we arrive, hop out and set up your barrier around the Hummer."

"Aye, sir!" Karson said, readying his weapon.

The mission in Russia had led to Karson's mission in China, having been a success. Before heading to Pakistan, Karson had said goodbye to Captain Paul and his team as they were called to Africa to combat the terrorist influences in Madagascar. The mission for SEAL Team Two was so top secret that no other branches, not even SEAL teams, were to know. That was the case for all SEAL teams. The less people knew, the easier it would be for the United States to deny involvement. Probable ignorance. All teams, unless on joint missions, worked in secrecy. While Victor headed for ISDN, Karson's mission was to capture Hatyara. The two friends had made plans to meet up after the war was over. That is if they both survived. Americans were the most undesirable people in the world by enemy forces, especially in Death Nation's most allied countries in the Middle East and Africa.

Even though it was sad to see Victor and his team off before being activated and mobilized to deploy with his team to Pakistan, as long as Karson was with his brothers, it didn't matter where he was. To hell and back he would go.

Richardson drove to a gas station. People hurriedly finished fueling and left the station, fearful of what Americans would bring. "Out."

Karson stayed in the vehicle, looking at a document that he'd been sent the day before with barely any new information. *There has to be something I can find in this...* Karson looked at Richardson who was staring at Karson through the window. "What?"

"I want you out with the team."

"I was just-"

"Don't care. Out."

Karson sighed. "Yes, sir." Karson hopped out of the Hummer and stretched his legs, looking around at the surrounding buildings and houses.

"So, where should we flaunt our power and influence after this deployment? Papua New Guinea? India? Fiji? We have actionable intel for Africa!" Private Laukins asked, walking up to Karson.

"Don't care where we go, Laukins, as long as we can bring the battle to some Sissy Nation soldiers."

"I'll drink to that, brah!" He said to Karson.

"Hey! HEY!" A Pakistani man came running at the Navy SEALs.

Karson turned but was tackled by the man before he could react. He hit the ground so hard, all the wind was knocked out of him, and his canteen slammed into his side.

Karson moaned as the man was yanked off of him and slammed into the Hummer. Richardson helped Karson up into the Hummer. "You okay?"

"Yeah. What's he want?" Karson asked.

"Don't know. Do you feel up for interrogating him?"

"Sure." Karson stepped out of the Humvee and hobbled to the back to find the man handcuffed and sitting on the bumper. "Do you speak English?"

"I sorry for hit you. I just need tell you something! Der is large group people in Quetta."

"You speak English very well. How did you learn?" Karson asked, having Davis plot a course to Quetta.

"I went to University. Dis is not relevant to dis situation. You need go Quetta. My family is der. I tink something is happen der."

"Explain." Karson ordered.

"JUST GO DER!"

"QUIT JERKING US OFF, MAN! WHY WOULD WE GO THERE ON YOUR WORD?" Karson shouted to the man. *Did you not understand my English or somthin'?*

"You need go der. Bad tings happen."

"Okay, man. Whatever you say." Karson turned and walked over to Richardson.

"Let's go." Richardson opened his door. "Finish the fuel and get in."

"Oh, you cannot be serious," Karson huffed.

"I am. It's the newest lead we've had in months. I'm tired of being here. I want to do something more than patrol. We are a SEAL Team. Not a standard Navy patrol."

"I-I... This is so dumb. What if it's a trap?"

"Then we'll be ready. Team, cut him loose and mount up."

The Americans were driving fast on the highway, causing cars to swerve out of the Humvee's way. The locals didn't want to mess with the SEALs' hardware. The team reached the city of Quetta, a city in the North Western part of Pakistan near the border with Afghanistan. Another hostile area where violence and hatred, sexism, racism, and death were the ways of life. As the men approached the area, the Sailors' state of alert went up tenfold. They were the only U.S. warriors in this vicinity, and this was the most dangerous city around. Thirteen Green Berets had lost their lives near here, defending civilians on a Missionary trip from Vermont, of all places, where a study showed that only twenty-two percent of people identify as religious. Their desire to spread the word of God wasn't reciprocated in the area, and multiple civilian and military lives were lost in cowardly acts of terrorism on American citizens.

That needs to stop. Gone should be the days of American assassinations. In Roman days, one need only say I am a Roman citizen and the mere fact that he, or she for that matter, was a Roman meant that they received respectful treatment and was even slightly feared. Same for Americans. We should be able to travel anywhere in the world and be shielded by the ways of American life. Woe be to those who attack us. Really, any country should have this as well; we should respect each other, man, woman, whatever from wherever.

"Captain Richardson: I need to talk with your second."

Karson looked at Richardson with a question. "Command?"

"Hunter. Admiral Thompson. You failed in China."

"Sir, all due respect…"

"Where are you with Hatyara?"

Karson was caught off guard. "Well, sir… uh… I'm on the trail, sir!"

"Well, my boy. Being on the trail usually means you will always be on the trail, never grabbing the prize." Admiral Thompson said.

"You want to come out here, sweat your balls off, and find him, be my guest," Karson growled through the communications. "I take my pants off every day and smell rank down there. I LIKE CLEAN JUNK! SO BE MY GUEST! I COULD BE SCREWING MY-"

Richardson bored a warning into Karson.

"Excuse me?" The Admiral growled back.

"I've got it handled, Admiral." Karson dismissed the leader of the Navy.

"For your sake, I hope you do." Thompson's voice was sinister.

"Serval! You dare talk to an Admiral like that?" Smith asked.

"Look fellas. When I work this hard on something like this, don't question my resolve and my deliverance. We'll get this dick-head; it just takes time. They know that. We know that. They just need someone to bust their balls."

****

CHAPTER 18 - The Broadcast

"First up on NPR. Thirteen Green Berets and seventeen missionaries for the Church of Jesus Christ in Vermont have been killed today in the first major attack on U.S. Citizens and Soldiers since the attacks nearly two years ago where one Marine, the first woman death on camera, was shot down over Iraq. The Green Berets were protecting the Christian teachers in Pakistan, but with tensions high, heading to this area of the world was a major mistake. One beret is said to be alive. Wait… we have news coming in.

"Ladies and Gentlemen of ze world. We have your Soldiers. We have your lives. We have your nations. When will you decide just to give in to the inevitable? We will raise our dark flag over your White House, over your

Kremlin, over your palaces. No need to struggle. We have already won. And we prove it today with sheer terror. Dis man is in direct violation of our nation, serving a separate leader and flag. He will die, and you will watch. Let dis be a view of what is to come to you. We not afraid. We not ashamed. We will enact a reign of terror that far outweighs that of France. We will bring blood and order to your lands. You will serve. Or you will die. Make your choice. Note. Not even your own Soldiers can save der own lives."

The shot switched to show a Green Beret in full uniform tethered to four horses, four axes in the hands of four Death Nation soldiers' hands. A whip cracked, and the horses pulled, at which point the man screamed in sheer agony. For ten seconds the man suffered, to be released as his limbs were hacked away and blood showered the ground, his limbs being dragged off and his body plummeted to the ground. The soldiers lit a fire and the man burned alive on live television.

"Join us, or you will face a torture far worse than dis man. Starting with you. Bonjour." The man pointed into the camera; then the feed went back to the NPR correspondents.

"We had no control over what you just saw, but it would seem that the Beret that fought so valiantly even as his brothers died to save those teachers, missionaries, men, women, and children has died. I-I... I have no words, but hopefully, our nation can pull together. Our sources are saying President Elding will be broadcasting tonight. So quickly after this national tragedy. This video also proves that even in nations deemed safe, foreign influences still have some sway. Stay tuned, we will have more information as the day progresses."

****

CHAPTER 19 - Ambush

The SEALs mission statement was as follows:

- **OBJECTIVE ONE: INFILTRATE INTO PAKISTAN UNDETECTED** ✔
- **OBJECTIVE TWO: OBTAIN INTEL ON LOCATION OF HATYARA (KINDA)**
- **OBJECTIVE THREE: VECTOR TO WAYPOINT AND ENGAGE ENEMY TARGETS UNDETECTED (PRESENT. TRYNA DO THAT)**
- **OBJECTIVE FOUR: CAPTURE OR KILL HATYARA AND EXIT UNDETECTED WITH PACKAGE**
- **TACTICS: SILENCED/STEALTH KILLS IF DETECTED, OR IF OBJECTIVE THREE AND FOUR ARE COMPROMISED**

- INSERTION: 20TH SPECIAL OPERATIONS SQUADRON UNITED STAES AIR FORCE TO PAKISTANI BASE WHERE OPERATION IS EXECUTED ON SEALS DISCRETION (COMPLETED WITH OBJECTIVE ONE)
- EXTRACTION: WITH HATYARA (BREATHING OR DEFLATED); UNDETECTED-FROM PAKISTANI BASE; IF DISCOVERED-GIVE LOCATION. 20TH SPECIAL OPERATIONS SQUADRON UNITED STATES AIR FORCE AIR SUPPORT WILL DEPLOY AS QRF
- WEAPON PAYLOAD: SUPPRESSED MODERATE WEAPON LOADOUT
- SUPPORT: 20TH SPECIAL OPERATION SQUADRON (GREEN HORNETS 20TH SOS)-CV-22 OSPREY AND APACHE HELICOPTER
- OPERATION: OPERATION BULL MATADOR
- HIGH VALUED TARGET (HVT) CODENAME: BULL
- BRANCH: UNITED STATES AIR FORCE AND NAVY JOINT OPERATION (TASKFORCE)
- UNIT: 20TH SPECIAL OPERATIONS SQUADRON (GREEN HORNETS 20TH SOS) UNITED STATES AIR FORCE AND NAVY SEAL TEAM SIX
- ROEs: RULES OF ENGAGEMENT: FIRE IN SELF DEFENSE WHEN FIRED UPON.

1. SOURCES SAY HATYARA IS IN THE AREA
2. MULTIPLE BRIGADES OF MEN HAVE ENTERED THE AREA
3. CIVILIANS KIDNAPPED; POSSIBLE USE OF HUMAN SHIELDS
4. FOOD CAPTURED
5. SHOTS FIRED
6. EXPLOSIONS IN THE AREA AS WELL AS SMALL SKIRMISHES OF RESISTANCE
7. LIVES THREATENED
8. GRAFFITI PROMINENT

Based on the mission above, the SEALs had discovered that on local intelligence and interviews and interrogation-Hatyara was not the leader of the operation, rather, secondary. In order to find the leader, however, Hatyara would still need to be captured. The mission briefing above, after relaying the new information to command stayed the same with some minor differences. The SEALs' cover was blown, so going loud was now an option, giving the SEALs a little more wiggle room to work. Suppressed weapons were no longer needed unless infiltrating enemy fortresses. Hatyara now needed to be captured alive; the no-kill mission was authorized. Also, Hatyara was a mastermind in war. He led the attacks on allied lands, and he would be a slippery pig to capture. The allied nations had spread out to their own enemy countries to try and regain order. The United States alongside the United Nations had the daunting task of overseeing all military operations, the U.S. sending troops to all areas of the campaign. With people of all countries now dying and the world's population diminishing every day since the enemy vendetta began, order had to come soon, or nothing would be left to fight for.

As the SEAL team was driving through different areas of Pakistan who now joined in what was being called the Third Great War, with no clue of where the HVT was, and no new leads, they continued to stop and ask locals if they'd seen the 'good' tyrant. Each time, they would have no luck. The language barrier never helped much either, nor the resentment of the United States invading the Pakistani country.

Should have taken up Arabic! Nah!

As the team drove past a group of men, Karson ordered an 'all stop.' Karson watched the people in his side mirror. Reaching for his weapon holstered in the roof. As the military Hummer came to a halt, the group all turned and squared up to the Hummer.

"What's up, Hunter?" Richardson asked.

"Those guys are suspicious."

"For just standing there."

"Look at what they are doing. They are sizing us up. Let's talk to them."

"Alright. Team, dismount. Follow Serval's lead on this one, team."

"Aye, sir."

"Aye, sir."

"I'll stay up top." The gunner called down, rotating the heavy weapon to the rear area of operation.

"Stay frosty, dude," Karson said as he pulled his gun from the roof and opened the door. "Keep on the swivel."

"Aye, sir." The gunner replied.

The SEALs made their way to the rear of the Humvee and formed a line, safeties off. Karson noticed a female in the group and made his way for her.

"Ma'am, may we speak to you?" Karson asked calmly and softly.

The men stepped in front of her, each raising their arms in a 'what do you want' motion.

Karson stuck a hand out. "Relax. Hey, relax. We just want to talk." The men looked at Karson, sizing him up, like tigers squaring up to fight. The men stood taller than Karson. In a country like this, if you weren't up to these men's standards, then you were a mere boy. Seeing that Karson was younger than them, as well as smaller, they took no attention to him. They pushed him backward. The SEALs all stepped forward. As they did so, a man in the rear of the group pulled a weapon.

"GUN!" The gunner shouted, and he honed in on his target.

Karson pushed through the crowd toward the man. As the Pakistani aimed, the SEAL team did as well, but Karson with democracy on his mind, pulled his knife and flicked his knife underhand, hitting the man in the face with the hilt. As the man's head flung back, three shots were expelled, but Karson closed the distance between the man and swept his leg, knocking him to the ground. He grabbed his knife and the man's weapon, pointing it at him. The woman, obviously the man's wife, screamed and lunged at Karson, but Karson's medic had made it to his side and restrained her, too.

"Restrain the group, team," Richardson said, taking the woman by the arm and sitting her down. "DO NOT MOVE."

"Me?" The gunner asked.

"No, stay up in the nest, and keep on the swivel. This won't take but a moment." Richardson radioed as Karson's captive got feisty again. Karson, ands on trying to role his opponent over, dropped his weight, unleashing the full force of his elbow to the man's jaw and forced his arms behind him, hearing a watery noise come from the man's shoulder, obviously an injury.

Whoops. Sorry, not sorry.

"YOU DON'T DRAW ON AMERICANS! UP!" Karson gestured and yelled. "GET UP!" Karson yanked on the man's hair, and the man obeyed. He turned the man around and slammed him against the wall, weapon pushed into his back. "WHERE IS HATYARA? WHAT DO YOU KNOW?"

The man refused an answer.

Karson put the gun against his face. "LAST CHANCE." Karson snarled.

The man smiled at Karson.

Karson smiled too. "I am kinda funny, huh? American scum pushing you around, just like always, yeah?"

The SEAL operators stared at Karson in shock.

The man started laughing. Karson did too, patting him on the shoulder, turning him around and letting him go.

"Serval!?" The sniper asked.

The man started to stand fully up when Karson drove a knee into the man's balls and forced the gun into his mouth. The man kept a straight face, but as Karson noticed with any terrorist or enemy he had encountered when facing down the barrel of a death stick held by any soldier, they feared. Their eyes widened, their hearts raced. They too were humans. This man was no terrorist. He was a human portraying human emotions.

I can work with that.

The wife spoke up fearful that if this Navy SEAL didn't get what he wanted, that she'd be going to a funeral in the not so distant future.

They love too! Karson thought as she began. *Wow. Surprising.*

"People in Death Nation when allowed to stay alive, are not permitted to know of leader's activities. If he enters a district of Death Nation that is a former country," she explained, "you hear through whispers. The whole district shut down. Not allowed to move around or see him, or if you are, it is severely security. 'Hatyara' as you call him entered four months ago. He moves on and on through de nation all de time, never staying somewhere longer den to view, rally, and deploy troops. He has more important duties, like taking more countries under his and Savior's grip. Once unified, we will be powerful once again. We will be freed from de hell hole we live in now."

"Where does he go?" Karson threw the man aside and moved over to her, holding his pistol in plain sight.

"Were you not listening?" The woman spat.

"Okay," Karson said, sympathetic to the stupid question. "Have you seen him?"

"Once, two years ago."

"Two years." Karson looked at his Captain, shocked by the duration of time. "Describe him. What's he look like?"

"Tan. Indian by how he talks." She said.

"Explains the name. Richardson. India. Someone goes to India." He directed his voice to Richardson. Back to the woman, he said, "You said Hatyara and 'Savior.' Who is this Savior of yours?"

"The man who will unite de world." She smiled. "Better than any man ever known. The Messiah."

"What do you know about him?" Karson pressed, dropping to one knee, leveling out with the sitting woman's sightline.

"Dat he is leader, and Hatyara is merely his mastermind."

"Okay. Name?" Karson put his weapon away.

"We only know him as Savior. He is hidden. No one knows who he is."

"He could be a myth." Karson stood and turned.

"No, we've heard him speak. Hatyara had his voice piped in via phone." She defended her 'supreme leader.'

"What does he sound like?" Karson said, his back to the woman, looking across the street at people gathering and staring. *We need to get moving; this is a bad spot to be.*

"He spoke in Arabic. I do not know!"

"BULL!" Karson turned and pushed her back. "Every language spoken by a foreigner has an accent, woman! What did his sound like?"

"You cannot touch me like dis! I will-"

Karson drew his weapon again and aimed the gun at her husband's face behind him. Karson's SEAL friend stood back, pinning the man with his rifle.

"Hey! Watch your gun!" He said.

"Tell me or I redesign your husband's face!" Karson glared at her, his sympathy replaced by American justice.

"African!" She gasped. "African."

Karson holstered his weapon. "Thank you. See, that's all you had to do. Give us what we want, and we let you live and go throughout your days unharmed." He pointed his finger at her. "I bet you wouldn't have the same experience with your 'supreme leader'."

"The punishment I may receive, the fear of Death Nation, far outweighs your threats." She murmured to herself.

"Maybe so, but you gave us what we wanted. You are no longer our problem." He turned the pistol-wielding man around. "Translate this for me, ma'am." She nodded her head, not looking Karson in the face. Karson cut the wrist binds and handed the man his weapon back. "We are here in your country to help you, sir."

"نحن هنا في بلدكم لمساعدتك يا سيدي." [Arabic: Nahn huna fi baladikum lamusaeadatik ya sidi.] She translated.

"We only battle your and my enemy. Not you. We are leaving now. Hopefully one day, our children or we can be friendly, and we don't have to fight each other or invade your country. Look up Dr. Martin Luther King's *I Have a Dream* speech. It relates to us now. Have a good life."

The wife started translating as the SEALs turned away, never actually taking their eyes off their confused civilians. Karson's gunner had them in his sights. Karson wanted to trust that the man would not shoot the SEALs in the back. They left the others bound, knowing that the husband could untie them with his wife.

"نحن المعركة فقط، ولك عدوي. ليس لك. نغادر الآن. نأمل يوم واحد، نحن أو أولادنا، يمكن أن تكون ودية، وليس لدينا لمحاربة بعضها البعض أو غزو بلدك. بحث عن الدكتور مارتن لوثر كينغ لدي حلم الكلام. ما يتعلق بنا الآن. لديك حياة جيدة." [Walays ladayna limuharabat bedha albaed 'aw ghazw baladik. bahath ean alldduktur martin lawthr kyngh laday hulm alkulama. ma yataeallaq bina alana. ladayk hayatan jayidat.]

Back in the Hummer, the SEALs breathed a sigh of relief.

"Thought you'd stay in the Hummer, Captain." Karson teased. "You move fast for a grandpa."

"Watch it, bud."

Karson laughed as his team started to chip in.

"Good move, Serval, spotting those guys. Oh, and saving the man's life; so much compassion." The SEALs made puppy eyes, teasing Karson.

"You wanted to kill those men?" Karson punched back at the Sailors, as the vehicle started moving again.

"Not really. Too much paperwork. Just glad they gave us information!"

"The only easy day was yesterday my friends," the Captain said, smiling. He radioed in the information to command.

"HALT!" Karson shouted.

"Again?" Richardson growled, screeching the Hummer to a halt.

Karson grabbed his rifle and hopped up and through the hole in the roof and took aim at another group and fired, dropping three.

"Serval! What are you doing?" Richardson shouted.

Shots were exchanged, and the SEALs covered their heads and screamed as Karson dropped down on top of them, thinking he was dead.

Karson slithered across the laps of his team and opened the right door, firing out the door and killing two more men.

"You enjoy that lap dance fellas?" Karson smiled and got out of the Hummer, weapon raised, searching for more enemies.

"WHAT WERE YOU THINKING, SERVAL? WE HAVE ROEs. THIS CLEARLY VIOLATES-"

Karson held a young girl to his chest and turned. She was crying, and Karson was trying to comfort her. "Those 'men' had their guns pointed at her head. Why would I have reacted any differently? You have kids, correct?"

Richardson nodded.

"You'd have done the same thing," Karson replied. The other SEALs peered out the Humvee and started to pipe up, but Karson didn't want anything to do with it. "We have to find her-"

A woman's scream echoed in Karson's ears, and a woman ran up and took her baby out of Karson's hands, thanking Karson with a slap with a force that snapped his head to the side and knocked him on his hindquarters. She ran away down an ally. Karson watched her disappear.

"You're welcome!" He shouted after her.

"I suppose you want to go after her?" Karson's Captain asked.

"Nah. I want to go find the terrorist that keeps us here!" Karson said, getting into the humvee. "We're never going to find this guy." Karson yawned, laying his seat back into the SEAL's lap behind him, his legs spreading quickly, but forgetting he was male, allowed the seat to crush his bits. At the manly groan, Karson looked up into Smith's pain filled, watery eyes and smiled.

"You're a jerk, you know that." Karson's friend groaned again.

Karson blew him a play kiss to taunt him suddenly closing his eyes flinching as the Sailor lifted his hand to smack Karson's face. Gunfire rang through the street up ahead of them and Karson slide out of his seat belt as Captain Richardson screeched the vehicle to a stop. Karson jerked his seat upright again fully alert. Smith, Karson was messing with, took a direct strike to the face from Karson's seat flying back to the upright position. His whole body lifted from the seat and shook the armored vehicle when he crashed back into his seat.

The SEALs in the back busted out laughing.

Karson looked back to see him rubbing his chin.

"Oww." He mumbled.

"Sorry 'bout that, Smitty!" Karson said to his brother, sincere. "You okay? I'm trained in medicine too, if ya want a checkup!" He reached back.

"Yeah." He glared, smacking Karson's hand away. "Don't think I need that, I'm fine!"

Karson chuckled and mouthed 'I'm sorry' again, and turned back to the front. "See anything?" He asked his captain.

"Notta." Richardson pointed up to the gun sticking out over the front of the Humvee.

After a moment, not seeing his Humvee's gun moving above, Karson looked to the back seats and yelled: "Laukins, get on that gun, man! What are you doing?"

"Just eating lunch," he said nonchalantly wiping his mouth and smiling. "They aren't even shooting at us." He said pointing out the window.

"I'm not asking. Up. Now." Karson said again.

"Relax, dude! Nothing is happening." His subordinate fired back.

Karson glared. The senior SEAL stared back, chewing his sandwich defiantly. Then, Captain Richardson turned in his chair so fast and ferociously and gave his Sailor a glare. The Private's eyes grew wide.

"HE'S A COMMANDER. AND HE'S RIGHT. DO AS HE SAYS." Richardson shouted.

"Sorry, Captain." Private Laukins whispered, crawling up into the nest.

"Not me. Him." Richardson growled.

Private Laukins climbed up on the machine gun and aimed at the fighters after he mouthed "Sorry, sir," he said to Karson as he had received an angry glare from the Commander, too, and a punch as he passed.

The scene on the road was like watching a duel in the Wild West; revolvers aiming and shooting at each other. Instead of revolvers, though, AK-47 wielder shot at AK-47 wielder. The team focused in to see what would come as more and more people arrived to watch the dueling men. Karson had a bad feeling.

"Twenty bucks the guy on the right takes it to the face, bro!" Smith said.

Jacobs nodded. "You're on!"

As the two SEALs in the back were placing bets, Karson's heart rate increased. "Something is not right, Captain," Karson said. "Backup."

"Just keep an eye out." He replied, relaying their position to command.

"Aye." Karson punched on the roof. "Keep your eyes open. See anything?"

"Nope. Just the --- up ahead of us!"

"Don't call them that," Karson muttered under his breath after blocking out the derogatory name calling from his teammate. *These are still people… I hope.*

As the men in the street kept fighting, the Sailors made more bets for each move the civilians made. "Commander? You want in on this?"

"They aren't even shooting at each other." Karson looked closer. "It's a distraction. Laukins, keep looking around-"

Something moved to Karson's right. Pulling his gaze from the front, he saw the threat. Karson grabbed his Captain's shoulder and ducked as low as he could with Richardson. Gunfire pierced the bulletproof glass of the Humvee's passenger window where the heads of Karson and Captain Richardson once sat. Laukins dropped down into the Hummer. The men in the back ducked down as well.

They shouted in fear.

Karson sat up equipping his P226 pistol from his leg holster and aimed out the smashed window. He fired into the reloading enemy combatant's chest three times with his weapon. The man went down like a rock. Limp. Dead.

"Wow, good catch, Serval!" The Captain screamed. "Laukins, get back up there. We're getting out of here!"

The Sailors were freaking out. "What's to come?"

"What if that's the just the beginning?" Another chimed in.

"We almost died, man! We almost died!" Laukins shouted down, firing at the men in the street converging on the SEALs.

"But we didn't," Richardson said, throwing the vehicle into reverse.

"Just watch your sides. Pull your assault weapons down." Karson always put his assault weapon into the roof holster when he got into a vehicle so he'd have room to relax and maneuver (paid off this time) if he had to, and so it wouldn't discharge a round if he hit it.

Karson reached for it, when suddenly yet another gunman came from the left side, but luckily as Richardson started to duck, and Karson aimed, Laukins found the enemy. The roof gunner was faster and turned his sights on the enemy and shot him with the large caliber bullet. The man's head exploded from the impact of the bullet like a watermelon, and his body slammed into the wall.

Karson tore his eyes away from the disgusting sight and gagged. *That was gross.*

"Nice shot!" Smith shouted.

"It's not over yet! Look ahead!" The gunner replied.

The situation would get much worse still. Private Laukins took a direct hit into his helmet which knocked him back down into the Humvee.

"Tits!" Karson shouted. "I'll do it myself!"

As Karson was about to take the high caliber weapon above him, Corporal Jacobs yelled, "RPG! GET OUT NOW!"

Karson looked ahead and saw an Arab man about to shoot the Navy Humvee. Karson kicked open his door, grabbed his M4A1 and dove into the alley, away from the Humvee. All he could hear was the explosion of his Humvee as the missile slammed into the engine, blowing it apart, and throwing Karson into a wall. Shrapnel hit Karson's armor and helmet with a tink, the force knocking Karson into black before he could curl up in a ball to protect himself.

****

Karson heard ringing in his ears from the blast wave, and the impact of hitting the wall was disorientated as well.

Breathless, Karson came to his senses. He was covered in debris and dirt. He pushed a door away from his line of sight and immediately began searching for his team. "Captain? Corporal? Privates? Team, check in." Now desperate to find his men to ensure he wasn't alone, Karson crawled through an open door. He dragged himself into the center of the room and radioed one last time. Karson pulled himself up onto the seal of the window, hearing only the ringing, even though bullets were flying, even pelting the building around the window he was leaning on. Suddenly he felt an impact into the back of his Kevlar, knocking him back down from the window. He screamed a pathetic scream and looked back, seeing an armed man stepping back and winding up for another stab.

The man sprang towards the downed SEAL. Karson rolled to his side, and the man drove the knife into the wall. Karson kicked the man to his side and struggled with his M4. The man was up in a flash and grabbed the gun and threw it over the table. He grabbed a pan and smacked the side arm from Karson's hand and wrapped his fingers around Karson's throat. Karson grabbed at his hands, trying to release the pressure as the man pushed him up the wall, off Karson's feet. The man leaned in close to Karson's face.

"You die now, American." He hissed. "You friends will feel pain similar if not more den you feel now. Sleep. Die. Die."

The man's breath stank, his body stank, and he didn't feel like a human.

This is why you want two guns in every fight. So you don't die!

More like an animal! Hell bent on killing.

Karson kept struggling, desperately thrashing to save his own life, losing the fight. The man kept stabbing the knife into Karson's armor trying to penetrate it. The force rocked Karson's body, but there was nothing he could do to halt the blows, going deeper and deeper through his Kevlar. *I'm gonna die!* He whimpered in his head. Karson's training and life force were draining from his body. Gasping, Karson let his left hand go, feeling around for anything he could use, his eyes starting to close. Finally, his hand brushed against a hard metal object. Karson searched for it and found the pan. Grasping the handle, he slammed it into the side of the man's face. The only thing it did was make the dude angrier. His grip tightened. Karson felt himself losing his life. It drifting away, his life flashing before him. Falling in love in elementary school. Distancing from love. High school. Thinking he had love. Being bullied. Dropping out. Being bullied. Wanting to join the Marine Corps. Navy stealing his heart. Boot camp. Growing up and finding himself. Missions. Friends. Family. Brothers.

Karson's hand found his knife on his back and slammed it into the enemy's arm, Karson finding his feet, then stabbed to the man's neck. The man's face darkened. Karson's eyes widened. *He's not scared.* Every time an enemy is dying, Karson felt their fear. This man smiled as his life pumped out of his neck hole. Karson shoved it into his eye to get the Arab's arm off of him. The man fell over. Karson felt the grip slightly lesson, and he knocked the hand away and slid back against the wall and stared at the man, watching this man's life flash in his eyes, his soul depart.

"Man, that was scary!" Karson whispered rubbing his throat. "Damn!" The blood was starting to reach Karson's boots, he moved. He cleaned his knife, grabbed his pistol and his M4. Karson slithered back to the window and crouched, peering out the window like a house cat trying to escape to the wild.

Looking around the sandy street, Karson saw camouflaged people fighting robed men down the street.

I have to get to them!

His team disappeared into an ally. Time was running out before Karson possibly would be surrounded and overpowered and killed. "Team? TEAM! I'm on the right side of the street and injured! TEAM! CAPTAIN?" *Our radios are down.* Karson stood and moved to the door, yanked it open, and fell back. *Balance, stupid.*

Karson stood and sprinted out the door, cringing in pain. His dash, which looked like a gallop with his limp, took him out into the street behind a car. There was a sniper in the building in front of him. He looked at his team and waved to them. Then gave them the sign to move through that building and to rendezvous at the corner building.

"ATCH- OR- D!" Karson's radio statically assaulted his ears.

"WHAT?" Karson shouted, ducking back down as the sniper's bullet struck the hood right in front of his face.

"ATCHOUT-ID."

What's he saying- Suddenly, an explosion flipped the car onto two wheels and back down onto its side.

IED. Watch out for IED. "Perfect," Karson muttered.

His ears were starting to calm, and the ringing quieted to a soft buzz.

Karson stuck his thumb up over the vehicle and motioned them through the building again.

Karson's Captain nodded to his most trusted SEAL on his team and moved to do as Karson directed. Karson then took aim at the sniper and fired. The man rolled over the ledge and into the street, dead, right in front of Karson's teammates. As the man fell, the SEALs shooting his corpse, startled, Karson moved into another spot behind some sand bags as rounds hit all around him. Karson's friends stared at the man, saluted Karson in thanks, and moved into the building to meet more enemy combatants. They heard the entrance of the SEAL team and AK-47 fire was met by M16, Scar, and M4 fire soon to cease. The SEALs then made their way through the corner building, clearing it out.

Karson dove through the door, and his team spun around aiming at him. One screamed and fired a shot, hitting Karson in his breastplate, knocking him back out into the street.

"HOLY GOD ALMIGHTY PROTECT ME!" Karson screamed, rounds again directed at him.

Richardson stepped out into the street and fired at the enemy across the street, giving Karson a split second to get up.

"GET IN THE BUILDING!" Richardson shouted at his subordinate.

Karson dove through again. "YOU SHOT ME! WATCH IT, DUDE!"

"SORRY! WE'RE IN A WAR!" He shouted back. "YOU SCARED ME! DIDN'T KNOW WHO IT WAS!"

"IT ME!" Karson shouted back at Smith.

Karson felt his body for blood, but none. "Captain, what are we going to do? We're surrounded. Your men are incompetent." Karson said winded.

"You're on the same team. We're not incompetent. Alright, team. Look here. See that radio tower at the end of the drive here? If we can just make it there, alive that is, we can hook our emergency radio to it and call for a dire extraction. We'll have to fight until we can get into the chopper, though. Karson. I want you on this building with Smith and snipe the enemy. Smith will snipe; you just call out targets okay? Don't get caught sleeping."

"I am a better sniper, Sir." Karson dared pipe up.

"Do as I say," Richardson said curtly.

"Sir."

"Thanks a lot, Commander," Smith said.

"Hey, am I wrong?" Karson smiled.

"No, but still!" He turned and readied himself for the battle down the street.

"Laukins, you, Jacobs, and I are going to get to the radio and hook it up. You guys will place yourselves at the entrance to the building while I head up there and hook it up. If anyone comes in your line of sight, you blow them away. Got it?"

"Yes, sir." Jacobs spoke up.

"Alright. Let's move. Jacobs, you last. Can't have medics getting killed."

Smith challenged Karson again. "Dude, I'm still pissed. I can easily out snipe you. You're not better than me!"

"I am. We're in a war. Your feelings come last. Let's go!" Karson said in reply.

The team formed a line at the door.

"On three." Richardson held up three fingers.

Karson readied himself, tensing, then relaxing his muscles.

Richardson clenched his fist, the three fingers disappearing. "THREE!"

The highly trained American Sailors broke from cover and bulleted into the street against the walls toward the radio. Karson and Smith scattered to the other side of the road dodging enemy fire and laid down cover fire from their side. They took cover in doorways and fired from around the corners, Karson and Smith firing on targets nearest Richardson and his team, and Richardson and team firing at targets closest to Karson and Smith-their bullets crossing each other. Finally, Karson and Smith made it to the tallest building on the block and worked their way up the stairs. They kicked down doors and shot the snipers that the SEALs couldn't hit from the street in the rooms, then made their way up to the roof. Karson put a claymore mine facing out the door into the stairway and took a seat next to his teammate and called out targets. However, the Captain was still street fighting.

"Men, there are two tangos in the building to the right." He instructed his team. "Karson, have you set up a sniping perch yet?"

"Aye, sir, I'm calling out targets now. You'll have a clear street in Three...Two... One..."

BANG

"You're good. There are men in the radio building when you get there. You are nine meters away." Karson said, looking through his rangefinder, counting down their distance. "Nice shot, Smith."

The Captain kept moving with his commandos. When they reached the building, they placed C4 on the door and breached it. They entered the building and killed the men on the first floor. Then the Captain headed up to the roof with Jacobs while Laukins sat and watched the front door. When Captain Richardson finally reached the roof, Laukins faced the door while Richardson hooked up the radio and radioed for help.

"Command, this is Trident Eagle 1-1. Captain Richardson, SEAL Team Six. We need immediate extraction from Quetta city. Where heavily engaged and outnumbered. Look for green flares on the roof of my structure. Any other bodies besides those on my structure, are fair game for instant execution. Repeat, we need an immediate extraction from this battle. GET US OUT OF HERE!"

"Trident Eagle, stand by. We have a Black Hawk en-route to your location. ETA: thirty minutes. We'll send an Apache that can be there within ten minutes."

"Hurry. We're being overrun. Fighting a city here!"

****

CHAPTER 20 - Camera Woman

"Sidewinder 3-8, com check."

The com system inside the Apache assault chopper burst to life as the pilot entered into the aircraft, ensuring all systems were a go. "Sidewinder 3-8 copies. All systems stable, and ready to fly."

"Sidewinder 3-8, Falcon 5-2. I'm assigned as your support, ma'am. Good flying out there."

"I've never flown with a raptor before, 5-2! What would happen if I were to be shot down? You can't just land and get me out!"

"3-8, then I'll fly around in a circle over your crash site, shooting any person who dare shot at one of my sisters."

"You're Air Force, though."

"So? And you're a Marine. That doesn't matter to me. We fight for the same team. Wear the same flag. I fight for fifty stars and thirteen bars. Don't you?"

"I guess that's true."

"Then you're my sister."

"Alright, my man. I'm spinning up and taking off."

"I'll be flying over the northeastern part of the territory, quadrant 7b$_3$. Holler if you need anything."

"I'll be in 3b₇. Weird. You do the same-."

"Hey, you best be careful. That patrol zone is not secure. Uncharted. Possibly crawling with enemy."

"Did not know that. Thanks for the tip, Falcon. Out." The Apache pilot lifted off from her air base for the fifty-mile journey into an enemy no-fly zone, and an area that was devoid of people. Her mission: to patrol and find enemy activity undetected while gathering Intel on forces in Iraq to be sent Pentagon. The pilot, Lieutenant Commander Nancy Dennin, turned to her copilot, Lieutenant Sara Jacobson. "Once we cross into the zone, no radio. We can't be discovered. The sound will give us away, but not before we're on top of the enemy. The radio traffic will give us away far sooner. Make sure you stay on that thermal imaging camera. Tell me as threats appear."

"Yes, ma'am."

The pilot went back to watching her instruments, after sharing a fist bump with her sidekick.

"Dennin, do you ever get afraid?" Jacobson looked up from her duty.

"No. Well, technically... Yeah... Yeah, I guess I do. But I don't let myself feel it when I get in the air. I make sure I'm all combat-ready as soon as I sit down in this seat. People rely on us, Lieutenant. Some fear is healthy, but don't let it get the better of you."

"Good point. Thanks." She went back to her camera. "I won't."

The landscape below flew by faster and faster as the pilot opened her aircraft full throttle. From time to time, the pilots encountered civilian areas flying directly over the hidden villages.

"There's another one!" Jacobson would say, unable to see them in the valleys.

"Are these not coming up on your camera, Sara?"

"No, ma'am! I swear. I don't see them until we're right on top of them."

"Falcon 5-2, so that you know, we are known to be in the area. Please listen carefully to our radio traffic."

"I've got ya." The static voice came across, barely audible.

"Falcon 5-2? Your coms aren't coming through completely!"

"Nancy, dive!" Sara pushed down on the controls and as the ground came into view, Nancy took back control of her aircraft.

"Sara, what the-" Nancy fired a missile to pull a stinger away from the helicopter as she maneuvered around the explosion. "Sara. Machine gun."

"Right." Sara positioned her hand around the fire controls as Nancy locked onto where the missiles were coming from.

"Sidewinder 3-8 in contact. Falcon 5-2, where are you? Can you assist?" The weapons opened up on the small hut where a human form was on the roof. For a moment before he was riddled with bullets. "FALCON 5-2?" Another missile lock signal hit the aircraft, this time from behind. Nancy maneuvered the aircraft, firing chaff as she spun the chopper and dropped altitude.

"Nancy, go up! Higher."

"That's the opposite of what you want to do. You want to go down."

"You're not seeing it. I'm seeing it. There are people right-"

Nancy gasped as a warm red liquid filled the helicopter and Sara's face split in two. Nancy stopped what she was doing in shock. Suddenly the back of the chopper spun from Nancy's control as a fire alert flashed on her screen, her attitude diminishing. The entire plummet was a blur and Nancy unconsciously slowed the fall, saving her life as she smashed into the ground somewhat gently. She exited the craft, as it engulfed in fire and started walking into the setting sun.

"3-8, what are your coordinates?" Were the last words of English the young pilot ever heard. She pulled her phone and read a message from her friend.

> Happy flying, sis! Hope to see you home for the holidays! -K

She smiled and typed a reply.

> I love you, Kar. I hope you have a happy holiday. I won't be able to make it... -Nanny

The impact of the rifle hurt as I woke up the next day. I'd never felt an impact like that. I can't remember anything, and these men don't speak English. I can't ask them to relay it to me. Even if they did, I doubt they would. Whatever these guys are called, they don't really let you talk to them, especially to ask them for information. They take from you; easily is not in their equation. Even if you want to spill your mind's knowledge, they still want to spill your blood and torture you tremendously. Then they lead you to execution. They plug your ears with super glue, giving you no sense of hearing. They place contacts in your eyes, taking your sense of sight. They put glue in your nose so you can't breathe and they rake your tongue with nasty tasting food, making you long for the luxuries of your western civilization. I don't know where my capturor is, however, I know he's behind me somewhere, with a knife. I know from what I've seen and trained that this is my last moment. I feel the blade at my throat. I feel the size as my jugular is slashed and my blood exits my body in a spray. The pain is incredible and I feel my body shaking as tendon and vein after tendon and vein are cut through. Then comes my spine, and as it is severed, the pain ceases, the convulsions, but the brutality of my murder is still the same. My vision blurs, and off I go.

****

BUZZ

BUZZ

Karson looked down at his phone as he sat with his friends in Texas after passing the prescreening test on the USS Ford three days before he went off to BUD/s.

I love you, Kar. I hope you have a happy holiday. I won't be able to make it... -Nanny

"Hey, Mr. Navy Pilot. Come get your dinner!" Karson looked up at his friend Elizabeth holding out her hand. "What's wrong?"

"Nancy was supposed to be back today. She can't make it apparently... but this message is from like a month ago... Why am I just now getting it?"

"How do you know a month ago if you just got it?"

Karson showed her the phone. "Navy. I have friends who gave me some sweet tech!"

"You're a nerd. Come on. Eat, then we'll talk about it."

Karson smiled and threw the phone on the couch and turned the TV on as he walked into the kitchen to the smells of pure bliss. Turkey, ham, green beans, stuffing, mashed potatoes with garlic, pie, pudding, all kinds of stuff. He filled his plate and walked into the living room where his friends sat and ate, the news playing in the background. They talked about relationships, Karson's relatively new, juicy relationship at the top as Karson blushed and ate a mouthful so he couldn't speak.

"Oh come on, Karse! Talk!" Laura gently cuffed him on the back of the head.

"Wanna know," he choked on his potatoes, "name?"

"Yeah!" The girls cooed as Karson rolled his eyes at his buddy Jack.

'With the recent number of deaths by camera being brought to light, another just surfaced on the dark net, and on social media. A US Marine Pilot was shot down in Jordan last month, and her whereabouts were unstated and unknown. Unfortunately, they will remain that way.'

Karson stopped eating and snapped his attention to the television. *No.*

"Karson?" Lea tapped him on the shoulder, impatient. "Kadin Karson-"

"Shh, shut up!" He swatted her hand away.

"Nancy Dennin, a 24-year-old Marine pilot, is shown here on video, no statement, nothing, just her and her executioner. He then proceeds to behead the Marine woman, the latest in the violence against our nation. The first woman killed on camera."

Karson's phone began to ring. It was the Navy's Chaplin service, and a knock rocked Karson's heart at the door.

"Karson?" Stephany asked. His friends came to him; Jack looked at Karson, then the door, and walked over to open it to reveal a Navy Chaplin.

Tears streamed from Karson's face. He buried himself into his present friends' loving arms as the Chaplin confirmed to Nancy's next of kin that his best friend's death was true. Karson's friend was gone. The one who helped him into the Navy. She was gone. Her job finished. His just beginning. The job of bringing these murderers to justice.

I have to miss her funeral.

****

CHAPTER 21 - Pack Mentality

At Karson's building, he heard the radio broadcast head out. Karson could see the enemy bugging out. "Okay, they are going to regroup. We need to-"

BOOM

"Incoming!"

Karson and Smith both saw it coming. A tank warhead was flying right at them. Karson launched himself up, Smith right behind him. They got to the end of the roof in that same second and jumped down to the building's lower level rooftop. It was a ten-foot drop. Still, the force of the warhead going off so close to them pushed the Sailors off the second roof and dropped fifteen feet to the ground. Both SEALs hit hard, but

Karson landed on his injured ankle wrong, and he collapsed from the searing pain that jolted through his body

"OW!"

Smith slid over to Karson, keeping his head down in case rounds ricocheted around the corner into the ally. "You okay, sir?"

"No. That hurt. I think it's broken or at least will take a moment to stop aching. Smith, you're going to have to carry me to the tower. We have to get there before the tank gets in here with reinforcements."

"Yes, sir, hold on." Smith picked Karson up on his shoulders and went down alleys behind the major buildings, the 'back way' essentially, through the city, and made his way through the smaller, abandoned streets, towards the Captain's position, when they heard growls coming from their left. They both turned their heads, staring into bright yellow eyes. A pack of wild dogs stepped out of the shade and looked at their meal. They growled and launched themselves down the street, barreling towards the SEALs. Smith dropped Karson at once and grabbed for his pistol, but was too late. The dogs were on him. Karson grabbed his and shot the dogs on Smith until he could fight back, and then shot the dogs coming up at him from the entrance of the alley. He was on his back now, upside down and shooting at the dogs from over his head. Everything was inverted.

"You okay, Hunter?" Smith asked, brushing off fur.

"Yeah. You?" Karson tried standing.

He spat out a hair ball. "Yeah, I believe so."

With the dogs dead or retreating, Smith stood and helped Karson limp on towards the Captain's position. Once inside, Smith joined Laukins at the front door, while Jacobs patched Karson's leg up so he could at least walk and gave Karson the Barrette .50 caliber sniper rifle he was carrying to shoot the tank. Karson ran upstairs, ignoring the pain, and took aim, waiting. He wanted the tank to turn a little bit so he could shoot at where he believed the gunner station was, hopefully disabling the gun. The tank was searching for a target, and slowly, Karson finally got his wish. The tank turned slightly, and Karson fired center mass of the tank into the gunner station. He fired continuously, punching holes into its hull each time the bullets hit it. However, he still didn't seem to hit the gunner. The tanks main gun turned its attention towards the building the shots were coming from.

Beating blades pounded Karson's ears. The sun bright explosion brought relief as the shell that was supposed to end the Americans' lives never came.

Karson sighed relieved, and rolled over and had to slow his breathing and heartbeat.

"Thank, God!" Richardson nodded. "That one... that one was close."

Small arms fire kept the SEALs busy as they waited for their Black Hawk extraction. Their Apache was keeping up with the larger, more dangerous forces like enemy vehicles trying to make it into the city to kill.

As the chopper was making its way towards one section of the city, Karson saw a trail whiz past his post towards the helicopter. He turned his weapon towards it; he wasn't fast enough. An RPG fired at the Apache helicopter hit the midsection of the chopper, disabling the prop.

"Mayday, Mayday, Hellbird 3-2 is hit, and we're going down. I repeat, we're going-"

The chopper rose into the air and slammed into the side of a building, tearing it apart and it crashed down into the street. Enemy troops were closing in on it.

Richardson leaned over the lip of the building towards the crash.

"Dammit. It didn't explode. I can see small arms fire coming from the cockpit. We don't leave men behind. Karson, do you think you can get down there and help them with that leg?"

Not again. "Yeah. I'll get them. I lost my best friend to something like this, and I'm not going to let it happen to them. Jacobs, Smith, come with me. Captain, you snipe, and Laukins, you guard the door."

With that, Karson made his way across the roof towards a ladder firing down into the massing crowd of enemy forces and slid down the ladder with his team towards the chopper. "Okay guys, with the chopper down that means all the enemy will be around that area. Expect little resistance moving up the street, but when we reach it, Satan is going to unleash his army on us. Move quick, smart, and with purpose. Kill anything that moves. No time for risk taking. Smith, you'll blow it up. Jacobs, if they can't walk, I'll get one, you get the other, okay? If they are fine, I'll guard you while you help them. Clear?"

"Aye, sir."

"Richardson, you lay down over watch and kill anything that moves that isn't American. Got it?"

"Aye."

"Good. Let's get this done."

They spun around the corner and headed towards the crash firing at the enemy they could see surrounding the crash. Troops were spilling into the city from all directions, and the SEALs were having a rough time fighting. "THIS IS INTENSE, DUDE! I'VE NEVER FOUGHT THIS HARD!" Karson yelled.

"I KNOW! NEITHER HAVE I!" Smith stumbled over a body he'd dropped.

Jacobs readied a grenade to throw. "SAME BRO!"

Karson had taught the men that in a situation like this, if they smiled while fighting, it would, one, ease the tension, and two, make it easier to kill. Three, it'd give them a reason to keep fighting.

Karson slammed against the wall of a building near the chopper, the firefight still exploding in front and behind him. Karson started to take more steps towards the prize when he felt a blast from above and felt himself fall to his face. The SEALs behind him opened fire.

"Sir, you okay?"

"He's still up there."

Karson stood and shook it off, aiming up. "You guys shoot the pack in the street. I've got this dick. He shot me. He's mine." Karson pressed himself flat against the wall, still looking up. As the combatant poked his head around again in a different spot for a different SEAL, Karson grabbed his teammate as he fired, and pressed him to the wall too. Karson guessed his new 'friend' would go back to the first spot and aimed there, as his man thanked Karson for pulling him from where the bullet now had made a hole. Karson watched the spot so intently; he could see flies crawling on the wall, then fly away as a head poked out over the edge of the wall, and met a bullet from Karson's pistol. Blood rained down on Karson, and he walked back into combat, his kill confirmed.

Moving up to the chopper, Jacobs radioed the news to Karson.

"Pilot-KIA."

Damn.

"Copilot-KIA."

Karson had had enough. "I'm coming. Set charges."

"Aye, sir." Smith moved to position.

Karson made it to the downed Air Force pilots and saw that the force of the impact had been intense. The pilot's eyes had blown out of her head, and her body was mush. The copilot had similar injuries, and a slash to his throat.

I'm gonna kill a lot of people today.

"I'll get her. Jacobs, when Smith is done, help me carry her."

"Aye, sir."

They got the dead and headed back. The Commander was helping with his shooting and Smith had placed the explosives, helping Karson move back to safety, shooting behind at the enemy spilling back in on top of the chopper, trying to see what they could take. At a safe distance, Karson ordered the explosion. The faster it was out of commission, the better safety the U.S. intelligence and technology would be.

The enemy were all gathered around the chopper like the pack of dogs desperate to give and feed off of death, and Smith deployed the charge, blowing them sky high. The thundering of a Black Hawk roared to life as the explosion subsided, and the SEALs could see their ride above. They hurried into the building, Richardson disabling the charges, the team mounting the chopper. The helicopter, closing the door, turned and flew towards safety. An RPG flew past, the pilot took precautions, but the sudden jot as Laukins sat down caused him to tense to try to regain balance, and his finger slipped into the trigger well and he fired a round that hit the Black Hawk pilot in the head. The craft started to spin out of control, but Karson grabbed him from the controls. "Sir, can you fly by yourself?"

"Yes, sir." The copilot said shocked. "Sorry, that just took me by surprise, sir!" The copilot started his duties.

Karson looked at Laukins who was just as shocked and distraught. "Hey," Karson grabbed his friend by the neck and put his forehead to Laukins's. "It was an accident, could have happened to any of us. Focus up. We still have a job to do." Karson patted his head. "You hear me?"

Laukins nodded. "Yes, sir."

"INCOMING!" The copilot shouted.

Karson ducked down as a missile flew at the aircraft, leaning forward and twisting the tail around to miss the shell, by the skin of their teeth. The maneuver was so close and drastic that the chopper lost control and the copilot attempted desperately to try to regain control as fire erupted from below, sending hot metal at the Americans.

"Get us out of here." The Captain yelled as Karson began first aid on the pilot's face.

"Serval, you get up there and fly with him. I'll have Jacobs take over this task."

Karson made his way to the front, sitting and strapping in. "Aye, sir."

"Where are you flying?" The copilot asked Karson.

"Captain?"

"What?" Richardson asked from looking out the window.

"Where are we flying to, sir?"

"Base."

"There is a Pakistani base forty miles west of here. I forget the coordinates." Karson looked back at his pilot.

"Doesn't exist anymore. Overrun. I could fly you there, but we'd be either shot down or captured as soon as we get there. It would seem Pakistan has renegotiated its alliance to support Death Nation."

"Our stuff is there-"

"It is the property of the enemy, now. An Air Force strike team will try to fly over and destroy what they can, if they get the chance to. For now, it would seem the enemy have access to some of our equipment and information."

"Dammit." Karson punched the air.

"I'll fly you back to our base. We're in the process of bugging out. Death Nation is closing in. We need a coalition force, not our puny little operating base."

"Where are you going after that?" Karson asked.

"Israel, only allied state left in the Middle East. Australia. Home. Pretty much anywhere that isn't dark is fair game right now."

"Is there an accurate account of who's dark and who's not?"

"From what we've been told, a lot. So many places in the Middle East are known to be dark. Intel suggestion nothing else. We think... well... That is, I think Asian and African countries are out, too."

"Same intel. Alright."

"Do you know anything I don't? Have you been anywhere else?"

"You know I can't say."

"Yeah. Special Forces, always keeping secrets." The copilot looked forward again.

"Normal flyboy, always bitching about Special Forces." Karson grabbed his shoulder.

He smiled. "Yeah."

"We have a mutual understanding," Karson said. "Tell you what, I will say you are correct in your assumptions."

"Hey, can we turn on some country music? My boys calm down when they listen to it." Richardson called up.

The copilot looked at Karson. "Really? Country? Yes, sir. That is fine."

Karson winked at the pilot. "Thanks." Karson flipped the switch, turning on the radio. "There you go, boys. Pick what you want."

"Serval! Just got word from Command. We're heading to the Air Force base, then will be heading back to the ship at some point after that. We'll ride with some troops from the base, but will dive into the water. Chopper needed elsewhere and it would take more fuel to land."

"Aye, sir." Karson said. "I could use a bath!"

"That seriously all the intel you boys get?"

"Normally, we know what we're doing, who the target is, or whatever, like, thirty minutes before we takeoff. This is a treat to know that much!"

"Hey, did I ever tell you my blow job story?" Laukins's voice piped up in the background.

Karson rolled his eyes.

"They always like this, sir?" The copilot's words were covered by laughs.

"You're flying Navy SEALs. We do anything and everything." Karson rolled his eyes again.

He nodded his head. "I think we all do, sir."

"This chick was hot, man! Her ass, man, that ass was something. But she dissed my job. I couldn't let that go!"

"She probably thought you were a freak!" Karson called back.

"Nah, man! She said it's the biggest-"

"Hey, let's talk about the mission-" Karson tried to interject.

"When you're done, I gotta tell you my story! Her dad walked in and-" The copilot called back.

Karson turned to the front, of course listening in, but was annoyed that he'd been ignored yet again. Interrupted by the copilot of all people. People died today, and the idea that more and more nations were falling was terrifying. They needed to plan, not talk about the past.

We don't live in the past, nor future. What we do now, the present, is what leads to our futures.

****

CHAPTER 22 - Whistle Tones

Karson sat on the hood of the Humvee watching his friends playing ball. Karson was eating the papaya his love back home had sent; for some odd reason, his stomach had been perpetually uneasy for the duration of his deployment. The men kept bickering about who got what point.

"Alright, ya'll. Ya know what? Let's do it this way. Everyman for himself. And I'm getting in this. Winner gets the pot." Karson placed a twenty-dollar bill on the hood of the Humvee.

"Damn, Serval! That's a lot of money! Ya know what kind of job we have?" He looked around. "Let's do it!"

Another twenty. "HEY! We're overseas. Money doesn't work here!"

"No." Karson smiled, "But word just came in. We're going home next week!"

"What!?"

Karson smiled. "After ship check, we get a mall leave before next tour. Now place your money in and let's play!"

"Alrighty. One hundred and sixty dollars!" Karson smiled. "Nice!"

"Eight men! On a court. Who will be deemed the winner, and the richest SEAL or serviceman here?" Laukins took on a sports announcer personality.

The SEALs laughed as a female Sailor walked by.

"You can join us, Tiny!" Karson tempted her.

"Hey! You're just as little as I am, Runt!" The female flipped Karson off over her shoulder.

"Get over here and play with us, Tina!" Smith called.

"Ohh, you'd like that wouldn't you, you perv!" She chuckled as she turned around and walked over. "You're on!"

"Hey, chick! Money!" An Airman on the base stepped up to her.

"Yah, I don't have any money..." She said, looking at Karson.

"Hey, she can't play. No money, no playing." Laukins threw the ball into Karson's hand.

"It's cool. I got shit to do anyway, I guess." She started to turn to leave.

"I've got'er!" Karson pulled out forty bucks. "Let's make it an even two hundred, yeah?"

Smith took the money and put it on a Hummer's windshield. "Damn, you're wealthy!"

Karson winked. "That's what happens when you rank up. You make more moola!" Karson chucked the ball over his shoulder. "Your ball." He turned as the Sailor came dribbling up behind him for a layup. The Sailor got passed Karson, but not the tree of a SEAL nicknamed Leviathan. The Sailor ran smack into the behemoth's chest, knocking Smith backward, at which point Leviathan picked both the Sailor and the ball up and walked down the court, everyone laughing as Smith kicked his legs and as Leviathan tossed the ball into the basket.

"One." He said, dropping the SEAL on his rump.

"Ow!" He said, rubbing his coccyx as he looked up at the giant man.

Karson walked over to Tiny as the play reset. "Hey. How you doing?"

"Why you got to go and do this, Karse? I'm fine. Honestly."

"I know you are. We're friends, though. I'm just looking out for you."

"I wanted the upgrade, Karson. More money, more safety..."

"Tiny, I am part of a team where everyone has to operate under one hundred percent efficiency. I cannot allow someone higher up to jeopardize that."

"You think I would dare endanger my brothers and sisters?"

"Tiny, I've seen someone reject our ethos for much less than this."

"Now you're questioning my loyalty."

"I'm saying that anyone who is unable to solve their own problems can't address the problems of a group of people in combat. I'm sorry, but that's the truth. Not like you can't try again in a year."

The ball came nearest Tiny, and she lashed out, snatched the ball and threw it into Karson's junk. "Whoops." She got the ball back and tossed it into the basket. "Sorry. Didn't mean to send you that **curve ball**. My mistake."

Karson nodded. *Probably deserved that, but my decision is valid.*

She walked back up to Karson. "You know, I almost forgave you for screwing me like that, Karse. I always told myself he's got my back, he's got me, but then I realized that you were promoted again and again after that and I realized you're in this for yourself. You want your money. You want the praise. You could never cut it in your dreams for fame; you have to take it here. I could be up there, dude. Now I'm stuck working on the machines that could make my dream job a reality."

"Tiny," Karson started.

"Chief Scott. It's Chief Scott, Commander."

"Chief Scott." Karson nodded. She walked off the court.

Karson turned back to his friends and continued to play ball, scoring three points while everyone else scored higher. "Alright, rematch?"

"Man, no! I ain't losing all this cash!" Leviathan snatched the doe.

Karson smiled. "Let's play some pig, then. Pass some time."

"Cool!" He said, pocketing the money.

An eerie sound stopped Karson in his tracks. The sound of a whistle. He looked up and saw ordinance slam smack into the ground right in front of him on the basketball court. Nothing happened. Like in the movies, everyone stopped and stared as the alarm at the base started to sound. Karson felt the urge to stop and stare and praise his lucky stars, however, his legs thought different.

"RUN!" He shouted as he took off in the opposite direction of the base. He made it around a corner of an ammo shipping container when he heard the explosion. A blast wave doesn't stop for man-made materials and it sliced right through the metal sending Karson flying through the air. The only reason he survived was landing on top of the tarp of a troop transport. The 20mm Phalanx CIWS systems started engaging other ordinance from an unknown enemy. However, they all shut down after a minute of defense, ordinance still raining down on the military base.

I have to get to the radios. That meant running through the base showered with explosive death. Karson jumped down from the tarp and searched for where the bombs were coming from over the walls of his base, facing the mountains. "It's always the mountains." Karson sprinted around the outskirts of the compound seeing limbs scattered over the ground. He reached the communications depot where he found no one operating the only way for assistance.

"Commander Karson Hunter Joint Force Base Mammoth Tail. We are in dire need of assistance. We are being overrun by ordinance fired from an unknown location in the mountains to our south. Repeat, we need help! How copy?"

Karson heard footsteps behind him and grabbed a pin about to kill whatever threat ran up on him.

"Karson... Get ready to fight." Richardson said to his second in command.

"I almost killed you, sir."

"I see that." He handed him an MP5. "We have troops coming to our aid, but an enemy force is on its way."

"Paint the targets, sir, and I'll throw rounds to them!"

"Get up on the wall. Keep your head down you have no Kevlar or helmet. There's a sniper up there. Take the rifle and trade him your MP5." The two walked out into the chaos of the burning base.

"He's not going to take kindly to me taking his weapon."

"You outrank him."

"Oh. Duh. Right." Karson climbed the stairs and found an Airman setting up a M14 Sniper Rifle on the wall. Karson slithered up to him and relayed the orders. He was right, the Airman didn't like being told he was off his weapon, but Karson had to move the sniper to the other side, as the Airman set up on the completely wrong side to find targets. As soon as Karson lay down to fire, he felt rounds pelting around him and scrambled to find targets. Numbers of heads exploded from Karson's precision, and he turned his attention to the mountains and sure enough, located at least three enemies lobbing mortars down to his position. "RADIO! I NEED A RADIOMAN!"

Karson checked the coordinates and relayed them to the man who ran up. "Have the fighter's fire on that location and tell them we need choppers!"

Fifty minutes of death and destruction rained down on Mammoth Tail as the Americans tried so desperately to hold off enemies. Finally, the mountains exploded from American explosives and metal rain fell from choppers bringing in a QRF to aid the base.

"Karson." Richardson's voice called to him. "Gear up. We're being activated. We have multiple bases mobilizing in the area. Multi TICs. We're now a quick reaction force to these troops in contact. We are supposed to stay here, but we need to get on a chopper however possible. You have five minutes."

"Aye, sir." Karson jumped down, leaving the sniper rifle and ran to his locker inside. Destroyed. The entire building. Karson looked around for anything he could use and found enough to get by. A helmet, a Kevlar vest far too big for him, a SCAR and enough ammo, Tiny… "TINY!? TINY!" Karson ran over to a body lying under debris. "MEDIC! MEDIC!!" *Not again. Please, not again!* Karson remembered his friend who died by the hands of the enemy, and now his other friend at the hands of Hatyara. "Tiny…" Karson knew his friend was not breathing as a medic came in.

"You need to go, sir. You have a job to do. I'll take care of her. GO!"

Karson tore his eyes away from his dead friend and tried to block out his feelings, forgetting her. He sprinted outside and found a chopper landing, and ran to the bird and jumped inside. "I need you to take us up."

"Not going to happen. We are here to stay as cover."

"You don't understand. There is a man here in the area we need to find and take captive. We need you to take us. I'm a commander for SEAL Team Six."

"I wouldn't care if you were President Elding himself. We're not going anywhere."

Richardson and the team with their added SEAL were running up to the chopper now, and Karson drew his weapon, dragging the first pilot out the helicopter and throwing him into the soil. Richardson took the other. The SEALs mounted into the aircraft and Karson held the pilots at gunpoint as Richardson took the helicopter up. After they were high enough, Karson crawled through the doorway and into the Copilot's spot.

"You know, sir… I am a pilot. I'd fly a lot smoother than-"

Richardson dismissed Karson flatly. "I'm flying."

"Okay…" Karson responded curtly.

****

CHAPTER 23 - Look to the Flag, the Stars and Stripes forever!

The sun was setting as the men and women came back to the city of Lahore, Pakistan, after a long day of work in the fields. Farmers, pickers, businessmen-people of every job known in the region. The United States Marine Corps was initially stationed here after the wars of the Middle East to help check the flow of people entering the city and ensure a the bad never again were able to form anywhere else in the world. Maybe this city could be the start of peace in the country. Even though extremism was outlawed by the redesigned Pakistani government set in place in the early 2020's, some terrorists still made it through the brittle New Pakistan government. That's where the Americans came into play.

No terrorists, weapons, explosives, or other contraband items were to be allowed past the Marines and into the city. With this job, the Marines took their post very seriously. Nothing could slip through their fingers, so it would seem.

For the United States, The U.S. Marines would serve until the end, no matter how big or small the task was. Marines knew that what they were doing was for the greater good of the community they were serving in, wherever the United States of America sent them. The Marines had stopped on this particular day, two attempts of men attempting to smuggle weapons in, and one attempt of a man carrying heroin into the checkpoint. Drugs, weapons, intruders; it would just add more and more chaos and lead to possibly more attacks and bloodshed. No different than any major city in the United States.

Not. Needed. Period.

On the other side of the checkpoint, a younger Marine addition, recently enlisted, fresh out of boot camp, a mind full of the idea that he could make a difference, had just deployed to the region with the United Sates Marine Corps' First Battalion, Second Marines. "Timberwolf" as they called themselves, from Camp Lejeune in North Carolina. This young Marine served as a Military Police Officer in the unit, which was shipped out as a security measure as the United States decided what to do about the ever-growing numbers of Death Nation. This new Marine, unaware of the intel race going on back at home, stood guard at his post as the other Marine law enforcers checked for illegal items that could cause more death and destruction to the civilians, as well as the Americans present. Looking around, he felt strange, oddly left out, in a sea of new culture. But that didn't stop the Marine, and he smiled as a young lady in her black gown, and her child, walked up to him at the checkpoint.

"تهدأ قليلا من واحد." [Arabic: Tahda qalilaan min wahid.]

Translated as 'Calm down little one, the Marine didn't give this a second thought. He had to admit that to a youngling, in her own country invaded by a foreign military force, even a friendly Marine could probably seem a little scary. He smiled and gave her cheek a soft squeeze. He looked the lady and her baby over, then turned away to let them through. The woman's eyes followed his as he stepped aside.

His body's instincts immediately sent a pulse through him. 'Danger.' His body started to tense as he felt threatened. *Why is she… maybe it's because I'm sexy!* The nineteen-year-old Marine refused to let his guard rise for this innocent bystander, and he started to chuckle inwardly at his stupid self, looking up at his comrade in the tower. The lady walked past him and towards the break area for the Marines.

Racism runs rampant through us too often. She's just a civilian.

As the woman neared the structure, another Marine MP saw the woman and child making their way at a brisk, steady pace towards where Marines would escape from the heat as another shift would take over. The Marine walked a path to intercept her. She noticed him and walked faster. He reacted immediately.

"Ma'am, halt. Now." He released the safety on his weapon.

The woman's eyes widened, and she decided to make her move prematurely.

The Marine at the entrance stood, unaware.

Suddenly, one metallic click clinked among the pitter patter of animal hooves and human voices. It didn't sound like that of one of the fellow Marines un-safteying his weapon.

"STEVENS!!!!!" The intercepting Marine yelled at the Corporal who had let the female through. "MOVE! BOMB!" Corporal Stevens's fellow Marine called as he ran towards the Corporal.

The Marine Corporal turned his body and weapon in the way of the sound as an explosion detonated and ripped out of the woman's head wrap. The Corporal was hit first by a shock wave, imploding his insides and sending him airborne, then he felt the pain of shrapnel hit him riddling his body. White hot, razor sharp, cracking body armor metal, piercing deep into his body. His breath was knocked away, never to be regained fully again as he hit with a devastatingly hard and bloody thud against a pole, wrapping his Kevlar body around it. He slid down the pole, leaving a red streak showing his path.

His team screamed: "Men down" as other Marines had fallen too, and rushed over to their fallen brothers. Small arms fire took them by surprise, stopping them in their tracks. Panic overtook the local men and women. The Marines were plunged into shock as more Marines were killed in the ambush, until their training slowly kicked in and they finally returned fire, trying to overwhelm the enemy force with superior firepower and training. Body parts pelted the walls; blood splattered over people and animals as civilians and animals were blown apart as well. Terrorists didn't discriminate between innocence-men, women, elderly, children and warrior. The little checkpoint was sent into turmoil. Bullets. Grenades. Explosives. Bone, flesh, agony.

Blood. Lots and lots of blood.

In all of the pain Corporal Stevens was in, however, watching his brother's fight and die in addition to the pain throughout his body, nothing could contend with the pain he felt as his eyes fell upon a disfigured body of a little girl and her mother. How did he miss it? How did he miss the threat with all of his training?

She was a woman. I'm so stupid. Women are just as deadly, if not more, than men. Why would she do this? Especially to her baby girl? The light was bright in his eyes as he turned and looked up at his best friend who's tears pelted his face.

"Ethan! ETHAN! Don't leave me, Marine. You're gonna be okay. Ethan? ETHAN! PLEASE! YOU'RE MY BEST FRIEND! PLEASE!" His voice cracked. "Please?"

But Ethan was too far gone. He touched his friends face and drifted into a bright, white sleep.

"Don't do this to me! Don't make me have to tell your family!" He hit Ethan's chest.

"HEY! MARINE!" All sound was drowned out by the battle, and the Marine didn't care to listen. "CARAL! HE'S GONE!" The Marine shook Ethan's friend Carl as he ran up to him. "ETHAN IS GONE, CARAL, AND THER IS NOTHING YOU CAN DO! FOCUS ON THE BATTLE OR WE'LL ALL END UP LIKE HIM. YOU CAN COME BACK-" The Marine's head disappeared in a spray.

Carl screamed in terror and agony.

"HELP! WE'RE BEING OVERRUN! TIMBERWOLF! WE NEED HELP NOW! LAHORE!"

****

Country music filled the skeleton painted chopper, skull on the cockpit as the SEALs bounced from funny, insulting stories to their sex lives. The SEALs were getting louder and louder in suspense from the sex stories, as if talking about it brought them closer and closer to their much needed climaxes they hadn't had while away from their wives or 'significant others' back state side.

Yeah, I feel it too... Karson rolled his eyes at his Captain.

"And then when she went down on me, I pissed in her mouth and she-"

"HELP! WE'RE BEING OVERRUN! TIMBERWOLF! WE NEED HELP NOW! LAHORE!" Gunfire erupted in the radio frequency; then the radio went silent.

Karson grabbed the radio from Captain Richardson. "Just fly. I'm afraid you'll end up flying us into the ground if you don't. You've always sucked at flying anyway."

"Not as much as you suck dick! Serval, give me the radio. I'm your Commanding Officer." Richardson was focused on Karson, the stick pulling back.

Alert tones went off in the chopper. "STALLING. STALLING. STALLING."

"CAPTAIN!" Karson pushed the stick down towards the ground as the helicopter started to reduce speed, and fall back in the sky towards the ground.

Richardson fought back for control of the aircraft, finally gaining stability to continue flying forward, and not backward into the ground.

Karson retorted on him, terrified. "SEE, YOU DO SUCK AT FLYING!" Karson was fuming.

"Just answer the radio!" He said.

"Give me a second!" Taking deep breaths and calming down, he looked back at Richardson. "I got it." Karson cooed, shaking the radio.

Richardson swatted at it.

Karson laughed and responded to the Marines. "Marine Check Point, Timberwolf. SEAL Team Six, squad 'Trident Eagle' ten clicks out. Do not lose that checkpoint." The sound of the helicopter speeding up and the engine roaring to life made Karson smile as Richardson turned the chopper on its side as it made a sharp turn to the north.

"Marine, can you tell me what's happening?" Karson was saying, not fazed by the maneuver.

"The shots, they're coming from the overgrowth. We can't get our eyes locked onto the enemy. And people in the city are against us too now. We're fighting two fronts, sir."

"How many brothers de-" More shots interrupted Karson. "Respond. Are you still combat effective?"

"There are too many dead, sir! We don't stand a chance!"

"Don't think of that right now. Focus on staying alive and holding your station."

"I'm afraid, sir."

"Me too! But you have to push, Marine. We're coming. We'll help you, but for that, you have to drive to win! You have to help us as much as we have to help you!"

To his Captain, Karson said, "Can you make this go any faster, Captain? We have to stop the slaughter." Back to the Marine, he continued. "Do me a favor. Are you near a flag?"

"NO!" He screamed. "WHAT WILL THAT BANNER DO FOR ME?"

"TURN THE RADIO OFF, LAUKINS!" Karson shouted back at the SEALs behind him.

"Aye, sir."

"Look at your arm!" There was a pause on the radio. "Do you see that flag?"

"Yes."

"Let that be your courage. Let that stand for your strength. That is your flag. Your fight. That is freedom, and it must be defended."

No one answered Karson. Karson looked at his Captain who continued to fly, stone-faced and serious.

After the deafening silence, the radio changed to ballistic.

"AYE, SIR!"

"RAH!"

"AYE, SIR!"

"YES, SIR!"

"GREAT WORDS, SIR!"

"OOORAH!"

"Sir, we all heard you, sir. This is our post. And we will defend it." Marine voices pounded the radio channel.

Gunfire splattered over the radio channel.

"That's the Marine Corps I know. We're almost there. Stay dug in!"

"Aye."

"Command, this is Trident Eagle, position two. Anyway a gunship can strike Lahore?"

Only static responded to Karson.

"Command? We are in dire need of an answer. NOW!"

"Eagle two. You are sadly on your own at this point. Multiple attacks are underway; our fleet is busy handling those, more dire targets. As soon as we can, we'll scramble someone to you. For now, fight hard."

"HURRY UP! WE MIGHT NOT BE HERE WHEN YOU GET AROUND TO US! WE'RE VALUABLE LIVES TOO! SCREW YOU!"

Karson shouted, furiously. "WHEN WE GET OUT OF THIS I'M GONNA REDESIGN YOUR FACE!"

****

Hearing that help was on the way made everything feel better. SEAL Team Six would be on the scene shortly, and everything would be okay. The Marine put down the radio, and stuck his weapon out the window, aiming at muzzle flashes. What he saw terrified him. Marines fighting an invisible enemy. across the way, some Marines were being pulled into a garage and slaughtered like cows, their throats slit and the blood spurting from their wounds. These PEOPLE were cashing in on the bounty set in 2014 on American heads. 'Any American killed by anyone and turned in was rewarded in cash.' This bounty needed to stop. Carl took aim at the men dragging Marines away.

"Carl?"

Carl jumped, and spun around, aiming as someone ran in.

"It's me, Carl!"

"Michael! You scared the curry outta me, man. I almost blew your heart out!"

"Thankfully you didn't! We need to secure the ammo depot! It's the only chance we have of keeping this place under our flag!" He pushed his shoulder into the wall under the windowsill.

"THAT'S SUICIDE, MAN! IT'S ON THE OTHER SIDE, AND IT'D BE A MAD DASH INTO THE ENEMY FIRE!"

"IT'S A RISK WE HAVE TO TAKE!" Michael smacked Carl. "WE'VE HAD NO RADIO CONTACT FROM ANYONE OVER THERE. FOR ALL WE KNOW, THE ENEMY HAS OUR GUNS, AND WE'RE NEXT TO DIE! DO YOU WANT TO BE ANOTHER DEATH NATION CASUALTY?"

Carl stared at Michael. *Death would be a relief right about now.*

Michael continued when Carl didn't speak up. "WE BOTH KNOW WE PROBABLY WON'T SURVIVE THIS, SO LET'S AT LEAST MAKE A DIFFERENCE! YEAH?"

"I hate it when you're right, dude!"

"Marines. There will be no air support for a while." Commander Hunter's infamously warm and calm, yet still in command voice, full of confidence, rang over the radio.

Both Marines smiled. "Alright. Let's do this!"

"That's the spirit!" Michael pounded Carl on the back.

Both Marines moved to the entrance and looked out. Bullets pelted the wall in front of them, so close, they fell back inside, bullets slamming into the door frame where their heads had been just moments before.

"Is there another way out of here? One that's NOT going to shoot me in the back?"

"The roof…"

"Okay, then let's go to the roof… is there cover?"

"If we stay prone, yes." Carl sad. "Otherwise, we'll be Swiss cheese."

They moved to the ladder and climbed up top. Staying low, they dropped down where no one would see them, and they slinked across, listening to gunshots, and bullets thudding into more people. The sound was horrible. If it didn't kill instantly, then noise of agony followed the metal hitting meat sound. It could make even the strongest of men cringe and puke. All of the blood, it would turn any sane person insane. Especially when every person that was dead was part of your extended family; the family that would die for one another. The family that was dying for one another at this very moment.

The good thing about Carl's thoughts right now was that they made time fly by. Michael and Carl had already reached the end of safety, having a mad dash ahead of them for cover, when a Marine sniper fell dead from the roof above, crumpling into a mess. Crunching bone sounds came out of her body, right in front of the two breathing Marines.

Carl puked.

Michael knelt down to see who had bit the bullet, checking her pulse.

"Julia." He said, removing one of her dog tags. "Dead."

Carl puked again, as a terrorist came around the corner. Carl ducked, Michael shot the keffiyeh from his head with Carl's pistol.

"We've got to move Carl. They are going to overrun this place. We have to secure that room."

"This can't be happening."

Michael spun Carl around to face him. "HEY! IT IS! IT IS HAPPENING, CARL. STAY IN THE FIGHT, DUDE! DON'T GO TO THAT PLACE YET. I WANT TO LIVE. HELP ME STAY ALIVE, DAMMIT!"

"ALRIGHT!" Carl screamed. More bullets hit the area around the Marines. The enemy force seemed just to keep growing and growing.

"Good. On three."

"THREE!" Not wanting to wait, putting off the inevitable any longer, Carl danced from cover, shooting to his side at the 'humans' who killed his family. Michael followed.

The ability to do something, even when not wanting to, was the job of the Marines. It meant sustaining freedom for anyone and everyone who wanted it.

"Oorah!"

****

CHAPTER 24 - Priority over Life

Richardson called back to his SEALs. "Ten minutes out, men. Serval, I need you to ready up for fast roping."

"Time to go to work, sirs!" The SEAL addition called up.

"Aye, it is." Karson climbed back.

"How much supplies do we have?" Richardson asked.

"Enough to get the job done."

"Alright, so not that much." Karson piped up.

"Precisely." Richardson called back "My worry. Conserve shots. Like the expression from someone at the Battle of Bunker Hill during the Revolutionary War. 'Wait until you see the whites of their eyes'."

"Who wants to gun from up here? Scratch that. We'll gun to thin it out, then drop down. We're going to make a few passes, then drop down."

"Ready, sir," Laukins said.

"Same." Hunter chimed in.

"I am ready to fight!" Smith continued.

"Ditto," Richardson said.

"Serval?" A Sailor asked him.

"Yeah, bud?" Karson asked, readying his weapon.

"Why are we going here? I thought our mission was Hatyara." Jacobs asked.

"It is, but we have to save our own as well. Maybe we'll find a trail..."

"I understand that, but this spying. What's the point? We should just go get him. Find him. Nothing else. Like, if I'm drinking a full glass of water, I drink it to half full and fill it back up. What is the point of that bottom half? Let me just go and kill him."

"I appreciate the dedication to this and that's a great analogy, but we cannot just go get him. We don't know where he is. Meanwhile, we have Marines being slaughtered that we do know where they are. We have to go here first. We'll get him. Just not yet. Sandstorm?" Karson asked the SEAL who had taken the gun.

"Let's spill blood!"

"Good answer! By the way, your name is my favorite by far."

"Same." He replied smiling.

The Captain took a serious tone. "Men, it's been an honor serving with you. If something goes wrong, know that."

All SEALs nodded. They put their hands in the middle and shouted a battle cry as the helicopter flew up onto the target. The surprise worked beautifully. The advantage of height, always fun to have. The enemy bodies could be seen in the bush.

"That's a lot of keffiyehs!" Sandstorm shouted over the thunder of the American aircraft. "You attacked our brothers. Now we'll rain down death on you!"

"No matter! We've got bullets to spare! Command. We've arrived at the incident center, engaging now. Excess reinforcements would be welcome. Force far outnumbers the checkpoint and our forces."

Bullets started pelting the chopper.

"SANDSTORM! LIGHT 'EM UP!" Karson shouted.

Sandstorm gave a war cry! "YEEHAWWW! GET A TASTE OF 'MURICA, BITCHES!"

"Again, we're engaging multiple areas. Help is far off. Hold as best you can." The voice sitting safe in a control center spoke.

"We'll try," Karson said. Karson readied to repel to the ground when something in the distance caught his eye. "Yeehawww, get a taste of 'Murica, bitches? Texas?"

"You know it!" Sandstorm kept shooting.

****

Meanwhile, while the troops engaged in battle, Hatyara was on the phone while watching the event unfold.

"Sir, your special troops are loyal to you, and it seems that the Americans are fighting for their lives. The attacks are going as planned, and will be completed as you wish!" Hatyara looked around as more and more troops gathered to invade the city. "Yes, sir. The Marines will be killed; this helicopter can't be but a measly way to try and get the troops out. We'll destroy it. Nothing will go wrong. We will be successful!"

"Sir…"

Hatyara held his finger up.

"But, sir, this is important…"

Hatyara glared at his insubordinate. "Yes, sir. As you wish. I will see it done. WHAT?"

"An alert cry was sent out before we could take the radio down. SEAL Team Six is on that chopper. The boy?"

"This is of no concern of mine. SEAL Team Six can suck my cock for all I care. You, on the other hand, interrupted me while talking to the Supreme Leader, and you failed me." Hatyara drove his knife into his soldier's throat. "I expect perfection. Not failure!"

As Hatyara withdrew his dagger, a harsh gurgling noise poured out of the man's throat as his life drained from his head, spurting all over the ground. Hatyara wiped his knife on his kill and walked off.

Bullets suddenly ripped through the trees that covered Hatyara and hit the ground around him. He dove for cover. *I have been found out.* "BLOW THAT CHOPPER AWAY!"

More bullets hit around him.

****

"Sir?" Karson prodded Richardson.

"Yes, Serval?" He turned in his seat, swatting Karson's hand away.

"That man over there? On the phone. Could that be... It can't be..." Karson pointed.

"Whoever he is, I want him. Serval, snatch him."

"Aye, sir. GIVE ME THAT GUN FOR A SECOND!"

"AYE, SIR!" Sandstorm replied.

The sound of the chopper nearly drowned out the door gun. Karson aimed at his target. From what he had deduced, Hatyara was a warrior much like Karson, if not more, and would be able to escape death by bullet. Karson's first shot would be near him. The second barrage at him if he moved fast enough to be the man.

Karson's deduction was sound. The man, Karson's target- Hatyara- moved with purpose, not fear, and was able to evade the second wave of bullets.

"SIR, THAT IS HIM. THAT IS THE MISSION. THE MARINES MUST WAIT."

"AYE! I'LL DROP YOU OFF THERE!" Richardson called over the noise.

"AYE!" Karson wrapped around the rope, ready to drop out.

Captain Richardson rotated the chopper and soon hovered over the area Hatyara was. Karson, Sandstorm and Jacobs repelled down. The gun on the helicopter was still operational by Laukins. Hitting the ground, Karson crouched to provide cover as his team hit too, shooting three enemies charging the drop zone. Once all SEALs hit the ground and the chopper moved to safety, they began moving through their AO.

"Team. We have to find him before he escapes. If he does, then we're tofu!"

The sound of men screaming orders and firing randomly surrounded the SEALs as they made their way through the tall grasses to the mini village that sat on the outskirts of the city. As they entered the village, they started meeting resistance. The SEALs shot the enemy soldiers and continued searching for Hatyara.

"Team. Split up. Cover ground. If you see Hatyara, shoot him. Less lethal shots."

"Aye, Sir." Sandstorm split off without worry.

The SEALs moved apart, keeping each other in view or radio contact as they were stirring a hornets' nest. Hatyara would be guarded and heavily or not, these men would stop at nothing to protect him like any Soldier would the President of the United States of America.

Karson found his way into the first building closest to where Hatyara had been standing. He entered and stood in the dark, damp, moldy and musty smelling hut.

CREAK

His head snapped up. *Upstairs.* Karson looked for the stairs. *There.* Moving up the stairs, Karson turned his weapon. He would fire if he had too; capture was the primary objective, but death would come to Hatyara if it meant that Karson would be killed if he tried to catch him.

Karson rounded the corner from the stairs and felt the stairs creak underneath him.

And behind me! Karson spun around and felt the full impact of a rifle into his face. Karson stumbled back up the stairs and hit the ground. His gun and helmet both slid away from him. Reaching for his gun, the dark figure grabbed it from Karson's hand.

Karson looked up, as the man threw the pistol out the window, shining light inside the room. Karson looked up to see a dark man with a full beard and a long set of dreads staring down at him. His teeth were yellow, and he smelled rank like death was covering him.

He bared his teeth. He was animalistic. No fear. Just hate. He now had his prey that like a crow does an eagle, had kept interfering with his affairs.

Only you're gonna find out that you're the crow, and I'm the Bald Eagle.

"Amerdican scum. You should know better den get in way of my plans."

"What plans? Who are you? Who do you work for?" Karson asked, rubbing his gashed skull.

"Wouldn't you like to know? I believe you call me in your language, Hatyara. I am now nightmare of your life. What's left of it. In two minutes, I'll be taking it from you. Your hunt for me will be over. Tell me, who are you?"

"I'll never tell you that. I am a United States Sailor, and I demand you let me go! NOW!"

"No. You give no orders to me. Commander. Das right, I see your fear now. I can read, and I know ranks of your military. Tell me, who will miss you when you're gone? Our plan is going perfect; Supreme Leader will be pleased I have won an easy and decisive victory over your so-called United States of America. Once done here, we will move on, our plan to take your country soon! Easy peasy!" Hatyara slammed Karson into the metal bars that hung in the room and cuffed him into the wall. "No way to escape. I think I'll have fun with you, my slave!" He slammed his massive fisted hand into Karson's rib cage, the force rattling Karson's smaller body even through the Kevlar.

"OOF! Let me go! And I'll be sure your treatment is as close to just as I can!" Karson gasped as another hit racked him in the stomach.

"You will not catch me. Without knowledge, I am a ghost. A figment of imagination. No one can ever take us."

"You underestimate me."

"I don't." He reached into Karson's pocket and pulled out an identification card. "Commander Hunter. So nice to meet you. Shame that I have to kill you now. Don't worry; I'll make it slow, that way you can feel... Every. Single. Incision." Hatyara's face was so close to Karson, he could smell his breath. Smelled of burned human, and rum.

"You eat humans?" Karson asked curiously. "Suits you. Makes sense."

"I do. Gives me their souls. Their power. And you look appetizing. Maybe a pinky to wet my appetite?"

Hatyara raised his knife and sliced a deep wound into Karson's arm down to his hand. Deep, but not enough to kill him. The pain, though, and Karson's fear of knives gave Hatyara his satisfied reaction. He placed the knife on Karson's now ungloved hand and started applying pressure. Karson squirmed.

"NO! NO PLEASE!" Blood started dripping from his finger when the

BANG

of a flashbang ripped through the stillness of the room. Hatyara flinched, Karson kicked, missing, as Hatyara slammed his fist into Karson's cheek, knocking him out.

****

"Serval? Commander Serval? Wake up, sir!"

"Waa… Where… What happened?" Karson asked hopping up.

"I was walking, in search of Hatyara, when I stumbled upon your pistol. I looked up to see the window and entered. I ran up and tossed the grenade, but Hatyara had disappeared, and here you hung. I let you lose. You've been out for ten minutes."

"TEN MINUTES? MOVE!" Karson grabbed his SCAR and rushed out of the room back into the streets, calling back a thank you to Jacobs. Hatyara had slipped through his fingers.

I screwed up again! Alrighty. Think it through, Karson. Where would he go? Grass? Obviously, but he'd want to be near his men and to see his work carried out. 'Sides… We have a helicopter. We'd be able to spot him, and knowing that we'd spend our time looking in the grass…

A man came around the corner, and Karson launched up, shoving his gun under the man's chin, and squeezed the trigger, looking away as blood splattered all over the place.

…and he'd for sure go somewhere else. High in the building, he'd be exposed… knowing that I'd look there, so he'd stay on the ground. Unless he obviously thought I'd go to the ground to look, in which case he'd pick the highest spot. Karson looked towards the highest place in the village. *He'd be sniping us. No, he wants us to look for him. He himself likes to watch death. A sniper rifle wouldn't give him the ability to watch us die instantly. The recoil would take his eyes off of us… What about the hill. Go through the grass in the back, head up that hill, easy escape into the caves or the area behind the hill, where he could have a vehicle waiting.*

"Team. The hill. Move on the hill behind the village."

The SEALs hurriedly rushed to rendezvous with Karson and hared up the hill after their target.

At the top, Karson tried finding his target through his scope, but the bullets kept pushing him back down. When he looked back over the top of the hill, he witnessed a grenade thrown by one of Hatyara's men. Karson honed in on the ball of shrapnel and fired a shot as bullets pelted Karson in his chest protector, knocking him back and down the hill.

The SEALs watched all unfold in slow motion; the SEAL falling away, the bullet spinning through the metal ball and an explosion in real time knocking them back as well as shrapnel pelted the grassy outcrop.

"OOF!" He rolled backward down the hill. The SEALs on the hill dropped down from the crest of the hill for cover.

Karson hit the bottom of the hill and saw an enemy vehicle to his right. He ran for it, hotwired it, and raced up the hill again, motioning for his team to get in as he crawled through the gunner hole.

"Serval? Are you okay?" Sandstorm asked.

"WHICH VEHICLE IS HE IN!?" Karson didn't take himself out of the battle. Like an actor, he stayed in the moment.

Hatyara was racing away in a convoy of vehicles.

"We don't know, sir. MEDIC! MAN DOWN!"

Karson had no time to tend to his men. It was priority over life right now. Priority of life replaced when this new war started. Death or the possibility of it was what this war was all about. Even in the enemies' name. He shot at the vehicles as they raced down the other side of the hill. The enemy returned fire. At the bottom, Karson jumped out of the vehicle and crouched in the road and loaded his grenade launcher to fire, but as he did, he heard a noise behind him. Looking over his shoulder, he saw a troop transport speeding up to run over the SEAL. Karson dropped onto his back, and the truck was over his head in a second. Karson lifted his carabineer up with some rope. It hooked the truck, launching out of his hand. The line sagged, then tightened, dragging Karson behind it. He had to work fast. If the troops in the truck noticed him, he'd be shot dead and dragged for miles. Karson moved his way closer to the speeding truck, hand cross by hand cross, the dirt keeping some of the road burn at bay.

Karson's team drove up in the truck, and Karson launched himself up onto their vehicle, and they inched closer to the truck. Karson unhooked from the carabineer, but as he did, the truck slammed on the breaks causing the two vehicles to collide, the SEALs vehicle flipping over its self, throwing Karson into the back of the troop transport flipping him onto his back as he slammed into the ramp. Karson looked up to see enemy soldiers lining the vehicle, sneezed, and was immediately met with feet kicking him, and knives coming out. He swung his legs around, kicking a few men to get himself to his feet, but as he did, a foot was thrust into Karson's chest, knocking him backward, losing his footing over the lip of the transport, he toppled out back onto the ground.

"Sir! Serval is down. Repeat, SERVAL IS DOWN!"

"Serval! Talk to me, Buddy!" Richardson radioed down from the chopper.

"He's not moving, sir!" Sandstorm ran over.

"Alright. Team abort mission. I will land, pick up any Marines left, and come to you. Lay down flares. Hurry up, we're running out of fuel."

Sandstorm rolled Karson over and checked for a pulse. "Aye, sir."

Jacobs started running down the road towards Karson, who still lay unmoving as the Black Hawk helicopter landed. Seven Marines boarded the aircraft under heavy fire, one taking a shot to his spine, a wound that would cripple him for the remaining days of his life to come. Taking off again, the chopper's rotors were hit, causing the chopper to limp along through the air only at forty feet. Fearing that the helicopter wouldn't be able to take off again, Richardson ordered that the SEALs strap themselves to the rope to fly with the chopper.

"Sir, we have wounded." Jacobs replied.

"You know what to do. Never leave a man behind."

"What about our men?" Marines clogged the coms.

"They are dead. We can come back for them. You are still alive, and my people are still alive. They are the priority."

Hovering over Karson's limp body now, the SEALs hooked in after a rope dropped to hoist Karson up to the crew cabin of the aircraft. A Marine medic took his vitals and shot him with some adrenalin to wake him up. Karson launched awake, striking at anyone near him.

"Serval! SERVAL! It's us. You're safe." Richardson called back.

"Did we get him?" Karson said drowsily. "Where are my guys?"

"Flying." A Marine said, pointing down.

Karson's eyes bulged from his head. He looked out the window. "But did we get-"

"No, Commander." Richardson answered.

"FOLLOW THE ROAD-" Karson ordered.

"Serval, we have to get back to base-"

"NO! WE HAD ONE JOB. GET HATYARA. LEAVE ME BEHIND IF YOU HAVE TO. I'M NOT ASKING I'M TELLING, FOLLOW THE-"

"HEY! YOU ARE NOT IN COMMAND HERE, SERVAL. YOU TAKE ORDERS, DO YOU UNDERSTAND? I AM IN CONTROL. I GIVE THE ORDERS. MY COMMAND IS THAT WE ARE GOING BACK TO MAKE A PLAN, AND GET OFF THE CHOPPER HOPEFULLY BEFORE IT BLOWS US AWAY! SO SHUT UP AND BE USEFUL AND HELP THE WOUNDED."

Karson didn't respond. He punched the side of the chopper and stared out the window.

I had him. I had him. Now he's gone again!

As they were flying back to the base and the SEALs had managed to climb in. An hour later the Captain noticed a compound. "Serval, look!"

Karson looked over from staring out his side of the window.

"Open the left door." Richardson ordered.

"Aye, sir." Karson did as he was told and stared out into the open at a structure with tracks. Many, many tracks leading from it.

"You think that's where Hatyara could be heading?" The Captain asked.

"Maybe, I'll mark down the coordinates and we can come back here sometime and search it."

"Aright. That will give you the chance to lick your wounds; all of us. We'll rest and be strong enough to storm it. Let's take another team with us."

"Okay. They can stay outside as we sweep and clear." Karson said with a smile, happily back on the trail of the enemy.

"Sure thing. Air Force drones will do scans tonight."

Sure enough, the Air Force was able to send a drone. What came back shocked them. On the cameras, they picked up armored trucks and tanks escorting supply trucks into the compound. What they also believe, based on a vehicle, presumed to be Hatyara's having disappeared into a small barn, the heat signature fading after a few moments, is that the compound has more than one level below ground. They also found it used to be American controlled. They just had to find the long forgotten blueprints to gain an edge over the illusive enemy.

****

CHAPTER 25 - Rewrite your Yearbook

"Serval, to the command post. Serval to the command post." The loudspeaker chirped.

"Serval. Get your arse in here!"

"Huh?" Karson raised his head. "Can I help you?"

"What did I just say?" The voice said, snarkily.

"I don't know who you are. I don't take orders from a nobody." Karson lowered his head again, resting after the long flight to the nearest allied military compound. Her Majesty's flag still flew, even though England, recently fallen, was now under the control of Death Nation.

"Your Captain wants you now. Don't make me ask again!"

"Alright then. Thank you." Karson said. He stood up from the ground, dizzy, and tired. The blow he took and the sleep deprivation was starting to get to him, and he had a raging headache, and his body's immune system was failing, giving way to a cold. Coughs and sneezes now ravaged his body, curable only by sleep which seemed so far off.

"Alright, gentlemen. This will only take a few moments. The number one enemy, Hatyara, has now fled U.S. custody yet again. We have, however, discovered a compound to which he could be hiding. Like any enemy; Bin Laden, Kaddafi, Hussein, they all run and flee and hide in their safe havens. We will destroy this one, and anyone who stands in our way should the need arise, just like our ancestors before us. This animal doesn't escape again. There shouldn't be too much resistance entering, but as we have discovered a multitude of levels, we fear that this may be a suicide mission. One needed of course, but without knowing anything about this thing, we could be walking into an entire army down there. No matter. Again, if need be, we'll just destroy the place." Richardson now looked at Karson with disgust. Karson's head dropped at the next sentence. "I for one am tired of constant fails, death, and chasing a man who excretes in a hole. The incompetence of some people in these allied militaries is the very reason war rages in the world. I will not accept failure again. If anyone cannot do their job, they should leave now."

Karson glared now. *If you want me gone, say so! Otherwise, let's go get this guy."*

No one in the room moved. Karson and Richardson stared, everyone stealing glances at the leadership in the room. Richardson continued, turning his head to face the screen now.

"Comparing this complex with our intel, and the intel of the British, we've concluded that this was an American held secret prison, deserted in 2013. We-"

"Could there still be prisoners in there, sir? In our assault, they could be in the way or attack us, or we may accidentally shoot them." A Sailor spoke from the back of the room.

"All expendable. Our mission is Hatyara. Besides, it was deserted over twenty years ago. No one could survive that long!"

Karson, pissed off now at Richardson, gave his own answer. "Even still, to keep us sane, and on the right side of things, **sir**, we should keep our weapons tight and our heads on the swivel."

"Whatever. We'll be going in on Black Hawks and fight our way inside. Serval, your team will be on the chopper that attacks the back of the enemy complex. I'll go on the one that attacks from the front. The SAS teams will lay overwatch until we're grounded, then land on the roof. Fight to kill, except for Hatyara, unless you have to kill him to keep him from escaping. **Again.** However, if you kill him, I'll shove my rifle so far inside of you. I'll have to find a different punishment for you, Serval. I know how much you like that, I'll find something better for you! BRING HIM ALIVE. HE HAS TO ANSWER FOR HIS CRIMES ON EARTH BEFORE HE DOES IN HELL! Hatyara will do anything to kill us and get away. Stay on your toes, gentlemen! This will be pretty tough. Questions?" Richardson ended his briefing.

Everyone shook their heads, itching to get out and complete this mission.

"Good. Let's go. One hour."

Everyone left the room, except Karson and Richardson. Karson shut the door.

"You have a problem with me, Captain? Or what?" Karson turned.

"Yeah. I do have a problem with you. WHY IS HE STILL OUT THERE?"

Karson threw a chair. "BECAUSE HE KNOWS HOW TO FIGHT! YOU HAVE TO BE A CAT IN THESE FIGHTS. NOT A DOG LIKE WE ARE. A DOG HAS ONE DEFENSE AND OFFENSE, TEETH. WE JUST RUSH IN AFTER THE FACT. THAT IS OUR TEETH. A CAT HAS TEETH, FRONT CLAWS, BACK CLAWS,

TAIL, AND SCENT. THAT IS FIVE. I'M TRYING TO BE A CAT, NOT A DOG! OOF!"

Richardson was in front of Karson in a heartbeat, slamming his hand to Karson's throat, and pinning him against the wall. Karson's hands struggled with Richardson's forearms, but the Captain was much stronger than Karson.

"You think I don't know that? You think I'd have sent you in after him if I didn't know he could fight?" Richardson tightened his grip.

Karson couldn't breathe. He was clawing at Richardson's hands, his legs loosing footing on the ground.

"If he didn't know how to fight, we'd just send the Army. I gave you an order, Karson and you failed me. The one mission that you shouldn't have failed me on, and you did. I got Victor's report. Inadequate to perform. Hero syndrome. Feels like he controls destiny. Well, guess what, Karson. I will not have that on my team. If this mission doesn't kill you, you'll be out of this team, either a mere Sailor scrubbing waste from ship bowels, or a civilian, dishonorably discharged and with the abilities to only kill, you'll be homeless. Hated. Unwanted. EXPENDABLE!"

He released Karson.

Karson wheezed and coughed. "That's what you honestly think, sir? That I'm inadequate? Unable to perform? IT WAS ME WHO SAVED YOUR SORRY HIDES MORE TIMES THAN NOT. IT WAS ME WHO COVERED FOR YOU IN AFRICA WHEN YOU LOST CONTROL OF YOUR TEAM, LOST CONTROL OF THE SECTOR, AND LOST CONTROL OF AFRICA!"

"I told you never to bring that up. I will end you. Make you disappear. Rewrite your high school yearbook to make you never exist. We're going to make some changes on our team, kid."

"I'm not friendly on this, sir. I don't like this at all."

"It's the way it has to be."

****

ARRIVAL

"There it is, men. The Gulf of Aiden. Ignore the ugly ship grave yards, there. Hopefully, we go nowhere near them! We'll be landed in no time! Now starts our trek to dock. Be on alert. All armed. Watch for threats on shore and on water. We may be the military, but we are not invincible. Keep watch, and be careful with your mission."

The intercom system onboard always gave a report of what was happening in real time. Karson enjoyed working on this vessel. It made everything run smooth in a world where nothing ran smooth. His missions had so far been to Europe. Now it was Africa, right after being promoted to Lieutenant. A land where he'd wanted to go for his entire life, he never thought it would be like this.

****

CHAPTER 26 - Cloudy Day

"Eritrea. How did we end up in this place?"

"Dude, I didn't even know this country existed."

The United States had ordered the invasion of a subtle country in the Horn of Africa, 45,406 square miles of land right above Ethiopia, as well as the invasion of many other nations on the continent of Africa, just a bit more under the radar.

The Americans stood on a street corner and watched people walk by. Especially the women. The fully covered female sex would travel on foot across the streets, around the Americans, and would continue on their way. Some however, would stop, squat, and stay in that uncomfortable way for a while, gaining the attention of the American troops, who would shift nervously, their fingers revolving the safety of their weapons, and placing them gently on the trigger, scanning the area high and low for threats, never taking their attention entirely from the one who had gained their attention in the first place. Then, much to the troops' disgust, the women would stand up and continue on their way, leaving a pile of feces where they had been moments before. The men would flinch. Karson was prepared for this, having been told that people would defecate in the middle of the streets and leave it, not caring to wipe their cracks or any other part of their private regions, triggering flies into hectic buzzing around the horrible smelling bodies of the people of this third world country. Karson's uncle, who had served in the U.S. Military years before him, had explained this phenomenon before Karson was deployed. Many Middle Eastern countries were like this: poverty-stricken, foul, hard lives.

"That is truly disgusting." Leaf growled, gagging in disgust at the woman who gave the most innocent look of 'I can't help it...' He chased her off.

"You bet your sweet face. And they don't even wipe! Them butt cheeks are crusty my friends. Maybe they could use a lick!"

"Eww, stop it, Lieutenant!"

"Tehe!" Karson mimicked a long haired woman, twirling his curls in his fingers.

"HEY! YOU TWO STOP BEING CHILDREN!" The Captain of the small insurgency of Americans shouted across the street. "No pun intended." He whispered, Karson assuming to him. "WE STILL HAVE A JOB TO DO!"

"YEAH! WATCHING PEOPLE POOP IN THE STREET!" Karson dared taunt and tease again.

The Captain glared at the Sailors.

"Okay, yeah… We seriously should stop." Karson said, elbowing his laughing friend.

"Fine." He said, trying to stifle his laughter.

"Good boy!" Karson said, sassy.

The Sailors continued to pace the streets of Beilul, a small cape town in the Southern Red Sea Region of Eritrea, just north of Assab, the main port of the country. The need of Beilul was simple: maintain control of people heading into the harbour. Should the port fall, the United States would not have as much control of the African Country which helps as a staging ground for the American forces' part of the war dealing with the mega-continent: the invasion by the United States, along with other allied coalition forces, into the forty-seven countries of the continent.

"Serval?"

"Yes, Sailor?"

"Sailor? Really?" The Sailor glared at the Lieutenant.

Karson chuckled. "What, dude?" Karson snapped his fingers. "Carrion?"

"Wah? Oh! Can we go get food? Pleeeaseee?"

"No, Carrion, we cannot."

"Why not? And just use my real name, dude. Seriously."

"Because we don't split from the group," Karson said as if he were scolding a stupid child. "And I don't think that is a good idea. If it were just us on a covert mission, maybe. But we're in the midst of crowds of people. These people might hunt your family. No, I'll use your code name."

"It'd only be for a few minutes. We're so hungry." Carrion whined.

"And I sooo don't care!" Carrion gave Karse puppy dog eyes. "NO!" Karson said louder, more stern.

"Mean." Carrion replied, taken aback at how his friend was acting.

"Excuse me?" Karson turned on him.

"Can we ask the Captain? He's probably nicer than you." Carrion continued to protest.

Karson turned across the street and waved at the Captain. Karson walked across the street and glanced back at the Sailor, who was frantically begging Karson silently not to ask the Captain. The Captain blew up across the street, pushing Karson aside rather roughly, causing him to lose his balance with the weight of the gear and hit the ground. The Captain stomped across the street and got right up in the Sailor's face. His mouth shut, his posture straightened, and he couldn't look his superior in the eyes. He gulped.

"We're in a war zone. Stop heckling the Lieutenant. NO FOOD! YOU'RE FINE! WE DON'T BREAK FORMATION!"

"Uhh… aye… Aye, sir!"

Karson came back. The Captain stormed back across the street.

"Thanks a lot, sir." The Sailor still wouldn't look up, but he was clearly pissed.

"I had said, 'no.' You said, 'ask him'. I did what you said! I sure didn't think he'd do that!"

Carrion muttered under his breath. "What did you stick up your-"

Karson turned to his comrade, having about enough. "You'll be cleaning the toilets when we get back."

"Sorry, sir?" He asked, looking up now.

"You heard me. You'll be cleaning toilets. We're friends, Samuel, but I'm still an officer. You need to learn to differentiate when I'm playing around and when I'm being serious. You do what I say when I say it in these areas. That might just keep you alive. Understand? If you don't, we'll take it up with Captain Richardson, and if that doesn't work, the Admiral, and even the President of the United States of America, to whom we serve out our orders for the good of our homeland. If you have a question with the POTUS, then you've got a bigger problem than just food. Besides, sometimes, these people jerk off into the food. The food here probably is poisoned, or rotten, you'd be on the toilet, or possibly in a casket taking a dirt nap before you could make it back to this corner." There was no answer. Karson turned and found that the Sailor was gone.

"Oh..." Karson growled. "SCREW ME!" He pressed his radio button. "Captain Richardson, Carrion is Absent Without Leave. Permission to pursue him and bring him back to his post?"

"YOU LOST YOUR SUBORDINATE... HOW DO YOU LOOSE YOUR... YOU NEED TO GET A GRIP, SERVAL! LEAD YOUR MEN. You know what! Forget it. Granted Lieutenant, but remain in constant radio contact. Every two minutes I expect a 'fine.' Do you understand me, Lieutenant? LIEUTENANT?"

Karson flinched, not used to being yelled at by his C.O. "Sorry. Was giving an order to another Sailor to guard his and my post. Yes, sir. I will obey and-"

"YOU TAKE MY ORDERS FIRST, SERVAL. UNDERSTOOD? I'LL DROP YOU BACK TO PRIVATE IF THIS KEEPS UP. UNDERSTOOD?"

"Aye, sir. I'll have him back soon. First 'fine' said now."

"Aye." The Captain curtly replied.

Karson walked up the street, chambering a round into place in his rifle, and clicking a bullet into the weapon on his leg. Taser ready as well, double checking his moderate gear loadout and armor. Karson rounded a corner and was met by a wall of people. "Ugh! Captain, I'm going to be heading into a sea of people. I'm going to leave my radio on open frequency. My distress signal will be shiny day."

"It's cloudy, Serval."

"Okay, you know what? Cloudy day then."

"That's better."

"I am not in the mood for teasing-"

"Watch what you say to me right now, Lieutenant, because I too am not in the mood. Get into the crowd and get your Sailor back before anything bad happens. Move."

Karson walked into the marketplace, passing stands, looking for the American man, while maintaining a constant level of alert. How hard could it be to find a man, dressed in jeans and a shirt, with a giant gun hanging on the front of him? Karson kept looking. "Fine." Karson found himself continuously saying.

People stared at Karson nervously, stepping out of his way quickly, and eyeing the weapons he was packing. He was ever vigilant himself. This country had lost some of its law abiding citizens to the ways of the enemy world, and they wouldn't think twice of killing an American, even if the American man was only there to help. The fact that Karson, and any American at that, are American, means that they have a hypothetical, giant, red, throbbing target painted on the back of their heads. Anyone who kills or captures an American can expect to be well rewarded by the many terrorist groups the world has procured. The police officers in the streets also were not free of corruption. The American Soldiers have been working with the government's law enforcing and defense forces, but still, some would love the chance to make easy money. *Easy?* It doesn't take much to kill an American, even if their country is the most powerful. All of man was created equally when they were placed on the earth.

An ally would make a good spot to disappear. Maybe there is food down there. Karson tried radioing the subordinate SEAL. Having not been in radio contact with his worthless Sailor, Karson started to think this was more of an emergency over a run to satisfy a young man's belly. "I swear Sam, when I find you, I'm gonna kill you," Karson said to himself. "Fine."

"Karson, it's time to come back to post. We will regroup and hunt for Carrion. I want you back here now. Something suspicious has come up."

"Aye, aye, sir. I'm heading back to you. Carrion, if you can hear me, you need to tell me now, or I have to leave you behind."

Karson had reached the end of the street. Karson took one last glance around the market, jumping up onto a table. The vendor protested. Karson dropped some Nafka, the currency of the country, into the man's hand so he wouldn't be rowdier and draw attention. He was nothing but thankful, and more appreciative of the Americans who had invaded his country. As Karson was about to turn around, he saw a bearded man with jeans come running out of an alley. His gun was missing, and he was bleeding from his nose. Karson turned and glared at his Sailor, and yelled across to him.

"Carrion! CARRION! WHERE ARE YOU GOING? GET OVER HERE!"

Sam stopped for a moment, looking around, and found Karson standing on the corner. He took off for Karson.

Karson now was worried. "Where are your weapons? Carrion!"

"Lieutenant! RUN!" As he yelled, Karson raised his weapon.

"Carrion, what's happening?"

"RUN DAMMIT!" He shouted.

Suddenly, Karson's fear of being deployed to Africa came true. A torrent of men came running around the corner; fifteen heavily armed police officers in their riot gear. They raised their weapons in return, including the American-made, extremely accurate SCAR. More officers would be surely coming now.

"Oh no," Karson mumbled. "I'm gonna kill him."

"Don't just stand there, RUN!" Sam called as he rushed past Karson.

"CLOUDY DAY! IT'S A CLOUDY DAY, CAPTAIN!" Karson was first to fire, taking down the first man, tripping three. The new enemy now returned fire. Karson and Sam ran into the mass of people, attempting to flee.

"WELL, WHY DID YOU DO THAT, LIEUTENANT!? THEY WEREN'T SHOOTING AT US BEFORE!"

"THEY WERE GOING TO!"

"Lieutenant Serval, you have used your distress signal." Captain Richardson said through Karson's earpiece.

"Yes, Captain, it's a cloudy day, sir. Multiple enemy heavy ground forces are in pursuit of us. One EKIA. We need a meeting place. ASAP! I'm the only armed with my rifle. Carrion is unarmed."

"Give us some time, Serval. Keep running."

"WELL, WHAT DO YOU THINK I'M GONNA DO? SIT HERE AND LET THEM SHOOT ME? SAM! I'M GONNA KILL YOU, YOU KNOW THAT? DEAD. D. E. A. D."

"IT ISN'T MY FAULT!"

"WELL, WHO'S IS IT?" Silence. "TELL ME WHAT HAPPENED!"

"WHAT HAPPENED WAS ARMED MEN ARE CHASING AMERICANS, AND WE'RE IN DANGER OF OUR LIVES!"

"Serval, rendezvous at the parking garage across the street from your position. I'm sending the map to your HUD!"

"LET ME GUESS, SAM; THEY HAVE YOUR PACK TOO?"

"UM, YES THEY DO!" Sam called behind him.

Karson reached around him, pulling out his helmet. On the visor of his helmet, the map of the city, which Captain Richardson highlighted in red like a GPS in a car, the path of which Karson and Sam should take to reach the blue highlighted parking garage, where their escape vehicle awaited. Karson ran faster, catching up to his partner.

"Sam, here is my pistol." Karson handed him a weapon. "I want that back. It's followed me everywhere and brought me luck. Follow me. We're going to that parking garage. They're going to be right up on us, so we need to be quick. Fast is good. No mistakes now. Can you keep up?"

"I'm in big trouble aren't I?"

"Yes, but let's not discuss that now."

"Aye, sir." He looked on his shoulder.

"For now, just start shooting!"

"These aren't our regular enemies, sir!" His conscious poked through.

"NO? They're shooting at us though and-"

"YOU FIRED THE FIRST SHOT!"

"HOW WOULD YOU RESPOND TO ONE OF YOUR SAILORS RUNNING AROUND A CORNER, COVERED IN BLOOD, TELLING YOU TO RUN AWAY AND THEN ARMED MEN WITH A MORE ACCURATE AMERICAN GUN COME RUNNING AFTER SAID SAILOR, FACES ANGRY AND WEAPONS RAISED? NOW YOU TELL ME HOW I SHOULD HAVE REACTED!"

"SURRENDER!"

"I SWEAR TO ALL THINGS HOLY I'M GOING TO PUSH FOR YOUR COURT MARSHAL!"

"IF WE DON'T DIE FIRST!"

"WE NEVER SURRENDER! Captain, we are a quarter mile away." Karson relayed.

"Good! We see you. Just keep running!" The team's sniper spoke up.

"WHAT DOES IT LOOK LIKE WHERE DOING?"

"Sir, is there any way we can leave the Lieutenant behind?" The fifth SEAL on the team laughed.

"SCREW YOU MAN! SCREW YOU!"

"Serval, we're going to start sniping your pursuing hornets!" The sniper spoke again.

"GET THESE GUYS OFF OF US!" Sam screamed.

As the men kept running, muzzle flashes came from the garage in front of Karson and Sam. Warning shots fired at the advancing Polices' feet. This did little to slow them down, so Captain Richardson gave the order. "Light 'em up! Smoke them."

"Aye." The two Navy SEALs beside the Captain fired shots in unison. But for every police officer they killed, it seemed like more were coming from side streets. The SEALs in the garage could see the cops flanking Karson and Sam. "Serval, they are- "

As Karson turned down a side street, his face met with the end of an AK-47. The cop turned the barrel towards Karson, but Sam came in and collided with him. Karson took his chance and jumped up onto the wall, running over the scuffling men on the ground, and kicked the second officer's gun barrel. It got lodged into the chain link fence. Karson pulled his knife and slashed at the cop's throat, but missed.

"Sailor, keep those other cops from making it into that ally." Captain Richardson said through the com links so Karson would know what was going on.

"AYE!" The Sailors kept shooting, as did Captain Richardson.

Come on son, make it out of there. Use your training, Karse.

The voice gave Karson a push. "DIE ALREADY!" He yelled as a bullet lodged itself in the side of the wall, where Karson's head had been moments before. The cop paused shocked, and Karson saw his opening and stabbed him in the side. The cop collapsed.

"Thanks, sniper!" Karson said.

Sam, having killed his opponent, then took the time to execute Karson's opponent. Karson stopped and spun around. "CARRION! HE WAS UNARMED. I HAD HIM DOWN. THAT IS NOT THE WAY OF A SEAL!"

"Times have changed, man." Sam winked and ran past Karson. Karson was about to argue when more officers came around the corner, seeing their fallen comrade, and started shooting at the fleeing Americans in rage, bullets flying everywhere. Karson stumbled but ran after Sam, yelling in fear, but also to give himself an adrenaline boost.

"WHY DOES THIS GARAGE SEEM TO BE RUNNING AWAY FROM US INSTEAD OF RUNNING TOWARDS US!?"

"HEY! JUST RUN FASTER, CARRION!" Karson yelled.

"I can't do it!" His voice was hoarse.

"YES YOU CAN! RUN BOY, RUN!" Karson tried pumping him up.

"I CAN'T!" He slowed.

Karson pointed his weapon at the cocky, larger SEAL's feet and shot the ground. Sam screamed and ran faster.

"I told you could do it," Karson muttered under his breath. Sam's middle finger floated behind his body as he ran under a bridge. It was a straight away now, and Karson let his legs loose, overtaking his subordinate. As suddenly as he reached his top speed, however, and with the garage quickly approaching, Karson's joy was demolished as a police car pulled in front of the ally. Karson dive rolled over the hood of the car, but a cop grabbed him and handcuffed him faster than Karson could react.

He dropped Karson to the ground, Karson breathing hard in pain. His face buried into the ground.

Sam hid behind a pillar in the ally.

"WHERE IS REST OF TEAM, AMERICAN?"

"SUCK IT!" Karson spat mud from his mouth.

"VERY WELL." The cop drove his boot down into Karson's neck.

"AMERICANS! WE KNOW YOU ARE HERE AND CAN SEE US! COME OUT WITH HANDS UP OR WE KILL HIM!"

SILENCE

The cop looked around the scene. He picked Karson up and put him in front of him. He noticed a flash coming from the multi-story parking garage. He turned to his colleagues and ordered them to do something in Arabic. The cops in the alley turned and headed towards where Captain Richardson was.

"YOU HAVE THIRTY SECONDS AMERICANS, OR HE DIES!"

Five cops surrounded Karson and the ally, the other police leaving quickly, with death and bloodlust in their eyes, hungry for American souls.

"Let's talk about this, officer!" Karson pleaded.

He slapped the SEAL. "Shut up. You're in bad spot."

"Serval, if you can move forward three steps, I can help you. I can kill him if you move forward. Move forward, and you're home free." The order came from the SEAL sniper prone in the garage.

"Look, we are just here on a peace mission. You attacked us, we responded with force." Karson took a step forward.

"DON'T MOVE!"

"More." Richardson ordered for the focused sniper.

"Look, I'm being nice! No one else has to get hurt." Hesitantly, another step.

"I said don't move!" The cop growled.

"One more step." The sniper couldn't speak while slowing his breath so Richardson gave another order.

"I'M SERIOUS!" The cop said.

"You're going to die if you don't let me go." Karson taunted.

"Yeah? What are you to do to me?"

"Come on man we can- "

"Serval, cut the compassion, this is your life, step forward." The sniper growled, losing patience and focus.

"Please, officer…"

"Serval, I order you to step forward." Captain Richardson had made Karson's mind up for him.

The cop started to shake. Another step. The bullet ripped into his head splattering brain matter and lifeblood all over Karson's face. Karson hit the deck as Sam came out of the shadows and killed one, and the two snipers, plus Richardson snipers killed the other three cops. The Sailors took off running again.

"Captain, the officers are coming for you!" Sam spoke.

"We know. Hurry up!"

"Thank you, Sam! You saved my life." Karson panted.

"Welcome."

Karson, as he ran, jumped as high as he could in the air, and repositioned the handcuffs in front of him.

"THAT WAS COOL! HOW... Here, Lieutenant, I can shoot those off."

"No thanks."

"Just hold out your hand."

"DO NOT BLOW OFF MY HANDS!"

BANG

The bullet cut the handcuffs in half. Karson pumped his arms and reached the entrance to the garage. A cop had been stationed at the door, but Karson jumped, wrapped his legs around the officer's neck, and twisted, knocking him off balance. He drove his knife into the cop's throat and grabbed the rifle and pistol.

"Serval, stay hidden, the combatants are here. We're moving. Radio contact in few minutes." A static voice met his ears.

Karson and Sam sat in an elevator and closed the door. "Sam, give me my pistol." The Sailors exchanged guns, Karson gaining his and Sam gaining the African's. Karson whispered, "What happened to you when you disappeared?"

Sam sighed. "I knew you'd ask. You know I was hungry right?"

"Yes, I know you were hungry."

"Well I was, but someone caught my attention."

****

"We're in a war zone. Stop heckling your Lieutenant. NO FOOD! YOU'RE FINE!"

"Uhh… aye, aye, sir!"

Karson came back. The Lieutenant left back across the street.

"Thanks a lot, sir."

"I said, 'no.' You said, 'ask him.' I didn't think he'd do that!" Lieutenant Serval said.

"What did you stick up your-"

"You'll be cleaning the toilets when we get back."

"Sorry, sir?" Sam asked, stunned at his friend.

"You heard me. You'll be cleaning toilets. We're friends Sam, but I'm still an officer. You need to learn to differentiate when I'm playing, and when I'm being serious. You do what I say when I say it in these areas. Understand? If you don't, we'll take it up with Captain Richardson, and if that doesn't work…"

Sam had had enough. He was hungry, his stomach growling. He was a young man. A growing man who had to eat to stay strong! His mother's voice sang through his head. He turned on his heel silently and away.

He went up the street and turned a corner. *WOW! That is a lot of people. Oh well, I'm armed and American! I'm invincible!* And he continued through the market.

"Shit. Shit. Mega shit. All of these stands look disgusting. Oh, now that smells good!" His head swiveled to the left, and he saw smoke rising from the cooker. He licked his lip and walked over. "English?"

"Money?" The man retorted.

"Course." Sam removed some money and placed it on the table, the man quickly taking the money and putting some meat on a plate and handing it to the American. "Thanks, man!"

"Yes." The man turned to help another customer as Sam moved off into the crowd, eating and looking for more food. He found an English sign saying Al Sicomoro Bar and Restaurant and walked towards it, finishing his dinner and throwing the plate on the ground. *Someone will get that.*

"Step to side, man." A man standing at the entrance said. "You may enter in a moment."

"Excuse-" Sam's words got caught in his throat. "Who is that?" The doors opened and four men in suits exited, followed by a woman. Sam's mouth watered. "She's beautiful."

"No ideas, American. She is actress. Asmarina Tsegay."

"Hello!" Sam stuck out his hand. The woman smiled and reached. However, the guards stepped between them.

"Move along." They said as they walked by. Tsegay waved, but followed the men into the alley. Sam followed the group, ready to woo the female of his dreams! *You could be so much more in America!*

The group of six rounded a corner and Sam sped up to catch up, but as he turned the corner, no one was there. Cars drove past at the end of the alleyway.

"Here pretty lady!" Sam laughed as he turned, when gunshots erupted from a side ally. He jumped around the corner and positioned his weapon against the wall. He slithered up the side of the wall and rounded the side ally to find Tsegay running.

"Mmm. Foreplay!" He said, moving faster after her. "Those gun shots can wait!" Sam turned and found the bodies of the security detail. A scream echoed from the way Tsegay had gone. He moved further into the labyrinth and finally came face to face with a female held by armed police, a blade cutting across her throat. Sam's eyes bulged as a man grabbed his weapon, slamming his elbow into Sam's face. Sam drew his weapon but again, the weapon was taken. Sam dodged lunges at him but took a strike to the jaw and nose. He turned and ran back from where he came, finding the Lieutenant standing there like an idiot.

"RUN!"

****

CHAPTER 27 - Blue on SEAL

"Right. Move to the stairs." Karson stood and slithered around vehicles, making his way towards the staircase. He peered into cars and checked to see if any were unlocked, but none opened. "Sam, keep moving towards the stairs, I'm going to check out that police cruiser... see if I can grab a radio or something."

"Aye, sir. Tread careful." Sam passed Karson.

The blue striped white car sat parked against the wall, and no one seemed to be in it. Still, Karson moved carefully to the shadowed area. As he approached, he could tell the vehicle had been running, as the popping sounds of the engine hinted it was cooling off. Karson ensured the car was unguarded and used his rifle to knock out the window, and reached in, unlocking the door. As he did, a shadow rose from the backseat and grabbed Karson around the neck.

Karson screamed and flinched away, but the grip around his neck tightened. "SAM? SAM!" Karson shouted for help that never came as bullets rang out in the garage. "Alright then." Karson twisted and turned, pulling his knife and slamming it through the man's leg when he had a clear strike. The grip loosened immediately, and Karson slid out backward from the car and took off towards the stairs, after shooting the cop in the chest. "Never thought I'd be shooting police officers..." Karson ducked as rounds struck close to his head against the concrete and ducked down behind the concrete walls where Sam was hiding.

"Smoke 'em?" Sam asked, pulling a smoke grenade from his vest.

Karson smiled and pulled a concussion grenade. "Throw."

Sam threw first, smoking the garage, and Karson threw the concussion grenade to slow the advance of officers. "Up. Up the stairs." The two Sailors turned tail and sprinted up the staircase, and Karson radioed his team. "Captain, what floor?"

There was no response.

"Great." When he reached the second floor, he looked for Richardson, but he was nowhere to be seen.

"LT, let's keep moving! We have a window here; we should keep moving up."

"If we get to the top, we're going to be trapped, man."

"If we stay here, we'll be shot and killed for sure. We have a chance right now!"

Karson weighed his options and agreed. "Go. Let's find our work." He followed Sam up the stairs, ensuring the police officers searching the grounds did not spot them. Karson moved around more vehicles searching for his team.

Sam looked Karson dead in the eye. "We should spread out."

Karson paused and thought. "I don't like it, but okay... Be careful." He moved through the darkened floor as if this were a forest. He advanced around pillar after pillar, like a tiger on the hunt, no one to be seen. Except when Karson saw the point of an AK around the pillar closest to the staircase on the other side, he hurried and slid around the corner, stalking turning into pouncing.

Karson halted, weapon raised as the realization of what stood before him struck his cognitive abilities. "You're like... Nine..." The child soldier raised his weapon too. "Drop it. Hey, drop your gun." *Please don't. Please...* The kid loaded one into the chamber.

Sam ran up to his leader. "Oh my…"

Karson looked at his teammate. "He was about to kill me…"

"You could have disarmed him… he's a kid… was a kid… he didn't understand… What the heck, man?"

"He'd have gone on to hurt others…"

"YOU DON'T KNOW THAT!"

"We have to keep going, dude…" Karson didn't take his gaze off the dead child.

The cops heard the shot. One was on Sam in a second. Karson took aim.

"No, child killer. I've got it. Don't want you to shoot me either."

"Alright." Karson lowered his weapon as Sam kept fighting, infuriated. "We wouldn't be in this mess, and I wouldn't have had to kill anyone if you'd not gotten us into this."

Sam started losing the fight. Started turning purple. He looked at Karson for help. Karson gave him none.

The cop stared at Karson. "You're next." The officer smiled.

Karson smiled back. He raised his weapon and popped his skull. "I'd have let you try, but that face was so freaking ugly…"

"You almost let me die!" Sam gasped for air.

"Said you could handle it. Up the stairs. Now."

"Go down the stairs, Serval." Richardson's voice corrected the Lieutenant over the radio as a car across from him revved its engine and raced from its spot. Karson smiled and pulled Sam down the stairs and ran to the ramp as officers stormed the floor from all directions. The car skidded to a halt, and Karson and Sam hopped in and fired out the window with the others as the car burst from the bottom of the structure and drove through the streets after a group of cops amassed at the entrance, to which Karson screamed: "DON'T STOP. DRIVE THROUGH THEM AND ANYONE! IF THEY DON'T MOVE THAT'S THEIR OWN FAULT!"

Sirens and lights were behind the car in moments.

"SAM I'M ENSURING YOUR COURTMARTIAL OR AT THE LEAST, YOU'RE OFF THE SEAL TEAM AND AT THE RANK OF AN ENLISTED MAN! DO YOU UNDERSTAND ME?"

Sam nodded at his Captain. Karson patted his shoulder. He looked at Karson. "Fight now. Worry later. We'll get through this together, you and I."

"I thought you'd be mad too?" He asked.

"I am. But we are brothers." Karson leaned out the window and shot behind him.

"Thanks, sir." Sam smiled and began his duty, to ensure his brothers got home. Alive.

****

CHAPTER 28 - Fatality

Richardson turned and glared at Karson. "How is that my fault again?" He hissed. "You lost control of-"

"Sir, I have done nothing but fight for our team. Fight for our Country. Sir, you are not the same man I met during my time at boot camp. I will not serve a corrupt leader. If this war has changed you, then this is not a fight you have my support on, and I will gladly take a dishonorable discharge rather than go in on clouded judgment and get ourselves blown up for nothing. If you can tell me that you know what you're doing and can lead us, then I will fight and die alongside you, brother. But if you can't lead these men-"

"You think you can lead these people?"

"I don't want to be a Captain, sir. I like where I am. Over everyone, but still taking orders to pass onto them. Leading teams on missions I have been ordered to lead on. Still being lead on how to lead others. I don't want to be the boss, making decisions. I'd be perfectly content still being the new guy on the team. I just want to get this over with so I can go get laid again and live happily ever after!" Karson said, the most honest he'd ever been. "I'm tired of being a Soldier. I 'm sick of fighting. I want to relax. I want to be a human again. I want to have fun again, not fight this stupid enemy. This isn't even a war. It's a group of people with no real nationality. They just fight because they can. Kill because they can. For some, it's about their religion. They believe they'll be rewarded when they get to heaven. But I'd rather be rewarded here and now, rather than the possibility that the story may not be true. Everyone has that doubt, but I'd rather fight a country, like Russia or China, or North Korea rather than a bunch of dead nations with one man calling the shots. This isn't worth my time. It's just my job. I want Hatyara dead, so it stops."

"He's part of a splinter group Hunter. Do you know what that is? If you couldn't find him how are you going to find him now?"

"I KNOW. I KNOW WHAT IT IS. I NOW HE'S A SPLINTER CELL, I KNOW. I'VE KNOWN ALL ALONG THAT THESE ODDS ARE AGAINST US!" Karson sighed. "Sir, you and I fighting is never going to get this done. We will crack this maze; we'll find him. We'll do it. I promise."

"Just help me find him, Karson. And maybe we'll end the war."

"I will. Just don't fall apart on me, sir."

The two went up to the flight deck and boarded the choppers. A British Soldier pulled Richardson to the side as Karson moved towards his chopper.

"I don't like the feeling I'm getting, Captain!"

"What do you mean?" Richardson watched his eyes.

"It just doesn't feel right."

"I don't have time for this. Spit it out or move along. You're SAS. Act like it!"

"Doesn't it feel a tiny bit odd to you that they'd hide in a prison or whatever this thing is? I know it's not operational, but we still patrol and check on old structures from forever ago. Even World War II structures that have withered away to nothing. I know you do the same; from when you went to Germany or Japan. When you invaded North Korea under cover of night so no one would know you were there. The countries civilians don't know or have security clearance to know about. And countless other missions both of us weren't a part of that we aren't allowed to know of because there are secrets and forces even above our pay grades."

"Hey! I'm not going to tell you again."

"But-"

"ONE MORE WORD AND I'LL FIND A WAY FOR YOU TO BE OFF THE MISSION!"

The SAS Soldier's eyes widened, but without another word, he stalked away from the American to his helicopter after sharing a look with the strapped in Karson. Karson glared at Richardson who held Karson's gaze. Karson had an uneasy feeling from that gaze. Unsettled Karson started to look away. *Sorry, sir, but I have a job to do.*

Richardson held up his middle finger, then sat down in his seat and closed his eyes.

I swear, Captain, when we get back, you and I are having a heart to heart, and you won't catch me off guard this time!

The choppers took off at 0530. They headed inland with the rising sun, so the brightness would mask the chopper by the shining of the sun rays into people's eyes. The mountains and deserts flew under the United States and British Tier One groups as they approached their destination. Finally, a mile out, they reached their first contact.

RPGs pelted the mountains beside the chopper as they approached the compound. Karson's sniper opened the door and hung out, picking off enemy forces as the helicopters kept flying. Arriving at the compound, the men in the mountains must have radioed in because men on the roofs were waiting for the joint force. Multiple bullets struck the choppers from AK-47s, various other assault rifles, pistols, and more RPGs launched at the Black Hawks. Karson noticed one coming from his right as he dropped a rope. "RPG PORT SIDE!"

The pilot was quick to react, swinging the chopper around and firing his weapon, so it exploded mid-air away from the chopper. However, the force of the turn had knocked Karson out of the Black Hawk, and he was hanging on to the rope, losing his grip. The pilot was trying desperately to gain control; he didn't see the other RPG coming. As it got closer and closer, Karson knew this could be the end. He let go of the rope momentarily as the RPG smashed into the side of the door of the helicopter failing to explode, the ordinance falling to earth, exploding as it hit the ground. *Now that is some luck!* The door of the chopper was heavily dented, but as the flying machines of the United Sates had been outfitted with newly fitted, heavy duty armor, the rocket-propelled grenade didn't pierce the hull.

Luckily for Karson, he had regained his grip and as the chopper pilot regained control, Karson pulled himself back up to safety.

The SEALs aimed out the doors. Karson hung out the door to shoot targets below the helicopter, held by a teammate. He shot the men on the roof who fired the rocket launchers. Alpha team's chopper flew too close to Karson's, the wind, almost unbearable.

This is not going to end well! "CAPTAIN! TELL THE SAS TO SLOW DOWN, OR MISTAKES WILL BE MADE."

No one responded to Karson. Karson looked back at his men. "I am about to lose it."

"This is ridiculous. He yelled at me, he yelled at the SAS; he has no respect for you it seems like, and this is going to get us all killed! We aren't prepared for this and we don't know what we're walking into!" The SEAL holding Karson said.

"Didn't know he yelled at you. Alright, just stick with me, and maybe we'll live. Richardson is right on one thing, though. Now, my order to you is shoot anything that isn't an ally that moves!"

"Aye, sir!"

Karson looked back out at the events unfolding and found the SAS team fast roping down at the front of the complex. Karson watched as the men fought valiantly and entered the compound, listening to their coordinates orders through his headset. Even with all the mayhem that was unfolding, all was going as planned. No friendly casualties. *Yet.*

Finally, Karson's team, Bravo, hovered over their LZ and fast roped down also, while the British came under more fire. Karson was first to slide down and as he hit the ground, he moved three steps so he wouldn't get squished by other commandos who were coming down the rope and crouched to provide cover fire while his operatives joined him, shooting the men who were endangering his brothers 'from over the pond' as some would say it. Karson continued to lay over watch as a shadow presented itself to his right. His instincts taking over, Karson swiveled his weapon and attention right and fired three shots center mass into his target, the target dropping. He repositioned himself in his original position and moved his finger to his coms.

"Commander Church, Bravo team has landed. We're moving inside." Karson radioed the SAS team leader.

Enemy combatants spilled out of the building to clash with the U.S. Sailors trying to make entry into their newly acquired home.

"TEAM! FIRE AT WILL!" Karson shouted the order again.

"Good, we just reached the lobby now. Move to the center. We'll regroup there. Be careful, Commander. We'll find the entrance to the bunker together, and hopefully Hatyara along with it. That bastard isn't going to get away again. If one of us gets him, say over the com channels, and we'll immediately extract."

Richardson took over. "I want British troops outside. My SEALs are fewer. We will take the enemy." He stalked past Karson into the stairwell.

"I've-"

"Your orders were to follow the SEALs. You will get intelligence when we are done."

"Aye, sir." The British Commander's voice was full hatred, but defeat.

Don't see why we don't get intel now...

Karson and his team continued to shoot at the streams of enemies gushing out of the doors. "Team! We're about to be flanked and pinned. We have to push! You three, shoot the men coming out of the doors. Trip them up! The rest of us, go direct to threat. Pick off all active combatants you see. Show them how many fucks we give!"

"Sorry, sir, I gave my last one to the guy I just killed. Now I'm just killing for the hell of it."

Karson chuckled.

"Just kidding, it's just to survive." Karson again smiled and kept fighting. The major firefights had Karson's blood pumping. When fighting, Karson's training, along with everyone else's, kicked in so that their mission could be completed. It's almost animalistic, the Navy SEALs way of fighting, yet it also has trained them to show restraint in battle if surrender is possible. Not animalistic.

The SEALs regrouped on the British, taking their place. They quickly entered and made their way down into the labyrinth of the enemy controlled fortress. The fighting subsided slightly. Still, a few pockets of enemies could be found.

They're in deeper, for sure. "Team, be prepared for a large force down here when we find where they are all hiding. There should be a bunker." Sure enough, Karson rounded a corner to find a heavy door. The SEALs wasted no time planting explosives.

"We found it, Hunter. We're-" As they began to move back, the door exploded prematurely, knocking Karson and Richardson back, and incinerating five of the American Sailors instantly.

The world rang in Karson's ears, much like when the Humvee explode. Only this time, Karson felt blood gushing from his face and ears.

"DUCK!" Richardson yelled as bullets flew out the hole in the wall. The other seven SEALs dove to the floor as Karson threw a stun and frag grenade in at the same time. When they exploded, the SEALs regrouped themselves and ran down the stairs behind the door. They split up around the large space continuing to battle towards Hatyara. Karson and a teammate had gone together around a curve and found another staircase.

"We have to check this, sir."

"No, wait!"

The SEAL didn't listen and went down.

BANG

BANG

"MAN DOWN!" Karson screamed as he killed the tango. The other SEALs had to keep fighting. They pushed down the stairs. The fighting was intense. The SEALs finally reached the bottom floor of the bunker and killed the guards of the SEALs' high valued individual.

Hatyara stood from his chair in front of the monitors.

"Ahh... You found me. Good! Good."

"Hatyara. By authority of the United States Navy, and the President of the United States of America, you are now in our custody. You will be extradited to the U.S. authorities after we return to be tired for your crimes. You will then suffer your life in a maximum security military prison, where I will ensure you suffer every day."

"What crimes, do you speak?" Hatyara smiled.

Karson stepped forward and tied the world's most wanted man's hands.

He raised them generously. "You speak. I no listen. You will die. I will cherish the moment."

Karson was now nervous as they all moved out. *What does that mean?* More of Hatyara's troops were moving on them, but that was to be expected. But, what they weren't expecting was Pakistani reinforcements, under the command of a new player in the war. As the team reached the first floor of the complex, troops split the SEALs up. Karson took Hatyara and headed towards the front of the building, and Richardson headed out back.

"This is crazy Karson. What's your total?" Richardson's voice sang over his coms.

"Seventy-five. Yours?"

"Ha, I'm at one hundred and one."

"Dang it! You're beating me!"

"Karson, I want you to know something." Gunfire erupted through the coms.

"Captain?" Karson asked, pushing Hatyara around the pillars of the building. There was no response.

"You were my most trusted SEAL. Anything I said was to make you stronger. I know you, and you alone can do anything. Oof. And I want you to know how sorry and appreciative I am. Call the choppers. You're in charge now."

"HEY! TAKE HATYARA AND GET OUT OF HERE!" Karson threw him to his friend, Austin.

"Where are you going?" Austin called after the Commander.

"GO!" Karson ordered, before a voice cried for help.

"Commander, the Captain is down. What do we do?"

"Status?" Karson responded to the SEAL engaged with Richardson.

"Don't know."

Karson went into shock and stopped. He had a job to do, but also a friend to help. Karson had to get his team out with Hatyara. Alive.

"Get to the choppers." Karson barely got the words out. He ran out onto the complex grounds to find the British Special Air Service team all dead around the grounds. Richardson and three SEALs lay on the ground with them, as the choppers were landing. The other SEALs ran, Karson looked back to see his helicopter taking off with Hatyara, heading towards the ship. Karson ran over to Richardson and knelt down.

"Karson, I-" Before he could speak, a bullet ripped through his throat, and slammed into Karson's chest protector, knocking him on his back. Richardson's head dropped, his spine severed. His fatality pumping his life source out onto the ground.

Struggling to breathe, Karson sat up to see a man walking towards him.

"Supreme Leader, let's go." An American accent shouted.

Traitor. You killed my friend! "YOU KILLED MY FRIEND!"

"NO! I WANT THIS ONE!" The Supreme Leader shouted at the American traitor, walking ever closer. "He's got some fight that I need snuff out." His voice was barely audible in the roar of noise surrounding the area.

Karson snapped a shot through his HUD's camera as the man raised his gun.

"THAT WON'T DO ANY GOOD, AMERICAN!" Suddenly, bullets pelted the men around the Supreme Leader, and they dropped. He ran. Karson had tears in his eyes as he stood up and fired at the man who killed his friend as the new most wanted enemy rounded a corner and disappeared. Karson ran after him, shooting at nothing as he rounded the corner. The man was gone, as if he were a ghost.

****

CHAPTER 29 - Jump

"COMMANDER! WE HAVE TO GET OUT OF HERE. THERE ARE MORE COMING. FIGHTER JETS ON RADAR! LET'S GO!"

"FLY!" Karson yelled.

Karson stomped into the ground, and raced back to Richardson, pulled him over his shoulder, and felt Richardson's blood glide down his face. He raced to the chopper as it took off and jumped up and in. The rest of SEAL Team Six who sat in the chopper pulled both Karson and Richardson up by Karson's belt. Bullets were fired, and the chopper bounced with turbulence in the steep climb away from the threats. Karson gently laid Richardson on the floor and covered him with a tarp.

"He deserves a Military burial. Arlington. Our enemy is not afraid to die, neither are we. We must make them fear. We are the demons in the shadows that even a fearless terrorist okay with death will cower and run from. We don't die. They are the ones to die. We will avenge Richardson. I will avenge Richardson."

The pilots, out of danger, lowered themselves below the radar line meeting up with the other helicopter. They flew over the desert finding a lake. Small, but still with water. Karson's pilot decided to fly out over the lake. Big Mistake.

"Sir, where are we going?" Karson asked.

"Shortcut."

"The other chopper isn't going this way."

"We made a bet. We're going to arrive ten minutes before the other one."

"I don't care about your bet. This is too dangerous, and we're exposed. Follow the flight path." Karson argued.

"I'm the pilot. I've got this." The pilot jerked his gaze back.

"EXCUSE ME!? I AM A COMMANDER-"

"And I'm a captain. Now sit down and enjoy the ride, or I'll have you thrown off this chopper."

Karson pulled his weapon. "I want you to follow that other chopper. NOW!"

"Or what? Risk a court-martial. I don't think-"

As the other chopper left eye sight, alert tones flipped out. Too late. AN explosion destroyed the tail rotor. The chopper lost control, spinning round and round.

"THAT IS WHAT I WAS TALKING ABOUT! TEAM, BAIL INTO THE WATER! LIKE A DIVER INTO THE WATER, ARMS CROSSED, CHIN TUCKED!"

At only twenty feet over the water, Karson and his SEALs dove and hit hard into the lake water, skipping across like bullets hitting a wall, then sank like a ton of rocks into the darkness as the pilots, slow to move, smashed into the rocks and incinerated with the aircraft. When Karson and his SEALs resurfaced after ditching their gear, they saw the wreckage and swam away from it. As they hit the shore, they sank onto the rocks winded and shocked. *Richardson! I have to get his body.*

****

When Karson woke up, he looked back at the smoldering wreckage and saw enemy troops. His SEALs started to stir, and when they came to, he put his finger to their mouths and pointed at the soldiers. "Let's get out of here." He whispered as he started moving, keeping his eyes on the troops moving around the wreckage and the lake. "No sudden movements."

"WOAH!" A SEAL shouted.

Karson dove on his SEAL. However, the Pakistani troops had heard and spotted them and started sprinting and shouting.

"Run!" Karson screamed, standing from his covered position as rounds hit around them. He bolted towards the cover of the forest, hearing the SEALs following behind. Rounds bounced off the ground, still whizzing past Karson, a tactic for the SEALs, firing bullets to hit and bounce off the ground into an enemy.

He and his team were so close to the trees when the SEAL in front of Karson was shot in the head by a sniper. They were done. The SEALs dropped to their knees hands above their heads.

You just killed my friend. "I was born to kill you." His voice was deep and gruff, filled with grief. He'd lost too many friends that day. "WHY DID YOU FREAK!"

"I slipped!"

"YOU FREAKED OUT BECAUSE YOU SLIPPED, AND NOW WE ALL ARE DEAD-" Karson could hear the men getting closer and blacked out as an AK-47 rifle stock cracked into his neck. Even in his unconscious state, he could feel the torture that was already being done to his body. A poke to the eye, and a step to the testicles... His body unconsciously reacted, revealing he was still alive. Karson dozed in and out of consciousness as he felt the warmth of the wreckage and felt the blazing hot molten metal sear his back as they passed the crashed Black Hawk. Karson felt air than hard metal and heard the sound of a troop transport truck starting and tearing out across the deserted landscape before a blood smelling sack was tied over his head, and he fell into a disturbing sleep.

Captured. Soon to be tortured. And killed. No hope. No rescue. Just assured death. Typical.

When a Special Forces team is captured, the United States denies the fact that they were there. This is called plausible deniability. In this case, help is a miracle if it is sent. No one was coming for these SEALs.

****

CHAPTER 30 - Unspeakable

Karson woke up to find himself and the rest of his team strapped to chairs. The room was dark, and though it was medium size, the stench of death hung in the air, along with the musty smell of urine and feces, puke and blood. Rats scurried around the edges of the room, nibbling on the bone that was left over by many, many tortured beings, and blood and brain matter were darkly splattered on the walls. Evening sunlight cast in through the tiny hole of a window. Karson's men were still unconscious and barely breathing. At least they were all alive. For now.

Okay. Ow wow, that hurts. My head's pounding! How do I get out of here?

Karson tried tugging his arms off the cold metal chair, but the bindings were too tight. His hands were purple from the blood pooled in his hands with nowhere to flow to, and he could feel pressure in his feet, and as he tried to move them, he groaned in pain, stifling a screech as something sliced through his calf. He looked down to see his feet, burned, bloody, bound to the rusty, sharp chair.

I'm gonna need a tetanus shot now! THANKS, DUDES!

Karson started to pant as panic overtook his body; he was still a human after all, even if he was trained not to be. His body shook from dehydration and hunger, and his head pounded from the pain he had been inflicted *while I was unable to fight back. Had I been awake you wouldn't be alive.* The sweat and the dirt from his face ran into his eyes, or was it more than dirt? His eyes burned as he blinked the biohazard into them. *And here comes pink eye.*

Making noise, Karson needed to get his teams' attention. "Wake up! Guys! Wake up! Hey! Please wake up!" *Don't be dead!* With no stirring from his men, Karson took a different stance.

Karson started to shout. "HEY! HEY I'M IN HERE! COME AND FACE ME YOU COWARDS. Untie me and let's see who wins that fight? Huh? Are you too dagum scared to face a small United States Navy SEAL trained for you! HUH? COME GET ME!" The door in front of them slammed open and Karson flinched as his Sailors jerked awake.

Really? You wake up when the bad guy comes in? Gah!

In stepped an officer, or at least what looked like an officer. He wore his robes, but still looked like scum to Karson. The man got right to business, after clocking each SEAL in the head fairly hard with a club. Karson bared his teeth and growled, receiving another, harder hit to the rib cage.

"MMMMMMFPPH. OOOOOOOO! IS THAT ALL YOU'VE GOT? LET ME GO AND I'LL SHOW YOU WHAT DEATH IS LIKE!"

"You answer in lie, I hit you. Let's begin. Who are you people?" The officer said in broken English, with a quiet, soft, subordinate voice.

Low. Soft. Deflated but trying to keep inflated posture. Shaking hands. He's not the one in charge. The one behind him. Glaring at him. Trying to keep composure. Not an English speaker. Needs this one to translate. Kill him first.

"Why are you looking at him? Look at me." The man smacked Karson over the head.

After a pause: "Well, if you say so... I know you're not in charge. He is. Anyways, we are a United States Air Force para-rescue team. We were here to extract a group of United States Marines when we were shot down." One SEAL improvised a fake story, which now, all in the room would go off of.

Karson and his team were taught to tell false information and trained to adapt to any story one made up so they would be able to keep their cover and hopefully their lives. If one story failed, they'd conjure up another and another.

Never revealing the true story. At least, Karson wouldn't. He couldn't speak for his friends, whose eyes shone with fear. It was one thing to be a SEAL on the outside of an enemy torture camp, but inside, even the most hardened could crack.

"Good." The officer seemed to buy the hoax. "What was the Marine mission?" He asked looking around.

"We were not privileged to that kind of information, sir. For this reason. If we were captured, we would not be able to tell U.S. secrets. The United States would pretend we didn't exist. Saying we were rogue actors in the military."

The interrogator stood up and smacked the SEAL. "Again, what was their mission?" He asked, his voice shaking.

"Sir, we are just Airmen. We are not allowed the information Special Forces are allowed because we are just regular Soldiers."

The interrogator had decided he would kick up his brutality. He picked the Sailor up by his hair and had the men standing around him beat the Sailor down with their fists, feet, and rifles, finally, grabbing him by the chin and opening his mouth, sticking a rusty, feces covered blade into his mouth, gagging him. "The truth!" He shouted. The sickening sounds of metal and wood dulling Austin's teeth and cutting through flesh sickened every American in the room as well as the groans and slicing, gurgling noises coming from his mouth.

Karson had had it. "Enough! ENOUGH! I'LL TELL YOU BUT LEAVE HIM BE! Stop it. STOP IT! STOP!" The torture slowed to a halt. "If not, I'll never tell. None of us!" Karson had their attention. The SEAL's breathing was shallow now. His eyes drooping, blood gushing from the wounds from his mouth. His tongue, cut, hung out of his mouth.

"Put him down," Karson ordered.

"You don't control-"

"I SAID PUT HIM DOWN! NOW!" Karson lunged forward in his seat. "NOW!

"YOU DO NOT TELL US WHAT TO DO!" The man smacked Karson hard with the baton across the face twice. Left, right.

"YOUR BATON DOESN'T SCARE ME, TERRORIST! ITS EASY FOR YOU TO ATTACK US WHEN WE'RE TIED DOWN. LET ME OUT AND I'LL SHOW YOU WHO WE REALLY ARE! LEAVE HIM BE YOU PRICK OR YOU'LL NEVER LEARN WHAT WE KNOW." Karson spat blood at the interrogator. "I PROMISE YOU; YOU WILL NEVER BREAK US IF YOU HURT HIM. I WILL TELL YOU EVERYTHING, NOW, JUST LEAVE THEM BE!"

"You care for your friends, no?" The man asked, infuriating Karson more.

He nodded. "Yeah. I just showed that to you. Let him go."

"Then proceed." He nodded at the other men who put Austin back into his chair.

Karson looked at him and nodded. He spat blood, a small smile. *Good.* "We were told to pick them up and their package. Ten of them were killed. They should have picked up someone, and got in the first chopper. They left after we were shot down."

"We saw only you. Where are your friends?" The man inquired further.

"They were closer to the trees. As we were hit, we radioed for them to leave with the HVI. High Valued Individual. They did as we commanded. We jumped from the chopper. Our friends died on impact. That's why I assume you found no bodies on the crash site?" *Richardson?*

"Good. I like you." His attention was trained on Karson now. "You. Leader. Yes?"

Karson nodded. "Yes, sir."

"Be a good leader and tell me where this person is. Now."

"We were following the first chopper, sir. They probably flew to a base." He left out the part that the chopper was flying to the U.S.S. Linda Kingsley, anchored right off the coast." *I'm sure someone knows about a giant warship parked right outside your front door...*

"Okay. Where is base?"

"No idea. I may be the leader, but again. Not privileged to information. Higher than my pay grade. Above my security clearance. If I were to be captured, I couldn't spill the goodies. My guess is the base that is miles to the west of here."

"We will find it then." He said.

Karson nodded. "Sir, did you find bodies? SIR?"

The man left.

"Sir. There is no base to the west of here." Austin mumbled.

"Yeah. Let's hope they don't know that." Karson began shaking his chair.

"Sir, what are we going to do?" The SEAL on the right, Chance, asked.

"Conserve your energy, Chance, but try to get free. We're useless in power if we're bound." Karson kept trying to get loose.

Chance nodded, needing a direction that he could follow. "Aye, sir."

"Thank you, sir. For helping me." Austin slurred his words from the damage he'd sustained.

"You're my brother. I will always help if I can." Karson stopped and looked at him.

"Same for us, sir. Same for us." Slug nodded, also trying to get out.

"We're in this together, guys. We're going to get out of this together too. As soon as I get out of these bind, I'll check your mouth." Karson said. "Let me see your tongue." Austin obeyed. Karson nodded. "You're okay, man, just a cut."

"I'm sorry I slipped." Chance apologized.

"Doesn't matter. It was going to happen anyways. They were closing in. Focus on what is important now."

"I'm going to throw up." Austin gagged.

"Austin, you're okay, just give me a second. Deep breaths. Sniper training. In and out. Slow your heart, that will slow the bleeding."

Ten minutes later, to the SEALs' unpreparedness, the man came back into the room with five other men to separate each Sailor. Karson was put in a separate room and tortured, just like the others.

"THERE IS NO BASE TO WEST! TELL US WHAT YOU KNOW, AMERICAN." The officer took Karson for himself.

Karson was waterboarded, electrocuted, frozen, heated, sleep deprived, starved, refused water, poked and prodded. He had toothpicks shoved under his nails, his tongue pierced. The men began to unbuckle Karson's pants, ready to mutilate his manhood. AK-47s were used to sodomize as well, still hot after rounds were shot through them. Luckily Karson evaded both of these. However, Karson believed his life didn't matter in the spirit of national security. *I will not break! I cannot break!* He could only hope that his team was as strong, because Karson could hear them screaming in agony as they too were tortured. A form of torture Karson was spared *thank God,* was when a man cut another man's skin away, pulled his muscle, tendons away from the bone, so the bone is left attached to the body and exposed, only to be sanded down to bone dust.

"He's mine." The interrogator began unbuckling himself as well, as Karson's clothes were removed. Karson squirmed and fought as hard as he could as the naked, disgusting man approached him.

"The more you squirm, the more I yearn." He smiled.

God! Don't let me break! Let us get out of this. In one piece. Alive! Have mercy on all of us, even these idiots! But please, make this stop! Karson lashed out as hard as he could as the men spun him around.

****

CHAPTER 31 - Leave us

Each evening, the Sailors were placed in cells with others. Every once in a while, an inmate would attempt to attack the SEALs, and even in their weekend state, they were able to fend off the measly attacks of the insane. Also, these men were so crazy; they decided to fight the guards, at which point, they would be gutted, and put back in their same cells and left to rot, leaving the others to deal with the consequences. Some of the SEALs were sickly, puking and bleeding and beginning to become infected. Karson was doing somewhat better than the others. However, the injury he'd been dealt to his calf was giving off a weird vibe and ached every day, more and more and more. His whole body ached, from the torture he'd received by penetration, toothpick nails, being pulled and tugged in every direction.

Karson could hear the enemy talking about the men, and eventually, Karson was yanked from his cell after being placed with an individual who had peaked his interest. The man was not treated poorly like the other inmates and was given time out of his cell, and from what Karson picked up, the name Hatyara was mentioned a lot. As Karson made his move, however, he heard the enemy say to move him.

"Get him out of there!" One guard shouted.

"WHY?"

"He's bad news." The superior guard asserted.

"He's a tiny kid from the states," the other guard argued with his superior.

"He's the one Hatyara briefed us on. The best the world has to offer. He is after our leader, and with the courier. Get him out. NOW!"

Karson looked at the man to his right. "Courier. Tell me what you know-"

The men were tortured for days. The same schedule. Never the same way, but at the same intervals every day. Unspeakable horrors had been done to Karson. Sexual torture, bodily torture, mental torture. As the sun started to creep over the horizon, Karson would be subjected to being stripped naked, and feel a hot blade drawn down his body, bleeding him until the sun hung in the sky, beating directly onto the structure the Americans were being held in. Just like other inescapable, torture prisons like Diyarbakir Prison in Turkey, La Sabaneta in Venezuela, Tadmor Military Prison in Syria, Carandiru Prison in Brazil, or Camp 22 in North Korea, Karson had no way to escape while the men went to have their lunch break, as he was always bound in chains. This was no *Prison Break.*

After an hour break, and Karson's cuts being somewhat scabbed over, he felt the horrendous feeling of ripping skin as scabs were peeled off his body viciously, and new injuries were added, in places untouched, and on top of still raw cuts. His gag reflex worked overtime as he was fed rotting food. If he managed to keep it down, then fingers were shoved down his throat to make him puke, fed and forced to excrete diarrhea. Everything kept in just long enough to keep him alive. Having all of his hair plucked off his body. Extreme sweating came after dinner, then extreme cold. Upside down torture, whippings, urethral probing, nails cut away, dehydration, starvation, ball taps, knives, toothpicks, eyes held shut, and punches to the body. Each time, something different but on the same schedule. Finally, after a waterboarding session, the men tied Karson to a chair in rope.

"We'll return after meal, American."

"You do that." Karson spat at the man. The man stepped forward and slammed Karson's jaw with a hard punch. Karson again was bleeding, having lost at least fifty percent of his blood every day, brought near the cusp of death, but never quite given the rest he deserved. But he took the chance of a lifetime. As soon as the door closed and the men walked away, he started to work on the rope that restrained him. He knew the SEALs had to escape as quickly as they could, so he squirmed and squirmed; clenching and unclenching his body, deep breaths to stretch the rope until he finally wiggled one of his fingers free, bending his hand awkwardly. Slowly, he wriggled each finger out. A day ago, the sounds of his friends were silenced. Worrisome, because in training, each SEAL was trained to make a noise to let the others know they were still fighting. Karson's phrase was 'FUCK A DUCK!' Others were grunts, groans, and chants like 'Hard work work... Hard work work...' These frequently pissed off the interrogator, so the phrases were used when a sharp pain was induced. Now, though, sadly, it was quiet. Too quiet.

Karson continued working until his hand was free, and once his hand was free he wriggled the arm out, giving him the chance to work on the knots, loosening them, so they looked like they were still useful, but really, all Karson had to do was move and they'd fall.

I'm coming men. Just hold on a little longer. Karson was working on the last rope while he thought when the soldiers came in with AKs and picked a spot around the small room in front of Karson.

"You are the leader of SEAL Team Six, are you not? You have lied to us. We know where Hatyara is. We will kill you now on our Supreme Leaders command to your old cellmate."

"The courier. Why are Pakistani soldiers helping a man whom nobody even knows? Why would you work for someone who takes your country out from under you, and slaughters your own people? Seriously, explain that to me!" Karson asked trying to buy time to wriggle the last rope loose slowly, and also see if he could take information from these clearly uneducated men. "This is not the purge."

The soldier raised his pistol. "Not for you to know, American." The man nodded, and they covered the window with a blanket, plunging the room into darkness. Blinding darkness.

Karson calmly retorted. "Alright. Time for me to be leaving then, fellas." Karson sprang up and grabbed where the pistol was with one hand, and spun to the man's back, kicking the man beside him into the others, creating a domino effect. Karson grabbed the knife out of the man's vest with his other hand as the man pulled the trigger, trying to make Karson lose his grip, when Karson slit his throat, adding enemy blood to the chamber rather than innocent blood. The flash of the muzzle gave Karson the locations of the other targets in the room. The other men had stood now, and the man in front of the door turned his gun to aim, but Karson threw the knife into his eye, stepped forward and struck it deeper into his juicy eye socket, piercing through the orbit and into the brain. As he died, Karson grabbed that man's pistol. Karson aimed the pistol and shot the other shocked guards now standing around the room.

"Three, two, one." As the last man dropped, Karson grabbed a weapon, and ammo while opening the door and exited the room.

Karson's team had obviously cracked and told the Pakistanis everything. Karson ran past an open door, sliding to a halt to peak in. Karson's heart ached and tears formed in his eyes as he found his dead colleagues, each and every one…headless. Karson's eyes opened wide at the gore, and he vomited and covered the door in puke as he thought of what the men had gone through in their last moments. The feel of a cold blade ripping through the tiny veins and fibers around the throat; the feeling of cold as your face emptied of blood and the stress one's heart would go through as it pumped double time trying to send blood to a head that wasn't there, instead sending blood splattering all over the room. The feel of a hand pulling your head the rest of the way off from your shoulders. The sounds you'd hear and the sights you'd see as your body spasmed as it died, your thoughts and eyes processing everything for the last ten seconds of your life as your head too, finally dies. Watching your friend go through that right before you were next. If you were the last one, watching all of them go through that, then you too going through it.

Karson stumbled in and touched each man and cried. "I'm so sorry, boys! I'm sorry I wasn't in here with you. Maybe we could have gotten out, or maybe I could have gotten you to live longer… Maybe I'd have gone with you… I'm so sorry!" Karson sobbed and noticed the camera beside the bodies. He grabbed it and looked through, to find the videos of his men, being beheaded, like James Foley and Steven Sotloff, and others of every nationality. *Like Nancy.*

"Death Nation. Enemies of the allied world." Karson muttered a warming. "WE WILL KILL YOU ALL!" Karson shouted. He heard men running down the hall to him. He had to leave his men as more troops came rushing into the prison, but took the camera, so the terrorists couldn't take and use it against the United States of America and everyone else who now fought the terrorists who brought death to any nation it could get its hands on. He realized that it'd been hooked up to a computer somewhere and threw it, shattering it after taking the tape out. *At least you won't have that camera. This will end. Or I'll die trying to finish it. Either way, it ends starting now.*

Karson snuck around corners of the building and finally found a back door, after saluting his fallen men, and taking their dog tags for their families and military records. He ran across a courtyard and down a road that led from the structure. The men would surely follow, so Karson had no time to walk. He sprinted, running through the tall grasses like a lioness chasing prey so that if enemy forces came down the road, they'd not see Karson running. He continued to follow the road, hoping it led somewhere to which Karson could escape, but after what felt like an hour, he discovered a small hut with an antenna.

Radio? Radio station? Help. Extraction. Karson was so disorientated; his thoughts were sporadic. He stopped and readied the weapon he carried, and checked the magazine.

"Seven rounds left." He mumbled. *That's enough for me. Six more than I need.* Karson's confidence up, he stepped forward and tripped on a vine and fired a shot. "CRAP" Karson dove for the structure and hid around the side as the outside was clear until the door opened. He ducked back around the corner as an armed guard walked out and quickly scanned the area. He walked a few feet again and looked around. Karson slipped inside the door and found only one other guard. Karson snapped the guard's neck easily so he could level the playing field and then hid by the door.

The other guard, a police officer from the looks his uniform and the uniform of the man Karson had killed, came back inside and noticed his deceased friend and raised his gun to scan the room. As the gun crossed Karson's body, he lunged, grabbing it, and pulled the officer towards him, but the Pakistani front thrust kicked Karson into the wall. The cop pulled out his large knife and lunged at Karson, slashing at him.

"Man! Why you need a long knife like that?" Karson ducked down and punched the man in the groin. The man responded by squealing words Karson didn't comprehend from his foul language and kept fighting. He grabbed Karson and slammed him against the wall again and again until Karson started to lose consciousness.

I'm always getting beat, man!

As Karson kicked the man away a few inches, the man lunged one more time at the SEAL Commander, but Karson grabbed the man's arm, snapped it over his shoulder, and threw the man head first into the wall. The man tried crawling towards the gun, while Karson turned and threw the other man to the ground. He started typing, trying to find the English settings to the radio so he could call for help when a bullet ricocheted through the room. Karson turned and saw the man standing, and grabbed the chair, and lifted it over his head. The man shot again, and the bullet hit the metal beside Karson's face, and he dropped the chair. Karson lunged, knocking the gun away, as the man locked arms with Karson and both stared at the other. Karson slammed his head into the man's nose, his grip releasing and struck his nose with the palm of Karson's hand, cracking it up into his brain, killing him instantly.

"You wouldn't die would you?!" Karson fell against the wall and slid down to catch his breath.

After a few minutes of listening to radio traffic, Karson assured himself no one else was coming and closed the door, pulled the chair over to the radio, and sat down to call for help. He switched its frequencies and radioed a code to the U.S.S. Linda Kingsley.

"U.S. Navy SEAL Commander Hunter. Imminent danger to the ship and Hatyara. They have blown my cover. Leave these waters. Leave us behind."

Moments passed, and Karson started to worry that they hadn't received his message. Finally, a sentence came through the radio.

"We have a team on their way to you. Stay put." The message replied.

"NO! DO NOT COME LOOKING FOR US. TOO DANGEROUS. SOLDIERS ARE EVEYWEHRE. NOT SAFE. MOVE ON WITH THE MISSION. LEAVE US BEHIND. THAT IS AN ORDER."

"All due respect, we are not under your command. We hear you but will not comply. We have calculated your current position. We will send a team to retrieve bodies. Town nearby you, due south. Eighty miles. There is a means of transportation possible to the south. Follow it. You'll be alright. Get there; we extract by park area. Tomorrow at this time. Good luck, Commander. See you soon. Out." With the mountains full of troops, traps, and animals, Karson would need the luck, and he most definitely had to get down to the small park that the Americans would meet. Karson had no time to waste and hurried to grab the dead man's AK and uniform and changed and set off towards the town, stuffing his camouflage into a backpack.

****

As Karson continued through the wilderness, he met a railroad that was about a mile away. When he looked to his right, he noticed a smoke screen shooting up, indicating a train was closing the distance. Knowing that could save him some time, Karson high-tailed it to the tracks. Finally, the train started to pass Karson, and he turned to run alongside the train, and as it passed him, Karson jumped up onto the back ladder, which began to break, leaving Karson no choice but to sprint again. He kept tripping, so he raised his legs.

Monkey bars, like at school when I was younger. Karson passed one hand under the other, and summoning his last ounce of power, grabbed the back of the car and hoisted himself up onto the back car, hanging his legs over the edge, panting, and laying back to watch the land flow away from him, oceans of sand. Oceans of sand.

****

The Supreme Leader watched as 'Washington' welcomed him into the district.

"Supreme Leader. We captured a SEAL team in Pakistan. They have a leader. They call him 'Serval'. When interrogated, he deflected every-" The Australian man who sat beside Ojore was interrupted by the American.

"I know who he is. Tell me you killed him. I hate his guts."

Ojore looked up to the front seat. "You know this man?"

"I worked with him. He shot me."

"What is his name?"

"Karson. I'll tell you all about him."

"As I was saying, sir... He escaped. He sent this message." The man flipped a laptop and handed it to Ojore. A bloodied young boy came across the screen, and Ojore laughed. "This... boy?" He spat, mockingly. "This is the 'man' you all say is the Cat? The one who kills and terrifies? He is tiny. Miniscule. He is not threat."

"He attacked the compound your brother was at. He's got some strength in his average reframe."

"Then he knows what I look like." Ojore snapped his head up.

"He snapped a picture of him." The man took the laptop and turned up the volume.

Ojore nodded.

"Death Nation. Enemies of the allied world. WE WILL KILL YOU ALL!"   The boy shouted and Ojore stared at his eyes.

"Do not kill this man. I want to meet this man myself."

"NO, KILL HIM! OH PLEASE KILL HIM." The American screamed.

"But, sir?"

"That is my order." *I am coming for you, Karson.* "Kill everyone except him. I want him all to myself."

"What, you want to molest him? He's probably got a loose-"

"You scream or talk to me that way again, I'll finish what the SEAL failed to do and shoot you in the face." The American was fearful. "You got me?"

He nodded, crossed his arms, and looked straight ahead.

****

CHAPTER 32 - There is Still Good

Eleven hours later found Karson waking up to the sounds of chickens and goats in the car he was riding. "I did not fall asleep..." Karson looked at the sun. "I had to have slept through the night... only alive from the heat from inside the car..." He stood up and looked around. Nothing in sight except... yup... oceans of sand. Karson opened the train car and walked inside. *Gross...* Animals looked at Karson and scattered as he walked through the train car. He looked through the window on the other side and found the train occupied with people. *Okay... I'm going to have to get off soon. Hopefully at a village.*

An hour later found Karson jumping off the train and staring at a large town a mile from the tracks. From up on the hill, Karson could see a small area of a few Kashmir trees. Behind the town. More like a city. This place was kina huge!

Rendezvous. Tomorrow.

The city was way too large to go around, so he had no choice. He would go through town. His Pakistani uniform would draw too much attention to himself being American, so he sat down to watch the flow of people in and out of the city, starting to get sleepy from heat and dehydration. Finally, he saw a group of nomads leaving the city and followed them at a distance. When one stopped to relieve himself, Karson decided to pounce. He stalked up to the man, grabbed him, and wrapped his arm around his neck in a sleeper hold, and put the man to sleep. Karson quickly stripped him and put the robes over his police uniform. He wrapped the head dressing around his head and face, stole the man's knife, and left the AK-47.

He hid the knife and pistol and backpack under the robes and headed into the city passing the guards easily. Inside the city, Karson was still on high alert, even if he was blending in. He had practiced acting in his youth, and being only twenty years old, he was still pretty fresh with it. He found a marketplace and got to an empty cart. What he found made him euphoric. He was suffering from hunger and thirst, but luckily grapes were great to quench his thirst and famine at the same time. This cart had a whole bushel of grapes, and Karson took as many as possible and ate some and hid some and walked off.

He continued walking through the city towards the forest when a knife hit the barrel right beside Karson's head. He looked around to find a giant Pakistani man running towards him, shouting. Karson could only assume he was yelling الابتعاد عن العنب! [Alaibtiead ean aleunb!] {Arabic: get away from my grapes!}

Karson had no money. He had to get away from those grapes.

"Oh no." Karson's eyes opened wide, and he spun around on his heel and ran the opposite direction. He was so tired, though. He went around bends and corners, but the man always found him and was gaining.

Finally, as Karson was running, something drew him to an open door, where he entered and slammed it shut. The man of the household stood up and looked at Karson. Karson's face wrap had untied, and some of the police uniform was showing, obviously worn by a foreigner. Karson dropped to his knees, pleadingly to the man not to reveal him. The man walked over to Karson, grabbed him by the arm, smiled, and led him to a bed. He said, "Sleep," in English. Then spoke more in Arabic. Karson had no clue what the man was saying, so the man rolled his eyes and took Karson's clothes off, said "sleep," again and a left Karson. Karson's head hit the pillow, and his eyes instantly shut. No matter what happened, a year of no sleep would be replaced by comfort. Whether he woke up didn't matter.

****

Karson did awake, eleven hours later and looked at his watch. He sprang out of bed and found his Navy camo folded at the foot of the bed replacing the police uniform, as if the Arab man was saying 'don't hide behind a different uniform. Be proud.' They were sewn from where they had been torn, and they were clean! He hurriedly dressed, putting his boots on, grabbing his pistol, checking the ammo, and placing the knife in a sheath, and Karson then left the room.

The man was not there.

I could have gotten used to this. I wanted to say thanks…

Karson found a sheet of paper and wrote the man a message.

Thank you so much. You saved my life. God bless you! You have shown me that in a war where Americans generally hate the Middle East, there is still good here, and I found that in you. Thank you so much. I am forever in your debt!

-KH

Karson left the letter on the table in the main room, hoping the man would be able to translate the message. Then, Karson made a mental note of where the man lived, hoping to return to say his thanks in person. Before he exited the house though, he saw something on the mantle that grabbed his attention. 'Ojore has control of leadership.' *Strange.*

Karson exited the house after replacing the robes over his uniform and slithered through the city, attempting to lay low in the bustling city, trying to find a way out and to his extraction, without anyone noticing him. As the time ticked away, leaving only ten minutes until his desired extraction, Karson had to plan a new strategy.

With only half way to the extraction point covered, and another half to go, Karson spotted a man on a scooter round the corner into an ally. Karson knew what he had to do. He crept over like a serval, his nickname earned here as it always was, and he peered around the corner. The man was dismounting and heading into the bar. Karson took his chance. "Hey…" He whispered. The man looked around.

Karson threw a rock. The man walked faster, away from the now eerie alleyway. Karson bolted around the corner to intercept him and grabbed the man, pushing him against the wall.

"Give me your keys."

This man, though, obviously knew how to fight. The raised his knee, slamming it into Karson's stomach. He grabbed Karson's head and started to twist to break his neck, but Karson spun with the force and flipped around, knocking the man's hands off his head and slamming his fist into the man's throat.

"I am not in the mood to kill today. KEYS! NOW!" Karson frisked the man, feeling everywhere. He found the keys. "Good. Stop." The man was trying to fight. "Stop, or you're gonna get hurt."

The man kept fighting.

"Your choice. Sorry about this." Karson punched the man as hard as he could in the balls. Karson's hand ricocheted off, hitting something hanging in front.

"What, you got an elephant trunk down there or something!?" Karson pulled the knife out and smashed the hilt of the blade into the man's temple-just enough to knock him unconscious. "Stay down!" Karson laid the man down, gently, then raced over to the bike and drove out onto the street, pulling the face mask over his head again, to hide his completion and beardless face.

"I'm used to being the predator; now I'm the prey. I'm the one hunted not the other way around… Tis wrong!"

He got on the road and headed towards the back of the city to the extraction point. However, even with it being time for the chopper to pick Karson up, there was no sign of an American Black Hawk vectoring towards the area. The military had no time to wait these days for people to make it to a point so if Karson weren't there, the chopper would leave. He'd have to find a different way out of the land.

"DID I MISS IT?" Karson shouted. "DAMMIT!" Karson moved around, trying to listen to the air to see if he could hear the thundering beats of helicopter blades, when suddenly, as he stuck his head out, a bullet spun past Karson's face and hit the tree behind him. Karson "hit the deck" and drew the pistol he had, looking for the shooter. His cover was blown, so he removed the robes so he'd have less to trip him up if he had to run. Karson looked down a street and saw a man crouching as he ran towards the Kashmir trees.

The grape vendor. "Really, man!? I took a vine of grapes. Big whoop!"

Karson stood behind a tree, hoping the man wouldn't notice him. But, of course, Karson had inherited the stroke of bad luck from his mother, and the man came by the tree Karson hid by, saw him first, and he tackled Karson to the ground, landing on top of him. The man towered above Karson in height and weight, and so Karson had no chance in a ground fight. His best bet would be to shoot the man, but his gun was out of reach. The man started beating Karson over the head. All he could do was protect his face, and hope that the thunder noise he heard was American and not nature.

The man rose up, lessening the weight slightly on Karson, who took his chance, wrapped his legs around the man's head, and twisted, pushing the man to the ground, allowing Karson to stand up.

The thundering was deafening now, and a huge shadow blocked the sun from the ground. Karson looked up to see a Black Hawk hover over him.

Karson waved for the crew to drop a rope.

"AMERICANS!" A shout echoed from in the distance and shots rang out. The helicopter responded by sending bullets into the crowds.

Karson started climbing the rope. "Ha. Suck it! We Americans look out for our brothers and sisters."

Karson put one hand over the other when he lost his grip and fell back down towards the ground. Karson gripped tighter into the rope, using his feet to hit the grape vendor in the face, knocking him down a bit so that Karson could climb higher and faster up the rope. But the vendor persisted.

You're gonna die! "HEY! SHOOT THIS GUY! SMOKE THEM!" *Man, they can't hear you! Just get up there and-* "Ahh! How can you catch me so fast?" Karson was at the lip of the chopper, and the men noticed him but were busy fighting the attacking people, who now had vehicles.

"GO!" Karson shouted, and the pilot turned the chopper hard, and flew off over the city.

"CUT THE ROPE! WE'RE CUTTING THE ROPE. GRAB THE DOOR!"

Karson grabbed the door as the rope was cut. The man, however, caught Karson's boot.

Karson kicked and kicked but to no avail. The man kept climbing. As his head broke with the floor of the chopper so he could reach out and pry Karson's fingers off the floor, the crew caught a break and shot the man through the head, and he plummeted, deceased, to the earth below. Karson hauled up over the lip and hugged them.

"Thank you! Thank you! Thank you!"

"We look out for our own, Commander."

Karson shook hands.

"GRAB ONTO SOMETHING!" The pilots shouted as the chopper turned.

Karson looked out the door and ducked as red hot flames burned his skin, and his ears rang as the rocket blasted his ears. An RPG-7 flew through the port side and out the starboard side door, thanks to the talent of these pilots.

"WAHOOO! WELL, THAT WAS CLOSE, FELLAS!" Karson laughed and everyone high-fived in success.

"U.S.S. Linda Kingsley. She awaits you, sir."

****

CHAPTER 33 - The First Female POTUS

United States Navy Ship Linda Kingsley: Indian Ocean

The helicopter flew for two hours out over the ocean. Karson could only stare out the window and think of the torture his men went through. The pain Karson was in didn't matter to him anymore. And it took all his strength to sit still in the chopper which was taking a slow time landing. *Maybe I should just jump out.*

"There she is, sir. The newest ship in the fleet."

"That is not a ship…"

"New class, sir. It resonates with the new era set by the first woman president."

Karson looked on in awe at the carrier. The helicopter came in for a landing on runway 4's helipad. This aircraft carrier had been upgraded from the two runways of the standard carrier. This carrier was far more advanced, with a plethora of decks added, a larger tower for ship operations, and eight runways. Four for takeoff, and four for landing, with eight heliports. The four take off runways were the four at the front. One straight off the front of the ship utilized as two, two a forty-five-degree angle from that. Additionally, at the back of the ship similar to the front, were the two straight off the back and two at an angle. Each landing was connected through the ship in the case of emergency. That way, if an aircraft missed the cable, they could take off again. Eight helipads were on the sides of the ship. Four on the port, and four on the starboard. This ship gave 'floating U.S. territory' a new meaning.

Karson finally had made it onto the flight deck of the U.S.S. Linda Kingsley, the newest ship in the Navy fleet.

"Sir, if you'll just follow me, Admiral Thompson would like to have a word with you."

"Didn't know he transferred from the Elding. I just want to go rest for now. I'm sure you're the man on the ship that takes care of its guests, so could you please escort me there?"

"Right away, sir." He replied.

"Thank you, sir." Karson followed the Sailor.

He started leading Karson in the opposite way he had to go when a voice called him to a halt

"Serval? Where are you going?" The voice was low, familiar, and definitely pissed off.

Karson and the Sailor both turned around, but only the Sailor saluted, pissing Admiral Thompson off ever more.

"I out rank you, son, show me my respec-"

"I'm going to shower and sleep, sir."

"We have a debriefing!" To the other Sailor, he ordered, "You're dismissed. I'll take care of this man from here on forth unless further orders apply."

"Aye, sir." The Sailor saluted, looked at Karson, then turned on his heel heading towards the middle of the ship.

"I got nothing to report, dude. Let me rest. I'll talk tomorrow."

"Really? Your dead Sailors aren't something to report?"

Karson glared and threw the camera he'd taken at the Admiral and started to walk away. "Here. That is my report."

"KARSON. NOW!"

Karson stopped, shocked and enraged.

"YOU DON'T SAY MY NAME LOUD ON A SHIP LIKE THAT! ONLY THE SEAL TEAM I OPERATE WITH CAN DO THAT DURING A MISSION IF THEY RANK HIGHT ENOUGH. THAT'S A SECURITY BREA-!"

"I AM YOUR COMMANDING OFFICER. YOU DO WHA-"

"NO, NOW YOU LISTEN HERE! I DO THINGS MY WAY. I'M TIERED OF TAKING ORDERS! I LOST MY MEN, I'M TIRED, I'M REALLY REALLY HUNGRY AND THIRSTY, AND I'M GOING TO TALK TOMORR-" Karson's Admiral stared deep into Karson's eyes. Karson's eyes grew wide and he shut up immediately. *You've gone way too far, Hunter.*

"You do what I say when I say it." The Admiral's voice had dropped an octave and volume, but the rage and force were evident. "You can clean the blood off and sleep later. YOU'RE LIKE A DOG, BRED AND TRAINED TO TAKE ORDERS. THAT IS IT! GET IN THAT BRIEFING ROOM! NOW!" He grabbed Karson by his shirt and threw him towards where the Admiral wanted to go.

Karson glared but obeyed his Admiral. He threw a chair back and sat in it, however, the force of throwing it back damaged it, and when Karson sat in it, it broke, crashing onto him.

"OW!" He shouted. Everyone stifled their laughs and listened to Karson debrief.

Karson told everything. Not wanting to keep it in now that he was talking about it.

"Y'all stormed the compound and found heavy resistance..." Admiral Thompson prompted his SEAL.

"Y-yeah but… but we split up, and that's when…" Karson paused. "That is when Captain Richardson passed away…" Karson wiped away the tears running down his cheek.

Even in his saddened state, Karson's briefing was continued. "As we came around the lake and lost him, we were hit. My SEALs and I thought quick enough to jump early. The crew… I FORGOT TO GRAB HIM! I FORGOT-"

"Serval, you had to save yourself and your men who were still breathing. Richardson will have the proper burial, just without his body. He would understand."

"We got captured… you have the tapes… May I go now? Please, sir?" Karson was fighting his tears, his eyes beat red. His face puffy.

Everyone looked at Karson, then the Admiral, then each other, wondering why he was crying. They'd soon find out why Karson was about to break down. But he was a SEAL. They don't do that. Right? It has to be something bad to break a SEAL.

"We'll watch the tapes… That's enough for now. However, Hatyara was a good catch. I understand the man in charge of everything escaped. You should have taken the shot. We know what he looks like and are sifting through images to find his name in our databanks. It's, however, proving difficult, if not impossible. When we do find him, he has now been ordered onto a CIA kill list. Everyone is looking for him now. He is to be shot on site. We want it first. The inability as long as this war has been going on to be captured-"

"Excuse me, but I don't see any of you battered and bruised from hunting the enemy-"

The Admiral continued as if he'd not been interrupted, though his voice was stern again. "-by anyone has made the government take the next steps." Addressing Karson, he said, even more stern, "You are ordered, Serval, that if you see him, to take a shot. You of all people won't miss. You are too good for that." The Admiral was complementing Karson so he wouldn't argue again.

"You're right. I will shoot him on the spot next time I see him."

"Thank you. I can't release you from combat missions, but you can go rest. Dismissed."

"But if I see the slightest ability to catch him, I will do so."

Everyone looked at Karson with disbelief. You don't do that. In the military, you don't back chat a commanding officer, especially the leader of the fleet, and the head of the entire United States Navy.

"That is the same tactic you have used this whole war finding Hatyara, Commander, and look at where that got us! A lot of dead people." An officer spoke up.

"Precisely. That's what I'm going to do again." Karson said.

The Admiral held up his hands like 'FOR REAL?'

Karson turned his blue gaze onto him. "Only this time, I will see it through. If he has the chance to escape, and I can't capture him, rather than hope to catch him later and sacrifice countless lives, I will shoot him, not even playin'."

The admiral sighed knowing all arguments were useless against Karson when he made up his mind. "Just see to it that we get him dead or alive."

"Aye, sir." Karson said, content that he'd won.

"Go to bed." The Admiral ordered. "We are sending a team to recover the dead. They will be going home."

"Thank you." Karson walked out, no salute, nor handshake and walked straight to the armory. He checked out an M9 pistol, much to the displeasure of the Master at Arms who made it his priority not to have weapons on board at risk of discharge and ricochet. After, it was loaded and handed to him, he made his way to his cabin, which typically didn't happen for anyone except highly valued individuals. However, as the Admiral was Karson's friend, he had made an exception for the young SEAL. He'd been through enough. More to come.

Entering into the room, Karson dropped his stuff onto the floor, and laid his pistol on the bed and jumped in the shower. After, he climbed into his bunk bed, removing the ammo from his pistol and laying it by his head. A rifle holster was on the side of the wall had Karson checked one out. *Shoulda.* Karson started to dose off, the only thing making his life bearable right now was that the United States had finally had a good break capturing Hatyara, but at a high price. Thankfully, the ship lulled Karson temporarily to sleep.

War never waits, though. The sleepy always pulled back in. At 23:27, the ship jerked to the port side. Karson was jolted awake as he hit the ground. He looked at the clock.

"Ah!" Karson said, blinking sleep from his eyes. "Five hours? For real?"

The alarms started going off, and the red light in the corner was flashing. Karson quickly got up and found some black clothing and hurriedly put it on, grabbed the vest that had been provided to the room, and hurried to find the armory. He passed everyone in line for a weapon as well as the new Master at Arms on duty, who pulled his pistol.

"Halt." The Master at Arms moved to intercept Karson.

"Commander. U.S. Navy SEAL. I need a rile. Already have a pistol."

"Oh." The Master at Arms holstered his pistol. "Grab what you'd like, sir."

"Thank you, sir." Karson replied.

Karson loaded an M4A1 assault rifle and rushed past everyone. The ship continuously rocked side to side.

Not strong enough to be hit by torpedos. It's the sea wizzes shooting ordinance out of the sky. Those are some heavy rounds to rock this ship like that. It was hard to move on the ship, as it had increased speed and was firing at an enemy unknown to Karson as he made his way to the surface of the ship.

"Sir! You need a helmet!" Someone shouted, Karson assumed to him.

Karson spun around as a Sailor came up to him. He handed Karson the helmet.

"Thanks, man." They high fived.

"Don't mention it." As Karson looked to take the helmet, the sailor shot Karson in the chest. Karson fell backward onto the ground as the sailor positioned himself over Karson.

Obviously not a drill, Hunter! Karson coughed.

"Death Nation is everywhere. You are an enemy of Supreme leader Ojore! You must die." He said.

Karson launched his lower half up towards the man and kicked the pistol away. Karson was on his feet in a blink of an eye and had the sailor in a sleeper hold.

"Ojore? Is that his name?" The man could only choke. "What is his-"

"HEY! LET HIM GO!" Bullets rang down the hallway.

"Can't let you live, man. Sorry." Karson snapped his neck and threw him at the men. Then he turned a corner and exited to the outside of the ship onto the deck.

Admiral Thompson. Have to get to the bridge.

This was the SEAL's first priority in a crisis on board a U.S. Ship. Find the Admiral and keep control and order on board. As he reached the deck where he could see, he looked up at the bridge to find it completely destroyed.

Okay, still not a drill. Karson thought as he grabbed a Sailor running past him. "What is going on, Sailor?" He shouted at him over the noise of choppers, fighters, and weapons discharging. "I was just attacked by one of our own."

"A transmission of our location was sent out when you boarded. Two torpedoes. One was detected in time and eliminated, but another hit the ship on the port side under the water. I think a jet hit the bridge. The admiral was not there. We don't know where he is, sir. Someone gave us up. Someone betrayed us for the enemy. I honestly thought it was you but apparently not!"

"Okay. Let's see what's going on. We need to find the Admiral and keep Hatyara in our custody so go-" Before he could give the young Sailor an order, though, a bullet ripped into his head, dropping the scared young man like a rock. Karson ducked down and found the source. It was an enemy in red who had boarded the ship, and Karson ended his life quickly. He ran over to the man and took a mental picture of his uniform.

United States Navy. Sanders. My old commander, makes sense. The United States of Death Nation? This is their plan? Red Navy uniforms? Turn our military against us? Take it for their own?

He looked around and what he saw shocked him because he thought it impossible to happen to an American ship, one this advanced at that. Enemy mercenaries were climbing aboard the U.S.S Kingsley and Sailors were turning against their country. The ship was to be taken or sunk. Whatever they did after wasn't known.

They want Hatyara. Karson saw flashing muzzles as enemy sailors and mercenaries clashed against loyal U.S. Sailors in a firefight. Karson saw five mercenaries climbing over the railing near him and fired. They plunged back into the water. Helicopters were landing enemy soldiers and shooting the U.S. Sailors. Karson sprinted out of cover firing at the landing soldiers making his way to the starboard side of the ship. Suddenly, as he reached the water locked door to drop down to the brig, another explosion, possibly a torpedo, rocked the hull of the Kingsley and knocked her to her side again. The deck, being metal and wet was slippy, and Karson had no hold onto anything. His feet gave out, and he slid towards the water, dropping his M4.

Grab the side- An enemy came rushing at Karson from the side and Karson rolled to the side firing the pistol, and rolled under the railing unable to grab it, hitting the water from fifteen feet up, his pistol disappearing to the depths.

Hitting the water un-expectantly, he gasped from the impact sucking in water to his lungs. He spluttered at the surface of the water again as two more torpedoes hit the Kingsley before she finally started firing back again. Her cannons started shooting into the water hitting the submarine and her machine guns spun and engaged the enemy choppers, knocking them out of the sky. She had managed to fire off the two helicopters and seven F-16's strapped down on her massive flight deck, and they combated the enemy fighter squadron with precession.

The helmet Karson had on allowed him to place a thermal goggle over his eye, and he dropped under the water to see what was hitting his ship.

That is a huge ship! That's a huge submarine. Karson took a picture of the image as the object floated away into the darkness.

That is creepy! The only reason that it would disappear like that is if it had its prize. Hatyara escaped. Coming back up to the surface, Karson gasped for air and grabbed onto some debris and also floated away into the darkness; only his trajectory was helpless to do anything useful.

****

After the ship had fallen out of sight of Karson an hour ago, and no contact with the ship, Karson felt sand beneath his feet and hauled his body up the steep slope onto a hopefully Death Nation undiscovered and uninhabited island. The trees would have to provide a place to rest tonight before he could work on anything tomorrow.

You have been going nonstop for a year, Karson. Rest tonight. You can take a one-day break.

He found an easily climbable tree and slithered up it, onto a low branch. He was unarmed so if someone was on the island and saw him;

he was a sitting duck. But he was too exhausted to care, and death would be an easy way out of this difficult time in his life.

Karson uncomfortably fell asleep on the branch almost instantly, exhausted from his wading in the water, with a current that seemed to want to drag him down. His dreams were cluttered with death, injury, gore, and the uniforms he'd seen.

The flag looks like a pirate flag, only more like Hell than anything else. Their uniforms red, like blood. Also like the dark side.

He continued to dream of a spider, the size of a person spinning Karson into a web and felt q-tips on his face. Karson's eyes flew open and saw the eyes of an enormous spider staring back at him, deciding whether or not Karson's boy face was edible. Karson's hand was on his face faster than The Flash could have run to the Grand Canyon. When he killed it and the guts slid over his face, he squealed like a girl as more spiders fell from the leaves onto his body. Out of everything in the world, bugs and sometimes spiders were his biggest fears. No enemy combatant or animal. Just insects and arachnids. Nothing made Karson more of a sissy than that.

As Karson bolted out of the tree and walloped the ground, he could hear buzzing, and that sent chills down his back.

Water. Bugs don't go in the water, right? He sprinted down the… Well, he sprinted, slipped, and rolled down the sand hill into the water. The coolness of the water made his aching bones chill, and the insects didn't seem to be on top of him, so he relaxed. That is until he heard a fast boat coming up onto the beach. Karson rolled over and swam along the shore of the island until he spotted a shadow walking up the hill.

I have to see who that is…

No, you don't. That is a 'Death Nation' crew. Stay away from it-

I'm still a Navy SEAL…

Ugh. You're gonna die.

It is my job… Stop arguing with your chiding conscious. Find your work. Eliminate it. Then get some rest.

Karson crept up the incline and followed the shadow into the trees. Listening, he heard the crashing of a person through the undergrowth and Karson stealthily closed the distance. In the cover of the trees, he called out.

"Who's there?" He shouted at the dark figure in front of him.

"Karson?" The figure spun in a circle. Looking around, he shouted, "Karson is that you?"

"Who... Admiral? Sir, you're alive!" Karson ran over to him and saluted him. "Are you alright, sir? That bridge was destroyed."

"I left just before the missile hit, thank God." He said calmly. "Now, we need to get to the boat and get back to the Kingsley before it leaves us behind. They took her, Karson. Our own men betrayed our ranks for Death Nation. And our other commandos are retrieving bodies. We were defenseless onboard. We have to take our ship back. We have Sailors and Marines still battle ready. We can do it. We have to take that ship back, Karson, or our own payload of ordinance can be used on any innocence around the world. Also, there was a Coast Guard Ship nearby being used as a battle vessel. It will be our transport now."

"Can our guys kill their own, sir?"

"If they have to, I think they will. But after, I don't know what will happen."

"Alright. Let's do it."

They both hugged and headed back to the small fleet of small craft. Karson hopped in with the Marines, to talk to the leader, who wasn't for killing his brothers and sisters.

"Look... They took on the Flag of Death and killed our people. I just want you to be prepared, cause you're gonna shoot someone who shoots at you and you'll find they wear the same uniform as you, but they don't support it. It's just a tactic to take you by surprise. You have to do your job and do what is right."

****

CHAPTER 34 - Lights Out

"You sure 'bout this, sir?" Karson asked the Admiral a mile from the ship as they split into sections to board the ship at four points.

The plan was as follows. The four crafts would disembark from the Coast Guard Cutter and race to board at their respective points at the stern of the commandeered US Naval Vessel: Karson and Thompson's teams, Alpha and Bravo teams would head below decks and flush everyone out to the top. Team three and four, led by the Marines, would stay on the deck and pick off people on the flight deck as well as people rising from the hull of the ship. Snipers were sure to be on the destroyed bridge so they would also take those shooters out. Once the major areas of the ship were cleared, all four teams would make their way to one of two places. Karson and one Marine team would join forces and take the weapons rooms-the armory and the war room where weapons and tactics were executed. Thompson and the other Marine team would make their way to the secondary bridge and take anyone who was holed up in there. Rules of engagement were limited to this: don't get shot, and eliminate anyone and everyone that was loyal to Death Nation and release the crew members still alive and held captive, wherever they are. Definitely shoot red, watch out for dirty blue.

Thompson decided the time to attack was now. "Use any force necessary to defeat the threat, no matter who or what it is." The dawn light starting to fill the openness of the ocean, would provide excellent cover still for the dark fast boats on the dark water, but also provide enough light to see any dark uniforms patrolling the decks of the gray ship.

"Alright. Move. Use the boarding equipment that each boat is equipped with. It has a harpoon gun that fires a three-pronged hook up to the railings where it will hook in, and with the rope attached, let you climb to the top. Once on top, drop the hooks back down to the boat pilots who will move away and behind the ship so as not to be detected. Any final questions of our assignments?" Nobody spoke. Admiral Thompson turned to Karson. "You up for this, Serval?"

"Aye, sir," Karson responded. "Let's take our ship back!"

"Do you want to kill?" A Marine asked Karson.

"Huh? For now, yes. Hell yes. They killed our brothers and sisters. That is unacceptable."

The fast boats powered up and tore through the remaining mile between the crew and the ship. Once on approach, the engines were silenced and the four boats glided into their positions, the light rumble of their engines masked by the massive ship's noise from the water she kicked up and her engines. No one on board could hear them coming; and because these fast boats were U.S. Navy made, they were harder to detect on radar, as the hull of the boats, the engines, and design work of the boats were specific to not being detected. Less noise, faster approach, material that cuts through, rather than pushing through water.

Karson's Defender-class boat reached the Linda Kingsley first and skirted around the bow of the ship to the port side. Karson grabbed the boarding kit and fired up to the railings, the hook sticking the first time. He went first up the rope, a basic drill from training that every Soldier, Marine, Sailor, and Airman should have gone through. The normal height from the water sixty feet, the Kingsley a bit more of a climb. He reached the top in moments, the one hundred and twenty feet from the water to the flight deck of the newest and biggest U.S. aircraft carrier an easy climb.

Karson's team started rising, but already a problem arose. Men were patrolling the fight deck. Karson had to wait until Thompson was up to go below deck, but to do that he'd have to cross the distance from the rear of the ship to the island (the tower of the aircraft carrier) to enter, as the hanger doors were sealed tight. Outside, in the middle of the flight deck. IF they made it, they'd have to break into the island, costing time in the open.

The patrol continued to close in on Karson's location as Thompson's hook clanked into a holding position, alerting the patrol of intruders. Karson and his team had thrown their hook back down to the boats below and had gone prone like their commander. Karson motioned for a Sailor to come up beside him and whispered an order.

"Admiral team cover blown. I take right; you take left. Fire on three."

The men raised their weapons and moved towards the back of the ship.

"Once their out of the light." Karson waited for the spotlight to pass over the patrolling men, and counted. "One. Two..."

Thompson's head came over the rail, and he and the man on the right locked eyes. The man raised his gun laughing. "Looks like your luck just ran out, sir!"

"Seaman, don't!" The Admiral pleaded, his free hand lifted in surrender.

"Three," Karson whispered.

Karson and the second Sailor fired. Blood splattered out of both mens' heads and they crumpled to the ground. Karson and his team scurried over, avoiding the spotlight, to where Thompson was boarding along with his men.

"Thanks, Serval." The Admiral shook his hand.

"No problem, sir. Team, dump 'em in the ocean?" Karson fulfilled his responsibility as SEAL commander.

"Aye. Quickly. I want to get in-"

"Island." Karson winked as he interrupted. "Always a step ahead of you, my friend.

The Admiral sighed as he and Karson tossed the bodies overboard. "I hope the Marines-"

"They'll figure it out, sir. For now, let's worry about ourselves. Everyone focus up. We're going to enter into the island and head all the way down. From there, I'll head towards the front of the ship. You guys head back. Clear each level, rising towards the bridge. Hopefully, by then, the Marines will have it, and we'll have located our crew."

"What happened to the Serval that boarded my ship earlier mid-panic attack?"

"Still here, sir. But, I'm working right now. Gotta keep a level head."

"Aye. Karse- Serval, constant radio contact, alright?"

"Yes, Admiral, unless otherwise unavailable. Let's move. Everyone, on me." Karson led the way towards the island, taking one more suppressed shot at the guard by the door. "The sharks will have a feast tonight!" Karson smirked. Two Sailors quickly pulled the man around the island and tossed him also into the ocean, then regrouped as Karson finished wiping the blood away, Thompson opened the door and all men entered into the ship after three tense minutes. The key code was changed. Luckily, Thompson had an override on his duty issued cellphone of all things.

Karson smiled. "Pretty sure that's not allowed."

"Shut up and keep watch." The Admiral punched Karson's shoulder.

Karson knew this ship like the back of his hand, but because it was now under enemy control, taken by the help of some of her crew, the ship now seemed foreign and unwelcoming. Like entering into the abyss that awaited the SEALs in China.

The men quickly descended into the bowels of the ship to the engine room which took the entire bottom of the ship. Karson and Thompsons' teams split, Karson's heading forward, Thompson's heading backward.

Little resistance at the bottom, Karson immediately found that the enemy crew were guarding those of the still loyal American crew, but because a giant ship like this needed manpower to run it, the loyal crew was under duress to make the ship move.

"Admiral," Karson whispered. "Weapons tight. Friendly crew engine workers guarded by enemy. Shoot wisely."

"Aye. Still vectoring through. No enemy contact."

Karson picked his targets wisely, shooting the men in the darkness and farthest away from the center as possible, so their deaths would be silent and undetected especially by the noise in the room. If the men were closer, they'd hear, but far away, not a chance. Once they were all down with no one the wiser, Karson's job got tougher. There were still eleven men, and he only had eight on his team, nine with himself. He had to drop the ranks of the enemy, but to do that, he'd have to be silent and to do that, he'd have to sneak and kill, and in order to sneaky sneak, he'd have to separate the men who stood facing each other in the light.

Think it through...

"Sir..." One of Karson's Sailors asked.

"Shh. I'm thinking..."

"The lights, sir. Shut the lights out." He ignored Karson.

Karson looked at the dumb Sailor. "That would mean we'd have to shoot in the darkness. We have no NVGs."

"Pick three men you're going to kill. Shut the lights out, shoot them. Knife them. Kill them somehow. We'll pick our eight targets. When the lights go off, for at least ten seconds they will be unmoving. Shocked. The lights come back on in about ten seconds so if you miss, lights back up, pop, pop, pop!"

"Sailor, I-I..." Then it clicked. "Sailor, I think you're a genius!"

"You'd have come up with it quickly too, sir. Had you seen the light switch on the wall there?"

"What is your name?" Karson asked. "Ya know what, later. It's Trip cause we're tripping these guys up. Ya know, we could use a guy like you!" He high fived the Sailor, then put himself back to his mission.

Karson snuck around in the shadows towards the light switch and picked his three targets closest to the switch. A clump of guys standing by the switch. Karson motioned to the Sailors who the three he was to kill were. As Karson approached the switch, however, a marine from the team rounded the corner and entered the door right beside the light switch and kicked Karson onto his back. The men beside the light post noticed the movement and sounds and turned. Karson looked up at the marine and the marine looked at Karson. Karson looked at the men in the room starting to smile and ready their weapons.

You guys must get hard and get off to this insanity, don't you?

The marine looked back at his team, then down at Karson again, the marine raising his weapon.

Bollocks.

****

The Marines hopped over the railing easy-peasy, their Defender-class boats speeding away into the dark, they noticed the door to the island already opened.

"The SEAL and his teams must already be inside. What are we doing, up the island and back down towards the secondary bridge?"

"Yeah. Except..." Gunshots rang through the night air. "We have different plans." Three of the fifteen Marines from Polar Bear squad lay dead from the bullets of their brothers. The marines hurried to the island, ready to hunt and fry some SEAL for dinner.

****

Admiral Thompson watched Karson and his team disappear into the darkness and too made his way into the dark towards the back of the ship and engine room.

The team came up on a staircase into the higher decks of the ship and Admiral Thompson pointed it out to his team.

No contacts, yet...

Admiral," Karson whispered through the communication links. "Weapons tight. Friendly crew engine workers guarded by enemy. Shoot wisely."

"Aye. Still vectoring through. No enemy contact."

The Admiral's Helmsman spoke up. "Admiral, do we head upstairs yet, or no?"

"Not yet. Wait until Commander Serval says."

"Why do you take orders from him, sir?" The Navigator now asked.

"I don't." The Admiral looked over his shoulder. "But for my orders to be useful, I need someone I can trust that has been in the field and knows how to fight better than any of us. And trust me, that SEAL knows how to-"

"ADMIRAL... MARINES. ENGAGE THE MARINES. TRAITORS. WE'RE UNDER ATTACK BY THE MARINES. REPEAT, DO NOT TRUST THE MARINES!"

The Admiral turned on his heel, hearing gunfire behind him and raced towards Karson.

"Thought you said he could protect himself." The Helmsman was struggling to keep up.

"He can. His team, I'm not so sure about. Have faith, Carter. Have some faith."

The Admiral raced along through the engine room until a figure came down the stairs and raised his weapon. A marine stood in the way, guarding the path to rescue the other Navy Team. Gunfire still ripped through the hull of the ship, and screeches of terror and pain and death called in agony for help. The alarms on the ship started going off, and the red lights started flashing.

"Just where do you think you're going, Admiral Thompson?" He didn't move from the stairs.

"Through you if I have to..." The Admiral's eyes widened as five marines joined the former.

"Really? Not if we have anything to say about it." Like hyenas, they laughed.

"Drop your weapons. Or don't. It doesn't really matter. We're going to execute you anyways, whether right here, or above deck. Makes no difference to us. Just as long as we get to pop, pop, pop your heads with a bullet or execute you at Guantanamo."

The marines chuckled satanically and raised their weapons.

Thompson and his team too raised theirs.

Suddenly the lights went out, and the weapons flashed in the dark.

Admiral Thompson felt something warm crash into him and hit the ground. Someone lay on top of him, the Sailor convulsing as a bullet ripped his throat veins out of his skin, splattering blood like a loosened firehose all over the room. Thompson had to escape. He crawled up the stairs towards the lit hallway. His mission was the same. Karson would have to take care of himself. The crew of the ship had to be found now, or else Death Nation would kill the tiny American crew members left, if any were still alive.

More Death Nation sailors, however, met the Admiral upstairs. And they too shot their weapons. Thompson fired as he ran for cover.

CRAP! This is impossible. How does… I don't know…

****

CHAPTER 35 - Red on Blue

I *have the will to win, that's how I'll succeed.* Karson stared down the barrel of the gun of the marine.

"We all fight for the same team, sir."

"Really? The Supreme Leader is the man you follow?"

"I meant the flag." Karson glared at the marine.

"We don't follow the rules labeled by a piece of cloth. We follow what makes a man strong. And that is-"

"You support a man who kills and rapes and drinks. He doesn't care about you. He only wants-"

"DO NOT INTTERUPT ME!"

Piss him off just enough to cloud his judgment. Check.

"Really? I thought the only person that could tell you what to do was your boy, Ojore!"

The marine took a step forward and grabbed Karson, pulling him to his feet. Karson screamed.

Make him believe you're in pain. Gain your feet. Check.

"You know what. For my final day as an American Marine, I'm gonna enjoy killing you. Just to prove that Marines still are better than the Navy. Then I'll be a Death Nation marine."

"See. You still think like an American service member." Karson put air quotes around his words. "'I'm so badass! My branch is fantastic!' That doesn't sound like Death Nation to me!"

"Goodbye, Mr. Serval." The marine produced a knife and hurtled it towards Karson.

Step three, disarm and take leader hostage. Karson let go of the man's hand and stiff-armed the man at his wrist, drove his other hand down and free from the man's grasp on Karson's wrist simultaneously, lifted the man's arm and ducked under, spinning the man in the air. Karson hoisted the man up, knife in his possession, and slid it into place, slicing ever so slightly the man's throat to cause blood and let the men and the marine know who was in charge.

"Wait! Hold on!" The marine whimpered.

Karson lowered his voice and jerked the man around. "Tell your men to stand down."

"WAIT!"

"TELL YOUR MEN TO STAND DOWN AND PLACE THEIR HANDS ON THE WALL OR I'LL HAVE NO PROBLEM SPILLING YOUR LIFE'S BLOOD ALL OVER THE FLOOR. DO IT NOW OR I'LL KILL YOU WHERE YOU STAND. ONE. TWO." Karson started adding pressure and pulled the knife towards him.

"Okay, okay! Do as the man says, guys." The marine croaked. The men did as their leader said.

Karson ducked his head to his coms and radioed the Admiral, as the man started to struggle, and a gun went off, hitting the man in the chest, piercing his armor and his heart. The man died instantly, and Karson threw him at the others lunging for their weapons. Karson's crew started shooting as Karson ran for cover behind an engine and shouted into his coms. "ADMIRAL... MARINES. ENGAGE THE MARINES. TRAITORS. WE'RE UNDER ATTACK BY THE MARINES. REPEAT, DO NOT TRUST THE MARINES!"

Karson drew his pistol and fired at the ten remaining combatants. Bullets flew every which direction, ricocheting off the hull of the ship, hitting Karson's teammates and the Marines.

THIS IS RIDICULOUS! Karson thought as he killed man after man. "Team. Keep firing, but make your way through that door up to the next deck. We need more fighters. We have to find the crew. Kill anyone, even friendlies who raise a weapon against the U.S."

"Aye, sir." A voice replied.

"Follow me!" Karson broke from cover, firing into the faces of the enemy sailors and marines, dropping two more as his team finished off the final survivor and raced up the stairs. The engineers in the room followed, hoping to get a little taste of the action as well, a break from having to slave away in the hot engine room. Karson made it up onto the next deck, alarms going off, people running up and down hallways with guns. Karson honed in on the people pointing weapons at someone running down the hall. "ADMIRAL!"

The men turned and fired at Karson, who shot back, ducking down a hallway.

Think, Karson! THINK! Uh... Where would the prisoners be? Huh? You just took a ship with your traitorous friends... Where would you place your former brothers and sisters? They'd not need to put them under the water line on the decks 'cause they know we're unlikely or unable to sink a multi-billion dollar floating United States of America... They'd want the prisoners far from the armory... They wouldn't kill them for leverage... Karson stopped. Eyes wide. *THE HANGER... THAT'D BE A GOOD PLACE TO START!*

Karson turned and made his way up to the third deck from the second. *Okay... Engine room, second deck, third deck, hanger!* Karson ran up the stairs again from the third deck to the hanger level. *Guards will be there. Stealth. They're banking on surrender so we don't shoot the explosive ordinance for the jets. But we have to shoot so we'll shoot precisely. No second chances here.*

Karson crept along the corridor. He turned down the hallway. This deck was quieter. When he made it to the door, he realized why.

Man. Every damn troop and their mother has to be right here, don't they? 'Protect the prisoners!' Why can't you just let us win? Huh? Or why not just stop fighting, how 'bout? "Admiral? Come in. Admiral, do you read me?"

"Karson. Where are you?"

"Outside the hanger. I need you to find your men and mine and send them up here; half on one side with you and half on my side with me. We'll flank these guys. All enemy troops are making their way to guard the prisoners in the hanger."

"Aye. Okay, let's get this done."

"Hurry, sir. They're getting antsy and as much as I doubt they'd kill these guys, they will if it means neither one can run the ship. We have to flank them hard and fast, let the prisoners escape. No. Nix that. Let's grab some weapons from the armory, and bring them up. Enter, and give our friends firepower and support. We can take the ship back if we have more hands."

"Alright, then meet you at the armory." The Admiral paused for a moment. "Allied teams, meet at the armory. Repeat, meet at the armory. Our Marine friends are still on board so watch your backs."

Karson started running for the armory. As he dropped back down to level three, a Marine stood in his way. Gun up, Karson ordered him down.

"Sir. I'm on your side. I-"

"Drop, or I'll drop you." Karson jerked his pistol at the Marine's head height.

The Marine hesitantly did as he was told. Karson approached him to disarm him, but this Marine was fast, and he smacked Karson's gun from him, and spun Karson around, putting him in a sleeper hold, but not adding pressure.

"Sir. I'm on your side. Stop struggling! I can help you."

"Let me go then," Karson yelled as he was released. "Why'd your men turn?"

The Marine picked Karson's pistol up and gave it to him. "I don't know. We were on deck, and the leaders shot three Marines that were ready to do their job. They then turned on us, and we all agreed we had to kill your teams for Death Nation. Thompson was ambushed simultaneously with you. My buddy and I were together because we got down and he squeezed my shoulder. I squeezed his. As the bullets started to fly, we stepped to the side and dropped our brothers. Sir, as much as I hate it, we have to shoot our brothers. We can't save them."

"I know. We're going to the armory..."

"I heard." He pointed at his communication link. "They'll have heard. You have to move quickly."

"Let's go then." Karson and the Marine made their way to the armory, dropping two patrols of enemies making their way to the armory as well. Inside, they loaded the bags with guns and ammo and hurried back up to position themselves outside of the hanger. Half of the force with Karson and the Marine, and half with Thompson. "Hey, bud. What's your name?"

"Sane. You?"

"Serval. Special Forces?"

"Recon. You? SEAL?"

"Aye. Happy to have you, brother." Karson and Sane shook hands.

"Brother." He smiled. "Same." Sane replied.

"Admiral. On three, we enter inside the hanger and fire at anyone standing with a weapon. Make your way to center with weapons. Drop the bag. Form a circle, and yell orders. They know you. They don't know me. They'll listen to you. I will drop my bag and continue to fight. If we can drop these guys, we can make our way to the bridge. Once done, we'll conduct final raids of the ship to flush out any and all combatants, then man battle stations until we can meet back up with our fleet."

Admiral Thompson agreed. "Aye. On three. One."

"Two…" *Three.* Karson motioned forward and charged into the hanger, firing at anyone standing, pointing a gun. The prisoners looked stunned and hit the ground. "GRAB A GUN! GRAB A GUN! GRAB A GUN!" Karson threw the bag of weapons inside the group of prisoners, and they scrambled for one as Thompson came in too, doing the same. People were falling dead left and right, trying to escape the room. Within moments, gunfire was throughout the ship, and the hanger was quieting down. Karson asked men to join him.

"Raid the ship. Too look like us, the enemy not in red wears our Navy vests. Remove your camouflage but keep your armor on!" Karson removed his vest and cammo as did his allies. "You will have to kill your brothers and sisters if they stand against you. We must take back this ship. No questions asked."

"Where are you going, sir?" A Sailor asked Thompson.

"The bridge." He replied.

Karson walked out of the room. Loaded his weapon again and turned towards the secondary bridge. *Kill the standing men with guns. The unarmed are the crew of the bridge.*

Karson reached the door and opened to find men pointing a gun at each of the operators' heads.

"Hold der, Amedican, or dey as vell as jou, vill all die!"

"Portuguese. Okay. We'll invade Portuguese and Spanish places next. No one else has to die today. Just stand down."

"Jou are in no place to bargain. Drop to knees."

Karson didn't move. "HEY! LET'S YOU AND I TALK, MAN TO MAN!" Everyone in the room quieted. Karson had the man's attention. "Let's you and I talk, man to man. Innocence is not honorable slaughter. To kill a warrior, that is something else. These crewmembers are not worthy of execution. They man a computer for God's sake. They have no weapons."

"Jou haven't fired at us yet, 'cause of dem."

"Because I don't want to die. There are more of you than me."

"Yes. So drop to knees. Now."

Karson slowly dropped to his knees. "Americans in here, you know what you took an oath to protect. You know how to fight. The only way to win is to face your fears and kick these bastards from the ship."

"Don't try anything guys, or we'll shoot you through and through." A traitor spoke up from the back of the room.

"Ya know, I hate when people like you try to take over something. Don't fear these guys, Navy! Fight!" Karson lunged forward, slipping past the Portuguese, his gun firing once, before leaving his hands to fire another bullet, this time in the hands of Karson through and through the Portugeuse man's head. Karson turned his gun for another target but found Sailors struggling with enemies. Karson helped a female struggling with a man twice her size. Together, Sailor and Sailor pushed the man, former specialist McComb, against the wall, and the female Sailor, Quartermaster Phillips, drove a pencil into his eye. Karson turned to see the remaining battles ending in many EKIAs, and three FKIAs.

"Hey! Nice work!" Karson congratulated them. "You can worry later, but you now have a job to do. Radio the fleet to intercept us. Sound general quarters and get everyone to battle stations once you receive the all clear sign from Thompson, or if God forbid he dies, me. Understood?"

"Aye, sir." The female hugged him. "Thank you."

Karson looked through the cameras onboard the ship to find patrols filing through the ship, ending enemy lives as he spoke. Karson located a team of his friends, in the island, flushing out residual enemy contacts.

SEALS still on board. Get to them.

Karson rushed from the secondary bridge up to the island. He shouted as his immediate family turned on him. "Friendly. Commander Hunter."

"Commander! We thought-" The older looking SEAL said.

"Man, you're one SOB, man. We thought you ate it, sir." Slink's eyes locked to Karson's brightening ones.

"Nah, man. I thought you'd left. Guess you stayed behind, huh? Hey, let's get this done, dudes. What you got?" Karson took point.

"Three Tangos upstairs. Serval, you need to go up and spin around and fire if you're going first." Slink relayed.

"Alright. Up and back maneuver. You got my back?" Karson asked.

"Aye, sir. Always." Commander Slink responded.

"Then I'll go first," Karson said. "Good to see you again, Slink.

"Same! Go!"

Karson launched up and cleared the last step, then spun around the light and fired into the darkness, lighting up three figures, surprised to find bullets fired at them. The other SEALs made their way up top and honed in on targets.

POP

POP

POP

THUD

THUD

THUD

"Enemies down." Karson said. "Nice work, gentlemen."

"Do we have the ship?" The final SEAL rounded the corner.

"Don't know. Patrols are sweeping through now. The sun is coming up. The fleet has been notified. Just have to wait and see. For now, keep searching. I'm heading back to the bridge."

"Aye, sir." Slink and Karson chest bumped and parted.

"Thompson, Admiral Thompson, this is Serval. Come in."

"Commander. I'm on the bridge. The ship is clear. The final patrol is wrapping up a firefight in the engine room. No other contacts on the video stream."

"Was just about to ask where you were. Ship secure. You should radio that to the entire crew."

"In about two minutes, the patrol will be finished, and I'll sound the all clear after a final sweep. For now, we have to lick our wounds and get this ship back in order. I'm ordering an all stop. Dump the bodies. Clean the ship. Hooyah?"

"Hooyah, sir. Will go."

****

CHAPTER 36 - In times of war or uncertainty, my Nation expects me...

"Why'd you come-"

Karson covered the dying American's mouth. "Shh... Rest. We come back for our own, man! Always have, always will, hooyeah?"

Karson walked through the ship, taking in all of the blood and gore that lay plastered against the hull of the ship. Bodies. American bodies littered the ground, more prominent than foreign. Some allied. A lot of betrayals, yes, but still, American bodies. The reach of Death Nation, it was unstoppable. Ojore. This man was predicted, but never had Karson thought in reading the Bible that this man could be in this lifetime. But, the more and more Karson thought about it, the more he could see it.

The 'anti-Christ' was a person the Bible predicts to be appealing, strong, and someone to "unite" the world.

To me, this man isn't appealing. At all. But I can see how some will enjoy the death of 'the Big Satan.'

Karson had to admit, to other nations, third world nations without the luxuries The United States of America couldn't share with everyone, Ojore could be appealing. What do you need to be an attractive leader? Fame. Fortune. Power. Ojore: infamy among enemies, fame among loyal subjects; they call him their 'supreme leader'. Fortune-the man has taken over nations and surely has their natural resources, their wealth, their military might which is part of his power. Power-the man with his followers has taken over countries. Starting with Europe, heading into Russia, China, India, Middle Eastern Nations along with Pakistan, Afghanistan, Kazakhstan, Turkey, down through the Koreas, the Pacific nations, coming up through South America now, and other areas. All heading towards North America. The United States, Canada, and Australia were all that were left of the allied world. The European nations still fighting against Death Nation were those of France and Spain. However, they wouldn't last long. It has infiltrated some of the Ranks of the United States. It's a virus. It just spreads and spreads. No cure and left untreated, it will plague the world for eternity.

Where will I go next? South America? Africa? I hope Africa. I'll get to see Vic again!

Besides the fact that Ojore killed all people indiscriminately, those who didn't know about his ruthlessness and followed him blindly were spared. Any who stood in his way were slaughtered.

Not attractive. I knew the United States wouldn't last, but I thought she'd survive more than two hundred and sixty years...

The gore on the ship.

Not attractive.

Killing Americans supposedly fighting for the same thing as you, then having to turn around and blow their brains out.

NOT. ATTRACTIVE.

More along the lines of...

...It hurts. It hurts bad.

The pain of what had just transpired over the last seventeen hours was starting to get to Karson, who desperately tried to hide the fact that his eyes were stained and stinging with tears and visions of what he had just witnessed. For some reason, though, the death and the events that had made everyone on the ship an animal motivated Karson that much more to bring the 'supreme leader' to justice.

Dead, or alive. More likely, dead after the beating I'll make him endure!

Karson couldn't let the pain affect what he was placed on the earth to do. Men who were friendly to Karson, who followed him and had his back would walk past Karson who had taken a seat on the wall to recuperate. All the Sailors, Karson thought, were angry at him for the orders and choices he'd executed. However, if their paths were able to be diverted, the men who understood, would pat Karson and other Sailors on the shoulder.

I never wanted to lead as much as I've had to. Richardson left shoes to fill, and that just isn't me... Why would I have ever thought otherwise?

"Sir?" A voice roused Karson from his thoughts.

He looked over to a Sailor who came to sit next to him. "Yes?"

"No one blames you for the tough calls, sir. A-at least, I don't, sir. We took an oath to serve that flag from all threats foreign **and** domestic. No matter what, we protect The United States of America. Even from brothers and sisters who commit treason. That's our job, sir."

Karson looked down the hall. "Thank you. I really appreciate tha-" As Karson looked back at the Sailor, the Sailor was gone, disappearing around the corner of the hallway, off to do other duties.

Karson got up to chase after the man, to say thank you for his kind words but was stopped by Admiral Thompson.

I can't catch a break, dammit.

Another Sailor Karson had never seen before approached, this time stumbling. He was drenched in blood, his weapon in his hand. "I killed them... I killed my brothers..." He mumbled.

"Hey! Buddy, give me that gun, buddy..." Karson said, following him.

"Huh?" He turned in still in his hands. "Oh... hi... I can't do this anymore!" He raised the gun to his head. Karson sprang for it, wrapping his arms around the kid's neck and dropping him into a deep sleep.

Yeah, can't catch a break.

"Serval, I need you in my quarters immediately. You two," he said to the medics walking past. "Take this man to the infirmary. Suicide threat."

Karson watched as they grabbed him up, then stepped up to his Admiral. "Who was that Sailor, sir? I want to talk to him."

"Don't care. I need you now." The Admiral said.

Aye, sir." Karson sighed, defeated.

The Admiral turned and walked away; Karson followed.

Yet another mission.

Karson looked down, took a deep breath, and then entered into the Admiral's cabin. Karson sat down at the desk and listened to the Admiral's briefing.

"Now this is a near impossible mission that you may not survive, Karson, but I'm giving it to you because I know that if anyone could come home, it would be you. So prove to me that you are worthy of being called a Captain. I'm promoting you."

Karson was shocked at this. "What... what do you mean, sir?"

"I mean that this is going to test you more than any other mission that you've had. You're so young; some men are scared that you won't deliver. But I have faith in you just like your Captain had in you, and that is why I'm asking you to fill his shoes and take leadership over the team. Oh, and you're going to brief that noisy room next door." Karson could hear the screams next door. "You haven't failed the world yet, no one has. I doubt that that will start now. Now, get in there."

"Sir?" Karson began to protest.

The Admiral opened the door to the briefing quarters. Karson groaned. As Karson walked into the room, tnsions were high from the events that had transpired from the previous twenty-four hours. Sailors were screaming at each other, throwing chairs, shouting curses at each other, and posturing like they were going to strike each other down again, committing more treason against the United States of America.

"YOU SAY THAT WAS A VICTORY? WE KILLED OUR OWN! JUST LEFT 'EM. I SHOULD SHOOT YOU RIGHT WHERE YOU ARE RIGHT NOW."

The continuing chaos was to be expected when Karson walked in. Not, however, when the highly decorated Admiral walked in. He glared around at the in-order of the room.

"Oh crap," Karson whispered and stepped away covering his ears quick as the Admiral took a deep breath to add more noise to the already deafening room.

"ATTENTION ON DECK. HEY! THIS IS UNACCEPTABLE ON MY SHIP! LISTEN UP! HEEEEY!" The Admiral tried and failed to gain order.

"AND WHERE WERE YOU MR. NAVY SEAL!?" The Sailors and Marines who had spotted Karson slyly hiding in the corner were starting to turn on him. "YOU AND YOUR TEAM THINK YOU'RE ALL THAT, BUT YOU'RE NOT. YOU ARE NEVER THERE WHEN WE NEED HELP! TO BE EXPECTED FROM THE BABY SEAL."

Surprisingly, Karson was the reason the noise died down. "Yeah, SEAL pup! Resign. Give your position over to someone who can actually fill the shoes and has the balls of a real Special Forces operative!"

"You shouldn't need help. You should work as a team. We aren't there to be your 911 call when we are in danger ourselves." Karson responded a bit too snippy. "Now, getting down to business-"

"WHY YOU LITTLE PUNK!" A Marine Private beside Karson turned and sprinted at Karson. He reacted. Karson stepped to the side, grabbed the Marine's shirt and twisted him off balance while sticking his foot out, knocking the young Marine onto his face. The Marine gave a grunt like when a child hits the ground after falling off his bike.

'DAYUM!' Everyones' look on their faces basically said the flamboyant version of the word as the Marine turned back over to keep fighting. His pride was damaged, and he needed it back. Karson put his boot on the Marine's chest. He was defeated and lay there. Karson could have beat him to a pulp from the way this Marine had fought. If a Marine were at his peak instead of grieving, Karson would have had a harder time.

Shaking his head from the random thoughts, Karson instead reached down, grabbed the Marine's hand, hoisted him up, and tossed him into the crowd, careful to keep his side arm out of reach. His rage was enough; even the Admiral felt a little uneasy at this new found strength.

"I WASN'T WITH YOU BECAUSE MY TEAM AND I WERE WORKING ON TRYING TO SAVE MORE AMERICAN LIVES. YOU LOST YOUR MEN, WELL GUESS WHAT! WE LOST OURS TOO! BY OUR BULLETS! THAT'S RIGHT! WE HAD TO KILL OUR OWN TEAMMATES BECAUSE THEY COULDN'T TAKE THE STRESS OF WAR. BECAUSE THE ENEMY BRAINWASHING PUSHED HARDER THAN OUR TRUTH. HARDER THAN OUR FREEDOM. AND HAD WE WORKED TOGETHER AS THE TEAM WE ARE, WE

WOULDN'T HAVE LOST ANY. NADDA! ZIP! NOT ONE AMERICAN ON THE BATTLE GROUND. WE COULD HAVE HELPED EACHOTHER OVERCOME THIS STRESS. THIS FEAR! NOW SIT DOWN!"

Everyone sat. They looked at Karson with hurting eyes, saddened by the loss of their friends, their family. Their loved ones. Saddened because they could do nothing as the men and women they fought for were murdered in cold blood.

"Listen up. What happened out there is over with. It can't be undone; we can't bring those we lost back, and we sure as hell can't win this war if we are going to argue and fight each other. We all lost family, no matter the branch. My mind is pained too. My eyes water. My heart aches, just like yours do. I weep and mourn with you. We are all brothers. Army, Navy, Air Force, Marines, Coast Guard! We are all brothers and sisters. Why do you think The United States is in front of each branch?" No one spoke. "Guys, gals, we all fight for fifty stars and thirteen bars. We beat each other in basic. Somewhere along the way, we mistook military to mean that we can go crazy after a war because we can't help someone because we don't want to seem like softies. Well, this is not the military I want to serve in. Where are the honor and commitment? What happened to making the world a better place to live? We all are on the same giant team. It's time we started acting like it. What was happening in here was unacceptable by the standards of the United States Military to which we serve with. UNACCEPTABLE. We are in a war. We are professionals. It's time we show the world what we are made of. Now, I need my SEAL team, and Staff Sergeant Danny Wilson's team to stay in here. The rest of you, GET OUT OF MY SIGHT!"

People shifted towards the door or up towards Karson.

"Fill in these seats gentlemen. We have a long briefing ahead of us. I have been promoted to Captain, so I need a second in command. Commander Slink. Would you do me the honor, sir?"

"A-aye, sir. My pleasure!" The man stared at Karson in shock that he'd been chosen to fill big shoes.

"Good. Get up here, and note the time. 1100 hours."

"Yes, sir." Karson's secondary man stood up and stood beside him. "Great speech. You're a good man."

"You're welcome." Karson winked. "Alright, gentlemen. I know we were expecting some time off, but we have new orders. At 0300 hours, a distress call was made from the HMS Queen Elizabeth, the largest ship in Her Majesty's Navy. At 0330, an Irish ship made contact with her. Here is the transmission."

Static filled the room…

****

British voices walked on each others' transmissions.

"What is going on?"

"I don't know, sir… We have our techs working on it, but nothing seems to be wrong…"

"This is bloody creepy!"

"WE'RE HIT! CAPTAIN, WE ARE HIT… THE BOTTOM OF THE SHIP JUST OPENED UP! WATER IS POURING IN!"

"Radio for help!"

"This is the HMS Queen Elizabeth requesting help from any allied vessel in the region! Please help us! An unknown assailant is attacking us! Hurry and help us! Anyone come in! The attack seems to be coming from underwater, but our scanners show a negative reading on underwater bogies!"

"HMS Queen Elizabeth, this is LÉ Ciara. We are forty nautical miles from your position."

"IT'S TOO LATE! THEY'RE KILLING US! WE NEED HELP!"

As the transmission cut out, an eerie organ like mechanical noise managed to break through the static.

"Elizabeth? HMS Queen Elizabeth? Can anyone hear us? Come in!" The only response was static.

****

Karson turned back to his crew. Karson threw pictures onto the screen, as well as the one he'd taken underwater.

"That is a huge ship!" Slink mumbled.

"0600. As you can see, when the Irish Navy came upon the distress beacon, all they found were a few bodies; the rest, lost at sea. The ocean was covered in blood, oil, and the ship's lights could still be seen under the waves as the water sucked in yet another victim. As you hard, it all happened very, very fast."

Staff Sergeant Wilson's mouth was wide open. "That is eerie, man! That is creepy! That sound... w-what... what makes that noise man?" He trailed off.

"Debris from the ship showed little, except that whatever sunk the ship was highly advanced in its weaponry. The U.S. sent the USS Alabama to take underwater pictures of the ship. The divers' reports are as follows. The metal on the hull of the ship was seared. Not cracked or exploded. But seemed to be cut through. Like butter. Along with drag marks like it was pulled down as well as breached, like the Kraken." The men were speechless.

"Anyone know what did it, sir? Or who?" The old SEAL spoke up.

"Well, Gramps, we believe it was a type of submarine, obviously. However, none like we've ever seen. Navy sonar and intelligence have been tracking water movement with buoys. Some have been disturbed by heavy duty water displacement, meaning that it's something human-made, not natural. And it's big. Analysts say it seems to fight by distracting the ship to threats not there, and when men hit the water, it savagely maims them. It fights dirty and is trying to scare us. It won't work. This technology is just that. Technology. That means it can be destroyed. This is similar to the UN headquarters attack. A virus, mock threats, and then death."

"I don't know... That is impressive, man... it's kina working..." Gramps wrote down a note.

"How do you know it's a sub, sir?" Slink looked at the pictures. "Maybe it's a distraction?"

"We're not completely, but think about it. If it were a massive ship, even though the ocean is huge, we believe that we could spot it. Drones, radar, civilian witnesses..."

"Ahh."

"Russians, man. It's the Russians." Wilson scoffed.

"We're not sure who it is. Doubt it's the Russians. They were one of the first to fall. We went to their aide. They aren't going to have the ability to fight dirty like that." The Admiral interjected.

"The Novorossiysk-451, sir. We can't track that ship, sir." Slink said.

"That ship is way smaller than this ship. It may use the same technology, but it is not Russia. We're not sure who made it." Thompson continued to argue his point.

"As, I was saying, this ship whatever it is-is an extreme threat to the allied forces of the world. And we want it. At 0800, the Admiral was given orders from President Elding. When I arrived a short time ago, I was called to his quarters and briefed as I am briefing you. Listen carefully, and we all may survive this battle. This is something the Navy or any other branch has never tried, or deemed possible until now. Now, desperate times call for desperate measures as our security, our very lives, are at stake. We can do this. This is something DARPA has been designing, and I've devised a plan, with the help of our Admiral. Our job is to board this vessel and take control of her as our own ship. This ship will be too large for us to catch up to by swimming or to place explosives to bring her to the surface. And if we go outside, we'll be crushed by the water pressure. We will be deployed in Antarctic waters, where we will dive in our mini-subs. It's going to be freezing, even with our gear on, so be sure to focus on your body and protect yourself. Now, we will be near Antarctica because that is where the enemy vessel is going, we believe, based on the path it's been taking. This drop zone is subject to change, however, so keep your ears open."

Karson set down a picture and bar charts. "This is the largest ship on the planet. The Pioneering Spirit was the largest ship, weighing in with a gross tonnage of four hundred and three thousand, three hundred and forty-two tons, takes up one thousand five hundred and sixty-five feet in length, has a beam of four hundred and seven feet, draft of thirty-three to eighty-two feet, depth of ninety-eight feet, has a speed of fourteen knots or for you less educated men, sixteen miles per hour, and can accommodate five hundred and seventy-one crew members. This ship displaces the buoys by three hundred and twenty-five million, one hundred and twelve thousand, four hundred and forty-eight pounds in freshwater, and three hundred and thirty-two million, nine hundred and fifteen thousand, one hundred and forty-seven pounds in salt water. This ship we're hunting, analysts believe weighs in at four million, thirty-three thousand, four hundred and twenty tons and displaces ten times the water that The Pioneering Spirit does. This enemy vessel displaces three billion, two hundred fifty-one million, one hundred and twenty-four thousand, four hundred and eighty pounds of freshwater and three billion, three hundred and twenty-nine million, one hundred and fifty-one thousand, four hundred and seventy pounds of salt water."

The men all stared at the charts with the data and formulas, then up at Karson in disbelief.

"Buoys have been displaced all along the southern part of the world, so we think that this is the vessel, codenamed 'Big Momma.'" Everyone gave the slightest smile.

Karson continued. "We have actionable intel to deal with this threat promptly. This will be an intimate mission. Wet with blood. Up close and personal. When 'big momma' gets close enough to the 'DZ', we deploy and take our mini-subs to the enemy vessel. Now our mini-subs are newly furnished. It's a bit larger and it connects to the entrance of the enemy vessel. When it connects, the first Sailor will open the hatch and we'll slide down the ladder. When we enter, the alarms will sound, and enemy forces will be coming towards the hatch armed to the teeth ready to kill us. Our best chance to succeed is to escape into the sub and hide, closing the hatch like nothing happened. We must locate the camera to the entrance and disable it to ensure they don't see us if there is a camera there. We must be quick to disappear like phantoms. They will believe it was a malfunction and go on their way, granted, the patrols may be more pronounced throughout the ship after the incident. Then we will attack. We do not take any prisoners except for those on the bridge. Once prisoners are taken, we immediately start interrogating. It is imperative that we trip no alarms while on mission. If we do, we could easily be overrun. If all goes to plan, I will then split us into four teams. This is Alpha Teams mission by the way. When-"

"Wait! We have two missions?!" Karson glared at the interrupting Marine. "Sorry, Sir, please continue."

"Alpha team. My SEALs. Bravo team, this is your team, Staff Sergeant Wilson. Now, when I split alpha team, it will become Charlie Team, led by myself will go to wherever the bridge is. Delta, you'll go wherever their control room is and gain intel. Feeding the team on the fly. Echo, you will head towards the engines and see what damage you could inflict there. Every ship has flaws. Foxtrot, you will be the sweepers of the ship, ensuring that all enemy personnel are where they should be, helping to guide us all along. This will be the computer room. Charlie team, we will learn, and pilot the ship back to the United States Navy yard. Philadelphia. Also, we will gain contact with our country, so they don't blow us out of the water when we bring a giant enemy ship to the doorstep of America."

Karson's team nodded in complete and total understanding to what their orders were.

"Good. Now onto Bravo team. Staff Sergeant Wilson. This is something you've never done before. Marines are the Navy's so-called land based branch. You'll be underwater this whole time. You are taking pictures and sonar readings, anything you can gain from this massive ship. Of course all of the instruments you'll need are attached to the subs, so you'll be controlling these from the inside! This is to ensure that the United States knows what it's dealing with, even if we fail, which is still not an option. Both of us have this to face. Now, we all know dangers of the people and the ship, but let me tell you of another danger we face. If we breach our little submarines' hulls, we will be crushed by the water. If our subs' seals break and we don't enter right, we'll destroy everything. Ourselves, the enemy vessel, everything. We cannot survive in the water alone, so no escape that way if things go sideways. The amount of force from the water would be too great. All teams, stay out of the ship's sonar areas. You must stay close to the ship. The ship will destroy you on sight. We know this because sonar hasn't developed past this, at least we hope." Karson crossed his fingers.

He kept on with his briefing, Thompson nodding in support. "To approach the ship, we must come from the back. This gives us more chance because, though they have sonar, it doesn't wrap around any ship well enough. They'll believe we're sea life. My team, and Wilson's team, we absolutely cannot be detected. Stealth is our friend. If this goes sideways, we blow the ship inside out. Wilson, if we fail, and you're still alive, your job is to deploy your torpedo into our submarine attached to 'Big Momma,' then connect yours to it. Open the hatch, and then disengage your lock. This will flood the enemy vessel and destroy it. This will ensure the survival of many more lives, even if ours are lost. This ship does not sink another allied ship. We must gather as much information as we can. Weapons payload. Crew types. What the ship is. Her mission statement. Etcetera. Clear? Any questions? We deploy at 2100 hours into our subs."

"Sir, we are expecting a sub. What if it is truly a ship?" Gramps asked.

"Same rules, with some adaptations along the way. For example, rather than entering a hatch, we climb to the deck; all of us. We've already done this, recently… Anyways, Wilson's team would fragment into our four SEAL teams. Things like that. Honestly, I hope it is a ship. It'll be easier. Anyways, stealth is still our friend. Now, if there are no more questions," Karson turned back towards the screen and his papers, "go get some sleep. We leave at-"

"Ugh, this is impossible! This is a suicide mission!" A Marine addition whined.

Karson stopped mid-sentence and looked down and behind him. "Did I just hear 'impossible'?" Karson whispered.

The Marine gulped. "I-uh, I…"

Karson turned around and looked at his men. He spit at their feet. "Impossible. IMPOSSIBLE?" Karson glared around the room. "We are a Tier One group. Special Forces of the United States of America! Ha, and you say this mission is impossible." Karson sniffled and rubbed his nose. "We are brothers and sisters in arms, armed to the teeth, and this task is just merely 'impossible.' We have a job to do. It's what we get paid for. But we're too chicken because we might meet our maker before **we** want to. Do you think, back in 1775, that the founding fathers thought that independence was impossible? Do you think they whined when they knew they had missions they had to take care of? NO! THEY KNEW, THAT FREEDOM, WAS WORTH THE RISK, WORTH THE BLOOD AND SWEAT, WORTH HARD WORK, TO ACHIEVE FREEDOM, SO THAT THEIR BROTHERS WOULDN'T KEEP DYING. THEY DUG DOWN DEEP INTO THE MUD, AND PUSHED FOR FREEDOM, MORE, THAN ANY OF US COULD EVER DO!" Karson sighed. "And that's what we are doing now. You see, we are SEALs my Marine brother. We don't chicken out of anything we are ordered to do for our country. And I don't accept dead weight. We may be afraid at times, but we don't let it get in the way of what needs to be done. Like a wise man told me a few days ago, 'we are like dogs, trained to do what we are ordered to do with no questions.' That is it. So, if you are going to pose a threat to myself and my team, and to the security of the United States of America that we swore to protect even at the cost of our own lives, you can hike right on back to your base by yourself to get neutered. I'm sure Mad Dog would love to neuter you, wittle puppy."

Karson patted the Marine on his shoulder. "Because we have a job to do." He turned to his team, addressing everyone again. "Now, we've been given a job. We deploy at 2100 hours. Anyone leaves, I will personally ensure your court martial." He turned around facing the door, head bowed, eyes up in the proud view, like when a fighter has been knocked down but is mustering the courage to fight more, and succeed. Karson had this view-finding the strength of a tiger before the pounce, before the sinking of teeth into flesh, the warmth of blood spraying up onto the teeth; only because he knew he was heading his team to their probable, nay, most definitely leading them to their deaths. "We have a country to serve. And we will deliver." Karson whispered. "Call your families if you wish. I don't promise that you will come home alive, but you will come home. I will see to it that you will come back home. Dismissed."

"Aye, sir!" Everyone filed out of the room as Karson stayed behind and gathered his papers. He walked slower than ever as he headed to his barracks to get some much-needed 'R and R' before the mission. His mind drifted off to his family, friends, his love, the sweet scent of his love, and then to what lay ahead. *Maybe I am leading my brothers to death. It's our job, though. We knew what we were signing up for. We'll just have to kill everyone else before they kill us.*

As Karson made it into his barracks, hoping to still his throbbing, drifting mind, he noticed something out of the ordinary. The air was cooler. A figure sitting at his desk. A single candle lit in the room. *When did I gain a candle?* Karson made for his weapon but realized his gun was missing from his leg holster. The figure stood up laughing.

"Oh, jou Amerdicans are so predictable. So afraid jou'll sink jour precious ships if jou carry jour weapons on jou. It's quite simple to sneak onto jour ships. As ve sveak, ve are boarding all of jou. Oh, and ve know vhat is coming. Jour precious plan will fail. Jou vill fail. And jou vill go down in history as ze United States Navy SEAL leader who failed his country and led to ze destruction of a 'free world.' Ze United States of Amerdica vill fall, and I'll have jou alive just long enough to see it, and know zat jou vere ze reason. Zen, jou and every uder Amerdican vill all die! Ah ha ha ha!" The figure lunged at Karson and drove a knife into his chest. Karson grabbed for it, but the man yanked it out. Karson collapsed onto the floor. Panting. The figure was gone.

Karson stood frantically and looked around his room and felt his chest. Nothing was wrong with him. Karson's pistol was back and he unholstered it and crawled to the wall and sat against it, laying his head back trying to calm himself. "It was just a dream, Sailor. Just a dream."

Karson sat there for thirty seconds when he heard rushed footsteps and a knock at the door. "Karson?" A low voice called. "You in there?"

Karson stood and opened the door, aiming his pistol at....

The Admiral stood there looking down at the smaller Navy SEAL. "You look horrible, kid. Let's take a walk. You need some air, a smoke, and a drink!" He didn't even flinch from the barrel of a gun being forced into his face.

That is how you know you're a threat.

Karson obeyed the order, holstering his weapon and wiping his ever moistening face and glistening blue eyes, following his Admiral mentor who had become one of his best friends to the flight deck. They both stood looking out over the water, listening to the powerful all American ship push the water out of her way, lifting up a soft mist that refreshed Karson's quivering and heated body.

"You're shaking, Karson."

"I'm alright, sir. The water is soothing. I've always had a quenching relationship with the water."

"You're not fine. You're sweating in the cool air, and you're shivering at the same time. You talked about combat ready men and women for the briefing, but yet you definitely aren't combat ready or effective at this moment. You're broken down and crying. So now tell me. What the hell is wrong with you? What is going on?"

Karson just stared out over the water, his eyes shining even more blue, as the moonlit water was reflected in them, making them glow in the dark. "How many more people have to die before this war is over, sir? I mean, I just ordered that we kill our own men. I want our lives back. I want my Captain back. I want to quit. I'm not cut out for this!"

"Would you want another job, Karson? Because you can walk away right now."

Karson looked straight into the shadow of his Commanding Officer. "I wouldn't have chosen any other job. It's why I signed up. Best damn job I could ask for. The best $4,586.40 a month I could ever make. I serve with my best friends, my brothers... I have everything I could ever want. I've found myself here. It just sucks. I just didn't think I'd have to shoot my brothers and sisters. And I didn't hesitate. I didn't hesitate, sir. It was just another battle for me. They were just more lives that I had to take. I've become a savage. An animal. What makes me different than the enemy?"

"You know it's how you're trained, Ka-"

"And now you're sending me on another suicide mission. I'm going to get everyone killed, Josh, I'm going to getaaaa-" Karson gasped when the hand forced his head to the side. Karson put his hand to his face, gulped, and slid down the rail.

"You are a Navy SEAL Captain now, Hunter. This is not you. You never second guess yourself."

"Yeah but…"

"DO NOT INTERRUPT ME!"

"Sir." Karson sniffled.

He sighed and let go of Karson's chin. "You know we are friends now, Karson. But in war time, we are C.O. and Sailor. You will treat me as such. Do I make myself clear?"

"Aye, Sir." Karson wasn't looking at his Admiral anymore, rather at the deck.

"Look at me," Thompson said, more gently.

Karson did as he was instructed to do.

"You need to forget what has happened to you. Focus on the outcome. Focus on winning. Focusing on protecting the world, your family, your piece of tail waiting for you to complete this step in your life. Yeah, I remember you confiding your secret to me."

Karson smiled a rather small smile.

"This is post-traumatic stress. You're allowed to be soft, Karson. Just not when you're on duty. You can be soft and cry, and worry after this is all done. For now, let it go, and you won't develop a disorder over it. You can be human, but not too human. You are a warrior. Don't humanize yourself with enemies. They deserve whatever they get."

"How can I forget everyone I killed?"

"Karson, for goodness sake... Sometimes you have to stop feeling compassion. These people, these animals... they attacked you first! Us first. The United States first. Our loved ones, our people. The enemy attacked us. You did your duty, to God and our country. Against any, enemy foreign and domestic. And that includes traitors. Don't forget the duty you are sworn to adhere to. Forget the pain of it. You did it for you. You did it for the United States. You did it for the world. And you did it, more importantly, to protect your loved ones back home and abroad, as well as your brothers and sisters here. Do you honestly think the enemy will hesitate to put a bullet in your mother's head? What about Victor's head? You've got to stop them before they stop you. You are an American warrior. Act like one. We trained you to be extremely dangerous. Death comes with the job, Karson. That you knew when you joined."

Karson stared out over the deck of the ship. Then stood and turned around. "You're right. I am an American. Sailor. A fighter. A warrior. I am, a SEAL. I AM PROUD TO BE AN AMERICAN." Karson shouted out over the roar of the water, his voice carrying miles into the dark over the sea.

Maybe that will strike fear into my enemies!

"That's my boy. How are you feeling?"

"Feeling dangerous, sir! 'In times of war or uncertainty, there is a special breed of warrior ready to answer our Nation's call. A common man with uncommon desire to succeed. Forged by adversity, he stands alongside America's finest special operations forces to serve his country, the American people, and protect their way of life. I am that man. My Trident is a symbol of honor and heritage. Bestowed upon me by the heroes that have gone before, it embodies the trust of those I have sworn to protect. By wearing the Trident, I accept the responsibility of my chosen profession and way of life. It is a privilege that I must earn every day. My loyalty to Country and Team is beyond reproach. I humbly serve as a guardian to my fellow Americans always ready to defend those who are unable to defend themselves. I do not advertise the nature of my work, nor seek recognition for my actions. I voluntarily accept the inherent hazards of my profession, placing the welfare and security of others before my own. I serve with honor on and off the battlefield. The ability to control my emotions and my actions, regardless of circumstance, sets me apart from other men. Uncompromising integrity is my standard. My character and honor are steadfast. My word is my bond. We expect to lead and be led. In the absence of orders, I will take charge, lead my teammates, and accomplish the mission. I lead by example in all situations. I will never quit. I persevere and thrive on adversity. My Nation expects me to be physically harder and mentally stronger than my enemies. If knocked down, I will get back up, every time. I will draw on every remaining ounce of strength to protect my teammates and to accomplish our mission. I am never out of the fight. We demand discipline. We expect innovation. The lives of my teammates and the success of our mission depend on me - my technical skill, tactical proficiency, and attention to detail. My training is never complete. We train for war and fight to win. I stand ready to bring the full spectrum of combat power to bear to achieve my mission and the goals established by my country. The execution of my duties will be swift and violent when required yet guided by the very principles that I serve to defend. Brave men have fought and died building the proud tradition and feared reputation that I am bound to uphold. In the worst of conditions, the legacy of my teammates steadies my resolve and silently guides my every deed. I will not fail. The only easy day was yesterday! Hooyah! HOOYAH!"

"The feelings you have, Karson, are signs that this war hasn't made you into an animal. You're still a good man. You have a job to do. It doesn't make you bad to use your skills even if it means taking a life, justifiably. Don't let your thoughts consume and/or change you. Keep these thoughts, but do your duty. Do what you're paid to do. Do what is right, okay?"

"Aye, Sir."

"Cigar?"

"Oh, please." Karson practically jizzed in his pants at the offer. "Sir, why is this war happening? I mean, what has the United States done to provoke this violence? We're the good guys, aren't we? Aside from some severe corruption, we have a good system... I think?"

"I don't know, Karson..." The Admiral sighed. "I can't think of any reason but to this... According to Albert Einstein, 'everything that happens, happens for a reason." He handed Karson the cigar.

"Thank you, sir." Karson paused. "For everything."

The Admiral nodded, the zippo igniting the paper, and he and Karson shared a smoke as the ship continued to the drop point, where the Marines and SEALs would be thrown into a never before attempted mission, the realm of the unknown, that could spell disaster for everything the world has tried to build up.

****

CHAPTER 37 - HLD

F woooooshh

Kcshhhhhhhh.

Mmmmmmm. I love that! "That's tasty, isn't it?"

"That's the U.S. Navy at its finest, sir!" Karson smiled and nodded at the random Sailor walking by who gave his two cents.

The water mist started sprinkled the Sailors like rain, slowly revealing a smaller but still significant, Virginia Class Fast Attack Submarine, newly upgraded, and redesigned to be stealthy, faster, and more powerful. The original carried only a small crew and eleven SEALs in the lockout trunk, along with only one dry dock shelter mini submarine. Now, the U.S.S. Des Moines can carry thirty men, comfortably, as well as store four dry dock shelter mini subs. This ship would be hunting the enemy submarine, 'Big Momma.' Should the Des Moines come under attack, she would use her torpedoes, Tomahawk missiles, and her sidewinder missiles, adapted from the fighter jet version to the underwater submarine version to fend off her attacker.

Hopefully. Karson doubted anything could stop 'Big Momma' from the outside. All attacks had to be done from the inside.

As 'Big Momma' was far superior to the Des Moines, however, she would have to flee, leaving the SEALs and Marines to fend for themselves. The Des Moines would also be in the area to gather information and imaging, as well as maintain a lock on the enemy submarine for the fleets knowing for as long as she could.

"Alright, gentlemen." Admiral Thompson walked up. The zodiacs are waiting. Not to mention the fleet and the world. Mount up and board the Des Moines. I'll be monitoring your mission from here."

Karson saluted. "Aye, sir. You heard the man. Get moving."

"HIT THE DECK!" A Sailor from near front of the ship shouted, his voice miraculously meeting the distracted ears.

Karson and the rest of the disembarking crew dropped as a missile flew over the carrier and exploded near the submarine. The carrier fired back, sea wizzes halting the next three attacks, the enemy aircraft turning to show its payload to the Navy.

"Serval! Where are you going!?" Slink called.

"It will take a pilot two minutes to get up here. I'm gonna launch now. Get ready to lock me in." Karson sprinted to the nearest F-16 fighter jet and climbed into the cockpit and raised the lid. He hopped in, remembering his training as a pilot and fired it up. "Island control, Navy SEAL Serval. I'm commandeering a fighter, will be launching in moments."

"Serval, we cannot hit this craft. It's far superior to anything we've dealt with before. Never saw it coming, never had something get this close. Keep your eyes on it; it won't show up on your radar." The radio chattered.

"Thanks for the tip." Karson moved the fighter to launch as pilots hit the flight deck, running to their jets. Once locked in, Karson radioed for his launch, and felt the G-forces push him back against his seat, feeling the carrier disappear from beneath him. Karson flew up to altitude and found a sightline between him and the enemy craft. Karson flew towards the jet and fired his machine gun. "Frikin' missed."

The pilot shook his wings at Karson, taunting him. He flew out and away from the carrier, and drew Karson away from his allies.

I have to take this guy out now. He's far faster than I've ever had to fight before.

Suddenly the craft turned back towards Karson and flew right at him. Karson closed his eyes, ready to make the ultimate sacrifice for his friends, like the 9/11 fighter pilots who were left unarmed to face any airline that dared attack another building. They were to kamikaze into the plane to stop them. Karson too felt the call to service and sacrifice, however, the enemy jet right at the last second, launched himself up right before he struck Karson.

Sissy.

Karson took a deep breath and saw a strategy. As Karson turned, he found the enemy to do that same maneuver yet again. "Alright! Wanna play? Let's play." Karson spun the fighter around one last time to find the craft flying yet again at him. As they approached, the enemy started to lift off, and Karson turned his aircraft, slicing his and the enemy wing off from the fuselage. Karson ejected and was yet again freefalling through the air. He watched as the F-16 crashed into the water, then saw another free-faller in the air. Karson launched himself towards him. The enemy scrambled for his pistol, but Karson was on him like white on rice.

The man deployed his chute, knocking Karson off of him, but Karson grabbed his boot, then launched himself back up into the enemies' face, slamming his forehead into the enemy pilot's nose, blood cascading, knocking the pilot unconscious.

"Crap. Blood, in the water.... sharks. Damn sharks." Karson and the man both landed in the water, a mile and a half from the carrier. He sensed he wasn't alone in the seven minutes it took for his allies to respond. Karson heard the fast boats of his team and as they pulled Karson up onto the zodiac and detained the enemy, a fin breached the surface of the water. "Oh thank God! They left their new friend and raced back to the sub and carrier.

A Corpsman checked Karson over. "Your mission is delayed one hour, sir, so that we can check you out to make sure you're combat ready."

"I just did all of that, didn't I?" Karson grumbled.

"We can also want to interrogate this guy and see if there are new details to learn." The Corpsman turned away from Karson.

"There won't be..."

"How do you know?" The Corpsman was checking the enemy pilot now.

"He's too young. Won't be in the inner circle. He was just copying the 2016 Russian jet skimming the destroyer U.S.S. Donald Cook." Karson climbed the rope ladder and had a nurse check his head, patch him up, and he changed his clothes. Then, the SEALs and Marines moved to their boats and were transported a football field to the submarine, whose captain was topside to meet the new crew. Stepping onboard the ship, however, would prove to be difficult. And wet. Karson was able to do it as he'd done it before, as well as the SEALs, taught by submarine training at BUD/S. The Marines, however, the **land**-based version of the Navy, were not so used to having their boots wet, and many slipped. Much to the pleasure of everyone around, a low ranking private hit the slick metal; his heel fell from under him, and he took a splash in the water.

"It's that hot out, you gotta cool off? We haven't even started yet, P!" Admiral Thompson shouted across the channel.

"SCREW YOU! IT'S WET ON THERE, AND MY BOOTS ARE RUBBER, DICK PUKE!"

"That it is, aye." The captain of the sub piped up. "Gentlemen. On a sub, the same rules apply as on a regular ship and Navy rules. Also, there is one important rule. Do not mess with anything. We are flying blind if something messes up, and being far underwater, there is no room for error. One escape pod for everyone. Most importantly, do not mess with the hatch. Got it?"

"HEY! IS ANYONE GONNA HELP ME?" The Marine private shouted.

"Better watch out, man… I was bleeding in the water earlier. May have dribbled a little blood on the trip over here. Met a friend. That sharks is a comin'!"

"HELP ME THAN!" He panicked.

"Climb back onto the zodiac and get yo' sopping self up here!" The Captain grunted.

"Anyways, captain." Karson turned to his new commanding officer. "I can assure you my team, and I know Wilson's team, will all stay in line, sir."

He shook Karson's hand. "Welcome aboard the U.S.S. Des Moines. Make yourselves at home while you're onboard! We leave in ten minutes. Enjoy the sun while you can. It's a long trek to the Arctic."

"Antarctic, sir."

"We've tracked it to the north, sir. Our intel is more sound than yours."

"How can a ship move from the south to the north so fast? It doesn't make sense. I still believe we must go south." Karson said.

"Captain, is it?" The ship captain asked.

Karson nodded. "Aye."

"I remember when you were a young Lieutenant, hearing about you. Congratulations on promotion. I'm good friends with Admiral Thompson. I called Heath Richardson my brother. Now, this ship is made for intelligence. Our officers have tracked the ship based on the signature of the enemy vessel, and the size and movement under the water. I can assure you, your ship is in the north, sir."

"We have only one shot at finding this ship, sir. Ensure you are correct. I will not accept a mission failed." Karson started to walk towards the entrance to the sub.

"Same. We'll get you there, Captain. Just relax."

Karson stopped and turned his head slowly, slightly looking over his shoulder. *If people don't stop telling me to relax, I will shoot someone. The greatest mission of my life is at stake.*

"We have a course set from here in the Indian Ocean to the middle of the Arctic Ocean. That's eight thousand two hundred and twelve point six nine nautical miles or nine thousand, four hundred and fifty-one miles away, and traveling at our top speed of forty knots or forty-six miles per hour, that should put us there in forty-nine hours. Sir, you have two days to prepare, plus anytime extra it takes to confirm the enemy subs location one hundred percent."

"Just get me there as quick as a falcon, or I'll have your rank. Clear?" Karson turned to the Captain.

They shook hands again, and Karson stood looking over the glassy water as the men entered the ship. Admiral Thompson stood watching from the bridge and waved at Karson. Karson waved back, hoping he'd get to see his friend again.

I hope to see the sun again, man. I don't want to die under the water. Blech! Karson turned and made his way down into the ship, a similar path he'd be taking in fifty hours, hopefully.

Inside the tight metal ship, he could still hear the water lapping at the sides of the hull, more pronounced now. When he stepped under the water line, the temperature cooled, and the sound became more of a whooshing sound, as the currents passed over the smooth sides of the stealth attack sub. When it started moving, Karson barely felt it, but like in a plane when going up in altitude and the pressure makes your ears pop, so too did going down, under the water, where more and more pressure hit your Eustachian tubes.

There was something strange and claustrophobic at sitting under the water in a giant metal death trap with no margin for error that had Karson strangely calm. There wasn't much down here, and aside from the giant enemy ship they were hunting, everything seemed to be peaceful.

"Captain, you hungry?" Kayak called to Karson.

"Hey. Yeah." Karson said, looking up from his bunk. "Where is the mess hall?"

"This way. Come on!" Kayak led the way to the mess hall, where Sailor meshed with Sailor and Marine, bonding before the mission that could end in disaster. Even the ship captain and crew were down here.

There just here to see the men they believe are going to die. Karson got his food but refused to take part in the meshing. He had a job to prepare for and to execute, and now with the title of Captain of a subsection of SEAL Team Six, he had to be able to deliver the United States the product he had to give. 'Big Momma.'

****

TWO DAYS LATER

The trip into the Arctic was smooth and quiet. Karson had learned quite a lot of the functioning of America's finest submarines. He'd even gotten to pilot the craft. Training was done in large amounts. Everything had to be done perfectly. Briefing after briefing.

Discussion with Admiral Thompson and higher-ups. This was one top secret mission; even President Elding was not made aware of this mission. Strangely, people skirted the subject. If Karson or any of his team failed to sink or take the ship and were captured or killed, there would be no help, and the United States would deny all involvement, ultimately still leading to ensured disaster and destruction. The allied nations were cautiously growing thin, and nothing was stopping the spread of the Death of the nations. Death Nation had no distinction. They destroyed even the Nations that they held. The only one they kept were those of the Middle East. Everything else was destructible.

Karson lay in bed, in and out of sleep. Every time he was to go on missions, he'd have this time where everything was calm, and he'd reflect through the mission briefing and all of the key points. He'd visualize who (if he had one) his target was, the order (capture, kill, recon, tail, assassinate, etc.), the training he'd done (which way the handles turned, the directions he'd be traveling, the weapons, the number of enemies, the number of friendlies, etc.), who he was traveling with and the chain of command, stealth or loud, and the list continues. When he was at home in Texas in his pretty fancy one story 2,091 square foot, three bedrooms, two and a half bathrooms, and two car garage with a basement before heading on a mission, Karson would not allow himself to get off at least a week in advance of his mission. No sex with his lover, nor would he permit himself to masturbate if his lover wasn't home. When one does no eject his load, testosterone runs rampant through his body and with Karson, it made him aggressive. Really aggressive. For being a smaller guy, Karson needed to be aggressive. Gave him strength. When he was on a boat like this, it didn't matter; he wasn't permitted to have sexual acts onboard or on base. Somewhat difficult cause he had been sexually active since extremely young, and to not be sexual was tough as any male and female could tell you. *No wonder they tell you not to give up sex for Lent.* As soon as this mission, and every other mission was over, though, he'd head straight home if he could for a date, and should that date with his lover not take place, he scheduled a date with his right hand and some lube or spit.

And of course, now I'm horny!

Karson never really was nervous except for this mission. He always went through his checklist in bed the night before. His schedule for mission was like this the day before:

1. 1000 hours: awake
2. 1005 hours: Pushups, sit ups, pull ups, treadmill.
3. 1030 hours: breakfast: eggs and sausage patty, hash browns, three pancakes with syrup.
4. 1100 hours: review mission briefing, gun gauntlet (running through a course and firing), go to the firing range and test weapons. (Video games on the sub) Lunch at 1300 hours.
5. 1500 hours: review gear. Battle check it. Lock it up.
6. 1600 hours: Home. Spruce, watch the news.
7. 1700 hours: call the loved ones he had who'd pick up, (mom and dad, not liking the lifestyle Karson had chosen, never answer, so leave a message all the same).
8. 1800 hours: dinner (restaurant usually with team or friends)
9. 2000 hours: shower, get in bed. Television or movie (usually action to get pumped.)
10.   2200 hours: Lay and review.
11.   0100 hours: eyes shut.
12.   0600 hours: Eyes open. Stretch.
13.   0605 hours: Pushups, sit ups, pull ups, treadmill.
14.   0630 hours: Shower.
15.   0700 hours: egg, flattened. Water.
16.   0710 hours: off to work.

17.   0800 hours on: ready to work. Training,   review,   talking   with friends/team, etc.
18.   Hours: deploy and execute.
19.   Hours: home.   Nonchalant schedule returns after battle gear is put away unless new mission or instructed otherwise.
20.   The schedule is subject to change depending on missions, orders, or when the deployment is and where.

Karson lived a pretty normal life when not on duty or deployed. He was a man after all, even if he was an exceptionally dangerous one. *I still interact with people, I'm not a threat. I just defend our Nation more deadly aggressive than anyone else!*

Karson finally managed to drift off to sleep early, around 0045 hours after much will power not to jerk off. Being only twenty and all hormonal, Karson's especially, his hormones and urges were pretty difficult to overpower. *I can't break here, Karse. For my brothers.*

It worked because all he wanted to do was run or fight or punch the hull of the sub, which ultimately would break his hand with how hard he wanted to punch it. Karson's night was peaceful, no movement on his part, just lying flat on his back, dreamless, just the black of the back of his eyes and room. The gentle hum of the stealth sub, the soft rocking of the ship side to side, and the fresh and crispness of his bed, all clean and soft. This could be his final night on earth. His last night of pure bliss.

I could be dead by this time tomorrow. Huh. Weird. This is the job I chose.

****

"All companies. Man your battle stations."

Karson's eyes flew open as lights started going off. He could hear the sounds of a ship waking up and ensuing chaos. People were running around. Orders were flying, and maneuvers were being taken. Now he could feel the craft moving.

Karson was up and out of his bunk in seconds, gear on, weapon in hand. Karson could slip on his standard battle gear for a mission in sixty seconds: uniform bottom to top, boots tucked in, body armor. His gearloadout was modfied for the submarine.

Once calm after his combat breathing of four in, hold four, out four, and hold four, he raced to the bridge of the ship and hurried through the door. "What's going on?"

"Steady, men. Hold her steady!" To Karson, the Captain of the Des Moines reassured him. "Captain, we're not sure yet. Hold up."

Karson stood, staring at the screens and the crewmen. "I DO NOT WANT TO HOLD UP. ARE WE SAFE OR NOT? DO I NEED TO DEPLOY? DETECTED? DEAD? GIVE ME A SITREP!" After a pause. "NOW!"

"We're assessing and defending the situation."

"I want an answer now."

"I can't give you an answer now, Captain. There was a large blip on the radar, and now we're not sure where it went. It was a silent moving ship. Submarine. We-"

"You're not going to find it. You need to man your battle stations and be ready to fight. That sub, if allowed to approach, will sink you in an instance if it doesn't from afar. I don't know what it will do to a sub, but drowning is something that I wish not to happen to me. Nor being crushed. Call my SEALs and Staff Sergeant Wilson to deployment stations in the mini submarines. We are going in right now. Where was the last location of that submarine?"

"Twenty miles out, sir." The captain said. "Honestly, though, sir, that sub couldn't have spotted us, we are a stealth ship."

"So it is as well. It has technology we don't even know it has so I don't want to take any chances. Turn the ship around and follow the way you came. This is a one-way mission anyways. We either capture the submarine or we die trying. You have no chance with this ship. You need to get out of here. Send the coordinates to my HUD and feed me on the fly if you have any information to give. Alert my crew. Good luck."

"Good luck, Captain. You will be successful. You are SEAL Team Six. You have to be."

"Yeah, we're more than SEAL Team Six. I apologize if I've come off as a dick lately. I have big shoes to fill and want this to go smoothly with minimal casualties and-"

"I understand. No need to explain, my friend. Now go."

They shook hands and Karson ran to his deployment station and addressed his men. People were running around the battle group like chickens with their heads cut off. Karson radioed the bridge. "I forgot to tell you something, Captain, are you there?"

"Yes, I can hear you."

"When we deploy into the water, you best go silent. Just to be certain the sub doesn't find you if it hasn't already. Hopefully, we intercept it and take it before you have to battle it."

"God speed, Captain."

"Alright men, this is it. The day has arrived where we will see if the American Special Forces training has paid off. Man your subs. You all know the plan. Once we leave this deck, it is silent sailing from here. The pressure down here is too much for opening the mini-subs so rely on our training and radar. Follow in single file, and remember, five feet from the sub before you turn the minis on again. Shut them off once we determine the subs path and paddle into position. I need all radios and communication devices shut down now." Karson shut his off; got in the mini-sub. "God-speed, gentlemen. May the mission fate be in and only in our hands. Let us overpower our enemy and win this war, save lives, and keep the peace!"

"OORAH!" The Marines cheered.

"HOOYAH!" The SEALs cheered along with Sailors assisting in the deployment.

As they started closing the subs up, water came filling into the compartment. Karson got the all clear on his HUD to deploy and knocked on the side of his sub to alert everyone else as he was closed into his tight space. Then, the chamber opened, and out they went into the dark, cold Artic waters.

The mini-subs creaked and groaned as the pressure increased, and the temperature inside the subs dropped to freezing. Water dripped onto Karson, and he couldn't help but panic a wee bit. *If this sub breaks I'm going to be pissed for the ten seconds I am being crushed.* Karson guided his sub in the direction the ship Captain had told. Interception time: twenty-five minutes.

With every mile they inched closer, the scanners showed something moving towards the joint USMC/Navy SEAL SPEC-OPS battle force. The sound instruments picked up the faint humming of the sub that was undetectable to ships above and below the water until it was right on top of them.

Karson started to fall into full focus mode as they reached five miles from their target. At four miles, the humming was a lot louder, drawing the SEALs on, beckoning them, calling to them, death in the distant open waters of the Arctic Ocean, drawing them closer to their possible final mission. At three, a distant robotic sound lapped through the vast, empty ocean, as if massive industrial parts were moving. At two a blip appeared on Karson's radar and continued until mile one, when everything went silent and dark. Karson slowed his sub to a halt. The battle group slowed and stopped too, one line of mini subs. The water was visible for about a football field, so Karson looked out the small glass periscope.

"Captain, it just stopped." The SEAL in Karson's sub turned on Karson's radio from behind and spoke.

"I said no radio traffic, Slink!" Karson said worriedly. "Turn it off! Now."

"Can you see it? On radar, I mean?"

"No," Karson replied curtly, reaching behind to disable his radio signal.

"This is spooky, man." Another SEAL, Bullet, spoke up.

"Turn your radio down. Why aren't they shutting their sub down?" Karson started typing a message through his HUD to the others. *I hope this is encrypted enough.*

"Aye, sir. Signing off." Bullet whispered.

"Ditto," Slink said.

Karson shut his radio off again and scanned around through the periscope. Waiting. He had to admit that this was kinda creepy and he was scared. What were they to expect? *God, I know I'm not the best child of Yours, but protect us on this mission. I still have my whole life ahead of me; I'd like to travel Your great earth. And though I'm not great, my faith to You proves I love you. Protect and provide for us!*

Suddenly movement. A huge, dark shadow appeared a football field in front of Karson heading at a diagonal to him and the battle group. *It's coming right at us.*

The SEAL behind Karson tapped him on the shoulder. Karson stuck his hand up. *Hold on everyone.*

The sub drifted closer and closer, revealing its vast size and girth. It was the size of a fifteen story building at least, and long. Really long.

That's as long as a skyscraper is tall. An underwater One World Trade Center. Has to be. That's a lot to take... And I can't even see all of it! It disappears into the dark. Karson took pictures through the periscope.

Suddenly four torpedoes left the front of the sub. Karson did not move. He typed a new message.
'HLD.'

The Marine Staff Sergeant in sub Three behind Karson's typed back.
'THY R FRNG @ US'

Karson was frightened that he might do something stupid. *This could just be a test, to see if the weapons work, or to see if there is something in front of them. If we are hit, we'll be detected, and the mission will fail. If they miss us, we can still maintain the element of surprise.*
'HLD. TRST ME. DNT KNOW WE HR HD STL.'

The torpedoes floated closer.

Karson dare not move.   'HLD.'

Closer. The ship too. A quarter of a football field and closing fast.

Suddenly the torpedo was right on top of the group and coming right for Karson's sub. He squeezed his eyes shut.

The torpedo soared right overhead. The second went low, third right beside the subs. The fourth, however, nicked the last sub and knocked him lower into the sea, the torpedo veering off at a slight angle.

The mini-sub corrected itself, and Karson sighed. *That was close, but I was right.*

'C! NO PBLM. HLD. 5 FT FRM BM SO NO DETCTN. PDL 5 FT OR CLSR TO SP.'

Karson started rowing the mini sub towards the ship by the peddles below his seat with the help of his team. Closer and closer to the submarine. His submarine. 'Big Momma' would be his. 'Big Momma' was floating past now, and if it passed completely, there was no way to catch backup with her. If they turned the subs on too soon, the ship would know they were there, and if they get in the no radar zone but are too late, the massive roaders could cut the team up.

Almost there, almost there. Got it! Karson made it to the ship, scraping his sub along the side. He powered up and full steam ahead, heading for the entrance port. He inched his way closer and closer, flipping up as the port came closer. As soon as it was in distance, the hooks would fire and dock the sub to the port. His other SEALs would dock to the side of the mini sub and enter that way. Should the mission fail, the Marines in the third sub would be forced to torpedo the two SEAL Team's subs off, and dock themselves, open the hatch, and detach, firing a torpedo at the hatch as they did to keep water flowing in. But for now, the plan was the same. The SEAL at the front would open the hatch, and the team would slide in. So far, the mission was going as planned.

As the port sailed by, Karson fired his docking cables. The first attached no problem, but the second was unsuccessful. The sub started to tilt. Karson retracted the inactive hook and inched closer to the port. He fired the second again, and it hit its mark, allowing for the mini-sub to reacquire the target. Once on target, the sub sealed to 'Big Momma,' allowing SEAL sub two to attach to Karson's sub. The second sub SEALs opened the portal to Karson's sub and awaited entry.

"Alright, men. Once we open this hatch, there is no going back, and the alarms of the ship will go off. Patrols will be stepped up, and death will be rolling our way. We have no clue what is in here. We don't know if there will be an army standing there waiting for us, or what. But this is what we are trained for. The realm of the unknown. And we will meet it with heads held high, hooyah? Whatever happens, we do not leave without this ship, and we do not get captured. Fight until you're dead. Take as many out as you can should the need arise. Don't give up. America shall continue to be the land of the free and the home of the brave, not some desolate, terrorist run landscape. This is our fight. Give 'em hell." Karson turned to the front SEAL.   "Kayak, do it! Watch for a camera."

"Aye, sir. Hooyah!" The SEAL slid the sub mouth open, no water entered, and everyone sighed relief.

"Thank God!" Gramps grunted from the second sub.

Next, he bypassed the encrypted keypad, and turned the knob, and open the hatch came. Alarms, of course, started going off, and the SEALs lowered themselves into God knows what. Eighteen men.

Kayak saw no camera. "No video, sir."

Slink, Ricochet, Bullet, Kayak, Trip, Teepee, Gramps, Picket, Lizard, Bobcat, Manamal, Kite, Osprey, Dill, Tooth, Snipe, Stinger, and Karson/Serval. In that order. Multiple missions encompassing one.

Oh, please let this work!

CHAPTER 38 - Penetrating Big Momma

Karson was the last to drop down. He closed the entrance to the sub.

"Looks as if it'd been closed this entire time and it was only a malfunctioning sensor." Karson's second in command, Slink said.

"Good. Let's hope they buy it!" Karson replied.

"Hooyah!" Slink replied.

"Sir? Where do we go?" Ricochet asked.

Karson scanned the area. "Kayak, you disabled the cameras for five minutes correct?"

"Aye, sir, but only where I am. I have a signal disruptor. I'd have to find a computer to disable all." He replied. "If there was a camera, they hopefully missed us."

"Good." Karson made his way through the massive hallway to the T in the hall. "Looks like they can drive trucks-" Karson heard a noise to his right at the T in the hallway that sounded much like tires screeching on the smooth floor and raised his rifle, ready for a firefight. He looked both ways. No one was in sight, but he could hear the noise of tires and now boots closing in, heading from all directions, as well as shouting and the occasional bark. *If only you were here to cuddle...* "They don't know we are here, but they are coming armed to see what happened. That is good. Depending on how many there are, we can set an ambush. We need their uniforms to blend in. Aim for the back of the neck. If there are only a few, let's hand to hand it. Right now, that room looks as good as any. Kayak, open the door."

"Aye, sir." He moved into position and started tinkering with the keypad while the rest of the joint force stacked up, aiming their suppressed weapons down the hallways, exposed.

"Slink, Tooth, Dill, Bullet, Bobcat-cover the right. Ricochet, Trip, Pops, Picket, Manamal, Kite, Snipe, cover left. Teepee, Lizard, Stinger, Osprey, cover Kayak as we enter the room." Karson ordered. More urgently, he spoke to Kayak. "Hurry Kayak." Karson shifted nervously. "I don't want to be caught out here with our pants down."

"I'm trying!" Kayak responded, frustrated. "This is advanced technology. Lizard, Serval, Osprey, Stinger, Teepee, be ready." He looked back to see Karson nod.

"Team, if those men arrive, fire at will should we be trapped out here," Karson ordered.

"What's up with the floor? Why is it all gratey and holy?" Osprey asked.

"Not the time, Osprey. Focus on what is going on! And hurry up Kayak, we are sitting ducks-"

CLICK

"There." Kayak jerked his hand over his crotch and exploded his fingers in the air. "Suck that, Serval." He smacked Karson in the balls.

Karson chuckled with his eyes, protected by his cup. "Never doubted you. Everyone inside."

The SEALs Kayak had named entered and cleared the-

- "Armory. Perfect!" Karson smiled. "Some good news! Quick, everyone inside!" Karson closed the door. Uniforms and weapons awaited. Karson removed his gear and put on the enemy uniform and gear and took the AK-47 closest to him. Each of the men did the same in turns. Now, eighteen Americans stood in 'Death Nation' uniforms. Karson grabbed his suppressor from his rifle and modified it to work on an AK-47. "Team do as I do."

"Sir, why weren't patrols or a few men around the entrance to the sub? Why was it empty when we arrived?" Picket asked.

"Did we have armed sentries surrounding the sub's entrance on the Des Moines?" Karson replied.

"No... We had cameras..." Picket started.

"Exactly. This deep, no one would be able to open the hatch from the outside." Karson reassured the man.

"No, but we did. We're Navy SEALs. Wouldn't they have thought of this?" Tooth interjected.

"It's a bunch of mercenaries under the command of a lunatic. He doesn't believe that we have the ability to defeat him. Maybe we don't. But we've made it this far." Karson said.

"Just another thought sir, why is the armory located here?" Bullet said, looking up from his modifications.

"That has me worried, honestly. Perhaps it's because, like I said, their leader is a lunatic. Maybe we were supposed to be allowed on this sub when he surfaced next, so that way we could believe we had him defeated, or so we'd think we have the upper hand? I don't know. Maybe he knows we're here now. We'll figure that out later. Right now, we do have the upper hand. Hear that? They have arrived, and we're not dead yet. That's what I believe!" Karson said proudly.

"As you say, sir." Tooth replied.

Karson looked out the small window of the armory at the gathering at the entrance. The seven men were scratching their heads, watching the dripping coming from the portal.

Then, what seemed to be their ship officer, walked into view.

"What the problem?" The man with long boots, a belt wrapping around his fat beer belly, and a large hat on his head told his story.

"Bulgarian," Karson muttered. "Another nationality for Death Nation."

"Un Fuga, Señor." A Spanish mercenary spoke.

I want a taco now! Karson thought.

"A leak? Alright then. Keep eye on it, and if anything happens, let me know. We have heading towards American ship. Submarine. Stealth by look of it. It time to sink it. All crew must die. We cannot risk being detected. We must arrive undetected for maximum casualty." He turned on his heel and marched away in the opposite direction.

"Alright team, here we go. Those men are splitting up, and the bridge is to the right of here. All we need to do is-"

"ਉਹ ਿ ਡੱਪ ਮਹਿਲ ਨੂੰ ਲੈ ਕੇ." (Uha ïḍapa mahila nū lai kē. -Punjabi language.) {Those drips lead to the armory.}

"Tunahitaji kupata nyuma maeneo yetu. Kuangalia ni nje na kutuambia Whatis kinachoendelea." (We need to get back to our areas. You two. Check it out and tell us what is going on. -Swahili.)

«Давайте идти искать в Оружейной палаты.» (Davayte idti iskat' v Oruzheynoy palaty. -Russian). {Let's go look in the armory.}

« Je n'ai pas une arme à feu. » (I don 't have a gun. -French)

"I know those words! Russian and French!" *Thank you high school foreign languages!* "They are coming for the armory, team. As soon as they enter, grab 'em! Alive!"

Karson readied himself beside the door. The access numbers were being punched into the panel.

BEEP

BEEP

BEEP

BEEP

BEEP

BEEP

Karson held up his fingers. *Three...*

BEEP

Two...

CLICK

"One." Karson whispered, dropping his final finger.

The door opened, and Karson greeted his target, smiling. Karson raised his weapon. "Run for your life!" The man's eyes bulged, and he started to turn, but Karson lunged, grabbed the gun from the Russian man, and disarmed him, tugging on his beard to drop him to the ground. He threw him into the corner and aimed the pistol.

Teepee did the same to the Frenchman who had tried to run, but was too slow for a taser, which hit into his left glute, and also, it would seem, his...

"OOOO!" Gramps cheered! "Right into his nut sack!"

Everyone 'giggled,' well, as a SEAL could giggle.

"Nuts!" Bobcat meowed with laughter!

Karson looked over his shoulder. "Nice!" He said to his friends. Karson now turned his attention back to his enemies. "Y'all speak English?" No one spoke. "Alright." Karson drove his knife into the Frenchman's groin, slicing it off, holding his hand over the man's mouth. The Russian's eyes bulged. "You're next, my friend." Karson winked at the Russian. "Monsieur, I just cut your cock off... So if you move, try to flee, make a noise, or disobey me, its gonna hurt, and its going to hurt bad." The Frenchman's eyes watered and he slid down away from Karson and puked.

"I sveak English. So does he." The Russian spluttered out his words in a higher pitch. "Please, I obey. Don't do dat to me."

"Good!" Karson removed the knife. "Medic, patch him up." Karson walked over to the Russian, opened his mouth and made him lick the blade clean. "I have no problem grabbing another man's junk, especially if it means shoving it either down your throat or up your rectum. Now start talking. Tell us about your ship, the flaws, the locations of everything. The manifest, crew, everything. Do it now, or I'll cut your balls off as well and make you a eunuch. Gramps back there has a liking of testicles of any animal. He'll eat them raw even, meaning, bye bye left nut right nut." Karson sliced into the man's cheek.

"Start talking, Ballsy!" Gramps said.

Karson chuckled.

"Okay, Amedican. But you make huge mistake! HUGE! Dis ship is impenetrable and unsinkable and-"

Karson slapped him. "I'm gonna need you to keep it to a soft, inside voice." Karson cut his other cheek. "This room is going to be soaked in blood if you don't do as I wish. Team, four of you guard the door. We may be here for a while!"

"Hooyah." Four SEALs replied.

The man grunted and barely flinched as he spit out the blood, careful not to hit Karson, as he was unstable and unpredictable right now. His tongue moved to both sides of his mouth, checking the damage. Not enough to need attention, but enough to hurt.

Whenever the Russian man spoke, he did not look into Karson's eyes like a civilized man. Rather, like an animal plotting its next move. The man's eyes moved down and looked straight ahead at the beginning of the sentence, and ended on Karson's blue eyes on the last few words. "I don't know vhat you plan to do, but dis ship is far too large. You vill not make dent in it."

"I'll be the one to determine that. You just need to tell me what I want to know, and everyone goes home! Even you. You'll see your family again. Just do as I say." Karson used his thumb and pressed it into the wound in the Russian's mouth. "See, Death Nation, the very same people you serve for, taught me mouth torture when I was in Pakistan. I think I'll dull those yellow teeth of yours."

"Alright. I vill." The man moved his head and readjusted the way he was sitting and his crotch, obviously still nervous of what might happen to his prized anatomy, getting ready to tell his story. "Before I start... You cannot frighten dem. You cannot subdue dem. You cannot control dem. Dey leeve in most frightened places, most frightened conditions. Dey deal vit dis before for hundres of yeers... Dere immunt to feer and dis. You step into dis sess pool, you de only one who gets infected, Amedican."

"We will deal with every single one of your friends no matter the threat they pose."

"You don't know terrain."

"We're SEALs. We train for all. If not, we adapt. We interrogate you. You lose with us. Every time. And I think we're doing pretty well for ourselves thus far!"   Karson looked at the Frenchmen. "He gonna be alright?"

"Yeah, he didn't have a boner so he won't bleed out, but he's dripping like a faucet. That was brutal, sir. I thought that was against the law." The team medic, Teepee said.

"It is. But I don't follow the law on non-Americans. Not anymore. Not when we need this. This is an area that Congress doesn't want or need to know too much about. War is not a pretty thing like many think it is. Human killing human for a long time will bring out the worst in you. Best in you. But will stick with you no matter what. I'll torture the life outta you guys until you give me what I want." Karson smiled wide at the Russian. "SEAL Team Six... We are not checked. We do what we do and are praised for our ruthlessness. We do bad things to bad people! We skew the lines between Soldier and Spy! Bleed him until he gives you your intel. Start talking. Or i'll bleed you dry."

The medic continued working on the Frenchman, but he spit in the SEAL's face, who responded by sitting back on his heels for a second, wiping the spit out of his eyes, drawing his side arm and pushing it against the man's head. "I'm trying to save your life, dude, but I guess terrorists have no end, do they?" The medic placed to fingers together and started fingering the man's wound. "Yeah, you like that?" He reached into his pack. "Better get used to it since you're gonna have woman parts here soon! Mmmm, just like a wet coochie! Delicious!" The Frenchman moaned as his former cock and now hole was being damaged even more. The medic stopped, pulling out a packet of feces from his pack.

"What is that?" Slink asked his brother.

"Dog crap. I'm not much different than Serval. I've got torture ideas as well. Maybe fill his cut with crap... let him feel the infection rise. Now, let me help you, and maybe you'll be spared all of this."

"See, I told you. The law escapes you in these situations." Karson grimaced. "Talk about brutal, dude!"

"Whatever!" Teepee put the feces away.

"Sir, respectfully, the mission," Ricochet said.

Karson now drew his lips close to the Russian's, so his eyes were with Karson's eyes. The Russian's, full of pride, but with a lot of fear as well. *Surprising for a Russian. Even these hardened veterans can be afraid!* Karson's eyes, pure calm and expertise. No fear. Just hatred. "I specialize in torture my friend. Just like the medic there, and the rest of us. I'm the worst. I've felt all, and will deliver it on you ten fold. Diablo, as some of your Spanish colleagues would say!"

"I told you! I said I'd tell. I don't vant to be here anyways. You have no idea how hard it is being dragged from your home and forced to train in deeze training facilities and vit no respect, just like animals being led to slaughter house. I vant to be home vit family. Finish university. Go to Amerdica. Most of us do. Nobody likes Death Nation. Vhat a stupid name anyvays."

"Good. Then start talking." Karson smacked him again.

"Oue! Stop doing dat!" The Russian pleaded.

Karson unholstered his handgun and flipped it around so the handle was facing the man's head. He raised it. "I'm 'bout to beat the life out of you, man. You're wasting my time with your sob story. I don't care. I really, really don't care. TELL ME... Tell me what I want to know. NOW!"

"Okay. Okay. Dis ship is like a city. No, more like bee hive. Ve call it Hivemind. People go through day to day like normal people vould, except zat zey are under armed guard. As vell, zey are loyal, even doe most also hate Death Nation. Ve all fear the vrath of our Supreme Leader! Ve are all trained on how to fight. Zat is middle of ship, vhere food is grown and cared for. Der is people of different jobs on dis ship. Trackers, workers, ze royalty, ze seekers, destroyers, assassins, guards, nurses, etcetera, etcetera, etcetera. Dis ship never needs refueled. Da fuel is made on board somehow if any is used. Not nuclear; I believe plasma or something like dat. Dat part of ship is in back. Da bridge is at front. Dis is not only armory, uhder one every hundred feet. Weakness: size. Vhile vell manned, it is also dispersed through da ship. In heavy guarded areas are major tings. Bridge for example: heavy guard. Gun in ceiling and gun in hands of people. Video cameras all throughout. Control Center for veapons and systems is in bottom of ship. Very bottom. Uhh, uhh... I'm running out of tings... Can go through vents, but dey are narrow. **You** would fit, but vitout gear. You are small. Rest of you, vay too big."

"Weapons. Ojore? Locations?"

"You have me vrong, Amerdican. I am low on... food chain, I tink is, how you say, 'vould put it...' I not gifted major locations of ship. Just basic structure as I am basic soldier. Only vay to take ship down is from inside. No vay sink. If hole, it will be plugged."

"Yeah... We'll see about that." Karson said. "You have been very helpful, so I'll let you live, but it has to be that you go into a deep slumber for now. Medic, drug him and the Frenchie. We have a sub to take."

****

CHAPTER 39 - Алоешенка Щекочихин Ёжиков Цирюльников

T roops on mission:

1. **Slink**
2. **Tooth**
3. **Dill**
4. **Bullet**
5. **Bobcat**
6. **Ricochet**
7. **Trip**
8. **Gramps**
9. **Picket**
10. **Manamal**
11. **Kite**
12. **Snipe**
13. **Teepee**
14. **Lizard**
15. **Osprey**
16. **Serval**
17. **Kayak**
18. **Stinger**

Karson poked his head out of the door, weapon raised, checking to see if anyone had come back to check on the two missing Death Nation soldier. Ensuring the coast was clear, Karson made his way out of the armory and turned to his men.

"Sir, the Russian said we can't sink it. What if we fail to take her, sir?" Snipe asked.

"Make sure we succeed," Karson replied curtly.

"Even you can't be that stupid. If this fails, like it mostly likely will-" Picket said.

Karson was in Picket's face faster than a cheetah running after her prey. "Hey! If you think like that, we will not succeed. You think I don't know this is an impossible mission? Our job is still the same. Succeed. That is the order. That is what we will do. Remember where you work. We are in creation because we can make the impossible a reality. So shut up! We can do this!"

"Sir, we respect this fact about us. If we do fail, though, what do we do? We can't sink the ship." Manamal commented.

Karson thought for a moment. *What if they are right and this mission is flawed? Then we die, no one knows we are dead for hours, and by then it is too late. No ability to stop this ship. That destroy our sea power. What then?* Then his eyes widened. He snapped his finger. "I know what happens. If we fail, Staff Sergeant Wilson has his radio on of course and I will order him to execute his same orders."

"Sir, that is what we are saying, it won't work!" Kite shouted now.

Karson turned, smiling viciously. "You didn't let me finish. I'm sure you're familiar with the birds and the bee's gentlemen! I will order him to execute his orders and fuck the ship's hatch! He'll shove the mini-sub into the hatch of the sub, keeping anything from plugging up the torrent of water that will come flowing in! It won't be as fast, but it will be an unstoppable tidal wave all the same!"

"You don't even know if that would work, sir! All due respect but-" Picket added another comment.

"I'm about to consider you insubordinate and sit you out. You are paid to execute, not argue. You are trained to do the impossible, not whine like that Marine in the briefing room. You are on my team, and so you will treat this like we have already succeeded. You are a Navy SEAL, so nothing is hard. You are an American, and so your resolve must stand. You are a man, so grow some balls to live up to that bulge you got there. Trust me. Trust the mission. Believe that if we die, we will still succeed."

"Alright, sir. As you say. You have to understand my concern, though. All I want, like you, is to succeed in this mission and go home and see my family. Especially my baby girl." Picket stated.

"Aye, I do, and you will!" Karson responded, looking up and down the corridor again. "Alright team, we are on a sort of schedule now. They are after our brothers in blue on that ship of ours. We have to intercept this ship's control before they reach target range and make our ship look like a piece of Swiss cheese." Karson turned to his men. "Now for the fun part, gentlemen! Charlie team: heading forward towards the bridge, eliminating and disposing of any enemy personnel we find. Subduing the bridge operators if we can. Interrogating and learning how to pilot the craft. Ensuring we deliver it to United States custody. Tooth, Dill, Gramps, and me! Delta, control room, hack into computers and steal information. Eliminate all personnel. Hack system. Give us an advantage, feed team on the fly. Cover our tracks by looping their view of the cameras while you take control and watch from your view. Disable all traps and hidden dangers as you can, or inform us as we go! Kayak, Osprey, Lizard, Teepee. Echo, engines and fuel. See what you can learn and how you can cripple this craft should you be able too. Eliminate all enemies. Bullet, Kite, Picket, Trip. Finally, Foxtrot. You will be the sweepers. You are to head to the enemy quarters and disable them there. Take them all out. Once that is completed, head to the middle of the ship and gain Intel. Walk the ship. Learn from it. Feed us on the fly. Slink, Bobcat, Ricochet, Stinger, Manamal, Snipe. Eliminate any and all you can. This goes for everyone. Hide the bodies of our enemy. If we are detected, mission failed. Everybody understand?" Karson finished.

They all nodded.

"Good. Leaders of your squads, of course, are by rank. Let's go!" With that, Karson saluted his family and turned and headed forward in the ship towards the bridge. Not looking back. His team followed him up the long hallway in a quick but silent pace. Karson could feel the sweat dripping down his body as he continued to run. More running, and more running. Nothing seemed to change. No end seemed to draw near. No sounds were being made, besides the noise of the mechanics of the submarine. *Why are there no-*

"Sir? Does this feel right to you? There are no contacts. As SEALs, we are taught that if we are moving swiftly in a heavily enemy combatant field scenario, that we are probably doing something wrong, or missing something…" Gramps called up.

Karson slowed down and halted. He moved to the side of the corridor and pulled his canteen and took a sip. The water was warm and thick as it slid down his throat and he wiped away the beads of sweat from his brow. He looked at his men. Karson sighed. He looked up and down the corridor. "I honestly don't have any other idea of where to go with this… The commander walked in this direction. We're a mile or so underwater, so there is no need for a craft like this to have an armed patrol. All I can say is that we just keep heading in this direction, heads on the swivel, and wait for Delta's instructions, guidance, and help. I don't even know where the bridge is."

"I guess this works then, sir," Gramps said.

Karson took another sip of his water and put it back in its pouch and stood. A message popped up on his HUD.
DANGER'

Karson stopped in shock as five men with pistols strapped to their legs came around the corner. They stared at Karson and his team, crouched, looking as suspicious as possible, and Karson and his team stared at them, clearly up to no good. It clicked somehow, with the enemy first that this was a no good operation and one drew his gun, firing a shot into Karson's chest. Karson flew backward from the round he'd taken and slid on the ground, belly up.

"SIR!" Tooth shouted.

Karson heard silenced shots and thuds as five mens' lives were ended in five accurate shots to the heart. For this mission, Karson snuck his men hollow point bullets so no evidence could be captured. This worked here; the bullets stopped in their hearts after splintering to cause maximum damage and stopping power. Karson lay panting on the ground, his vision clearing. His breath knocked from his body as his colleagues came rushing over.

"That was a Desert Eagle .50 caliber, man! You took that and survived!" Dill was gushing and awing over Karson.

Karson grabbed clumsily to Dill's shoulder, eyes wide and was hoisted to his feet where he proceeded to lose his stomach's contents. His smaller frame convulsing with his body's provoked effort to relieve itself of some pressure. He gagged.

"Serval, you are alright. We need to hide these bodies!" Gramps said, grabbing one and dragging him around the corner.

Karson nodded and kept his hands on his knees catching his breath and sipping some water as his men continued to hide the bodies. Karson looked down and pulled the bullet from his chest and placed it in his pocket as a souvenir.

'SIR, ENEMY APPROACHING HARD AND FAST. GET OUT OF THERE NOW! 10 SECONDS

9

8

7

6

5… SIR THEY ON TOP OF YOU!'

Karson spun around as he heard the sound of more enemies arriving on top of him and his men. They too only carried pistols.

"Wat gaan hier aan? Ons het 'n skoot! Wat het gebeur?" {Afrikaans for: What is going on here? We heard a shot! What happened?}

What kind of language is that? Sounds Germanic, or Romanian?

"Antwoord my! Nou!" {Answer me! Now!} The man's hand moved to his weapon on his leg.

Karson needed something. "Здравствуйте! Я понятия не имею, что вы только что сказали, чувак! Я говорю на русском, французском и английском. Вы? Вы говорите на английском, французском или русском?" [Zdravstvuyte! YA ponyatiya ne imeyu, chto vy tol'ko chto skazali, chuvak! YA govoryu na russkom, frantsuzskom i angliyskom. Vy? Vy govorite na angliyskom, frantsuzskom ili russkom?] {Russian: Hello! I have no clue what you just said, dude! I speak Russian, French, and English. You? Do you speak English, French, or Russian?}

"Ek praat nie die taal. Jy moet my nou beantwoord!" {I don't speak that language. You need to answer me now!} He pushed Karson backwards with a blow to is chest plate over his Death Nation uniform.

I don't have the time for this dude!

"Sveak English?" Karson asked in his Russian accent. *Thank you high school theatre class dialogues!*

"Yes. We heard shot. What happened?" He replied.

"Oh. Uh…" An idea clicked in Karson's head! "Are you familiar wit da viral video 'Team Stay Vhere You Are and Follow Suit'?"

"No. Never heard of dat. Cut to chase." He took a step closer to Karson. "What are you doing here all alone?"

"Well, in dat video, it tries to see if you able to fire shot into chest protector and see if you take it… I tried video… I bored and thought no one vould hear me down here…" Karson said.

"You're lucky alarms not go off and cause mass panic. I can't let dat slide. Come wit me. Admiral will decide what do wit you!"

"I no tink dat necessary. Can't you help me out? Von't happen again." Karson fake pleaded.

"You and I bot know dat we need to be ahead on rank status. I can't let go. Face dat way. Walk wit us." He ordered. As he started walking, the man slipped in Karson's puke. "Why is vomit on ground?"

"Vhen you shoot self in stomach, you tend to lose your meal," Karson said embarrassed.

His HUD lit up.

'SIR? NEED INTERVENE? SAY 'I CAN CLEAN IT UP','

The man turned to Karson. "This is disgusting… You-"

"I'm sure Admiral vant to know vat is happen. It vill dry. I have date vit my cock later. I vant to be done vit dis!"

"You're messed up, man." The other soldier present said.

The hell kina accent is that? Karson looked over at him. "Var tend to do dat to Russians." He laughed and started following the enemy soldiers, looking back after a few minutes to notice his team following way behind, their red uniforms not blending to the dark of the interior of the ship. *Good, this will get us to the bridge fast!*

"Do you know if Admiral is on bridge?" The Afrikaans man asked his partner.

"Yes. He is. He went to check cameras and see why alarms went off." The partner responded.

"Good! This vill be over quick. Just tell story like you told us!" The South African soldier stated.

The men escorted Karson over to an elevator and pressed the up button. The number above the door was on thirty. It dropped down to twenty-three.

How big is this ship? The door finally opened with a ding and in the men entered. Karson noticed the man press the third highest number of forty-seven. *Dis ship is fifty stories tall!?* Karson was shocked. *Dayum! This is a lot of ship!*

The elevator rose quickly. *Wait. What are my men going to do? I guess they'll watch the number rise or take the stairs, or something... They're smart. They'll adapt and compromise.*

A sound reverberated through the ship, one of sheer terror. An eerie echo like the interior of a sci-fi spaceship with a creepy sound of a child's breathy moan. As suddenly as it started, it stopped. The men were unfazed, and Karson took his cue not to be either.

The elevator reached level-

"Forty-seven." A digital voice spoke to the occupants of the elevator. The doors opened and out the men went. This corridor was far smaller than the others and held doors Karson assumed were officer rooms and offices, or briefing rooms and bathrooms... Maybe a break room... Cabins to *porn? I bet y'all have massive orgies up here. That is STDs waiting to happen. Oh, lovely movie theatre! Wow! For ruthless people, they still have human tendencies!*

Karson followed the men around the corners of the hallway and through a set of water doors towards an opening in the hall to a lobby. On the right-hand side of the lobby was a huge metal door. *That would be the bridge, I assume!* Outside the bridge were two heavily armed guards. Full battle rattle. Fully enclosed helmet, body armor that wrapped around their throats and down their upper torsos, and pants that covered their boots. Armored. They looked like firefighters with guns!

"You guys look awesome, man! You hot in der?" Karson asked, politely. Admiring them, taking on the young new warrior look to these 'big strong veterans'! *I can play anyone! Especially a bad guy's ego!*

"No. Air conditioning." The one on the right said.

Karson nodded in approval. "Me vant!" *What?! You're an American!*

"Get on Admiral's good side, and he may just let you have one!" The one on the left now spoke up!

"Mmm… Dat vat you did?" Karson asked. *You too, huh? Traitors. Deserters. You're the first to kill! Nice and slow, I think!*

"Da!" He teased.

Karson chuckled! "As if you vere native to mother Russia!" *Air conditioning means there has to be a filter or a tube or a somewhat less armored section on their helmets. Good to know to shoot these bastards!*

The South African fiddled with a voice box by the door and finally got a response.

"Help you?"

"Have insubordinate here. Asking to speak vit Admiral!" The man said.

"Alright. Stand back." The voice replied.

Karson was forced back as steam appeared around the door and it moved forward out into the lobby and then up, down, and side to side. Four triangles with spikes and holes made this door an impenetrable force to be reckoned with. *Kudos to Death Nation for making this mission difficult!* Karson followed the men into the vast room. And what a sight Karson saw. *Gold mine! Right here! Alright, Hunter. Make your plan. What are you going to do?*

In the middle of the room sat the officer from earlier inspecting documents as he closed in on the enemy vessel. On the radar showed the submarine one hundred miles away and 'Big Momma' was closing fast. Also, a small fleet of Royal Australian Naval ships was closing in on the American subs position.

Good. Let the ship close in on the fleet and then take it, raise it, and hail the ships to board. The more people, the merrier!

The Admiral looked up and noticed Karson. "I have never seen you before."

"Large ship, sir," Karson said in his accent.

"I meet everybody once. I remember faces. Tell me, what is your name, señor?" The Admiral was clearly a wise man, very experienced and knew his way in order and respect. He was poised to rise from his seat but deemed it not the time to assert himself as of yet.

Karson stayed very calm. "Aloyoshenka. Aloyoshenka Shchekochikhin Yozhikov Tsiryulnikov." {Алоешенка Щекочихин Ёжиков Цирюльников.}

"Wow. That's a long-ass mouth full of words there, Aloyoshenka. Aloyoshenka, eh? That means 'defends mankind.' You have a rare name for a Russian man. Normally your names are Alexi or Vlad. Why this name? Why the hardest name to say? And, I assume, one of the hardest names to write... Hmm?"

"I don't know. I guess I special. From beginning, I knew I vas special. Maybe my parents felt same. Maybe dey vanted me to be memorable!"

"Ah, Russians do love their families and politeness, yet they are vicious and a formidable force when you're in battle against them. Every superpower need fear the Russians." The Spaniard came up to Karson and examined him. "You are far smaller than any Russian I have ever seen. Young. Very young. I feel like I would have remembered you."

That is absolutely correct, my dead 'friend.' Russians are pretty powerful, awesome, friendly people! Even to America! Rather than fight 'em, I'd rather just be their allies, and them ours! Hopefully, when the new world is formed, my wish will be granted. For now, continue engaging this man. "Da, sir! My guess, sir, is dat you ver distracted by how many people you ver meeting ven I came on!"

"Perhaps. You are a very exquisite creature, my boy! Well spoken. Polite. Handsome..." He removed Karson's chest protector and poked him in the belly.

Weird.

"Not firm but a slight layer of fat... I can feel your power, yet the softness of your body. Abs present but not a rock. I'm sure you cuddle up with someone special." The man examined him like an animal at the fair. "I certainly would have remembered you... What is the reason you are on my bridge?"

"I shot myself with a Desert Eagle," Karson said proudly, beaming, and puffing out his chest. *This man wants to be the father of everyone. Let me act as his son. He'll like that!*

"Mmm... And why do that, my boy?" The man took Karson's cheeks between his thumb and his index finger. "Perfectly white teeth. Sharp. Interesting."

"Because I vanted to be as strong as my oder countrymen who made video," Karson said. "I miss my home."

"Why do you smell good, have perfectly white teeth, skinny yet healthy, small, boyish frame, intelligence, silky soft hair, radiant blue eyes-deep in color, and perfect face? Yet full of muscle. You're also not pale. Rather, you have a somewhat dark tan, but not exceptionally dark, but it's not pale! Your family rich? Well off at least?"

"My family vas vell off and loved me. Kept me happy." Karson replied.

"I like you. Brave. Polite. Respectful. Smart. Daring. Just the kind of **man** I need in my company. You familiar with this ship at all? What was your primary duty?"

Think Hunter. Don't panic. Use your training. SEALs lie all the time when interrogated. Don't take too long; the man is waiting. Karson looked up into the man's face. Karson never really took in any enemy features he saw, but this man was an exception. Messy, somewhat long, reddish brown hair, deep dark pools of brown eyes with speckles of Amethyst poking through around the edges. Slight wrinkles showing age and wisdom and experience. Safety, it would seem for Karson. Admiration and liking for Karson. Meat on his bones but not fat. Strong. So strong from what Karson could feel from the grasp of his cheeks. Handsome cheek and jaw, white teeth. Larger, flatter nose. Lighter skin complexion. If you met this guy on the streets in Texas, he'd seem like an ordinary man to you. He could even have been *my father! But he's a killer, Karson. An enemy. Don't let him fool you. But he looks so nice...*

"Control room... Computers." Karson lied proudly, hoping Delta would notice what he'd said or even heard it from the cameras they should have taken.

RIGHT HERE WITH YOU SIR. COMPUTERS ARE HIGH TECH. I'LL ANSWER ANY QUESTIONS HE USES TO TEST YOU.

Karson relaxed a little. *Good! Bring it!* But to Karson's surprise, the man didn't test him. He merely looked at Karson for what seemed like a minute, smiled, ruffled his hair and sat back down.

"Aloyoshenka, come here." He beckoned Karson forward.

THAT WAS WEIRD!

Karson did as he was instructed. "Aye, sir?"

"I want to offer you a job. Here on my bridge. I'm growing older, and the man to take over my submarine decided he wished to pursue more military-political paths and went topside, and now has the title of second most wanted man in the world."

Karson's eyes bulged. *Uh, what?*

"Yes, Hatyara was second in command of this ship." The Spaniard continued.

Karson shut his mouth and listened more intently. *Wow, just out yourself, Hunter! That'll win you the ship! Maybe he didn't notice...*

"As I am without a second officer on this bridge," he continued, "I would like to know if you'd be willing to fill this position..."

"Are you sure you haf no oder people more qualified den me, sir?" Karson asked, shocked that his leader would realize that he was such a great Sailor after all!

"No, no one has the skill sets that you do. You're young, vibrant, a good leader..."

"Sir? I vork in computers... I hardly tink I'm-"

"Subs are basically computers. This one is just massive! That is all, my friend. Now, what do you think?"

"Uh..." Karson stuttered. *What are you doing!?*

"Come on. You have all the requisites required for my position when I decide to retire my command. You'll learn how to pilot this monster, conquer any enemy. You'll be good at leading the men. I mean, just look at how your boys will follow you blind into a trap. They must really trust you! Look at them!" To the other guards, he said leave and go back to your duty.

They saluted and walked to the door.

Karson nodded. Then he froze. "Wait… What?" Karson said, breaking character.

The two guards punched the code to open the door.

"TEAM, NO!" Karson shouted as loud as he could, turning to the door.

The door opened, and the men's heads exploded by large caliber bullets. Karson moved to retrieve his weapon, but the Spaniard pushed down on Karson's hand on his pistol and had his own pistol pressed to Karson's forehead in a matter of seconds. Karson gasped; *so close to death. Slight pressure… One finger spasm…* The men on the bridge too held weapons to the new SEAL guests, and four guns lowered from the ceiling and trained on the newcomers. Even a laser covered the now closed tight iron door.

No escape! I'm dead. We're dead. Delta, you'll have to tell the Marines to kill us! All of us! Sink this ship!

The Spaniard chuckled, eyes locked on Karson. Unblinking, and unmoving, even as he spoke. "I must give you Americans credit for making it onto this ship undetected, taking my guards undetected, making it here undetected Death Nation soldiers, and speaking to me, Karson, as a Russian. You are a very, **very** talented boy. You know that? You see, I know you're Americans. Didn't you think about cameras? Yes, you did, but a ship this size… backup camera systems?" He laughed. "But anyways, back to business. I know you like the position I have just presented you with. It was just a stall tactic, but now I'm really offering it to you. I know you know what you want. And this turmoil inside of you is temporary. But my offer still is valid and genuine. Just take what I am offering you. This sub is yours. Let me tell you how you get it, my son!"

My son? Father? Could you become my real father, rather than the one I thought I had back home in Texas for abandoning me for my life choices… For becoming and being- "How do you know my name, *dad*?" Karson asked, finishing 'dad' in his head.

"You are famous, my friend. You are the one everybody wants dead. You are the one who is so feared in the ranks of Death Nation. You are the one that may just end this war on behalf of the Allied Nations. The third world war will come to an end like her sister wars before. And the world will go back to normal. Well, that is until now."

"Sir, what are our orders?" Gramps asked. "Do we alert the Marines?"

"No," Karson said.

"But… But, sir!" Gramps stepped forward as a guard shouted for him to step back.

"I also must give your men props." His eyes were still on Karson's. "Well done, gentlemen. Those tanks of men out there are not possible to kill, and somehow you did it."

"How the hell did you kill Gigantor, out there?" Karson asked, smiling at his friend.

"Not difficult at all. Every design has some sort of flaw. You people are so predictable. 'It's no too hot in this suit; we need air!' There's a giant air pump on the helmet, meaning piping on the helmet on the back, so aim there, and splat. Brain matter everywhere. Anyone could have figured that out from looking at it!" Tooth smiled, defiant and cocky.

"I had to ask, dude!" Karson laughed. "I absolutely love you."

"See, right there is why I like you, Karson."

Karson looked back to the Spaniard. "Why?"

"Because even in this dire situation, you remain calm. You crack jokes… you still know what you have to do. You're plotting, and yet you can find the humor in the situation you're in. I like that. That is why my offer still stands. All you have to do is prove yourself to us. Then that is all yours. I have so much I can teach you! I can become your mentor! No more being in the fight. No more being hunted. No more orders to go into hostile territory. Only giving orders upon receiving orders directly from the Supreme Leader. It's a cruel world out there, Karson. Kill or be killed. On this craft, it is only kill. Simple." The Spaniard concluded.

"Except for right now. Right now, for you and this ship, it is kill or be killed. You know who I am. You know what I can do. You know that I have the ability to end whatever this is. That is why you are so afraid. That is why you want me to join you. You expect me to join you because if I don't, you have the high probability of dying. However, there is that slim possibility you win, and I die, which is still a loss to you because I'm so fascinating and 'talented' to you. I'm special. I would be a waste. If I join you, you receive a higher up identification on the totem pole for Death Nation meaning benefits for converting the most dangerous SEAL into a Death Nation killing machine. You are assured a victory against the Navy you're hunting, and possibly a win over the seas. Thin, you'd have superior air, land, **and** sea forces. Am I kind of close?"

"Yes. Spot on. Except for this part. Here is my offer. The offer before still stands if you prove yourself... worthy. Leave human nature behind. Your men right there need to die. Now, no matter how you play this, your SEAL team will die right here, right now. Either by your hand, by which they will be assured a quick and painless death. Bullet to brain. Or by my hands: where they are paralyzed by shot to the neck, not blotting out pain receptors, but disabling nerves. Then, they will be tortured for information, then burnt alive to the brink of death, then placed in a torpedo tube, about to drown, then crushed by being forced out of tube into open waters. Your choice. Your three men will die. You pick how."

Three men. He doesn't know about the others.

"As for the others... Well, let's just say they are being rounded up now. Let me ask you. What frequency does this subs internet system run on?"

"Easy. The internet system runs on-" *Come on Slink! What is the answer?*

"I'm sorry, is no one typing on your HUD? Yeah. They are otherwise engaged. Have a look." The Spaniard pointed to a monitor in the middle of the room. Upon the screen were sections of the ship where SEALs clashed with soldiers of Death Nation. "I'd like your answer now."

No! Kite is down! "How did you know we were onboard? How did you know about my team?"

"C'est moi!" {It is me!}

Karson spun around to see the French man bleeding onto the floor through his gauze.

"Looks like someone's period came earlier than expected this month!" Tooth chomped the insult!

Karson spit out in laughter, unable to control it.

"Silence!"

"Or what?" Gramps asked, ball tapping, rather, muff punching the Frenchman.

"Funny thing is, Frenchie, I think that is funny too!" The Admiral laughed. "Get some medical attention!"

"Hey, Frenchie? Pussy dripping a wee bit too much, eh? Need some pads?" Dill pickled in.

"I vill kill you right here, right now and no one will stop moi-" A shot rang out around the bridge and Frenchie's head split in two, blood and brain splattering everywhere. Even Karson's SEALs were in shock, staring at Karson in horror. Karson's gun was smoking, and he looked back at the Spaniard, weapon still in the opposite direction.

"You drew that so fast, even with my hand holding yours down!" His eyes were proud, holding his cheek from the backslap Karson had delivered him upon the draw. "You prove me right. You have a relentless evil side to you. You tortured him. You killed him in cold blood."

"He was threatening my friends. Much like you are doing right now. He was tortured by me, yes, but unlike you, I put him out of his misery. He was dying a slow and painful death."

"Even still. Now, I need your answer. Your friends die either way. Your 'merciful' hand, or my 'demonic' hand. Your choice, Captain. Make it now! This sub could be yours. You remind me of my son, my boy. I could be your new family. We could be your new family. I will take care of you! You can have anything you want. You know the world belongs to Death Nation anyways. Kill them and prove your loyalty to this Nation and me!" The Spaniard smiled at Karson. His smile was that of a father ordering his son to make a decision. Karson couldn't help but fall for it. *Am I on the wrong team? Could I let them die and figure out what this ship does and take it? Am I really going to give up working for this man, this man who likes me for a war allies can't even compete in? Is this choice even remotely as hard as I'm making it?*

"Is this how you get all your people to turn? Offering them niceties?"

"No, generally torture. Upheaval from homes. I know who you are though, and that wouldn't work. You are too highly trained for that, Karson. That is why I want you!"

"You're torturing me now, making me choose between two wants. The want to save my friends and the want to be on the winning side right now." Karson was stalling while he collected his thoughts. *Plans?*

"Your decision, Karson!" The Spaniard was impatient now. "I am sure you can relate. I have a schedule and agenda to follow and complete."

Karson looked up into his eyes. *I feel like Jesus on the mountain being tested by Satan. Only, Satan, you are sounding appetizing and making total sense right now. I honestly don't know what to do…*

"Alright. Here is my decision!"

****

CHAPTER 40 - The Room

"Alright, now for the fun part, gentlemen! ~~Charlie team: heading forward towards the bridge, eliminating and disposing of any enemy personnel we find. Subduing the bridge operators if we can. Interrogating and learning how to pilot the craft. Ensuring we deliver it to United States custody. Tooth, Dill, Pops, and me!~~ Delta, control room, hack into computers and steal information. Eliminate all personnel. Hack system. Give us an advantage, feed team on the fly. Cover our tracks by looping their view of the cameras while you take control and watch from your view. Disable all traps and hidden dangers as you can, or inform us as we go! Kayak, Osprey, Lizard, Teepee. ~~Echo, engines and fuel. See what you can learn and how you can cripple this craft should you be able too. Eliminate all enemies. Bullet, Kite, Picket, Trip. Finally, Foxtrot. You will be the sweepers. You are to head to the enemy quarters and disable them there. Take them all out. Once that is completed, head to the middle of the ship and gain Intel. Walk the ship. Learn from it. Feed us on the fly. Slink, Bobcat, Ricochet, Stinger, Manamal, Snipe.~~ Eliminate any and all you can. This goes for everyone. Hide the bodies of our enemy. If we are detected, mission failed. Everybody understand?" Karson finished.

Kayak nodded as everybody else did as well! Whenever he was briefed, he had trained himself to have the ability to block any and all information given that had no relevance to the mission as a whole, and any information that had no relevance to his stake in the mission.

"Good. Leaders of your squads, of course, are by rank. Let's go!" With that, Karson saluted his family and turned and headed forward in the ship towards the bridge. Not looking back. His team followed him up the long hallway in a quick but silent pace.

Kayak saluted and watched Karson move off and motioned for his team to follow him in the opposite direction. "Here goes nothing!" He whispered to his friends. "Let's kick some hiney!"

"Hooyah, Kayak!" Tepee confirmed.

Then men maneuvered through the hallways of the submarine towards the stern of the ship. Oddly, the ship, as much as a maze it was, had some signs on the ceilings pointing to things like restrooms, maintenance ports, offices, and sure enough, control room. The SEALs looked at each other.

"Too easy?" Kayak asked.

"Sir, up to you. If not the place, perhaps it will lead us there." Lizard lisped.

Osprey nodded and moved to the door, dropped his bag and placed a decoder to the keypad, while Lizard watched the window. A man walked past the window wearing a suit. The SEALs ducked down, and Osprey cracked the code and opened the door, all SEALs entering and taking the man to the ground. Kayak tied his hands while Osprey repacked his equipment and Teepee went to the computer.

"Sir... This is the right place. Check this out. I've got ship controls, cameras, alarms, manifests, all kinds of stuff here. Lizard, hop on that computer and hack it, see if you can get emails or something..."

"Sir... There is a word here. Erutrot. Never heard of it." Osprey asked.

"Same. Let me look." Kayak walked closer as Tepee and Lizard started copying all of the ships information to hard drives. "This is going to alert the ship, team, just so you know."

"We know. We'll be out way before they come." Lizard looked at Teepee and the two looked at each other and scouted around the room for anything else that could help them. They flipped on a television.

"Erutrot. E. R. U. T. R. O. T." Kayak stared at the word. "I don't know. Keep thinking. Write it down."

"Aye, sir." Osprey clicked his pen.

"Sir, I think I know what that means..." Lizard spoke. He showed Kayak the monitor. "Torture."

Kayak stared at the monitor. "Wah..."

"Kayak, I found something. A little town in Texas. We should ask the Captain about it. He's a Texan, maybe he lives near it, or maybe it's not so small… a grower, not a shower. Maybe we attack? But a lot of international calls, mostly from this ship are being transmitted to that location. It's in the middle of nowhere in the midst of the U.S. State." Teepee pulled out his HUD's control.

"Copy phone records." Kayak ordered, now moving around the room.

"Already on it, sir."

Kayak turned to his HUD and typed a message.

> Foxtrot. Possible
> torture chambers on
> board. Advise you
> receive and will check
> message validity

"Location found. Near our location." Teepee interrupted him. "Kayak, we can send two men to scout and engage. We still need to cut onboard communications and outgoing, just enough to still be able to reestablish should we recapture this ship."

"Alright. Osprey and I will go. You two cut the coms, and find out what the leaders of the world don't want us knowing about Texas."

"Aye, sir." Teepee buried himself in his work.

"Sprey, let's go." Kayak turned towards the door.

The two SEALs cautiously exited the room and turned left heading further into the ship, eventually following the iron smell of what Kayak swore smelled like blood.

"Sir, the smell is getting closer." Pounding confirmed Osprey's assumptions. The two men found a square in the ship, but the sounds were coming from behind them now, and they turned back to find red footprints going in and out of a heavy door.

"Should've brought the scrambler-" Osprey shook his head.

The two SEALs ducked behind the corner of the wall as the doors opened and screams now resonated from the closing window of opportunity. Osprey took the chance first, lunging around and shooting the man through the brain, his body going stiff. Osprey ran into the room; Kayak grabbed the body as it fell and dragged it in, dropping it and glaring at Osprey. "Don't do that again."

"No promises. Come-on." The two followed the corridor around the ship. "It just me or does this spiral around the ship?" Osprey was getting dizzy.

"Huh? What do you mean, Sprey?"

"Like? Are we upside down or something now, man, 'cause I'm feeling really strange."

"I feel it too; it's probably the passage playing tricks on us... Ahead. Window." Kayak pointed. Osprey nodded and took his position at the window and looked over. "What's he doing?"

"I don't know... Hypnotism? Brainwashing?"

"Film it..." Kayak walked further down the hall. It dead ended to the door into the room. The man's head snapped to the door.

"Kayak. It's one-way glass that door. He can see you; you can't see him..."

Kayak didn't move... immersed in the scene from the door.

"KAYAK!"

Footsteps

Osprey grabbed Kayak and drug his view from the scene and took him back up the hall.

As they wound around the corridor, the footsteps discontinued to be muffled and grew louder and louder until the two SEALs opened fire on a group of unarmed women, killing three, the rest running past them. The two SEALs stopped in their tracks and stared after them.

"What? Dude, you okay?" Osprey shown his light into Kayak's face, checking his pupils.

"I'm alright." He swatted him away. "Let's get back to the others... and find Serval and get out of here... this ship, something is up."

"That sounds good..." Osprey and Kayak hoofed it back up the hall to the command center.

"Anything happen?" Kayak asked.

Lizard looked up to answer as Teepee checked on Osprey. "Just talked to Hunter... He's in a bad spot right now, sir. Should we get up there?"

****

CHAPTER 41 - Plasma

"Alright, now for the fun part, gentlemen! ~~Charlie team: heading forward towards the bridge, eliminating and disposing of any enemy personnel we find. Subduing the bridge operators if we can. Interrogating and learning how to pilot~~

the craft. ~~Ensuring we deliver it to United States custody.~~ ~~Tooth, Dill, Pops, and~~ ~~me!~~ ~~Delta, control room, hack into computers and steal information.~~ ~~Eliminate~~ ~~all personnel.~~ ~~Hack system.~~ ~~Give us an advantage, feed team on the fly.~~ ~~Cover~~ ~~our tracks by looping their view of the cameras while you take control and watch~~ ~~from your view.~~ ~~Disable all traps and hidden dangers as you can, or inform us as~~ ~~we go!~~ ~~Kayak, Osprey, Lizard, Teepee.~~ **Echo, engines and fuel. See what you can learn and how you can cripple this craft should you be able too. Eliminate all enemies. Bullet, Kite, Picket, Trip.** ~~Finally, Foxtrot.~~ ~~You will~~ ~~be the sweepers.~~ ~~You are to head to the enemy quarters and disable them there.~~ ~~Take them all out.~~ ~~Once that is completed, head to the middle of the ship and gain~~ ~~Intel.~~ ~~Walk the ship.~~ ~~Learn from it.~~ ~~Feed us on the fly.~~ ~~Slink, Bobcat, Ricochet,~~ ~~Stinger, Manamal, Snipe.~~ **Eliminate any and all you can. This goes for everyone. Hide the bodies of our enemy. If we are detected, mission failed. Everybody understand?" Karson finished.**

They all nodded.

"Good. Leaders of your squads, of course, are by rank. Let's go!" With that, Karson saluted his family and turned and headed forward in the ship towards the bridge. Not looking back. His team followed him up the long hallway in a quick but silent pace.

Echo team raced around corners. Karson had made the mistake of putting all of the older, 'more experienced' cocky SEALs on the same team, his, so they believed they were invincible, invisible, and untouchable. Bullet and Kite held the lead, Picket and Trip took rear support as they followed the silent purr coming from deep down in the sub and at the rear.

"Team, halt!" Picket said. Taking the lead, "I hear something?"

"Yeah, I hear it too..." All four SEALs now stood facing down a porthole that led to the internal parts of an engine room, separated by a glass and metal door. "Kite, you're tallest. You look in there!" Bullet said.

"Aye." Kite moved forward, standing on his tiptoes, peered through the glass into the room.

"What is that roaring sound?" Bullet asked.

"Wow." Trip ducked down. "Sir, the sides of the sub are like a waterfall!"

"What are you talking about?" Picket asked, last to make it below deck to the party.

"There are large pools on each side of that room. There is a metal grate that walks across, but the entire thing is water, and the water pours in from the sides. I'm guessing sea water." He said, staring at his brothers.

"I have no clue what you're saying, but let's get in there!" Bullet moved towards the door. However, a keypad sequence stood in the way of entry.

"Any a' you know how to crack it?" Kite asked.

"I don't." Picket yawned.

"Ditto," Kite stated.

"Don't look at me!" Trip commented.

"Guys, we have to-" Bullet started to speak, but steps and a shout interrupted him.

"Hey! Intruders! Intrude-" A knife hit him in the ear. His hand flew to his ear as Bullet landed a punch straight into his temple, rendering him unstable. The SEALs dragged him over to the pad, but when his mind didn't allow a valid number, and a countdown to an alarm started, they used more drastic measures.

"Search his pockets! Feel him up! See if he has a key card!" Kite improvised.

The numbers kept counting down. The men felt everywhere for the card, pockets, neck, shoes... Picket's hand grabbed nut sack, Bullet felt around the taint; Kite searched butt crack and low and behold, with a smelly five seconds left; they rushed the 'racing stripe' card over to the pad, after passing it to Trip, the Navy Sailor Karson insisted join the mission. However, the brown covering the barcode wouldn't let the scanner read!

"Wipe it off, Rookie!" Kite ordered.

"Oh, yeah!" Trip smeared the foul smelling card over Bullets face, then with a second before cover blown, the keypad beeped and allowed entry.

The SEALs dragged the man into the room as the door started to close, and lay him on the side of the door, Bullet gagged over the railing.

"I'm gonna get you back for putting that crap on my face."

"Later. For now, we have to find out what the fuel source is. I have a pretty good idea! I mean it's genius. They never can run out. Thought it to be impossible, but it gives off no fuel slick to trace the sub and no emissions. For such a death-thirsty nation, this group of people couldn't be traveling in an eco-friendlier vehicle. And they're using the source that helps power the sun!" Trip smiled at his new friends.

"Okay, are you gonna tell us?" Bullet asked, still about to wretch.

"Hydrogen." Trip kept walking towards the center of the room.

"Huh?" Picket leaned on the rail.

"He said Hydrogen." Kite spoke up, wanting to move this along.

All that followed were blank stares from the team. Trip stopped and groaned. "Did you dudes not pay attention in high school chemistry? Or now, for that matter? Look around! We're in a room surrounded by water. That's all this room is. In the bottom of the submarine. The ship pumps in water to submerge. What better way to stay submerged and power the ship than to do both at the same time?! Look at the way the water all flows towards the center of the pool! I bet you that is a fuel cell down there that converts the water into hydrogen and oxygen molecules. That is what the water molecules are made out of! A continuous source of energy right there! They hydrogen is the source that burns, and come to think of it; there are no oxygen tanks or converters here. I'll bet you the ship makes up for weight by leaving off these converters, and the fuel cell takes the oxygen it doesn't burn from the hydrogen and pumps it into the ship! A continuous source of fuel. An endless source of air. This ship could stay under virtually incessantly!"

"Okay. How did you figure that out so quickly!?" Picket asked.

"Simple. I'm just super smart! And… I know Turkic. The dude had a piece of paper on his person, and when we were searching, I saw water fuel at the top of the paper!" Kite said.

"Sweet. Now all we need to do is relay this to Thompson." Bullet said.

"Don't you mean, Hunter?" Trip asked.

"He's busy. He'll find out in the debrief. Let's go through that control panel!" Kite dismissed Trip's question.

"Okay… if you say so." Trip followed the others.

The team moved to the center control panels and punched in the frequency of the allied submarine and sent the encoded message via their radios. The center control panel provided a way to shoot the signal a long distance, and the SEAL radio provided encryption.

SUB PWRD BY HYDROGEN FUEL CELL. HAS NO EMMISION WHEN BURNED WITH OXYGEN, JUST PUSHES OUT MORE WATER. USE OF ELECTROCHEMICAL CELLS TO POWER SUB! –ST6

"There. That ought to reach them! Let's get back to Hunter!" Picket moved towards the way they came when they noticed the man not laying where they had left him. "Where's that Turkish guy?"

The sound of feet hitting metal echoed behind the team. Kite spun around as a pen sliced through his throat, and blood dripped down through the grates in the metal walkway. Bullet grabbed the Turkish man and threw him into the water below. Kite lay bleeding out on the ground. Bullet was yelling curses at the man in the water as an alarm started going off. Picket guarded the door, and Trip tried stopping the bleeding, but Kite started to fade, his life flowing through the cracks, now providing plasma to the fuel of the ship.

The door to the room opened, and ten men entered, assault weapons in hand.

Picket closed his eyes.

POP

POP

POP

****

CHAPTER 42 - The Square

"Alright, now for the fun part, gentlemen! ~~Charlie team: heading forward towards the bridge, eliminating and disposing of any enemy personnel we find. Subduing the bridge operators if we can. Interrogating and learning how to pilot the craft. Ensuring we deliver it to United States custody. Tooth, Dill, Pops, and me! Delta, control room, hack into computers and steal information. Eliminate all personnel. Hack system. Give us an advantage, feed team on the fly. Cover our tracks by looping their view of the cameras while you take control and watch from your view. Disable all traps and hidden dangers as you can, or inform us as we go! Kayak, Osprey, Lizard, Teepee. Echo, engines and fuel. See what you can learn and how you can cripple this craft should you be able too. Eliminate all enemies. Bullet, Kite, Picket, Trip.~~ **Finally, Foxtrot. You will be the sweepers. You are to head to the enemy quarters and disable them there. Take them all out. Once that is completed, head to the middle of the ship and gain Intel. Walk the ship. Learn from it. Feed us on the fly. Slink, Bobcat, Ricochet, Stinger, Manamal, Snipe. Eliminate any and all you can. This goes for everyone. Hide the bodies of our enemy. If we are detected, mission failed. Everybody understand?" Karson finished.**

They all nodded.

"Good. Leaders of your squads, of course, are by rank. Let's go!" With that, Karson saluted his family and turned and headed forward in the ship towards the bridge. Not looking back. His team followed him up the long hallway in a quick but silent pace.

Foxtrot turned and followed Delta, however, split off to follow a group of men yawning and stretching.

"Team, we're going to allow them to enter into the bunk area, or mess hall, wherever. Indiscriminately, on my command, eliminate anyone and everyone in these locations. However, only on my orders. If there are too many, we will fall back and wait for these people to split into their bunk areas. We will then silence them there." Slink ordered.

Stinger nodded. "Aye, Slink!"

The men turned into a large room, and as Slink had directed, no order nor shots were executed as this mess hall had a load of people inside, chowing down.

"Well, we know these douche bags have some human tendencies! Slink, where are the bunks?" Snipe asked. "We could kill them in their sleep."

"I would assume around here; this seems to be the residential area. Manamal, do you have a bounce video camera? The throwable tactical camera?"

"Aye, sir!" Manamal removed his pack.

"Good. Tape that up high on the wall and transmit images. We need to know who comes in, but more importantly, who exits and where they go. Let's search this corridor. I need the thermal imaging camera, as well as a snake cam!"

The team moved their way right, up the hall they had entered searching for heat signatures of sleeping bodies. However, -

"Just like I thought. The camera can sort of give us a clue as to what's through the walls and doors, but there were hundreds of men in this mess hall, and I can only read one or two of them. Snake cam it is. We'll slip it under each door until we can find the hive!" Slink handed the thermal imaging back.

"Sir, two men just exited the hall. They turned this way." Manamal relayed information.

"Capture." Slink pointed at Bobcat and Snipe.

"Aye, sir!" Bobcat prowled after Snipe to hide further up the hall to flank the enemy.

Slink slid the snake cam into a room, found it occupied with a man on the toilet.

"Toilet. One inside. We can fit." Slink ripped the door open and slammed his helmeted head into the man's face knocking him into oblivion. The SEALs piled into the cramped and smelly compartment and shut the door, leaving a crack to peer through.

Ricochet piped up from his vantage. "On my go. They are getting closer. Closer…"

"This smells! Hurry up!" Picket hissed.

"Shut up!" Slink elbowed him, and as he flinched, the SEALs all fidgeted, pushing their way out into the corridor in front of the two enemy sailors. SEAL and Death Nation sailor both stared at each other, and the unconscious enemy sailor lay, naked, unconscious in front of his companions. Snipe and Bobcat walked up behind.

"INTRUDERS! INDTRU-" A suppressed pistol shot ended one man's life. The second turned to flee, and Bobcat lunged, but Ricochet ended his life too.

"Dammit! Now we won't- Wake this guy up!" Manamal smacked the smoking gun in Ricochet's hands.

"Aye. Question him, find out where the enemy rack for the night. Manamal, Snipe, and Picket do that. Ricochet, hide the bodies in the bathroom. Bobcat, come with me. We're gonna keep searching rooms. Manamal, keep on that camera."

"Aye, sir." Manamal sat against the wall as everyone holstered their weapons.

The SEALs split and executed their specific jobs. Ten minutes passed, Slink and Bobcat searched the remaining rooms, however, only found electric, air, laundry, and bathrooms. No sleeping quarters.

Returning, Slink saw his team leaning on the walls. "Info?"

"He's dead now, but the bunks are farther back. He said there'll be a huge opening and past that are bunking areas. It's a vast area he said, though. Not many hiding areas." Picket noticed.

Slink looked down the hall. "That's fine. We'll adapt. If able, we'll lay in the bunks. If not, we'll come back here and execute the men in the room. We'll find a way. Let's move."

The SEALs filed down a smaller corridor leading parallel to the main corridor the team had come from. As they moved farther back in the sub, they noticed the hallways widening, and a vast array of light was starting to fill the hall.

"There is no possible way they have sunlight filtering into this ship!" Bobcat said.

The team exited the hallway and found a huge square opening.

"Gardens? The ceiling looks like a giant lizard lamp. This must be how they have some oxygen production, as well as food production! Look over there! That door says animals. This is the area where they harvest, care, and grow food! This ship has a steady food supply to feed its inhabitants. It's like an underwater city! It's like Noah's ark. Let's grab some photos as we make our way around this towards the barracks!" Slink looked on in awe.

"Let's split in half and go around that way!" Stinger asked.

"Aye. Do that." Slink thumbs upped.

The team spread apart and slithered around the large square in the submarine. They could make out quite a few decks below and above them until the ceiling blazed with light. Surely this sub was larger than the men could see here.

From their vantage on both sides, men, woman, and children worked alongside each other as elderly sat and cleaned the crops. The smell of manure either came from enriching the soil, or the even greater possibility that there were animals on this ship to provide food for the meat cravers. If one laid in the middle of the garden, it would be just like laying outside on dry land, however, from the higher vantage point, the SEALs could still tell of the ominous area of operations they were in.

Numerous questions popped into each SEALs private thoughts.

How did these people wind up here?

Are they threats? If I went down there, would they say they are here as slaves? Or would they attack, loyal to the enemy?

Where are they from?

Why here?

Are these children combatant trained? Will I have to kill one?

Should we neutralize these people now?

Slink and his team rounded to the far side of the square junction, but as they were turning to enter into the rear of the submarine, a child screamed out as an adult started beating him relentless, drawing blood from the blows to his face. The kid screamed in agony as a man began to remove his belt and drag the boy to the side, undoing his button on his and the kids pants. Screwdriver in hand, stabbing slowly into the kids back.

Slink sprang to the edge of the wall and flipped back over the rail, holding to it by his legs.

"Slink, don't!" Bobcat whispered, trying to pull him back up.

"You'll blow our cover, dude!" Stinger whispered louder.

"I can't let him rape that child. The innocence must remain!" Slink steadied his breath and cleared his shot, readied himself to kill yet another man.

TFFT

The suppressed shot split through the two attacker's heads, one watching, and one about to penetrate the kid. "We protect the innocent. We maintain peace. We have to save even in the areas that don't want to be saved. That's our job." Slink looked up at his teammates.

Slink hopped back over the edge as screams cried out. Looking back over, the kid had made a break for it. People scurried from their spots in the garden to the sides, looking for where death had rung.

"Nice shot, bro. But, we're probably not going to achieve our mission." Ricochet patted Slink.

Slink winked. "Nonsense." He pulled out some grenades. "Let's get 'em now. Unleash all your rounds on them boys. It's been an honor to serve with you!"

"Hooyah!" They all said in unison.

The men smiled and headed to where the intel said the bunks would be. Sure enough, entering the room, people scrambling between bunks putting on their uniforms and weapons, the SEALs had plenty of targets to flush out. Like ants when you blast the ant hill with water. When you blast a room full of enemies with grenades, some die, the rest come out terrified!

"Throw them in!" Slink pulled the pin on two of his six grenades, waited three seconds, the tossed them into the center of the room.

"Grenade!" Was shouted by an American voice, before the explosions ripped through exposed flesh. The other SEALs did the same. Two by two, grenades were chucked in with three seconds expended before the timers ran out. They then retreated to the garden area and took up post, firing at anyone trying to escape the bloodbath. Alarms in this area of the ship now were going off, and for sure, enemy reinforcements would come to back their shipmates in red. Slink knew it could be the end, but he stood his ground, for as a Navy SEAL and any other service member, you sacrifice for the nation and the people you love!

That's the job I signed up for. It's what I believe in.

****

CHAPTER 43 - Oorah!

"Ugh! It's been hours, sir! What if they're all dead? We'll be sitting down here forever, uncertain of the situation inside, and maybe they'll kill more of us! We should get in there! SEALs aren't all that more special than us!"

"You saying that SEALs are not as great as they sound, Private?" Sergeant Blane spoke up. The Marine held a lighter close to his body, adding light to the cramped space, while also staying warm.

"Yeah! We're Marines, Oorah!" The first Grunt said.

"Oorah, bro, however, remember 'The Legend'? The man who provided us an Angel up high, taking out threats our brothers faced in Iraq in the 2000's? Yeah! A Navy SEAL sniper, Chris Kyle, God rest his soul, provided our men, and our other brothers from other branches safety, confirming one hundred and sixty kills. Kills that could have killed our brothers. Thank God for the SEALs. If they need help, we'll assist them. But that doesn't make them any less the warriors they are. Doesn't mean they deserve less respect. If anything, you should aspire to be like a Navy SEAL. All of us. Even though we have the courage to walk into the fires of Hell, SEALs somehow muster up the courage to walk into the flames of Hell's Hell." Corporal Young thought his mind out loud.

"The Sergeant is correct, but Private Scott has a valid point as well. Team, we'll begin to maneuver into position to board the SEALs' shuttle. We'll enter, and eliminate anyone and everyone. SEALs are wearing black. Death Nation wears blood. If you look closely, I always see patches of green. Move to position!"

"Aye, sir!" Young smiled, excited to be doing something.

"Do we have the photographs first? From the camera outside the sub?" Private Scott asked.

"I'd like to know that as well." Wilson said.

"Yeah, Staff Sergeant. We do!" Corporal Young checked the computer onboard the shuttle.

Wilson moved up towards the front of the mini sub. "Good. Start them to our leaders while we dock to SEAL sub."

"Already docked, sir." Young replied as he grouped the images into a message and hit the send button.

"Alright. Open the port." As they opened the port, the water started to drip in but the Marines were out and into the Navy sub. Next, they unlatched the door and dropped down, no alarms, nothing. "SEALs must have disabled coms. Nice. Means they made it somewhat far into their mission. Let's find them."

The Marines entered into the ship and came to the first T, realizing just how large this ship was.

"Sir, are you sure this was a good idea?" Private Scott asked.

"We're checking our men, and having an adventure. You think I want Team Six to get all the glory? Marines are down on funds and respect right now. Let's build it up a bit, shall we? Turn right. Let's start from back to-" Wilson was interrupted.

"CONTACT!" Sergeant Blane shouted.

Shots rang out in 'Big Momma's' opening hallway as the Maines opened fire in return on a patrol of enemy soldiers.

"Too many, fall back fall-" Sergeant Blane took a round to his chest and fell backwards. The Marines dragged him back around the corner. "I'm okay!" He gasped.

"They're flanking us! They knew! Somehow!" Private Scott groaned.

"No time for that... Fight!" Wilson unleashed his courage on the enemy.

The Marines kept utilizing their weapons, surprisingly no one was hit again, as Young found a hole in the side of the ship and slid down, calling his brothers after him! "Here!"

The Marines all followed suit, throwing a curve ball on the Death Nation soldiers. There was no way they were going down into the-

- "Sewers." The Marines marched through excrement. "Well, not like anything different than basic." Scott groaned some more.

"Oorah to that, Brah!" Young laughed.

"Except it's a ton more crap!" Sergeant Blane plugged his nose.

"I feel ya brother. Let's keep moving. Two ports down." Wilson said, counting how many surface ports they passed.

The Marines swerved and followed the tunnels two more holes down. They came upon a room.

"Sir... White room, computers. Four combatants. Dick shots?" Scott asked.

"Ooohhh... Man, I don't know. If you get shot in the dick, you'll feel a pain you never thought you'd experience. Do it!" Wilson ordered.

"Aye, sir." The Marine took aim and fired a shot, hitting Osprey between the legs, dropping him like a ton of rocks to a moan only a man whose balls got blown away could make. Another shot hit between his eyes.

The Marines watched in horror as the three remaining SEALs shouted in English "CONTACT!" and fired on their friendly forces. The Marines died by unknown friendly fire, a mistake that would haunt the Americans on board for the rest of their, some long, and some short, lives.

****

CHAPTER 44 - Raise It

"I need your answer, Karson." The Admiral said. "We are approaching our target, and are about to attack. I either need your support or eliminate you as a distraction. I would be so sad to lose you, my boy."

Karson stared from the Admiral to his Sailors. "So, I join you and kill my men, saving myself, making myself treasonous, or I refuse you, and you kill us all. This is simple!" *I honestly don't know what to do.*

"That is the correct decision. Let me teach you something. You don't get to my position without making sacrifices. I was in this exact spot when I was young. See what happened to me?"

"I really don't want to die…" He looked at his Sailors. "I'm no good dead… If I see one man being tortured, I can't save him 'cause if I die, then the one man I saved turns out to be the reason that thousands die. For my team, I thought I would die with them and for them… If a grenade comes, one jumps on it 'cause that leaves three more to finish the job. Sir I- "

"Admiral, we have contact." A low ranking Sailor called to his commanding officer.

He looked over. "Commence attack. Wah-" Karson spun the weapon out of the Admirals hand now holding him at gun point.

"I will let you survive. Tell your men to lower their weapons." Karson ordered, spinning the Admiral around, pressing against him to use him as a shield.

"Si. Do as he says." The Admiral raised his hands.

"Incoming!" The ship rocked to the side as the torpedo from the U.S. submarine impacted the hull of the sub.

"They should know they can't hurt our-"

"Sir!" The Sailor interrupted the Admiral in a panic. "We are taking on water. We don't show anything wrong, and we're rebooting the system."

"This is impossible."

"Sir, the entrance hatch is wide open."

Karson's eyes widened. "Our subs…"

"Serval..." The intercom system of the sub spoke. "We had contact with the Marines... They were on the ship, mistook us for the enemy. The water is filling the ship. Osprey KIA. What are our orders? Speak, I rigged it to hear you, sir."

Karson's eyes were wide opened as the rest of the crew started to work on saving the ship. "Can you close the hatch, Kayak?"

"Sir, the entire ocean is flowing into the ship. We have to leave..."

"Or rise. Admiral, you must raise your ship to the surface. It is the only way to save her..."

"And we'll be taken into custody by the allied world." He growled.

"Sir." The Admiral looked at Karson in surprise. "That's right. Sir. You must realize that the world revolves around the fact that good always triumphs evil. No matter how far ahead you get, you will always find that good wins eventually. Elections. Wars. People like your 'supreme leader' never win the war in the long run."

"This is where you're wrong-"

"I'm not. I'm also not going to stand here while this ship sinks." Karson pushed his weapon harder into the Admiral's head. The Admiral smiled.

"You're going to have to, Karson." The Admiral drew faster than Karson could react and fired a round at the SEAL; *purposefully missing?!* Karson dodged behind a pillar as the other SEALs unleashed their firepower into people diving for weapons and into the ceiling turrets.

After the attack in the United Nations, efforts were made to inform Soldiers how to combat the machines of death.

"Team, remember the eye of the weapon. Fire into it, you render it inoperable. Karson had a ceiling turret in his sights and honed in on the tiny hole that emitted a laser that sighted in on living specimens. As he pulled his trigger, he felt his body spin around and the Spanish man was on Karson.

"I really like you, son... but I can't let you win. You could have had so much with this rebellion against the world. A plethora of women, opportunity, everything!" He slammed his fist into Karson's cheek.

Struggling against his grip, Karson retorted, slowly walking in a circle to face the opposite way they had been. "Well, I already am in love, I am a Captain in America's Navy, and so I think I have all I need." He knocked the Admiral's right hand away, holding it off. His left snapped to Karson's throat. Karson gasped out his words. "I like you too, sir… but I can't let you win. I'm an American. We don't kill innocence." Karson knocked his left hand away, and launched himself up, slamming both feet into the Admiral's chest, knocking him out into the open from behind the pillar, Karson falling out on the other side. The Admiral tried to stand, but Karson's bullet hadn't found its mark, and the ceiling turret found its target on the Spaniard first, turning him into Swiss cheese, penetrating his body more than one hundred times. Karson watched in horror. *I never knew the body had so much blood!* The weapon turned on Karson, but this time, he found his mark. He stood and found Gramps and Tooth down, Dill was fighting in the hallway. So many enemies down, but some still working, one, in particular, launching an attack on the allied fleet.

Karson had to leave the downed SEALs, and rushed the enemy at the computer as the ship rocked from a powerful laser firing from the top of the hull, slicing through the ship above's hull, a massive bubble escaping from the ship as it instantly started to sink as two metallic arms lanced through the Australian ship's hull, dragging it down. Karson grabbed the man by the throat, and tightened his grip, sending his knife into the most sensitive part of his neck, inflicting the most excruciating pains. "Release that ship and raise this one to the surface."

"इस जहाज बर्बाद है। इसमें बचत नहीं है।" {HINDI: is jahaaj barbaad hai. isamen bachat nahin hai.} (This ship is doomed. There is no saving it.)

Karson twisted the knife. "RAISE IT." The man started to spasm from the pain. Alarms started going off indicating a hull breach.

Karson spoke over the intercom system. "Team. Abandon ship. U.S. personnel, escape at the escape pod top of the ship. Try to get there." Karson pulled the knife out of the man's neck and drug it across his throat. It's not like the movies, a smooth cut. It's deeper, and you can feel, hear, and see the knife bounce as it cuts through veins, tendons, and arteries. Blood pelted the instruments, as the man was nearly beheaded by the sharp Navy utensil. Karson threw the man out of his chair, looked at the controls, deciding that there was no possible way to learn the systems of the ship in a mere moment. He looked around the room, equipping an enemy's rifle and vest and ran from the room. He knew from submarines that the escape pod was near the entrance, however, knowing Death Nation's leadership, it would have to be close to where they were stationed on the ship.

Cowards. "Right above me." Karson made his way to the elevator, finding it on the first floor. He pressed the button and waited. *There has to be a staircase near here. Team, please be there. Please get to the pod!*

Finally, the elevator arrived, and Karson stepped on, finding blood smeared around the car. He pressed the top floor of the elevator, but it dropped rapidly down to the middle of the ship. The doors started to open, Karson had his knife positioned in his hand resting on his chest by his head. No one was waiting so Karson pressed 'close doors.' *That was spooky.* As the doors closed, an arm shot through, and a terrifying scream pierced Karson's ears as he too screamed, and rammed the knife through the man's temple. As the doors opened and the man's body crumpled, Karson pushing him out to raise in the elevator to the top floor, he heard a yell of "man down!" and watched as Slink, Kayak, Stinger, and Lizard sprinted around the corner, aiming at Karson.

"Serval!" Slink ran and hugged him.

"Was... w-was he..."

"Marine, sir... We killed the rest. It was an accident, sir. Keep your head in the game..."

"You're right... Right." Karson shook his head. The men entered the elevator and pressed top floor. The doors closed and Karson's eyes locked onto the nametag. *Blane.* "The floor wasn't flooded. I heard the noise, but no water..."

"The sub is designed for a small leak, sir. The water goes through the graty part of the floor... but the bottom of the ship is filling and it's raising to the surface, sir. Is the ship salvageable?" Stinger asked.

"No. I can't figure out the controls-" Karson said staring at the door.

"Try voice activation... Where's the command center?"

Karson pressed the floor for control center and told his other SEALs to hold the elevator as he led Slink to the control center, passing a now deceased Dill.

Slink looked at Karson. Just so you know, we're all that is left."

Karson nodded.

"United Axis Front DN EL 114309." Slink said.

"English. Axis granted. Welcome to internal controls. What are your orders?"

"Axis?" Karson asked.

"Surface!" Slink said. Instantly, the ship started to rise towards the top. However, now thre miles down, it was a long way to travel, and a lot of water to enter the ship.

"Slink, we have to try to get out of here, man..."

"Hopefully she meets us at the surface! Let's go, sir!" Slink turned and led the way out.

The two headed back to the elevator and got in, letting the doors close. As soon as the doors opened, Karson knew the end was near for someone. Enemies had the same idea, and they were entering the escape pod, the ones that knew of it. Others were entering from a door, Karson assumed where the stairs were.

The five remaining SEALs opened fire on both sides, the enemies armed, shooting back. Only a few were in the pod, and they were taken quickly as the men rushed towards the pod. Karson arrived first and turned to see Slink engaged with a heavily armored troop like the one guarding the command center. Kayak and Stinger both took fatal wounds but were still fighting as their deaths sped up. They wouldn't make it to the surface.

"SLINK! Come on!" Karson begged, opening more vicious fire, trying to unpin himself from inside the escape pod.

"GO, SIR! SOMEONE HAS TO HOLD THEM OFF!" Slink shouted.

"Slink, get in here!" Karson fired at the man's helmet, trying desperately to hit the soft spot. Lizard tried to run out and took a round to the knee. Stinger was fading. Even this far down, it was still a straight shot to The Maker.

"Tell them about me when you get back, my friend. See you on the other side!" Slink took a bullet to the leg and fell to the ground as the man grabbed him by the head. The doors to the pod closed, authority of Kayak.

Karson screamed trying to get out, but the doors were sealed tight, Karson watching through the glass. Kayak pressed deploy, but the pod didn't detach. Slink kept trying to escape, the enemy surrounding the downed SEAL, starting to cut him up. He looked back at Karson, nodded, as a knife plunged into both eyes, another sliced out his Adam's apple, the doomed soldiers tossing it around like hacky sack. Another soldier deemed it necessary to castrate the dying SEAL in excruciating pain, slicing a hole so deep... Again, Karson found just how much blood the human body held as his friend was mutilated in front of him, when finally, the pod detached and fired into the ocean, heading for the surface. Karson slid down the side of the pod and felt the tears stream red hot down his cheek.

I killed a Marine. I murdered my friend. Fourteen SEALs dead, two mortally wounded, one minor, and I'm barely hurt. Four dead Marines. I got so many American's killed downhere...

After long minutes of raising, the pod reached the surface, and Australian troops intercepted, pulling the men onto their ship, sending them back to the U.S. Submarine, Stinger and Kayak pronounced dead. Karson tried debriefing, but he was a shell. 'Big Momma' never reached the surface, but the sub's captain wasn't swayed. "We know where she is. We'll find a way down to her, to salvage her. We raised Titanic and other ships. Lot of profit came from the buried treasures. This is the same. We charted her a mile below the surface, still attached to the Australian frigate; she'll be floating there for a while. The massive air bubble we saw pop about four hours ago alerted us something was wrong... Time flies in these situations, huh?"

Karson walked out of the debriefing and found a place to curl up and sleep until he could just go home. That's all he wanted.

I just want to go home. I'm done.

****

CHAPTER 45 - Alert Tones

The living room dimmed as the sun made its daily dramatic exit, casting shadows over the chair Karson sat in. He held a bottle of wine in his hand, his leg dangling over the side of the chair, his arm behind the back. Four bottles sat empty on the table in front of him. The thoughts of what had happened a week ago still racked Karson's mind. Information was coming in from the HUD downloaded enemy information from all SEALs active on the mission, dead or alive... One of much interest is the location and design of other submarines like 'Big Momma' being built off the coast of China on the Islands they constructed in the sea. Waves of pain came from Karson's shooting of the U.S. Marine and watching another of his friends sacrifice his life, Karson surviving, and being mutilated in front of him. Lizard's leg was amputated. *One of these drinks will kill me, please...*

Karson took another swig and heard a knock at his front door. Karson stood unbalanced and stumbled to the door, looking out the peephole. Nobody was visible. Another knock, still no one in sight.

"Okay..." Karson unlatched the door, opening the drawer holding his revolver. "Hello?" He said into the sunset night.

A body lunged around the corner pulling Karson into an embrace, Karson placing the revolver at the man's head. A face presented itself to Karson's, and his eyes lit up, and a smile plastered itself on his face. "Victo?" Karson put the revolver down.

"Hey, buddy!" Victor said. "Woah! You reek!"

"Yeah... To be honest, I don't tink I've taken a sho-shower in a week. I've been perpechoooalie drunk. I got a call, and I deploy in a day and a half now. Friay."

Victor stared at Karson in disbelief. He grabbed Karson around the neck and slammed his head into the door and kicked him back into his house.

Karson groaned and held his head as he stared up at Victor, slamming the door. "WHY?" Karson tried to stand, the broken wine bottle at his side making him angry. "That was expensive, jerk!"

"It's Wednesday night... You need to detox. And I didn't understand a word you said. This isn't like you. I know. Your character plays like a symphony, every note of your character has been heard. This isn't it." Victor growled.

"I'm fine, Vitow..." Karson sat up, rubbing his eyes, his scruff and neck beard disgusting, riddled with booze and food.

"Can't even say my name right. Come on, man. Bed." Victor helped Karson to his feet.

"Why are you here? You're stationed in Cali... Cali... Uh..." Karson slurred his voice and stuttered his words. "That's a hard word to say... Californicate..."

"California? Yeah, but Admiral Thompson wanted a buddy to come and check on you. So I'm here. He's right too; you look like a hairball thrown up by a cat." Victor laid Karson on the bed and threw the blanket over him. "I'll be on the couch. See you in the morning."

As soon as Karson's head hit the pillow, his eyes closed and his dreams were red.

****

Karson didn't wake until the clock on the dresser beside the bed read

3:45 pm

He found Victor playing videogames, but decided to take a shower first. Once he was clean, shaved, and woken up, he walked into the living room.

"Hey. Thought you'd never wake up..." Victor's focus staying in the game.

Karson rubbed his eyes. "JSOC Warriors? Seriously?"

"Hey, this game is pretty accurate, my man."

"Yeah, but we live it every day... Don't you get bored of it? People jumping on grenades? We see that every day and it's just not accurate. If something goes wrong, we can find a different way than to just jump on a grenade."

"If it came between leaving you behind and saving others whose feet the grenade landed at, I'd jump on it, not even thinking of you or anything else. Just them. I'd expect that from you too."

"Seriously? I thought you cared more about me and your family to the point you'd not commit suicide. Nice to know you'd leave me behind without worry."

"If I had to choose between you and another fallen SEAL, I'd probably choose you. But otherwise, during a mission... if I had to lay my life down to save others, I would do it, and you would too and you know it.   We're not friends during an engagement, Karson, we're teammates and brothers. We have to think of everyone."

"I'd jump on the grenade too, I'm just saying maybe there is a way to, ya know, maybe throw the grenade back and kill a bad guy instead of ourselves? We're not the ones who are supposed to die in these things, they are. The bad guys."

"The Team must come first. Real SEALs know this."

"I understand that and I put the Team first-" Karson's eyes bulged. "DID YOU JUST QUESTION MY LOYALTY AND MY UNDERSTANDING OF WHAT WE DO?"

"I didn't say that-"

"Crucify me for wanting to take care of you and me and hoping to live to do something else after the Navy. I'm sorry I don't think about committing suicide every day."

Karson's phone buzzed as a news story popped up on his phone detailing a broadcast interrupting all others with an eerie Middle Eastern prayer like music. *Probably a Death Nation propaganda or scare tactic. Nothing to worry about here at home.*

Victor continued on clueless to the news. "You know this is a pointless fight and that none of this is relevant to our lives right now. We'd try to throw it, or we'd jump on it."

"How do you know it's not relevant. What if the war comes here?"

Victor looked back at Karson, his eyebrow cocked. His mind clearly saying *you're stretching for comebacks and you're being ridiculous.*

"Yeah, okay... Dumb question. Put it on multiplayer."

"You look good clean. Is this why you were drunk last night? You're tired of your job? You're scared about the future?" Victor asked exiting the game and switching to two player mode. "I'm gonna kick your butt by the way."

"I don't really want to talk about it, Victor. I'm sorry I yelled, too. I'm stressing out. And you're on. Maybe this will cool me down."

"Well, we are going to talk about it. I'm worried about you. What's up?"

Karson sighed. "I'm just scared. I can't see a way out. I want to fight something that makes a difference, not something that gets everyone I serve or care for killed."

"You make a difference, Karse. You inspire people. You get the job done. Buddy, you bring us closer to an end every day you're active."

"I want to stay home. Look, I'm done with this. Let's just play the game and I'll make dinner when I destroy you."

Victor put his hand on Karson's shoulder. "Just, promise me you're okay." He handed Karson the controller.

"I'm fine. Just ready for the next thing." Karson smiled and hit start. "I know as peacekeepers, we have to be violent sometimes to keep the peace. I just long for the times when keeping the peace was merely saying 'we're not going to do this, let's think of a better way to accomplish our desires.'"

****

"Tomorrow? You deploy tomorrow?"

"Yeah. Do you want another? Do you want wine?" Karson asked, getting up from the couch with his empty bottle, having just realized he'd missed his twenty-first birthday and the New Year.

"You know I only drink beer, Kadin." Victor laughed. "None of that girl nectar. Besides, you should slow down…"

Karson burst out laughing and slipped on the still wet floor.

"Are you okay?" Victor asked springing up.

Karson laughed harder. "Yeah! Girl nectar?"

"Sissy man drink if you ask me, wine is."

"I was just seeing if you wanted some of the fancy stuff…" Karson said as he got to his feet and walked into the kitchen. "Why'd you use my first name?"

Victor shrugged. "I like it."

"You're a funny guy, Victor, ya know that?" Karson rolled his eyes. "Food will be ready soon! You're in for a treat! True to life, real Texas barbecue for **our** New Year's Day!"

"Smells amazing!" Victor and Karson walked out into the backyard, and Karson opened the grill, exposing ribs and steaks, corn and potatoes.

"Ever had a caramelized banana?"

"No! What is that?" Victor asked as Karson ran in to grab a banana.

"Ohh, you have to try one!" Karson was so excited.

"What is it?" Victor called, scanning over Karson's backyard; once deployed, never feeling totally secure anymore.

"All you do is- What? What is it?" Karson now was nervous.

"Nothing, what's this thing?" Victor shook his head and smiled at Karson's eager face.

"You put it on the grill and let it cook! Learned it from an Australian mate of mine!"

"Mate?"

"Don't make fun of me! I love Australia." Karson retorted, pointing the banana at Victor. He lost it at the banana.

Karson's phone began to ring inside as he flipped the food, the banana's skin blackening.

"Hey, bud… Your phone is ringing."

"Can you answer it for me? Please?" Victor was already ahead of Karson and picked up the phone.

"Karson Hunter's phone? To whom am I speaking to?" Victor said into the phone.

"I work with Hunter. I need to speak to him. Urgently." The voice on the other end impatiently ordered.

"Oh. I'm Captain Victor Paul, SEAL Team Two. Can I take the message for him?"

"Victor, Admiral Thompson. I need Hunter. Now."

"Karson, get in here!" Victor called into the back yard.

"I am flipping the food-" Karson sharply replied.

"Now, Karson." Victor sternly ordered. "Food can wait."

"OW!" Karson stomped into the living room waving his hand back and forth. "What!" Karson thundered, Victor glaring at him warningly, giving him the phone. Karson rolled his eyes. "I'm cooking right now and just burned myself, so whatever it is I'm not interested."

"Hunter, good to hear your voice. You're being activated early. An imminent attack on the Country. Need you at least at the naval station, but if you can be on the ship at that time that would be best. Two hours. That is nine pm."

"Seriously? But I thought I deploy tomorrow." Karson complained.

"You may be deployed tonight. Don't know yet. Something big is about to go down. Sorry. Victor will be getting a call soon as well; he may be deploying with you from here; we don't know. Tell him he'd better have access to some gear. Two hours. I want you on the base. Got me?"

"Yes, Admiral. See you soon." Karson put his phone in his pocket and took a beer. "You have your uniform?"

"Yeah, why?" Victor asked.

"I'm being activated. You will be soon. Thompson said something big is about to happen. Something on U.S. Soil possibly. Maybe somewhere else in the world. You might be with me!"

"Hey. Let's just have a good dinner, and we'll worry about this after, okay?"

"K k." Karson groaned, walking slowly back to the grill. "It's ready."

****

Karson stood looking out the window up at the stars. He opened the window and leaned out.

"What are you doing?"

Karson jumped out of his skin, slammed his head into the window, "OW!" and looked back into the room; his knife pointed right at Victor.

"DAMMIT VICTOR! I'VE TOLD YOU NOT TO DO THAT TO ME!"

"I stood back here!" He said innocently. "Happy late birthday by the way!" He smiled.

Karson rubbed his head. "You're a jerk!"

Victor laughed. "What did you want to show me?"

"Come here!" Karson motioned for Victor to follow him out onto the roof. Karson laid down and looked up at the sky as the sun dipped further under the horizon, Victor joining him.

"That was good, Karse! How'd you learn to cook like that?" Victor asked, taking a swig of yet another beer.

"I paid attention to my mother when she'd cook dinner at home. And when I was in high school, I was artsy like I said... My parents had me go to an all art school and put me in extracurricular classes, like a young chef's academy." Karson said, staring up at the stars.

Victor looked up too. "How's...?"

"I don't know... We haven't spoken. Didn't want me to be a SEAL..."

"I remember you almost quit because of that..."

"Pfft, not quit? Not even join. But... I don't know, it all worked out, obviously... said 'I don't want you to give up on something you feel called to. Not even for me. I'll be waiting...' You?"

"Not too good either... SEALs never really stay with their spouses, Karse..."

"Yeah."

"Why are we up on the roof?"

"It reminds me of my childhood. My friend and I would climb to the roof of his dad's house and would study the constellations. I don't know... I guess I like the cool night air." Karson slowly looked at Victor. "I don't want to go again, Vic... I really don't want to. It's my job, the best in the world, and I love my brothers, sisters, and the job... But I don't see an out. There is no end to this war. I thought we got him, man. I thought we'd have him right now. That I could confirm the kill. That I could rest. But no… I have to face him again."

"Maybe it's not him… Maybe they just need you to train others. You don't know what the mission is. They didn't seem too excited."

"Something is about to happen. An attack on U.S. soil? I always said we needed to be more prepared before something like this happened again… Victor, something is about to go down. I can just feel it. You need to be ready too, man. You're probably going out again…" Karson rebutted him.

"I think it could be a revenge scenario." He said. "Remember Bin Laden? They hit the US on September 11 in Benghazi. Maybe he's not directly responsible for this…"

"I don't think so. Feels too personal." Karson said.

Victor looked at his watch. "You have forty-five minutes, Karse. Don't you think you should pack your stuff?"

'It's already packed. I pack two days before a mission in case things get out of control like now. Have an emergency pack always ready."

"How far is the base from here?"

Karson looked to his left. Victor did as well. The top of the ship Karson was assigned to be on was in plain sight.

"Thanks for being my friend. My best friend. If I don't make it back, all my stuff is split between you and Co-"

"I don't want to hear you talk about that, Karson." Victor put his arm around Karson and hugged him. "We will be here again, having dinner with our spouses, staring up at the stars. No matter where you or I go, we will have each other's six. Hey… Hey, look at me!"

Karson was staring down the road. Flashing lights and a fully armed Humvee escort were charging up his street, rolling to a stop in front of Karson's house. Karson and Victor looked at each other, then sprang up. "Come on!" Karson said crawling back through the window and running down the stairs out onto the front lawn.

"Captain Hunter, I need you to come with me. Now." A Sailor said.

"Why?" Karson asked when suddenly he flinched when he heard the boom of a warship firing its weapons. People outside of their houses screamed as the emergency warnings started howling in the night time air. People were exiting their houses and staring at the military motorcade on their street.

The Police were ordering everybody back inside. "Stay off the streets. Turn on the news and listen to instructions."

"I'm going to throw on my uniform and grab my pack. Victor-"

"Sir, I need you back inside." A Police Officer said to Victor.

"He's a SEAL Team Two captain," Karson said, stepping in between the two men.

"He comes too. Get in the Humvee." The Sailor said.

"Vic, I have gear for you. Basement. Sir, if you can load my pack that would be great. I need two minutes. Where are we going?"

"Houston. Go."

"That's away from my ship-"

"LET'S GO!" He shouted at Karson.

****

Karson sat in the vehicle, watching news feed of the attack on the USA. New York, Los Angeles, Chicago, Indianapolis, Portland, Miami… "There are so many coordinated attacks. This is insane." Karson whispered, hugging his rifle to his chest, his legs pulled to him, feet on the seat, still ready for any enemy at any moment.

"Yeah." A voice spoke behind Karson.

Karson looked back. "Yo! You're the cop that pulled me over when I was late for my flight to basic!" Karson smiled.

"Yeah. Names Jackson. Small world, eh? You inspired me to join the Coast Guard, sir. The quickest way to start serving was to join a branch, so I went to the closet recruiting depot. Sent me off, came back, and now we're a fighting force as well as rescue force."

Karson reached back. "Any branch or local service is a brother of mine." The two men shook hands.

"WHAT THE! Karse, look at that!" Victor said from behind the driver seat, smacking Karson's shoulder. Karson looked out his right window.

"That is not a shooting star! It's heading straight downtown! There's a PP concert there right now…" Karson said.

"Patricia Parke?" Victor asked. "Seriously?"

"Yeah. They are hitting the biggest concert in the world. There are so many people there…" The military convoy hit the highway as fighter jets and Black Hawks headed towards the attacks. Karson watched as the city went on as if nothing was going on. "The hell… Why aren't they fleeing? The emergency tones are going off…" Karson turned on the radio.

ALERT TONE

ALERT TONE

ALERT TONE

'This is a national emergency. Important instructions will follow. This is not a test.'

ALERT TONE

'This message is transmitted at the orders of the United States Department of Homeland Security and Department of Defense on orders from The U.S. Government and President Elding. NORAD has detected long range missiles as well as an invasion force heading towards major cities of the United States. At least one missile is believed to be targeted to Houston, Texas area while others are en-route to other capitals and major cities. All residents within a one-hundred-mile radius of the city should evacuate immediately and head to rural, low populated areas. Shelters are being set up at Red Cross and emergency centers outside of the one-hundred-mile radius. A representative from our government will be speaking shortly when everything is settled down and information is received. Emergency services as well as the military are mobilizing. Please follow the following instructions. If you are still in position of self-defense weapons after previous elections, arm yourselves. The U.S. Constitution makes it clear that state militias may be formed. Acting within the law, we authorize any civilian to fight alongside U.S. forces. Make yourself known to these forces by heading to local Police departments, state buildings, and other government facilities to be given identification to wear. If you do not, you may be fired upon. If not armed with firearms, arm with knives or any other weapon. Be vigilant. Help fellow Americans. Exit densely populated areas. Evacuate to non-major cities one hundred plus miles outside of major cities. Seek shelter immediately. Unless urgent, leave 911 and other emergency services open. Keep off the streets. U.S. Military Martial Law has been enacted. Follow the instructions of local emergency services and military personnel. Make way for emergency crews and military personnel. Look to the flag. It represents freedom. We are American. We will overcome this threat to our nation. To repeat,'

ALERT TONE

'This is a national emergency. Important instructions will follow. This is not a test.'

ALERT TONE

'This message is transmitted at the orders of...'

Karson looked back over. "Come on... Get out of there! Get out of there!" Karson whispered under his breath as explosions rocked the city. "GET OUT OF THERE? WHY ARE THEY NOT LEAVING?" Karson yelled. Karson felt the blast wave strike the Humvee, rocking it into the next lane.

"They are Americans, Karse... Defiant of anything attacking the nation." Victor's surprisingly and infuriatingly calm and soothing voice replied.

"Patriots," Karson said. The emergency sirens grew louder as the troops approached the concrete jungle and traveled the concrete rivers through the city. "Alright, guys... This is our state. Our land. Our nation. Texas once was its own country, defiant of any attack. We are the same now. It's our job to keep it that way. We will be fighting in the streets of the United States of America. We are dealing with terrified civilians as well as enemy troops. Our mothers and fathers and brothers and sisters and siblings and family and people of any identity are in the streets, in danger. Check your fire and head on the swivel. Any threat, if you do not know whether to fire or not, shoot first and ask questions later. Protect each other. Protect our fellow Americans. Defend America. It's always better to ask for forgiveness after the fact"

The Humvee exited the freeway and entered the combat zone. Karson readied his weapon, closed his eyes and calmed himself, entering into his warrior state. "I am the reaper. I will kill any enemy both foreign and domestic. I am a Navy SEAL. Trained to deliver on my mission. Trained to spit death like a cobra, protect like a wolf, and battle like a lion. I am unstoppable. I am death."

The Humvee rolled to a stop near the blast site. "Oh, now I'm pissed," Karson said as he exited the Humvee. "They just ended the greatest music ever known to man. It put all the old pop singers to shame." Karson looked around at people gathering.

Victor shouted. "CLEAR THE STREETS. EVACUATE THE CITY. SEEK SHELTER!" Karson was looking for threats as shots rang behind Victor who spun around raising his weapon to see heavily armed enemy forces making their way up the street. Explosions in the air revealed enemy aircraft battling the United States Air Force, and tank blasts a few blocks over gave way to the city being invaded.

Karson opened fire on any person he deemed a threat, armed civilians joining his side as a united fighting force, hell bent on protecting the American way of life. Karson nodded after identifying them as fellow Americans.

"Be careful! Help your fellow Americans." Karson broke from cover leaving them with less of a force to face.

"Go careful, sir!" The civilian followed him. "We need you!"

"Same to you!" Karson called back as he met up with Victor, placing his hand on his shoulder as they readied to breach the JPMorgan Chase Tower. "You sure we want to enter this building? Not sure why the tallest building in Houston wasn't hit, but I'm sure it's a target..."

"We need higher ground, Serval. Need to also have a view of the city. Formulate a plan." Thunder rumbled in the distance.

"Great. We'll be fighting in a storm. Always wanted that!" Karson smiled. "Breech it." Karson, Victor, and Jackson from the Coast Guard entered the building. The driver and Police escort continued to lay support in other important areas of town.

"Serval? Admiral Thompson. Are you relaying this channel?"

"Admiral! My Lord is it good to hear your voice. I am a team of three inside the JPMorgan Chase Tower. Tallest bundling in Houston. We are laying recon over the city, as well as taking shots at the enemy in the street."

"The invasion force is numerous. Every state at once. Distracting from an attack on Washington, then entering from all sides. Canada is being hit as well. I am sending a Black Hawk to your location; our vessel is heading into open waters. It was a mistake to send you there. Any intel you get before you hit the ship, relay to me. Chopper at the roof in twenty minutes. Your team call sign: Liberator 1. You are Liberator 1-1."

"Aye. Liberator 1 copy's all, sir. Liberator 1-1 out."

"Be careful, Serval. This is the last fireplace in the world. The rest of it is against us. Make it to this ship, you and Victor both."

Karson moved to the elevator. "I say we risk it. Maintain our strength. Head up to the thirtieth floor. Bust a window and snipe as well as recon. We need to be on the roof, floor seventy-five up to roof access in nine minutes to lay down flares."

"Your lead, Serval," Victor said.

Jackson nodded. "I'm just here for the ride!"

"Aye." Karson pressed the button and entered the elevator, pressed thirty and up the lift they went. Within seconds the SEALs and Guardsman were on the floor. Karson looked around the city in front of him as Victor equipped the longer range rifle he had. He placed a blast on the glass and blew it out into the air and let gravity rain down glass on the street below. "Victor, open fire. Jackson, with me, we're heading to tamper with the power supply to the floor below and up."

"Where is that? Shouldn't I stay with Victor to cover him?" Jackson argued.

"He's a SEAL. No offense, you're Coast Guard. He doesn't need your help. I need you to cover the hallway I'll be in. I know it sounds ridiculous just do what I say."

"Okay." Jackson followed Karson to the stairs and descended a level, finding the maintenance room. Karson pulled a lock pick kit from his pack and got to work wiggling and jiggling the lock to unlock the room. Jackson watched the hall, looking down to the streets below. Not much was going on, but he could hear gunshots from Victor pretty frequently.

"Karse, enemies are entering the building. Better hurry." Victor relayed over Karson's coms.

"I'm in the room. Jackson, watch the stairs." Karson looked around the room and found elevator access and pulled that peg to off. He then found lights and turned them off and exited the room. "That will buy us about seven minutes. One more than we need. Let's go." Karson held the door for Jackson, placed a claymore at the bend in the stairs that led to the top floor and followed. He opened the door and called Victor to regroup on him, and the three men went up the stairs onto the roof. The sound of rotor blades had the men looking up to see the Black Hawk approaching steady on their position. Karson waved, and the chopper turned and hovered. A crewman hung out the door with his hand outstretched.

"You'll have to jump. I've got you." He yelled.

"Vic, you first," Karson said, crouching, his weapon pointed at the door. "He'll need all his strength with you both. I'm lightest."

Victor stepped to the side of the building, and hopped, making it into the door perfectly fine, on his own.

"You next, sir," Jackson said.

Karson was about to argue when the doors flung open and enemy troops filed onto the rooftop and fired at the helicopter. Karson turned and started to spring when Jackson took a round and knocked Karson off balance. Karson slipped and felt air around him. Jackson flipped backward over the edge and plummeted, Karson for some reason was suspended in air, watching his brother fall to his death, the building floating away from him.

Karson looked up and saw the crewman had his hand.

"You gonna just hang there, or do you want to get in?"

Karson gave his other hand and was pulled into the chopper by Victor and the crewman and lay panting on the ground as the door was closed.

"Hey, what's your name?" Karson asked.

"Corporal Wayth. Pararescue."

"Glad to see you guys," Victor spoke up. "Mind if we join you?"

"Not at all, sir... Any SEAL is fine by me! We all fight the same battle!"

"Mind getting us back to our ship?" Karson piped up.

"Yes, sir. What's your name?" He asked, hand outstretched.

"I don't have a name. If you need me, call me Captain Serval."

"As you wish!" Wayth shook his hand.

"I hate these guys, Serv. We should kill every single one of them. This is our land. If you don't like it, don't come here, but don't come here and kill our people. How would they like it if we killed them? Huh?" Victor punched the door of the chopper as Karson slid into a seat beside another Para Rescue commando.

"Vic, not all people are terrible people... Not all of these guys agree with what they are doing. Did you ever read about the Pulse Club in Orlando attack in 2016?"

"No. Terrorist attack?"

"Yeah, it was a-"

"He deserves to die!"

"No. Vic, I know you're mad, but... People of all walks of life were marching in the street supporting the LGBTQ plus community -

waving the American flag in defiance to horrendous acts. Not everyone is bad, just some."

Victor looked at Karson and opened his mouth to speak, but the pilot interrupted.

"Hey, open the door and check out the West."

"Did you hear me, Vic?"

"Yes, sir. I did. Apologies. It's how we were brought up."

Karson opened the door and found a flare floating through the sky, the trail leading towards a tall building. *What is going on?* Karson pulled a pair of binoculars out from his pack and looked through them to find Police engaged with heavily armed terrorists on the roof of the structure. "Pilot, move towards that building and-"

"I've lost all control... Hang on to something!" The pilot said, the chopper starting to spin. "EMP!"

The chopper spun lower and lower towards the ground.

Huh? Karson wondered, stiffening as the butterfly feeling crept into his belly.

"I see a pond; I'm aiming for there!" The pilot tried regaining control of the bird, slowing the spiral, and giving the rotors manual power. The bird slowed down in its decent, but still smacked hard onto the ground, turning on its side and burying the props, missing the pond completely.

"EVERYONE OUT!" A PJ shouted, opening the other door and jumping through, helping his brothers out. Karson jumped down last, following Victor to find themselves in the Houston Zoo. Animals were freaking out and people were scattered throughout the zoo. Karson moved to the pilots and found they were dead. The aircraft took most of the impact nose to belly.

Karson lowered his head. "I'll send someone back for you, brothers." Karson turned to see the others crouched, pointing out. "Hey! Remember me? Captain Serval? Our mission is to get to those men in that building."

"Sir, we have orders to get you to the vessel so you can regroup with a SEAL Team. You need to come with us."

Karson pointed to Victor and himself. "We are a SEAL Team and those people do not have until-"

"Rice University is right here. They were in class today when the attack started. They need extracted."

"That's great... But someone needs to go help those Police Officers."

"They're probably dead, sir... The campus needs to be evacuated! Priority of life! Cops, Soldiers... we all know what we signed up for."

"Serval..." Victor spoke up. "Make a decision. Arguing gets us no closer to the prize. IF we split, just us, that is fine but-"

"Oh yeah, always turning to me to-"

"No. Take command. You outrank me now, it's your turn."

"THEN LET'S GO NOW!" Karson yelled.

The Airman stared at Karson. "Okay... Let's go then."

Karson marched past Victor towards the entrance of the building, finding a set of keys on the ground under a bench. Karson moved and picked it up. "Wonder if we can find transport..." Karson smiled, waving the keys. "You want to drive, Vicky?"

Victor glared at the feminine nickname. "Aye." He swatted the keys into his hand and exited the zoo. "CONTACT!" He ran back into the zoo, taking cover behind the brick wall, the SEALs and PJs hidden, but about to be discovered and slaughtered along with the inhabitants of the zoo.

"We could be here a while. We should drink up and be ready to get out. When a lot of people die, we'll have our chance to escape. Right now, we'd probably die if we attached this big of a force. We'll probably die here soon, but we'll survive for now." A PJ stupidly gave his own plan.

Karson looked back at the animals, his eyes wide. "We have to push them back... Lead them away from these people and animals." Karson shouted at the people, defiant of the PJ's plan. "EXIT THE ZOO IN THE BACK!"

Karson opened fire round the wall into the enemy wave, his new team fired with him dropping many, the force too large to be pushed back, pushed the American men back into the zoo, past the red pandas and the sea lions. *Please don't strike an animal... please do not hit an innocent animal!"* Karson unleashed his full might through his weapon, picking targets and popping their heads like acne. Seventeen minutes of fighting gave way to nineteen dead enemies, and four dead civilians. Karson heard the screams of animals, but his mission was to protect American civilian lives first. He was forced to leave the zoo and enter the Escalade Victor's keys found leaving animals to an uncertain fate. The SEALs and PJs raced from the parking lot in the direction of the University of Houston, six and eight-tenths of a mile away.

Karson stared ahead, saying nothing, wanting nothing of this war anymore.

"Hey, Karse..." Victor touched him. "You need to focus, man. I know you want to go back for them, but we can't have you being useless and broken down on me. No panda repeat, okay?"

"I'm not broken down. I'm pissed. It isn't fair. This shouldn't have happened."

How did we miss this?

****

CHAPTER 46 - Waterspout

"Y ou always chew gum when you're fighting?" A PJ asked Karson.

Karson stepped out of the vehicle, arriving at the University. "Only when I'm a bit nervous. Not nervous, edgy. I don't know... It helps focus me sometimes. This whole situation is all kinds of messed up. How did they get in? Why are they here? How many civilians are dead? Brothers, sisters, people of service? How long have they planned? Why, how... what is that creepy noise playing through the city?" As if a call to service, a speaker played the same music that Karson had seen on the news when he argued at home with Victor. It soared between the buildings in the attacked cities of America.

"Serval," Victor's voice snapped Karson out of his banter. "Focus up, okay?"

"Sorry," Karson muttered. To the PJ he added, "I have a bad feeling, that's all." Karson looked around the lobby they were stepping through as thunder rumbled outside and the winds began to pick up. *This is a big school!*

"Serval. Take point." Victor said. Karson had his gun pointed at the second floor and was spinning around, ensuring no ambush.

Karson stopped dead in his tracks. He held up his finger to shush everyone. He tilted his head and listened. "Footsteps." He whispered. He pointed upstairs and slithered past the rest of the crew, crouching slightly, putting foot after foot softly on each marble stair as he moved to the second floor, their steps softly bouncing off the walls, hopefully not enough to disturb the person above; it was far too quiet in the building for a nearly seven-thousand-person school. Crouching under the wall and lifting his head just enough to peer over, the footsteps were nearing rapidly, and Karson lunged up and pointed his weapon right in the face of a frightened red headed, freckle faced girl who screamed bloody murder and swung a hammer.

Where'd you get a hammer?

…at Karson, who lifted his rifle up, spun it around like a clock and disarmed her from her weapon. She took off in the other direction.

"Hey! I'm with the U.S. Navy! Stop." Karson ran after her. "You are safe! Stop running and let me help you!"

She looked over her shoulder and Karson ripped the American Flag patch from his shoulder and showed it.

"See! American. Like you."

She stopped and turned and ran at Karson, grabbing him in a hug. "Thank, God!" She whimpered. She let go and motioned for the Americans to follow her. "My friends and I are locked down here."

"Wait! Stop!" Victor called after her, but she was turning the hallway, and Karson started after her.

"Serval, you stop right there. We don't know if it's a trap or not."

"She needs our help, bro. Gotta help her." Karson raced after her, checking his corners and swinging wide around them, following the girl to a classroom. She knocked what Karson assumed was a code and the door opened.

"I found some Navy guy. They are here to help us!" She said to the class. "I'm sorry I attacked you with the hammer, you look like the swamp man with that dark, flimsily hat round your head.

Karson walked in slowly, his weapon up, and the four PJs and Victor followed. Karson scanned the room and nodded to the five males and seven females. "It's called a Boonie. Why are you here?"

"This is where we go to college, sir." A boy piped up.

"I know that... What are you doing in this classroom at seven in the evening?" Karson asked.

"We have a late class." Another said standing in excitement. "I'm sorry, but you look so cool!" He started to walk towards Karson.

"Hey, back away from him and sit down." Victor entered the room with his weapon up as well, only dropping it once Karson did. "Is this all of you?"

"Our professor went out to find some help... we heard shots..." The red head piped up. "You never think you'll have to go through something like this... until it happens to you..."

"Which way?" Karson asked, checking the boy who approached him over for injuries and ensured he was doing alright. He did this for everyone, his medical training kicking in.

"We're all fine. Right, out the door." She said. Karson checked her, then moved onto her friend who smiled at him.

"You're cute!" She pushed slightly into Karson. Victor chuckled as Karson pushed her away. She fended off his gentleness and hugged him. "Thank you for saving us! And for your service!"

Karson looked back and nodded to Victor, who took two PJs with him to check for the professor. Karson finally got the fearful and star struck college girl off him and walked over to the window and looked out and around the grounds. "It's my job, ma'am."

Police, enemy, and student bodies lay strewn across the beautiful campus. Sidewalk and greenery stained with blood and riddled with casings. Karson's heart sunk. "This is all messed up. It'll be your jobs to fix this, ladies and gentlemen. Alright... Happy to know you're here. This Pararescue man will check you guys out more thoroughly. We," Karson pointed at the other PJ and himself "will return momentarily."

Karson stepped outside as Victor was returning. "We need to check the rest of the building..." Karson nodded to Victor, the PJ he called into the hallway, and the PJ right of Victor. "Pharaoh, you, and you, come with me. You, go and guard your buddy." Karson began walking the direction of the stairs. "Captain, you come with me. You two take the basement. No rules of engagement. Protect yourselves and each other. Up here when you finish. Ten minutes tops."

"Yes, sir." The two PJs split and hurried down the stairs. Karson pulled a sticky note out of his pocket and jotted down the class number, placed it on his weapon, and Victor and Karson hurried up and began clearing the third and final floor. Victor took the lead, as he always did.

"You know... I may have ended up here had I stayed in school... Some of my old friends go here. Not that I had many friends, to begin with, but I had some close acquaintances..." They came upon the body of a professor and two students, shot in the back. "That could have easily been me..." Karson checked for a pulse, knowing- "Nothing." He stood and caught up to Victor. "Shot straight through and through."

"What do you think you would have studied?"

"I told you I went to an art school, so probably something with Theatre or music... film. Always wanted to be an actor or pop star. But now I shoot people for a living." He smirked. "I wonder where celebrities go or what they do in times like these? Do they just disappear to their private islands in the Bahamas? Go home with their families? They probably don't suffer like any of us do, or get their hands dirty like we do..."

"Hey, no better job than killing the enemy."

"Hooyah, only I wish we didn't have to... wish I was still staring up at the stars, chillin' on my roof, maybe eating chocolate, drinking hot cocoa."

"Hot cocoa?" Victor looked back at Karson with his brow cocked. "Seriously?"

"Hey! I'm still like, 12..." Karson laughed.

"No kidding! Hey, if we get out of this, I'll get you some hot cocoa! Deal?"

"Deal!" Karson followed Victor and took the lead, approaching a corner. He slid his weapon around the corner to check for enemies. Karson's eyes widened, and he put his hand up in the peace sign.

Karson and Victor slinked around the corner and slithered up to two red clothed men sitting and smoking on a bench pulled to watch another staircase. *'Idiots.'* Karson mouthed at Victor. A pen lay on the ground beside Karson, and he picked it up, emptied it, and pulled his knife. He pointed at the one on the left, his target and slammed his knife into the man's lung through his armpit, pulling out and slamming the pen in, listening contently as the air escaped out of the pen. Victor merely slit his target's throat. Karson held the man's mouth closed with his hand and watched as his eyes started to glaze over and his soul began to depart. "Any more of you?" He asked as the man gasped for his last breath. His eyes flicked further up the hallway and Karson's head jerked up to find two more people turning around.

"CRAP!" Victor shouted, ducking behind a pillar. Karson dropped down the staircase and readied to move to intercept the enemy, but Victor walked by. "Dropped them."

"Nice!" Karson high fived him, ran up the hallway, to ensure that it was empty when he found another patrol. Only this one was different. Karson motioned Victor to him.

"What? Let's get back to the classroom… Oh."

Karson looked with Victor to young children being beaten by enemy soldiers, their moans so soft and quiet, and their lives being taken from them by a brutal foe. Probably family of on campus living staff members. Karson wasted no time in taking these lives and shot several rounds into each torturer. But even had the SEALs had medical attention, there was no saving the three young children. They looked up at Karson, and their last sound was the kiss of death, where the Reaper sucks away the final breath from one's body. Karson looked down, his eyes burning as he fought tears. He looked up to Victor who placed his hand on Karson's shoulder.

"Why these people kill I'll have no idea…"

"They are sadists, Vic. Nothing more. It's their orgasmic way to get off. Let's get back to the classroom." He looked at his rifle's sticky note. "313."

"I know. I remember numbers."

"Well, I'm sorry I've got more to do than memorizing room numbers." They walked back to the room.

The PJs followed suit later, stating no contact and entered the room.

"Serval, no injuries." The PJ medic informed him.

"Cool. Let's go then. Need to move on. Get to the ship. Send someone back to them." Karson started to walk out.

"Everyone needs to stay put. Shelter in place. Lock the door, keep the lights out, and do not move through the halls again." He looked at the red headed girl. "We are needed elsewhere right now, but we will send someone to come retrieve you soon." The medic said.

"Excuse me?" A male student stood and approached Karson, grabbing his shoulder and turning him around from talking to an Airman. "You're in charge... when can we go ho-"

"You need to sit down." Karson pointed his finger in the student's face and snapped his thumb. He turned on his heel and headed for the door.

"Don't snap your hand at me!" The student followed him.

"You know..." Karson turned again and stared at the kid. "You know we're in a war zone right now, yeah?" He walked towards the kid, his feet moving heel to toe heel like on a tightrope. *Scary swag!* "You also know that you could die at any time, any place, right here in your university. In your own country. Right here where you stand? Right here, where you sit? Right here, right now, at this very second on this very day of this very week, month, year, this exact moment of time in the universe?" Karson stood nose to the nose with the kid, who stood slightly taller than him. "America is not safe anymore, kid."

"You're obviously younger than me. You should treat me with some respect. **Kid.**" He glared at Karson and began to raise a hand to him, but Karson raised his hand first. All five fingers, each finger dropping on each word. "America. Is. Not. Safe." His middle finger remained. "KID!" He punched the kid to the chest, knocking him back. "Yeah, I'm younger than you are, but I'm doing more to save your sorry rich kid ass than yourself, or anyone else sitting in this room. We all are." He gestured around at his brothers. "America is no longer free. Not safe. Enemy troops are right at your front door. Your colleagues lie dead right outside your window. Right outside that door. Now I ask you..." Karson drew his pistol, spun it around and handed it towards the kid. "Want to join my team? Hmm?" The kid just stared at Karson. "Go on. Take it! Or do you want to stay here, safe, and let the professionals go and save all our sorry lives like always?" Karson stared him in the eye, holding his gaze until he looked away. "Didn't think so."

Karson holstered his weapon. "That's what I thought. Now you sit your ass down, shut up, and shelter in place. Someone comes to harm you, run, hide, jump out that window, or fight. Don't sissy out. Don't be a victim. Don't let them harm you. Find the will to survive, because they certainly will. Boys, you may have to worry, but you'll probably just get shot. You're men. Girls, you are women. You'll probably be raped. Fight if you must. Win. Escape. Do something. But when we come back, we don't want to clean you up nor a puddle of piss from the ground because you got scared and tinkled. Kinda like the Pulse club in Orlando back in Sixteen. You study that in school? Those people showed so much courage... if only they had fought back. Fight and it might let you survive." Karson snapped in the kids face again, winked and turned to leave. "Leave the lights off. Help each other. Listen well and be quiet. Barricade the door. We'll send someone to you soon. I cannot emphasize this enough. Be. Quiet. Take your writing utensils and use them as a weapon. You all will be fine. Good luck." Karson had the men close the door and started walking towards the stairs.

"What would you have done if he'd said he'd join the team?" Victor asked.

"I'd have given him the gun and said, let's go!"

"Captain Serval? Do you not hate this war?"

"Not really, dude," Karson replied to the Air Force medic. "I don't like war, but I know it's a natural cycle. There will always be a war of some kind my friend, each one getting worse and worse as you go. If this one ends... when this one ends, a new one will begin. Worse than before. Someone new. Always fighting. Never sleeping or resting. Always killing. Blood. Gore. Violence. Treachery. Men like you and I fighting for what is right against satanic demons walking the earth. It never ends. It's the circle of war. It's the way the world works." Karson looked at Victor who nodded. "Can we get to the ship now?"

Thunder crashed as the men reached the front door and a downpour of rain and hail barraged the building.

"Great," Victor muttered.

"I kinda like storms. Mainly operating in them. Straight through and out of the city. The ship is about fifty miles away." Karson checked his GPS. "Don't see why they couldn't have taken me to the ship from my house, but whatever."

"Thompson needed you in the city to get some information, apparently." Victor said.

"War. It's just war." Karson said. "That's all the info I got."

Victor laughed. "You obviously didn't sleep much last night."

Karson glared.

"Serval?" Thompson's voice came through his comlink.

"Yes, sir?" Karson was surprised his leader was talking to him again. "We're Oscar Mike. On the move!"

"Chopper inbound to your location. Get to the top floor of a building nearest you, drop a flare if you have one. I need you to listen to me; this is your mission briefing. We have a window of opportunity no one else has or knows, and it's a mistake by the enemy. Victor too."

"Right here, sir!"

Both SEALs headed into the building directly across from them.

"Building is not the smallest, but it's not tall, sir. I have a flare." They took to the stairs and climbed the ten stories to the roof.

"Hatyara, Ojore. We found them. Based on the information your late teammates recovered from that submarine, we have tracked them to Latin America and Mexico. Ojore had been running free throughout the states, setting up these attacks. He fled to Mexico to rally his troops after this offensive, to invade our great nation in ruins. We cannot let that happen, and we will not let that happen. We believe Hatyara is at the Mexican consulate, and Ojore is in a palace like compound or resort, whatever you call it. Once on this ship, we'll be briefing, you'll be resting, and tomorrow you deploy, hopefully for the last time."

"Wherever you need me, sir. But one condition. I'm tired of these foreigners jerking us off. If I can't succeed, you blow Mexico sky high! I don't care if you have to break down Elding's door and do it yourself, nuke this guy."

"Karson, we'll get him. We have his ship." Thompson said.

"You salvaged it?" Victor patted Karson. "Told you good would triumph. Those lost coming home."

"We did. It's on its way to... Well. It's on its way." Thompson said. "Our troops overseas have found the shipyard. We will take it soon, adding a new breed of ship to our fleets.

"I see! Nice. Good work, sir." Karson said. "Out."

Karson and Victor reached the door to the roof but heard steps behind them. The Air Force PJs were accounted for. The steps were a floor down.

"Here, Vic. Take the flare, I want to check something out."

"I'll come with you-"

"Take the men to the roof and get the chopper. I'll be fine." Karson lowered a floor, looking for the source of the sound, finding a shadow just inside a ninth floor door. He raised his weapon as a civilian stepped out, a pistol in his hand. "Drop your weapon, and state your name and intention."

"I'm gonna kill you, terrorist." The civilian cocked his weapon.

Hearing someone say they were going to kill you, it sends a chill down your spine.

"Sir, I'm an American Sailor. Please don't make me shoot you. Drop your weapon."

"You invade my apartment building, putting my family in danger all the same." He raised his gun at Karson.

"No! Drop it!" Karson fired a shot, the man returned fire, hitting Karson in the chest plate. He fell backward up the stairs, the man's weapon jamming, he lunged at Karson. Karson's drew his pistol and punched it into the man's shoulder, his finger on the trigger, the force of the impact pushing down the trigger and sending bullet clean and clear through the man's shoulder. Karson kicked him back and turned and sprinted up the stairs. *I'm not about to kill a civilian of y nationality. I'm sworn to defend these people!* He reached the door to the roof, and out he went, followed closely by the civilian who met the butt of Karson's rifle, knocking him out cold.

"Serval… Who's that?" Victor called over the chopper noises as Karson dragged him inside. Karson looked up to see the Air Force helicopter landing on the roof of the apartment building.

"Civilian. Confused. Let's go!" He ran over.

The Americans loaded up in the chopper and flew towards the ship and eventually watched the land dip down and turn to ocean H_2O. Karson smiled. "Victor? You think we're being teamed up again?"

"Wouldn't see why not… I mean-"

The helicopter dropped and flipped to the side, sending Karson cascading out of his seat, Victor trying to grab him. The choppers alarm systems loud, and the electronic woman's voice screaming at the pilots

"Altitude

Altitude

Pull up

Pull up"

Karson screamed, having looked out the window and seeing the ocean approaching at a fast rate.

"Waterspout. Hold on to something!" The pilot was surprisingly calm for a man who was battling the winds of a high powered water tornado.

Finally, the expensive military helicopter was put back on level flying pattern and en-route to the ship, landing on the massive new aircraft carrier the United States created.

"AF3213 clear for landing pad Linda Kingsley S3." A static voice came over the communications.

"Clear, LKAIControl, AF3213 on final." The Air Force pilot spoke through the coms.

"S?" Victor piped up, questioning the aviator's lingo. "S3?"

"Means starboard." The pilot said behind him. "Linda Kingsley's starboard helipad three.

"Ah." Karson smiled at Victor's ignorance of aviation. "What? I didn't know… I'm a Military Police Officer, not a pilot like you guys."

"Uh huh." He mouthed, smiling wider, looking out his window at the approaching floating USA.

Upon touchdown, the Admiral was on the flight deck to greet the SEALs. Karson scampered up to him, about to ask his question, when the Admiral held up his hand. "Yes, you're being assigned to each other!"

Karson jumped a 360 as Victor glided up rolling his eyes. "We're together, Vic!" Karson shouted, the other crewmembers looking over.

"How you become a SEAL, Hunter, I'll never know." Admiral Thompson too rolled his eyes, motioning for the Sailors to follow him. "We found him. Both of 'em. Tapachula, Chiapas, Mexico. Victor, you deploy two days. Morning. You fly to the base of the invasion; you drive in, and you take the city. Lots of civilians. Be careful."

"I thought you said-"

The Admiral placed his hand over Karson's mouth, stopping him from his complaints. Karson talked into his hand, inaudible, certainly explicit language.

"If you'd just wait, I'll tell you, Karson." The Admiral removed his hand and stared at Karson, licking his lips, flinching at the taste and looked from Victor who was struggling to keep a straight face to the Admiral who always stared at Karson with disapproval.

"Literally waiting." Karson stomped his foot.

"Hatyara is in Mexico City. He has a meeting with the Mexican Secretary of Foreign Affairs. Kill him. Get to the invasion force. You leave tonight. You'll be there early morning, you get in, you get out. You have an hour to sleep, an hour to get ready. You leave at Zero five. You arrive zero seven. You have 'til noon to get set. Meeting at one. Clear?"

Karson sighed. "Yeah, sir."

"Something else to tell you... President Elding went missing in North Korea last Month."

Karson and Victor stopped dead in their tracks. They spun around looking at each other.

"Wait... What?" Victor asked.

"We weren't notified because?" Karson stormed up to the Admiral.

"You're both the top SEALs in the Navy. You had your own missions. The Secret Service is handling it. Just saying, considering that both of the men are in Mexico gearing up to finalize their world-conquering agenda with our nation, President Elding may be in the area of the invasion. Watch your weapons."

"How'd he go missing?" Victor asked.

Thompson looked at Victor. "Convoy destroyed."

Victor's eyes grew wider. "How do we know he's alive?"

"Admiral?" Karson said. "How-"

The Admiral held up a photo of a barely recognizable Elding. "Taken three days ago."

"We'll find him, sir," Karson said.

"Karson, he's okay..." Victor said.

"Secret Service, man," Karson said. "Remember the accusations of Obama's detail? It's never been resolved. We need to be his security."

"Agreed, but we're not. Go to bed." The Admiral smiled. "You leave in an hour and fifty-seven minutes. I need you combat effective so you need some rest. Go get it."

Karson nodded and looked back at the States, nostalgic for the bed, his bed, that he was supposed to be curled up in tonight. Then he went down the stairs to his rack and got some shuteye.

****

CHAPTER 47 - oh hey cow

"Here's your first aid kit, sir." The Corpsman explained to Karson.

"Thanks. I needed that brush-up." He winked at the female and turned, noticing a young child who instantly gave Karson the most insane flashback. "Who is this?"

"Child soldier. Trying to check his wounds, then rehabilitate him." The Corpsman said.

You were there... Rage filled Karson's body as his memory resurfaced of the woman who held one of the deepest parts of Karson's heart.

"Captain?" The Corpsman looked at the drained face of a fuming Navy SEAL… "You alright?"

"He should be cuffed…" Karson managed. Slowly regaining his composure.

"He's a kid, sir… Yeah, he's so, so scary!" The Corpsman said, offering more sass than she meant too.

Karson's sadness returned in the form of fear. "Hey, ma'am, do not underestimate-"

"A CHILD? This is coming from a child killer like yourself." The Corpsman turned to the Masters at Arms. "You two may go. Take the Captain with you. I do not need anyone in here who doesn't share my views."

The Masters at Arms began to leave and laid their hands on Karson to bring him with them. He jerked his sleeves out of their grip. "Get your hands off of me. I can move myself… HEY! GET OFF, MAN!"

The Masters at Arms got more aggressive, attempting to yank him to the door.

Karson threw one over his shoulder and backed the other against the wall, slamming his knee between the Master at Arm's legs, adding pressure. He held up a picture of the boy beheading an American. "Marine Pilot. One of the best. Taken by this 'kid.' To me, I don't see a child… I see a monster. A killer. I've killed these people before, and if he steps outside of this room, I will kill him as well. Either restrain him, or I'll restrain him permanently." Karson walked over and forced the picture into the Corpsman's face. "She was your sister. She was my best friend." Karson turned and exited the room, storming into the armory, arming himself with a pistol and a broken down newly advanced sniper rifle, before heading up to the flight deck to brief one last time with the admiral, who was enjoying an early morning cigar.

"Sir, those will kill you…"

"Karson…"

Karson tensed.

"None can hear. Besides, people slip all the time. They know your name. Even the enemy knows your name. Serval, it's kinda stupid…"

"I like it…" Karson looked out over the water.

"Remember to kill him on sight. This mission came unexpectedly, no one really knows what is going on. It all happens way to fast in war, my friend."

"I know that, sir. I fully understand that…" Karson took the cigar from his friend and puffed it once, handing it back. Thompson smiled.

"I know what Richardson liked about you… you do whatever you want. Like him."

"Kinda have to when you never know if you're coming home. Oh, sir. I need you to have weapons for me when I arrive…"

"For Ojore, we will." He stuck out his hand.

Karson shook. "Thank you, sir. I'll have this done soon."

"We're counting on it. We have undercovers in the area; one will drive you to the location from an airport. The same airport is your extraction. You'll fly cross country and ready up for invasion. We'll be through the Panama Canal-"

Karson gave a look.

"We have to risk it if we want to invade in time."

"They'll know we're coming."

"Ojore knows his hideaway is so protected. He will not worry. Same for Bin Laden. He thought it was safe, thus why he lived there."

"I guess…" Karson nodded as the pilot motioned him forward to the chopper.

"Five days Karson. We'll see each other in five days."

"Stay safe, sir. The first sign of trouble-"

"It's a United States supercarrier, Karson. We're totally fine."

"Yeah, but we've lost one once…"

"Won't happen again. Shoot on sight." Thompson saluted, Karson returned it, and began traveling across the nation holding his enemy. He watched water give way to landscape and at zero six thirty, Karson was met by an undercover at the airstrip and raced into the city.

"I have a perfect place located for you, sir. It's a restaurant roof; it has a clear sightline to the building. Your Sierra shot will be ideal for side one and two. They are easily sighted as it's a corner. The three side another building, and the four side, another building. Only entrances on sides one and two." He handed Karson a file showing the street corner.

"No chance of escaping into the buildings on the back or right side?"

"It's a government building. They must have wanted heightened security so no one could sneak in. Only two entrances, the massive main gate to a lobby, one, and a side door for important people on the left, side two."

"Great. Thank you for the information." The SEAL was delivered under darkness to the location, opting to walk the sidewalk up and down the street with groups of people. He bought a sombrero to blend in and also protect from the sun. He'd be waiting for a while. The information was sound. Only two entrances. The government building opened at seven and Karson moved inside to gain his bearings. Massive lobby. Elevators in the center; heavy doors led to secure locations, stairways, and offices. *No need for this... but just in case we need to enter inside, I want to know.*

With security being drawn to the really not so blended in American man, and the ever-present risk of being compromised, Karson slipped out the way he came and disappeared into the crowds of people, maneuvering around the Seven Eleven to find a dumpster out back that gave a better vantage to the roof. With a pipe somewhat above Karson's head, he jumped and clung onto it, providing an even easier access to the roof. He set up in the corner, watching people.

"Zero eight thirty." He set up the compact rifle and zeroed in on the side door. What was perfect about this newer rifle was that, even though he was watching the side door, he could also see the front door he merely need move his eyes a few inches to see through the other scope lens. The scope also had a wireless mouse on the side that when a target was offset from a perfect shot, instead of risking losing the subject while readjusting, the sniper merely slid the mouse, clicked on target and the barrel repositioned itself to lock onto target, leaving the shooter in his original position. This reduced risk of being comprised. The less movement a sniper makes, the more hidden he remains. The weapon also had a secondary barrel and magazine whilst still maintaining a compact size, in the event of another target that had to be taken out at the exact same moment. Command fire, when two snipers take out two different targets at the same time. This weapon allows for command fire with one shooter.

"He's obviously not going to enter through the front, though… right?" With the device setup, Karson laid back and took his time to rest, setting his alarm for noon, dozing in an out until the time to watch the door nonstop arrived. *I'll know when you get here… won't I?* Karson pulled up a picture of his enemy one last time. *Come on, Hunter. You have no room to doubt and cause an error here… You're trained for this. You're a SEAL. Where is he?*

1300 turned into 1310, 1320. At 1333, when about to move into the building to see if his mission was still a go, Karson noticed a rare sight, it would seem, in this part of the nation. A luxury vehicle approached the front door, and out stepped four armed men in *suits? That's weird for Death Nation terrorists…*

One remained unarmed, surprisingly normal looking. Karson quickly moved his rifle to hone in on his prey, mentally preparing himself in a split second to take what was left of this man's humanity… the mere fact that he was breathing. Karson clicked the button and the rifle barrel certainly did lock on target. But something halted him from what he was so desperate to accomplish.

I can do this… It's what you've trained for. Aim small miss small. Aim for his shirt button and you'll still hit near that spot. Aim too large and you'll hit little Miss Princess chowing down on that corndog! Gross! Karson took one final deep breath and…

I can't shoot him…

What was weird still, was what happened next. The man scurried up the steps and reached for the door handle, looking over his left shoulder and up to the roof of the Seven-Eleven on the corner of Luis Moya and Av Independencia. He smiled. He looked right into Karson's eyes, it seemed, through the scope. Into his soul… sending a wave of fear through the already battle worn SEAL.

"How did you know?" Karson smiled back knowingly defeated and removed his sight from the scope as the man nodded and slowly swung his body into the building as if he wanted Karson to shoot him. The Secretaría de Relaciones Exteriores was full of security; there is no way he'd not be compromised.

Or- "INCOMING!" Karson left his weapon, and hurried over the side of the building, dropping onto a dumpster and springing across the street. He had noticed a flash from on top of the target building, most definitely a Death Nation sniper.

Don't hit me, don't hit me… Oh hey, cow!

He sprinted up the steps and into the building. But with a sea of people pouring in and out, this was going to be even more challenging. He looked at the elevators and slithered through the crowds, sighting closing doors, and watched the number raise. It stopped on level ⑥ and Karson raced up the stairs directly behind the elevator, reaching level ⑥ in moments. Bursting through the door into:

An empty warehouse-like office suit. There's nothing here. The entire floor was void of any furniture, people, anything. Just concrete floor, metal pillars, empty office rooms on the outskirts and windows, aside from the elevator and stair island in the middle. Karson looked around, and around, inside the offices, out the windows, but there was nothing. He could go up and down, but that risked his death, especially not knowing where the target individual was, anyone could know who Karson was.

"UGH! I LOST HIM AGAIN! DAMMIT HUNTER… YOUR ORDERS WERE 'SHOOT ON SIGHT!' AND YOU SCREWED UP!" Karson fell to his knees defeated and outsmarted again. "Kind of SEAL am I?" He stood and marched to the door. "Maybe we can get Ojore…" Karson pressed the button for the lobby and headed into it, finding a seat to grab his bearings, having taken a newspaper and hiding his weapon inside, he sat and thought. "Certainly, that will stop the war… Probably be court martialed, or worse. You know what, I should have just taken that Spanish Admiral's position. I'd be underwater; I'd be safe… Maybe Hatyara and I would be teammates, I wouldn't have to worry about the targets he wanted to be taken out because" *NO ONE I'VE EVER FACED HAS BEEN THIS HARD TO KILL AND-*

The ding of an elevator to Karson's right caught his attention, and he looked at his watch to see some time had passed and then to the door.

The door opened and five men stepped out. Suits. Pistols under their coats. Death's orgasmic nature in their eyes. Karson stared at Hatyara, and Hatyara stared at Karson. The men protecting the terrorist looked on in shock, knowing what was to happen.

Karson was first to react as the two front men turned to protect their leader. Karson fired a shot that pierced both brains-the shot coming from inside a newspaper Karson had picked up to conceal the weapon-without even moving. The sound of the unsuppressed shot and the graphic sight sent everyone in a panic and Hatyara remained unscathed and took off around the back of the elevator through the thick metal door that revealed the staff staircase.

"You're not getting away." Karson took cover around the corner as the men disappeared after their boss. Karson ran after them, the door about to shut when Karson slammed through it, pistol raised as a henchmen grabbed his weapon and shoved a knife at Karson's gut, the young SEAL turning sideways and arching his body in a 'U' fashion, the blade missed. He spun the man's hands around on him, as his father, believe it or not, had taught him, and plunged the weapon into the man's eye socket, slicing through the bridge of his nose into the other. He leaped and spun midair, shoving the man with a kick into a laundry bin, slamming the wooden door on his head. "Nighty night!" Karson called as he took off up another flight of stairs after the man who killed so many of Karson's brothers. Up they went, so too pursued the SEAL.

"Floor two? Not that stupid. Level three?" Karson heard movement inside the room as they frantically called for the elevator, trying to evade the SEAL, and now the mobilizing security guards. Karson entered the room, wasting no time in killing the last henchmen standing by an open window not the elevator button. *Typical civilians, trying to get away!* Hatyara was not here, and everyone cowered down.

"THERE WERE TWO MEN IN HERE, AND ONE OF YOU SPEAKS ENGLISH. WHERE'D THE UGLY ONE GO?"

After a brief moment of screams and fear at the vicious voice, a man stood up, shaking "Up."

"All I needed, thank you!" Karson looked up and jumped, placing his fingers on the ledge above him and hoisted his body out over the street and up and over into the window above, laying on his belly, spinning around and standing up to find Hatyara with his hands up.

"You're way too calm at what is about to happen next. I've waited too long to do this, my man." Karson said, raising his weapon, his eyes, dark and evil, just like the man ahead of him. "I've learned a lot from you, Hatyara."

"Freeze!" A voice shouted from behind Hatyara, Karson's weapon jerked from his target to see white uniforms entering the room. Hatyara raised his pistol, Karson's eyes widened, as bullets flew past his head, and Karson opened fire at the Mexicans to push them back, not Hatyara.

Hatyara spirited at Karson. "You going to stand der like idiot or get away?" Hatyara ran up and pushed Karson towards the windows, both now firing at security. Karson screamed as they crashed through the shattering glass, the two mortal enemies fell towards the street, landing in hay.

"Oh, hey, cow!" Hatyara said as a cow ran away from the insanity that was unfolding.

Karson surfaced. "Thanks for that!" He raised his weapon towards Hatyara's face.

Boot.

Meet face.

Hatyara sprinted from the hay loft and ran towards the corner of the building, moving faster and faster every massive stride he took.

He's good! Karson, disorientated, sighed and took aim at the man he needed so desperately and watched as he came closer and closer to his deadly, reign of terror continuation. "Everybody always wants to run, huh."

Shots rang from above down at the SEAL, but his breath slowed, and time stopped as his wrist buckled and a bullet flew from the weapon, forming the most intimate penetrative bond a man could ever experience to the back of Hatyara's head. Karson looked up as the spray of blood evaporated midair, and hopped out of the bale, pushing the guards back one last time.

He ran to the man on the ground. Relief swept over him, and Karson snapped the photo as sirens touted through the streets and people ran for safety. Karson drew Hatyara's blood and took a finger, then found a scooter in an ally, and raced away towards his extraction point after retrieving the rifle, careful to elude authorities for the seven-mile journey. He found the grassy runway and leaped from the bike, sprinting to the black Dolphin helicopter waiting for him.

"Mission accomplished?" The pilot asked Karson.

His first half of the war was complete. Now to finish the final part. Karson nodded.

"Let's go then!" He smiled and fired up the chopper, taking them to fifteen thousand feet, two shy of its max ceiling.

"HELLO!" A voice shouted from the back seat.

Karson spun around and raised his fist at the man in black combat apparel. "WHO ARE YOU?"

"Special Agent Garrett Moore. United States Secret Service-I'm the one tracking our president. Your SEAL Captain told me to intercept you. We found Elding; we're going to need-"

"Oh, that's... that's fantastic! Where?"

"Mexican Consulate to the United States."

"That seems too obvious..." Karson looked out the window. "Trust me when I say, you're chasing a false lead."

"We thought so too, but it was actually genius." The agent clambered over the seat.

Face.

Meet ass.

"Wait, so how'd you lose him in the first place?" Karson pushed the ass away.

"This war has changed so many people, including our own and I'm sure you know that full well." Karson nodded as the agent continued. "North Korea. Our motorcade was attacked. Agents had turned. I'm shooting at my friends; I'm shot, knocked down a hill. Hit my head. Out cold. Helicopter takes Elding... Blah, blah, blah... I run through a few countries, and voila! I'm here! Not much different than your story! Anyways, here's the mission! Your friend, Victor, was it? He's leading."

"Perfect!" Karson lit up. "At least someone I trust. How long until we get there?"

"Here's your parachute. We jump in three minutes!"

"Yup. Just perfect!" Karson sighed. "Do I at least have weapons?"

"When we meet up with your team, yes."

Tight.

****

CHAPTER 48 - Leyri Gindle

"Here we are." Karson pulled his journal from his back pocket. The entry read:

Paseo de la Reforma 305, Cuauhtémoc, 06500

Ciudad de México, D.F., Mexico

"Your handwriting sucks, Serval." Agent Moore snatched the journal from his hands.

"Not as hard as you do, Garrett." Karson retorted, lunging for it, trying to take it back.

"Man, come on. What are you a middle schooler?" The Secret Service Agent thumbed through the book to the page Karson was on.

"Yeah, I admit that was bad." Karson finally got a hand on it and yanked it out of his colleague's hands, only to spin losing his footing to fall on his stomach. "Oof!" A small dust cloud drifted up.

Everyone laughed. Moore was disappointed. "It's all just mission information! Nothing juicy? I wanted some deets on your life! What was the page you were looking at?"

"It just has the information for this place on it. My personal stuff is back in my quarters on the ship. Paseo de la Reforma 305, Cuauhtémoc, 06500, Ciudad de México, D.F., Mexico." Karson stood up and brushed the dust off of him, putting the journal back in is pack. "Anyways, do we have a plan?"

Victor returned from his small scouting mission. "You say that someone big is meeting here today. Don't know why. It's not an embassy. It's a **consulate**, but the government trusts you to be right. Anyways, you make the plan."

"Well, I just have part of the plan. The rest will be up to you, Pharo, sir." Karson smiled at his friend.

"Okay... Well what's your part?"

****

"Hunter! Do you see that house across the street from the Consulate?"

"Hookah!" Karson shouted, already making his way that direction.

"I wasn't done yet, kid... whatever." Victor used his radio. "Serval, get inside, restrain that family, and take down the insurgents inside. It'll be messy but use your-"

"Knife, the suppressor is too loud even." Karson interrupted. "I already told you my plan, so shush!"

"Yeah. There are at least ten guys in there; it'll be difficult to fight them all with a gun."

"Aye, sir!" Karson replied, about to shut his radio down for a couple of minutes.

"Oh, and Serval?"

"Yeah, sir? I'm at the door. Make this quick." Karson assumed Victor was going to piss his pants at his rash tone, so he added an innocent "pwease?" to the end of his demand.

"You are on your own, Karson. When we're down and dirty in the consulate, you are without support."

"Just how I like it. Now let me get to doing my job, sir. Respectfully."

"Watch your six," Victor told his best friend. *Please be careful.*

"You as well." Karson skirted the eight-foot wooden fence into the backyard of the enemy occupied house directly across the street from the Mexican Consulate. He hurried to the back door as the man on patrol of the yard made his way around the side of the house. Karson hurried and picked the lock, opening the door slowly, checking to see if he needed his pistol right off the bat. Empty. The back door led straight into the kitchen. Karson hurried inside and shut the door, his gun holstered, the assault rifle strapped to his back, and his fix bladed knife at the ready. He could smell the horrible conditions these people were forced to live in. Rotten food, scraps for dinner, feces all over the place, no ability for baths. These people were forced to stay alive for the barbaric pleasure of torturing innocence. These people, innocent or combatant both may not like Americans, but Karson's job was to protect those foreign and abroad from heinous acts like these. *As much as I don't enjoy killing, I'm gonna have no problem putting you people down.*

Karson heard movement and crouched low, hidden by the square, wooden table and chairs. The man made his way down the hallway and into the kitchen. Karson could hear the sound of a zippo and the puffing of a cigar. The man relaxed, Karson could see, as the shaking in his legs subsided. *Maybe these guys are haunted by the kills they've scored.* The man's feet turned and walked towards the side Karson was on and he scrambled in a superhero climb around the corner of the table as the man looked out the window, waved and smiled at his partner, then moved to the refrigerator and grabbed a bottle of rum.

"I deserve dis, mon." The man said.

Dammit! I like Jamaica! Karson reminisced on the cruise he took with his parents when he was nine years old. *I masturbated in so many countries and international water… Basically all over the world. MY CUM COULD BE ALL OVER THE WORLD! I SPERMED A WOMAN AT NINE YEARS OLD? Not much different then what I was doing at five… that's kina cool!*

The trip went into Jamaica and the only person to make him laugh during the entire trip was a Jamaican ventriloquist named Azibo who constantly shouted "Yeah Mon!" in a high-pitched shrill, making Karson forget his sea sickness for the time being.

Karson thought his way through the kill. *Lunge up, straight into his throat, hand over mouth, bend him over knee, and roll him off and behind the table.* Karson slithered around the table into prime position, waiting for his moment to strike. Waiting for his prey to bend his head and take a drink from the water directly above the crocodile's head. The Jamaican man moved his way back around the table to look out the window. Karson knew his time was now.

"Yo, mon!" Karson said, reaching down an octave lower. The Jamaican man turned and Karson, using the floor as his trampoline, pushed through his glutes, thighs, hamstrings, calves and down through his feet, thrust the knife straight on through the man's throat, hand over his mouth, and pushed him silently against the glass, just as the man outside was walking by.

Karson's heart pounded in his chest. *Please don't see me, please don't see me!*

Luckily the man was oblivious to the SEAL inside the house killing his friend, or the SEALs making their way into the consulate directly opposite the thin wood that made the barrier to the double story house. Karson looked into the man's eyes, missing the chance to read his eyes as his soul faded away. He crouched, the man on his thigh, and rolled him off. "Goodnight." He whispered as he stepped on his chest, helping along the kiss of death as the Jamaican air escaped his body one last time. Karson walked to the sink to wash off his knife. "Next."

Karson heard the flushing of a toilet and made his way around the island in between two hallways. He knocked on the door and ducked into the room opposite the bathroom.

"Hallo?"

"German," Karson muttered.

"Ist der anyvon der?" The man unlocked the door and swung it open, looking across into the dark room. "Hallo?"

Karson pivoted around the door, threw his knife into the man's eye, launched forward, and pushed him against the wall, covering his mouth to silent the possible noise, and forced the blade through the man's skull, slow and painful. The man spasmed, then was still. Karson stood back, pushing him up against the wall, staring into his remaining eye, watching his life ebb away, and yanked the knife from his skull as he laid his enemy down, head propped in the sink, the blood draining from the basin. "Two." He whispered. He made his way out of the restroom that smelled of horrible, runny, curry encrusted diarrhea and up the second hallway, as a sneeze from the side yard halted him in his tracks. He tilted his head back towards the direction of the room he threw his knife from and moved back into it.

The door to the side yard opened slowly, then fully and revealed a large, Scottish brute, whom Karson wasted no time in drawing his blade across the Scotsman's throat. The man halted, grabbing at his throat, wondering what that cold metal pain was, as Karson came into his sight, smaller, holding the knife between his legs, looked up innocently into the man's eyes with his finger on his lip, reading this man's eyes too as if Karson were saying, 'whoops… did I do that?' Only this time, Karson saw no anger or fear. Rather, he saw pure disappointment as the Scotsman saw the blood on his fingers. The Scot was 'caught with his pants down' as they say. Killed in the stupidest of ways. Karson kicked him out the door and shut it quietly behind him. *I need to take my boots off; they are too loud.* Karson unzipped his boots and slid his feet out of them and laid them in the dark room. *I'll get them after I finish this!*

Karson yet again walked out of the room, having killed three men now, and heard someone coming down the stairs. Karson scurried around the island and down the hall beside the staircase and looked up to ensure no one else was looking down. "Hey, Ryszard? You done vith your poo yet?" His head came over the side of the stair railing, and Karson grabbed him by his shirt and slammed the blade of his knife into his temple, killing him instantly, like they do in that Zombie television show. *Only I'm actually killing living dead souls.*

He moved to the bottom of the staircase and carried the man into the front room and laid him down, removing the knife from his head. *Ryszard, huh? That means powerful ruler. Wasn' much of a challenge, your poopy friend.*

Karson had eliminated all men downstairs. He moved up the stairs, sighting a room on his right at the top of the stairs, the door closed. Another door in the middle of the hall, one at a diagonal, a bathroom with the lights out, and one more room on the left. The diagonal room had at least two men in it, the one on the left had one. Karson lay prone, again in a superhero pushup position, and made his way up and into the hallway, careful no one saw him.

He checked the door on the right at the top of the stairs and found it locked. *That must be where the family is held. I'll check in on them later.* Karson moved three steps to the door in the middle. As he started to look in, a man appeared and Karson had to act fast before he said anything. Karson grabbed the man on both sides of his head, pushing him back into the room, and twisted his head sideways, however, he lost his grip, and the man thudded onto the ground. The men in the other rooms shouted.

"WAT DE ACTUAL HELL!" A man squealed as he choked on coffee, and Karson brought his sleeve up to his face to stop his chuckle.

Karson quickly drew his suppressed pistol, ran out the door and to the right, shooting the first man in the doorway, the second in a revolving chair, the third standing from the couch. The fourth was fumbling for a grenade. As he pulled the pin and was about to throw, Karson lunged forward and launched himself into the air, slammed both feet into the man's chest and knocked him through the glass window. Karson then turned and ran into the last room and slammed the tip of his pistol up the man's nose, as a boom shook the house from outside-most certainly the grenade- and knocked the man he was pointing his weapon at back, then shot him twice, once in the chest and once through the skull right between the eyes. It was like watching a death on a Hollywood movie screen. The man's entire body stiffened and fell backward, his soul instantly gone, and his chin crumpled to his chest as his head smacked against the wall and he slid down. To top it all off, the shelf on the wall fell down on top of him. Karson flinched. "Sorry about that, bud... I'm sure you used to be a good man. Probably... depends I guess..." *At least that covers up that gruesome sight.*

Karson dropped his hands to his knees and panted. "Well, that could have gone smoother. Ten down." Karson moved to the open window and looked outside. The last man who was making his rounds around the house had died in the blast from the grenade after having checked on his friend who came cascading like a waterfall out the window.

Karson checked the bodies, found the key to the room on the poo man, put his boots on, and made his way back up the stairs and opened the door, revealing a mother and her three young sons.

She looked up in terror at Karson, pleading in her eyes at her new threat to her family. Her face spoke to him. 'There is nothing I could possibly do to stop you. Please don't hurt my boys or me. If you must, just take me. But leave them be.' She held Karson's gaze. Unsure. Life? No more life?

These people live normal lives too. Not the same as America... Not as free. But normal lives all the same. America now was going through the same thing. Uncertain. Live? No more life? Where would our lives go?

Karson turned and pointed at his shoulder. At the American flag. "As long as I am in your house, you are safe."

"Thank you." She nodded at the safety that flag brought with it.

"I need you to stay here, though. You're going to hear shots. You're safe with me here. I promise. I will let you out when I leave. Here. Here is some water." Karson was one of the only military men to still carry a canteen along with his camel pack, so with both of those full, he could spare his unopened reserve plastic water bottle.

Karson closed the door, moved into the center room upstairs, readied his M4 rifle and looked around the consulate grounds. "Pharo, I have the house. I'm ready to lay down cover." Karson took out his journal again and read the phone number.

+52 55 5080 2000

"Clear, Serval," Victor responded. "We're ready to move.

"You have reached the Mexican Consulate in Mexico City, Mexico. We are currently closed for the day. Please, try one of our other consulates, or leave a message." The automated voice said.

"As I thought. Why would you be closed on a Wednesday, in a nation still fully functioning at the peak of its power, unless you had someone important on the premises? But why here? Why this Mexican Consulate. Why Mexico at all? I get that it's a neighbor to the U.S. but..." Karson trailed off as he closed the field phone and readied his weapon. Karson found Victor, the agent, and the rest of the team with his scope. Then he found the first enemy that could compromise the mission. Karson's rifle was beside him in case he needed to defend the house. "Alright, I've found my first kill. Enter in 3...2...1..."

TFFT

He hit the man under his throat. "Aim small, miss small! Maybe because it's the last place someone would look?" Karson continued to think over his previous thought. The man he shot crumpled as the suppressed sniper rifle kicked, and Karson confirmed his kill. "Clear. Go now." The Navy SEALs entered the compound and moved under cover of a balcony. Karson peered inside. *Poor dude didn't even know he was about to die. Didn't even see me. Nah well. Most people in war, like two out of three, don't see the man who killed them... Whoops. That's a naked grandma. Gag! And she's bending over! Double gag!!* "Okay... that is The Consul's office. Where are you...?" Karson continued to move his scope throughout the Consulate, peering into windows. Suddenly, something major caught his attention. Something so drastic that it could change the entire outlook of the war. He only need confirm it.

"Serval, can we move?" Victor asked.

"Sorry. Yeah, move to the small building to your east. Hold there." Karson directed, distracted. Blurred in his peripheries, he saw his team begin to move. Karson zoomed in on the person in the window. Karson's eyes opened wide. "What the hell-"

Loud shots rang out, and Karson ducked for cover.

"Man down!" Sang out over Karson's coms.

"No!" He said as he stood and fired out the window at any combatant he saw. "Who's hit? How bad?"

"Focus on keeping us as alive as we can be!" Victor said.

"Well, there are so many of you, it's kinda hard! I just like working with four! Now that makes it easy!"

Karson found the same window, but it was empty. The door wide open, people scrambling around inside. Armed men ran into the room. Karson fired upon them, killing two. The rest scurried to cover under the concrete lined windows. The snipers on the roof turned their attention to Karson's flashing scope and muzzle. They too fired upon him.

"I knew I should have brought the muzzle flash suppressor." He stood and fired across the Mexican street. More bullets entered the house, shattering glass upon him. "THIS WAS NOT PART OF MY PLAN!" Karson shouted out the window. He stood again and fired. He heard screams in the other room. *Just stay put, and you'll be fi-* "Oh, holy crap!"

Karson turned tail and fled from the room and into the hallway into the room across from his, jumped over the body on the floor, and dove. He landed on the small, child-sized bed

"WHAT, YOU'RE SLEEPING IN A CHILD'S BED?" he shouted as he grabbed the side of the mattress and flipped it over upon himself with a man on top as an RPG rocket exploded in the room, its shrapnel piercing through the bed and into the confused man...

After a moment of fear, Karson opened his eyes, to find the man dead... taking all the hot shrapnel Karson would have taken in his place.

"Least I didn't have to pump the bed full of bullets. Alright, team. I'm coming to you! Watch out for the VIP."

"WHO IS THE VIP?" Victor shouted into his radio as the fighting intensified.

Karson flinched at the sudden burst of noise in his ear. "OW! You'll know him when you freaking see him," Karson stated as he slid down the stair rail, reminiscing that as a child he used to do this, only to be cut off by a small squad of enemy entering the house. Karson ducked behind the cover of the island between both hallways.

"Spread out. Two and two. Canvas the house. Find him." A voice said.

"Easy!" Karson looked up the left hallway, stepped out, and fired two bullets, spun around in a 360°-back to wall, then chest to wall-taking up cover from the island between the hallways again looking at himself in the mirror on the wall, his breath fogging it up, listening for footsteps from the right hallway to get closer, stepped right and shot that guy, and took cover once more behind the island. With no more sounds, Karson sprang from cover to the right and ran up the hallway, only to sense a soul behind him. He slid on his knees as a bullet flew over his head and spun around to send his own bullet into the last man's cheek which ultimately ended up severing his spine, stood an ran out the back door across the street wihtoug even a moment's hesitation as shots rang out. He ran towards the flag raised over the consulate. *Just noticed that. A united axis front. Someone united all these nations. The 'anti-Christ. Just like it predicted. Whelp, Jesus, you must be coming soon! I'm ready. No matter what happens now, the world must indeed be coming to an end.*

****

Karson skirted the fence to the house and the consulate, noticing, no one else was around. No one in the windows, no one in the houses except the one he was at… *Weird. It's like a ghost town… Perfect to cover up the VIP. They are probably all dead. At least the ones in my house weren't. That's a plus!*

Karson found his team but found Victor running through the courtyard with an enemy behind him, a knife in his hand. He was running for his team. Karson set his rifle down on its bipod and aimed at Victor, who noticed the smaller SEAL about to fire. He ran and ran, then slid to the side, falling to the ground. Karson tracked the enemy for a moment and fired. Victor stood and ran up to him.

"Thanks."

Karson saw that the man down had only taken a flesh wound and everyone was still alive. For now, that is. Karson took point and entered the building. The fighting had stopped. Everything was quiet. Too quiet.

"HELP ME! HELP, PLEASE!" Karson slammed the butt of his M4 into a man's nose, knocking him back, him crumpling to the ground.

"HOLD! Serval, he's a civilian." Agent Moore stepped around the line of eight SEALs.

"What he doin' sneaking up on me like that?" Karson sassed.

"He needed help…" Moore pointed outside and told the man to run. He hesitated, still staring up.

The team entered inside keeping cover. Karson crouched and looked at him. "He'll be fine. You need to go now. Sorry for breaking your face."

The civilian nodded and ran.

"These people sure do put a lot into their government buildings, don't they? Look at all of these statues and marble doors, archways, and hallways." Moore stood up looking at Karson.

"That is their culture, dude. Nice things for the high rollers. Plus, we're in Mexico, not in an impoverished nation. Keep an eye out." Karson said.

"Can you just tell me who you saw?" Victor looked up.

"I cannot confirm," Karson replied, standing, ready to continue.

"Who do you think it is?" Victor pressed more.

"If I told you, you'd restrain me. Just trust me. It's important." He looked at the agent.

"Man… I swear, you Team Six boys are crazy. But, it's fun. A break from the suit and tie!" The agent said to Karson.

"That's us! Just the real men who actually do real missions." Karson said, smiling at Victor.

"Watch it, brother." He pointed hard at Karson.

"I'm just busting your balls, bro. We all do good work." Karson patted Victor's shoulder and made his way to the fork in the hallway. "You three, with Victor. You three, with me! Shoot any enemy, but check your fire. Agent, come with me-"

"Mr. President?" Moore now ignored Karson.

All weapons turned to the man in the suit, with four armed body guards aiming their guns at the SEALs.

"Told you," Karson whispered. "Well, Crikey, mate!" Karson smiled. "Mr. President. What are you doing here, sir?"

The president hesitated in his shock.

"U.S. Navy, sir. Why are you here? We were not informed that you were out of the country. Especially not on a deployment we were ordered by the White House to go on."

Elding composed himself. "I do not need permission to go anywhere. I go where I am needed. I was just wrapping up a meeting when weapons started to go off. I will be leaving now. Thank you very much."

"Shall we escort you back to Air Force One, sir?" Victor asked nervously.

Why are you a puppy with your legs between your legs.

"That will not be necessary; we can take care of POTUS just fine thank-" Moore spoke up more firm than ever, his playful sass replaced by authority.

Impressive act, Agent Moore. "I don't believe that was a question. Rather, an order. We will be accompanying you to your jet, sir." Karson walked up to President Elding and said his hellos. "Mr. President. Where to next on your quest for world peace, sir?"

"North Korea." He replied.

"Where you were 'captured' from?" Karson turned around. "He was the VIP I saw in the window. It is confirmed. You were making a dealing with the enemy. We know a lot more than you think." Karson turned back and looked at his face.

"How dare you accuse your Commander and Chief?" Elding stepped forward, asserting his dominance over the Sailor.

"You've lost that title, sir." Karson dared provoke more. "I have proof. Russia found an encrypted email. It read: 'with the help of –RE- and the excessive troop gain, Russia has fallen to our control... The Russian President is not needed. R.E. Riley Elding. It makes sense now."

"That could mean anything." Victor spoke up, trying to silence Karson.

"Your body tells us otherwise. Also, while I was in Pakistan, a gentle civilian took great care of me. However, I saw a painting over a mantle in this man's house. 'Ojore has control of leadership. I thought about it and remembered that at one point when you visited troops a while back in your first term, the news reported you took an unscheduled stop. I assume it was to visit the man we now hunt. I saw a piece of paper, Agent Moore, that you were looking at on our ride over here on the helicopter. What was on the paper was a relatively detailed plan. It involved an elaborate plot at Elding's life, but insisted on keeping him alive. Now, sir, this could mean anything, but it certainly doesn't mean nothing. I decided to pit pocket you, Agent Moore, and take the paper. It's safe and sound with me. You have very rich information one could explicitly want to take, but what does make this more interesting is the fact that you have four secret service agents with you, in a foreign country when our intel states you were captured, this agent told us you were caught, and yet you're talking in a ghost town at a consulate to foreign government leaders, and you're not even bound. When I was in Russia, the president was bound. Why aren't you? You don't even seem scratched."

Karson looked back at his team. They were confused, but they trusted their friend.

"Sir. You are my President. I just want the truth." Karson saluted.

"Sir, you need not tell dem about what went on here-" Karson shot the man over the President's shoulder, the agents raising their weapons, Karson grabbing Garrett and restrained him as the other agents choose to die where they stood.

"So, I shot him because he had a covered up accent. You need to tell us, or you'll end up like me. In a foreign bar, with enemy's zip lining in to kill you, with nothing to protect yourself except a piece of paper that details exactly what this agent said happened to him at the attack site in North Korea. Or I can sew your anus up; you'll just explode from a buildup of feces."

"To gain power, to rain havoc on the world, you have to talk and push the world to peace."

I can feel the power amass in my fist as I formed it and released it as I smashed it into his face.

The SEALs reacted, restraining Karson, the Agent, and The President.

"You talk. You do politics. I continue to kill until you fix the problem. See, you see the politics of a conflict. When you are in it, politicians never bringing fighting to an end, it's about making sure my brothers come home, and that my other brothers and my countrymen don't ever have to go through what I am going through, again and again and again. So many of us don't come home because you do dealings like this. This is your fault!"

The President looked up. "We had to put a crackdown on human rights violators, and smack down on immigration. I had to do something drastic. It was the enemies of our Nation that caused us to do this. We had to be corrupted to make the world less corrupted. We kill or be killed!"

"DO YOU HEAR YOURSELF RIGHT NOW? IT DOESN'T MAKE SENSE. YOU DON'T MAKE ANY SENSE!" Karson lunged.

"Sir, we have hostages here. What do you want to do?" A SEAL walked in the hallway from a room to the right.

"Get them out. Set them free." Victor said.

"Aye, sir. Stay close to us. It's your best chance of survival." The SEAL walked back into the room.

"Serval. We have to go. We'll settle this at home. Our job is to get in, get out, and ask for forgiveness later. Let's go." Victor turned and left the room.

"I hope you have a good lawyer, sir-" Karson began when,

"BOMB!" Victor sprinted back into the room and

BOOM

The entire floor shook as a white mist filled the room, the people closest, ingesting it, collapsed instantly as rashes formed on their skin.

"DIRTY! EVERYONE, OUT THE BACK!" Karson shouted, grabbing the President and exiting. "That's a noxious, aggressive chemical asphyxiate and it causes certain death and skin deterioration if inhaled. Out the back."

"That was there to kill me, I know it…" The President said.

"Why?" Karson shook him. "WHY?"

"Because, when I found out what I was in for, I refused to go along with it. But the damage is done. I've leaked codes, secrets. Your name is known... fleet locations... the ways to hack the ships... Your paper with the plot. Signed-"

"Leyri Gindle for Riley Elding... Put that together."

"Yeah."

"You will still be deemed a traitor Mr. President. I'll ensure that." Karson said as he exited the building with his President. "But you'll be tried fair and treated fair. Better than a white gas to kill you.

****

CHAPTER 49 - Coalition
**"United we triumph, divided, we'll tear each other apart." –
Karson Hunter**

The AC-130 transport planes took off from the fleet of U.S. and allied coalition aircraft carriers carrying their payloads of trucks, tanks, Humvees, and other military equipment and personnel.

"I WANT OFF THIS FUCKING PLANE!" Karson shouted for the tenth time since the extremely fast take off over the roar of the engine as another wave of turbulence rocked the old aircraft, unnerving the SEAL and bouncing him in uncomfortable ways. "My balls keep bouncing on the seat!"

"You didn't-"

"No, jack off, I didn't have the time to change into a cup or tight under-ware, the alarms went off, and I raced to get ready."

"You're gonna have a tough time then..." He sang as he and his buddy broke into laughter.

"Thanks," Karson grunted, holding onto the straps with one hand, his nuts with the other.

A low voice came over his radio. "Two minutes to drop."

"ALRIGHT, MEN! MOUNT YOUR VEHICLES. YOU'RE GOING DOWN FAST AND HARD."

"Mmm..." Karson winked to his buddy to the left.

He punched Karson and stood, smiling. "You're a dork."

"I ka-no!" He winked. Karson and his SEAL team unstrapped from their seats and quickly but unstably moved towards their vehicle. "Operation Trident Justice, bro, hooyah?" Karson looked in awe at his new vehicle. A tank that doubled as a troop transport. The M3A2 Bradley Fighting Vehicle variant operated by the United States Army Third Armored Cavalry Unit, with SEAL guests. It looked fancy, smaller, more streamlined, but more powerful. Black. Slick black.

"Sir! How the hell are you?" The Army Tank Commander greeted Karson.

"Commander, I'm Captain Serval. I'm doing well. Thank you for your hospitality in allowing us to ride along with you, sir."

"It's our honor. It's refreshing to have the branches working together for once." He smiled.

"I thought the same thing," Karson said impressed. "I'm glad you're one of the few who feel that way, sir."

"Sixty seconds to drop." The voice hit his ears through the comlinks of everyone involved in the engagement.

Karson, the tank crew, and the SEALs settled into the vehicle and strapped in as the gate lowered. The commander raised the troop ramp and closed the top hatch, and settled into the driver seat. "Here we go, gentlemen. Best hold on. It's a fast descent."

"Ten seconds."

The plane continued speed, and the locks were released from the tank treads. The vehicle was thrown into neutral and physics pulled the tank out of the plane without a countdown, sending it plummeting to the ground. IT was like a roller coaster. Everyone enjoyed the ride. The tank commander allowed five of the seven thousand feet to disappear as the SEALs, even in their straps, were lifted out of their seats. Finally, the chute deployed, allowing ten seconds of air time and relaxation towards the ground. Karson smiled at his friends. "That was fun!"

"Coming from the man who was screaming the whole plane ride here." Karson glared to his left.

The vehicle hit the ground with a small thud.

"Yeah, but we're on the ground now!" Karson smiled wider.

The commander cut the lines from inside, and the vehicle moved along in convoy with the joint forces whose vehicles insides were also full of soldiers. Karson unbuckled. "Okay if I stick my head out of the vehicle?"

"Yeah, you can man the turret if you'd like." The driver offered.

Karson smiled. "Nice." As he started to climb, though, the commander stopped him.

"Uh, sir. Before you go up, though, you need to wear your helmet. No one wants to clean your head off the interior or exterior."

"Aye, right you are. Toss that to me, would ya, Warty?"

Karson's teammate did as he was told.

"Thanks, bae."

"Shut up." Warty snored.

"Thank you, Commander!" Karson called down.

He saluted from the side as he focused on the driving.

Karson winked at his team and mounted, looking at the massive force heading towards the enemy city in Tapachula, Mexico.

Shame this pretty city is going to be reduced to rubble. Have to find Ojore doe. Helicopters flew over, scouting ahead; everyone hell-bent on their way to take out 'Supreme Leader' Ojore first.

Sorry fellas… But I'm gonna be the one to take him. He's too smart for you.

As the joint forces of the world inched closer to the city, the resistance increased as the enemy noticed the coming wave of the World's last hope. Karson was instrumental in pushing his vehicle and the starting vehicles forward into the city, the rear of the force fighting the exterior forces. More and more shots were fired as they entered into the city's refortified interior. Karson looked up again to see the Marines fly over the SEAL's convoy in their Black Hawks as they invaded the city trying to get a crack at Ojore. Karson and the other gunners of the vehicles were shooting everywhere now, and the tanks were pivoting every which direction, firing their massive rounds at responding police and enemy vehicles racing towards the allies. The Air Force fighters engaged the enemy planes that were launched and the battle turned from skirmish, to fight, to war in the most brutal of terms. Karson's tank turned down a street in a smaller convoy and found civilians disfigured, burning, and vehicles torn to shreds from the ordinance already pumped into the city from the ships in the Pacific. Foreign aid surrounded the city and stormed the civilian homes and buildings, searching for anything unusual or key leaders of Ojore's regime.

I already killed the second... "This is the weirdest thing." Karson dropped down to his team, to check in on them, stating what was on his mind. The SEALs were looking out the gun holes of the vehicle like fat kids staring at candy in a candy store.

"What is it, Captain?" A tank gunner asked.

"All these 'aliens' fighting alongside us, man. Never did I think we'd be the generation to battle in World War Three. I get our two branches fighting 'cause we're from the same Nation, but these are all people from different countries. I guess it's just the bad guy version of the French Foreign Legion."

"CAPTAIN, GET BACK UP TOP! WE'VE GOT A PROBLEM!" Karson did as he was ordered. Ahead of his tank was a Stryker, not doing so well. The Stryker gunner burned out his gun after hundreds of rounds were expended and when he climbed out on top to cool it with his canteen, he was hit and fell off into the dust. The Stryker stopped and Soldiers from Delta Force sprinted into the gunfire, grabbed their comrade, and jumped back in.

An impressive feat of teamwork! Karson thought as he jumped out of the tank, rolling on the ground as he hit and slipped in the dust, nearly rolling into the treads. He quickly regained his footing and sprinted into the gunfire like a canine officer helping his human partner on a traffic stop. Karson reached the Stryker before it raised the troop gate. The Soldiers freaked out, hurling curses when they saw the American flag on Karson's helmet.

"SEAL Team Six. Here to help!" Karson laughed as he took the machine gun and cooled it with his canteen. Karson aimed at the snipers on the roof and killed them as the Stryker started moving again, still on track to find the most wanted target in the world.

They drove under a bridge and linked up with another Stryker brigade that gave Skunk, the name of the Stryker, another gunner so that Karson could get back with his team and continue his mission. The coalition had one job; lock down the city and kill opposition and capture anyone worth capturing. SEAL Team Six would take care of the leader.

Karson climbed back into the tank, a new guy taking his spot on the above gun.

They rounded a corner and were driving towards Ojore's palace, a direction that led into the sun. The international Navy fleet had blockaded the coast and fired machine guns at the planes and missiles into key targeted buildings inland, killing high political leaders, while also engaging Death Nation's now incredibly powerful Navy. Even though the bullets and ordinance had to travel seven miles, it still impacted in the most effective of ways.

The palace fired back on the coalition, coming by sea, land and a low flying Air Force Black Hawks, Apaches, and the occasional Osprey or fighter.

"Anyone know the casualty count?" Karson asked.

"Three medivacs have been called, sir... I know of one fatality on the HMS Ocean." The Tank Commander said, swerving to miss a kid running across the road.

"Captain Serval... A Black Hawk chopper is down. We have to vector towards it. Everyone else is engaged..." Warty said.

"We need Ojore!" Karson shouted.

Warty growled. "They are men of the United States, sir. We never leave a man behind, remember."

"Alright, let's get them out, and continue. We don't want another 'Black Hawk down' incident." Karson reluctantly agreed.

"A Marine squad will join you, I've just heard." The Commander called back.

"Serval," Admiral Thompson watching from drone cameras above radioed to the young SEAL. "Word from Washington... Joint Chiefs. Head to that bird. Extract the survivors and get back here."

"Aye, Command," Karson said. "Inform me, Marines channel?"

"2.43."

"Thanks." Karson tuned is radio to the frequency and patched himself to hear and communicate with SEAL Team and Marine Team. "Marines, SEAL Team Six. My name is Captain Serval. Do you read me?"

"Oorah, Sir! Loud and clear." The static voice was covered by gunfire.

"Hooyah! Get behind us. We'll need your help."

"Yes, sir. We'll go!" The Marines behind the SEALs' tank said. "Oscar Mike."

"Alright. Men, battle check your gear. Let's hit it!" Karson called up to the Commander. "As fast as possible."

The SEALs and Marines joined up, SEALs in front, and raced to the scene. They raced through the city towards the chopper, rounding corners and shooting enemy soldiers scattered throughout the city streets. However, finally turning down the road where the fully engulfed military chopper lay dead, a large group of resistance stood in the way. The gunners above on both vehicles fired at the wall of men blocking the road, indeed mowing the horde down, only to have it reestablished by bodies.

"STOP!" Karson shouted, his vehicle coming to a halt, the Marines continuing. "Marines, stop your vehicle."

As the Marines raced towards the wall, the enemy finally scattered, and Karson's vehicle began moving.

"I said stop, Commander." Karson ordered, trying to get up to him.

"Why? Why would we stop, we have those bastards on the run?" The vehicle kept moving.

"It's a trap." Karson said.

"We defeated them so easily. They are pussies." The vehicle still didn't stop.

"No... Team, keep your guard up," Karson said. "Why would a group of people sit and let themselves be killed, play chicken, and then bug out? It makes no sense..."

"Sir, there is no way they can stop us... They are gone..." Warty said. "We're fine."

"There is always an enemy out there that can defeat you... They were ready for us. This could be the one..."

The SEALs' Tank arrived beside the Marines who had hopped out, laying cover. Karson's team dismounted and the SEALs followed their leader to the wreckage, the Army commander keeping the engine running. Both teams had their weapons drawn and at the ready.

Why no bodies? The SEALs moved closer, watching the alleys the enemy had disappeared to. The Marines relayed the location. *Why no sound? It's too quiet...*

Karson walked up to the blackened window of the chopper and rubbed off the ash, the sounds of fighting still in the distance throughout the city. As soon as Karson peered in, he knew what was going to happen next. He spun on his heel and beckoned the Sailors to move back, and ran to the vehicles, just as the chopper exploded. The Sailors flew into the air, and Karson landed beside the Marine Humvee as the Marines adjusted their attention. But as always, the trap was sprung and by the enemy 'wasp' like swarm, American body's started exploding by enemy vehicular fire. Blood sprayed everywhere and men screamed in agony as they died from the 'wasps' high heated metal stingers.

Karson crawled into the Marine Humvee keeping as low and out of sight as possible. The door opened on the other side, revealing Karson's number two. The tank fired one round of ordinance, indeed doing damage to an unknown enemy as fire stopped, only to begin again after an explosion of an anti-tank round dismantling the American armor. *And now we're next.* Karson floored the Marine Humvee, racing from the scene as a surviving Marine was shooting over his shoulder as the only route to life was taking off. He hopped in the opened door, a panic attack racking his body.

"Tha-Thahh... That happened so fast! They're all d-d-d-d-dead... Everyone..." As the man convulsed in fear, continuing to look behind him, his trigger finger accidentally discharged a bullet from the chamber, striking Dasher, the sole surviving SEAL teammate of Karson's in the arm.

"HEY! MARINE, GET A HOLD OF YOURSELF! WE'RE IN WAR! THIS IS WHAT HAPPENS!"

"I'm so sorry, sir, I-"

Karson's partner spun around, clenching his wounded arm. "HEY! These guys are the least of your worries now. If we survive this, I'm gonna hunt you down and blow both of your elbows out of your arm! Ya hear me?"

The Marine gulped.

Karson smiled. "Hey, relax, Dasher. It's a scratch."

"Dude! There is a hole in my fuc-"

Karson looked over and bared his teeth, receiving the reaction he'd expected from Dasher. "Don't care. We're still working. Shut up." Karson pushed his finger into the SEAL's face.

Dasher still stared at Karson's mouth. "You actually went through with it…"

"Aye."

"WHAT IS WRONG WITH YOUR TEETH!" The Marine screamed.

"Upgrade. Right before I left the ship. It's why I didn't have time for ball support." Karson drove the small team as far as the Marine Hummer would carry them, until its tires, rattled by bullet and explosion damage finally gave out, grinding the Humvee to a screeching halt beside a two-story building in the middle of the city.

Karson kicked the door of the Humvee open. "Come on, ladies. We don't have all day! Ojore still needs killin'." He moved around the building, finding an outside staircase guarded by a fence. He shot the lock, pulled the chains off, and pushed through the gate, running up the stairs, his friendlies behind him. The staircase landed them inside the building on the second floor, where a tiny hive of militants was hiding. Karson shot the targets as the American's made their way to a second staircase. Karson radioed for a helicopter to meet them on the roof.

"Serval, I'm getting dizzy, sir!"

"You can make it, Dasher. You'll be fine…" But Karson found himself doubling back as his teammate fell down the stairs.

"I can't make it, sir," Dasher said winded.

"Sir, we can't stay here, we have to move-"

"HEY! I'M NOT LEAVING A MAN BEHIND, ESPECIALLY MY IMMEDIATE FAMILY. GET UP THERE AND PROVIDE COVER. WE'RE ON YOUR TAIL!" Karson picked up Dasher in the fireman's carry and pulled his pistol as he made his way up the stairs, his rifle hanging between his legs. On the roof, breaking through the door, Karson threw two green flares to signal their location so the flyboys would know where to fly. Unfortunately, it also allowed enemy militants to see where the SEALs and Marine were.

Enemy snipers on the other buildings shot at the SEALs and Marine. Karson fired his pistol as he made his way towards an air vent. The Marine finally shot back, painting himself a target. He shot erratically.

"MARINE!" Karson shouted above the gunfire. "IF YOU DON'T HIT YOUR TARGETS THAT GIVES THEM MORE OF A CHANCE TO HIT YOU! YOU'RE AN EASY TARGET!"

Karson was correct. Continuing to miss his targets, the snipers got a better and better lock on his body. The Marine was hit in the shoulder. He collapsed. As he fell, Karson too collapsed as another bullet flew into Dasher's helmet.

Blood. It went through. Even before Karson stood up and got behind cover with his friend, he knew Dasher was dead. "NO!"

The Marine died shortly thereafter too, taking the easy way out. Karson flinched at the sight.

"REALLY MAN, REALLY?" *I don't blame you, guy! Death Nation drives the best of us insane, BUT THE LEAST YOU COULD HAVE DONE IS WAIT UNTIL YOU GOT HOME... I NEEDED YA!*

Karson had to leave them both. *Rotors.* Karson took four quick breaths and sprinted from cover as bullets flew past him and hit either behind or in front of him. His feet pounded into the metal roof, and as he made it to the edge of the roof, he jumped. He started losing air as a huge black flying mass materialized out of thin air. Karson fell through the cabin, grabbing a hook on the other side as the chopper righted itself, allowing Karson to swing his legs back in. He didn't wait for a job or an order. He had to be doing something useful in this war; a chance to end this war. He got on the gun and squeezed the trigger, lighting up the enemy troops who had killed his friends.

"HEY! PILOT! MAKE A NOTE OF THIS BUILDING SO WE CAN COLLECT THEIR BODIES WHEN THIS IS OVER, PLEASE." Karson shouted over the M134 machine gun.

"YES, SIR, WAY AHEAD OF YOU!" The pilot called back.

A flyboy placed earphones on Karson's head, so he could hear what the pilots and the rest of the coalition command were saying. Karson chimed in, after an order to return to the ship for fuel.

"We have to get Ojore," Karson said, looking down and seeing the city swarming with U.S. and foreign coalition forces as well as enemy soldiers and mercenaries aligned with Death Nation. There are those vehicles with that stupid flag on them. They painted them all red! Karson shot at the vehicles, taking out three. Hundreds still were high on death and destruction, whether they be civilian, military, or their own teams. Death Nation fools were all for killing indiscriminately and in the most gruesome and horrendously practiced ways possible. Maximum blood… Maximum carnage… Maximum pain… Maximally barbaric.

Karson honed in on another tank, this one, armed with surface to air missile defense systems. It too had a lock on Karson. It fired first, but Karson was able to halt the assault of missiles. The chopper disappeared behind a building, spinning around for another attack.

Karson was ready, but the pilot yelled, distracting Karson from his duty to now protect the aircraft.

"THEY HAVE MISSLE LOCK! EVERYONE! BRACE!" The copilot screamed as the pilot worked his magic and spun the chopper completely around in a circle, the first missile flying past the 360° maneuver of the aircraft. "ANOTHER MISSLE LOCK! HOLD ON!"

Karson looked back out the door as he saw it. The missile flew around the building and smashed into the tail of the chopper, knocking it off, and sending the bird into a plummeting, unsavable spiral down.

"I CAN'T HOLD 'ER! MAYDAY, MAYDAY, NIGHTWING SEVEN IS HIT. WE'RE GOING DOWN! HANG ONTO SOMETHING, FELLAS!" The Pilot cried out through his radio.

"WE'RE ALL GOING TO DIE, MAN!" The door man screamed.

You probably are. I still have a job to accomplish.

They spun past a window of the palace and Karson took his chance. He dove out of the heli and…

****

"Sir, they are two miles away, sir." A soldier of the Supreme Leader relayed as his crew continued to place the vests over his body, tying them at the sides, snapping over a second layer to cover his vital 'Achilles heel'. Mortality.

"Let dem come. We have massive force. We have huge surprise for dem."

"All the same, Supreme Leader, sir… We should leave this area. We don't want to make the same mistake every U.S. enemy has made in the past."

"I AM NOT DEM! WHO DO YOU SERVE? GHOSTS, OR ME?"

"I am a soldier of the Supreme Leader, sir. Long life, sir."

"Good. Now get out of my sight before I shoot you where you stand. You have no business- I hear a helicopter..."

CRASH

****

Karson shot the window with his pistol, shattering the glass, pushing his legs out before him so they'd hit the glass and shatter it more, screaming as he soared through the window and rolled on the ground, cutting himself to pieces as he rolled, still able to shoot and kill two guards inside the palace before they even knew what hit them.

"THAT WAS SO COOL!" He shouted, wiping some of the blood away. "That will clot! Keep moving, Hunter!"

He was on the middle floor. Floor three. Five levels, full of threats! This'll be fun!

"Admiral Thompson, I'm inside the palace, sir. Where do I go from here, sir? Can you tell me, or is there someone else on this?"

"Wow! Karson, you never cease to impress. We thought you'd gone down with that second bird. The enemy is picking up out here, so we'll be out of contact for a while. Well send Victor and his SEALs your way. ETA, ten minutes. Intelligence says that Ojore will probably be making his way to the basement. There is a road the runs out behind the palace into the mountains. Or somewhere. Double time it there, kid. It could be his way out of the city. If he tries to leave, do not pursue unless you have a team with you. You're better off with them, and you know it. Don't lose this guy again. You'll all go together. We have a drone up. We'll track you and him if he runs."

"Aye, sir. I'll get him." Karson ran down the stairs but a royal guard tackled him from behind and they fell down the rest of the way. "OW!" Karson shouted, shaking his hand. "That hurt!"

They hit the second floor and Karson launched the man over his head. Karson jumped up to his feet, but the enemy soldier stood up.

"You're mine, mother fu-" Karson's mouth dropped.

Five other men came down with swords. They laughed menacingly.

"Man! Why y'all got this? Katanas... machetes... a skinning knife..." Karson growled, swatting at one, who swung the sword, narrowly missing his injured hand.

"Still think I'm yours, cocksucker?"

"Well, bugger." Karson said as he jumped up and spun in the air sending the cleats on his boot into the man behind him. Karson ducked from the sword slashes from the others, two going over like scissors, then under, narrowly missing his feet. The men all lunged again, but Karson slid between one man's legs towards the stairs to the first floor, shooting his kneecap out of his leg. The man crumpled in agony and screeched as Karson rolled to his feet and front flipped over a man running up the stairs. His slashed up, but Karson hit his blade away with his pistol. Karson landed and slid down the railing of the stairs to the first floor and turned down a hall.

The men chased after him. Karson kept ducking as swords stuck into the walls in front of him. He pointed his pistol ahead of him as he ran and shot the guards at the end of the hall guarding a door.

ROOM. HIDE. NOW!

Karson ran into the door, it not being unlocked. "Ow. My NOSE! UGH!" Karson stood up, cracking his nose back and kicked through the door, and sprinted into the dark, only to fall down the steep slope as the floor fell away into small, barely big enough for a cat paw stairs leading to the underground cave where Ojore would most likely be lurking, ready to escape at any moment his city or precious palace was lost.

Karson couldn't see anything in the dark, dank room and as he moved through, finally noticing a light towards the east. He moved that way as he heard the sound of engines starting. He sprinted.

The garage door was opening to reveal a tunnel into the summer's day, and the jeep began slipping out of sight.

"ADMIRAL!" Karson shouted as Ojore's escape was set in motion, and the cars sped away. Karson fired at Ojore's, busting through the glass and hitting the driver. Ojore threw him out of the jeep and took control. A vehicle was waiting for Karson, and he raced for the driver seat...

"ADMIRAL? DO YOU READ?"

"AMERICAN FRIENDLIES COMING IN!" A voice shouted from the top of the stairs as four Delta Force operators fell down the stairs. Karson pulled his flashlight and shined it down the hallway.

"RUN! OR I LEAVE! TEN SECONDS!" Karson gave the ultimatum.

Footsteps replied, and the operators appeared, weapons raised.

"Team Six."

"Delta." The man saluted to Karson.

"Nice to meet you. Ojore is the leader of the enemy. He's in the jeep ahead of us. Shoot as much as you can!" Karson hopped over into the passenger seat. "You drive."

"Hooah."

"Thanks…" Karson looked at the Delta man's shoulder. "Captain!" Karson said panting, reloading his pistol. He hung out the window to take better aim at the fleeing enemies. "I'm out of range. Hurry, sir!"

The Americans caught up with Ojore as they came out from underground and were in the sunlight. U.S. Soldiers ahead spotted and fired at Ojore. Karson waved, telling them to stop. A U.S. Black Hawk came and tailed Ojore as Karson and his new team continued to race after him.

"Serval!" Admiral Thompson called through the communicators. "I've tasked an Apache to you. Get in it. It should be arriving."

Karson looked up as an Apache started to land.

"We can't stop, sir…" The Delta Captain relayed.

"I know. Tis fine. I'll roll." Karson swung his legs out and was about to let go, then ducked his head back in. "If you guys get a shot, I don't care what your orders are, take it. Kill this guy!"

"Sure, sir… With pleasure! Careful, and good luck!"

"God speed, Soldiers!" They fist bumped. Karson let go, rolling in the dirt, slowly sliding to a halt. Karson ran up the hill and loaded into the heavily armed Apache as it hovered a foot off the ground. His team stayed right behind Ojore. The chopper took off and quickly caught back up with the fleeing enemy troops and leader. Karson took a sniper rifle from a Soldier and aimed at Ojore's remaining guards, killing all four through the roof. Ojore never flinched, his stone cold heart accustomed to death. This man was an animal. No fear. Just evil desire.

Satan incarnate.

They sped onto a heavily traveled highway, the Delta Force leader slowing in the traffic.

"DRIVE!" Karson shouted down, knowing they wouldn't hear. "Idiot."

Karson tried taking aim on the vehicle again, above the driver part of the roof when a shadow fell over the entire helicopter, and a sound louder than anything Karson had ever heard pounded his ears. He looked up to see a Harrier fighter jet hovering above the small chopper.

"EVADE!" Karson shouted ducking back in as the pilot of the enemy plane fired his engines down on the Americans, engulfing the helicopter in flames.

Karson pushed the joystick forward, and the chopper bolted ahead, the Harrier reposition its jets to pursue.

"Sir, he is entering a tunnel... We'll fly to the other side."

"Any chance you were retrofitted with a parachute for each seat?" Karson asked.

"Yeah... Sir, our chopper is bound to go down. We need those..." The copilot pleaded.

"You, come with me." Karson pointed at a Soldier, pulling him to Karson's chest. Karson grabbed the parachute and put it on, strapping both men together. "Now you still have enough."

They all nodded a thank you.

"Temporary, man," Karson reassured the squirming man of the weird position. The chopper dropped around the tunnel, and the SEAL jumped, the chopper turning away, the Harrier opening fire.

Immediately, Karson deployed the chute, and both men hit the ground hard, rolling. They hoisted themselves over the railings up to the sidewalk to avoid the traffic and maneuvered themselves into the tunnel, seeing carnage on the concrete.

"ANIMALS!" The Soldier shouted.

"What is your name?" Karson asked as he picked up a weapon from a dead Mexican police officer.

"Mark, sir." He responded.

"Mark?" Karson asked as the man nodded. "Green Beret, huh?" He nodded again. "Okay, Mark. I'm Captain Serval, SEAL Team Six. Keep your head on the swivel. I haven't seen a vehicle matching Ojore s, so he's in here, and by the looks of it flying up here, there was a building at the top of the hill."

"Should we wait for back up?" Mark asked, starting to turn to his radio.

"Serval, we are arriving on scene." Victor's voice reached Karson's ears.

Karson smiled and held up a finger, everything seeming okay. "Right on cue. Vic, are you in a chopper?"

"Yeah, there is a helipad up here..." Victor informed Karson. "We're landing to investigate."

"Enter there... We're in the tunnel below you on our way up."

"See you in a sec." Victor clicked the radio button.

"My team is here, Mark... I understand if you take a vehicle and leave..."

"No, sir. You can count on me." He said. "Green Beret, sir. I'm right where I'm s'posed to be."

****

CHAPTER 50 - Thrill of the Hunt

"My teammate from BUDs is up top, Mark. This is almost over. A four-hour fight... I thought it would take much, much longer."

"You still never know, sir..." He said, scanning the area in front of him.

"True, but I'm hoping."

Shots interrupted Karson as a final enemy unit put up its last fight.

"MAN! THESE GUYS DON'T EVER GIVE UP!" Mark shouted. Karson and the Beret engaged them. "Captain, move to flank them!"

"Yeah. What's it look like I'm trying to do?" Karson shouted at the Soldier.

"Gah. I'll do it. Stay put..." Mark broke from cover, doing surprisingly well against the force until he ran into the butt of an enemy weapon. As the man turned his barrel down, however, Mark swept his feet out and elbowed the man in the face as he killed another enemy racing towards him.

"Dat skill, doe!" Karson said as Mark stood up. "Dayum!"

"Yeah! Let's see what you got, betch!"

"Yeah, you've already seen my skill. Try to keep up meow." Karson launched himself over a rock and flipped around, blowing brains out from the man behind the rock. As Karson landed, he rolled back between the legs of another man and shot up through his taint out of his skull.

"Gross..." Mark muttered.

"That tends to be my job." As Karson stood, another man appeared from behind Mark. And just as Karson acquired his target and fired, Mark too fired, only his bullet went through Karson's arm. Karson fell backward and down. "OW!"

Mark raced over to Karson his gun drawn. Karson couldn't reach his fast enough as Mark fired the killing shot. Karson lay still. Blood and brain matter carpeted the rocks. Mark turned and walked a few steps to his bags. Picked them up, and faced the stairs where Ojore had presumably disappeared to.

Out of all the people and things Mark had seen, no one was a greater challenge or greater evil than that of Ojore. Even though Mark had done some evil, evil, evil things as a Special Forces commando, Ojore put all the kills Mark racked up to shame. Adolf Hitler, Elizabeth Bárthory, Talat Pasha, Saddam Hussein, Heinrich Himmler, Adolf Eichmann, Kim Il Sung, Emperor Hirohito, Genghis Khan, Leopold II of Belgium, Mao Zedong, Pol Pot, Joseph Stalin, all evil people put together; Ojore put them all to shame.

Mark noticed that one enemy was still alive, and moving, but Karson pounced on him at once. Karson grabbed his captured enemy harder, "Thanks, Mark, for saving me. Next time, wait 'til I move before you rain guts down on me okay?" He slapped his enemy and yelled, "WHERE IS OJORE?"

The man merely giggled as he started to drift off.

"Sir…" The Beret breathed nervously as Karson's eyes widened.

"Screw you," Karson said to Mark. "YOU SHOT ME IN THE ARM." The enemy shut his eyes. "Oh, no you don't!" Karson cut into the man's stomach. He wailed in pain, his eyes flying open, and his veins bursting.

"Where is he?" Karson twisted the blade inside the man. "Where does he think he can escape too?"

The man cried now. His hand pointed to the staircase at the far end of the cave. "He leave country!" The man gasped.

"Anymore of you people?"

He shook his head no.

"Where does he think he can go?"

"USA."

"Thanks. Nothing personal. You're just nothing but a waste of life." Karson stood up and executed the man, then turned to Mark, pointing the blade at his face. "I'd gut you too, but this wound saved my life. Next time aim better."

"Yes, sir." The Beret smiled, shaking Karson's good arm.

"Let's go." Karson moved towards the stairs and pulled a pair of gloves from his vest pocket. The gloves had sharp points on the gloves, allowing for extra grip like a cat's claws. "I got this idea from my name…"

"Sir, is this a good idea?" Mark asked, getting cold feet.

Karson didn't respond as he put the other glove on, looking over his shoulder. "Not at all. But we have to move up." They did just that.

What met them angered Karson beyond belief? His friend was unconscious and tied up, blood on a man, Ojore's secretary by the looks of him, revealed that there had to be more casualties in the team Victor was with, while Ojore merely looked at the two Americans. Chris was smiling at Karson. Karson new this was a trap, but the Beret didn't seem to realize this as he raised his gun.

Chris shot first, and Karson felt the heat of the bullet as it spiraled through Karson's ear, searing some of his skin, and buried itself through the Green Beret's eye socket and pushed out the back of his head, taking some skull and brain matter with it. The Soldier stiffened and hit the floor. Karson closed his eyes and took four deep breaths, thinking of a way out. *Mark.* Karson sighed. *Thank you for your service, brother.*

"Karson, don't try anything stupid. I'd love a reason to just kill you. You just saw what I did to your precious teammate. One of your many downfalls. You care too much about your men. You're of course going to drop your weapon."

Ojore merely chuckled as he turned on his heel and walked up another flight of stairs towards the roof.

"I found you, Ojore …" Karson called.

A moment past and Karson thought his bluff failed. Chris just looked at him with a stupid, cockeyed, dumbfounded look on his face. "You think you can taunt-"

"And how did you do dat?" The face of Satan himself had returned.

"I think you wanted me to find you. It was all pretty obvious. Russia. Notes. The sub. Elding… I know you worked together. Your U.S. plot is done."

Chris's eyes widened, now feeling left out. Ojore looked at Karson with

Is that pride I see, Mr. Ojore?

"What makes you tink you are right, boy?" He spat.

Pride because I'm a worthy adversary. "Your reaction, you basically just did. I got you both to admit it. More, I knew earlier. 'RE' in the letters. B T dubs… This little coward you have working for you, he's no warrior. He's just a puppy that wants to hump your leg."

Chris advanced. Ojore called him back. "You like Genesis of an idea. De reason I followed through wit dis mounted, strategized, attack on our world. You get sense, you tink of where it came from, which is history, you decide to make it better, and you act on it. Exquisite, son. Exquisite." He smiled. "I'll leave you two to it. Chris, I expect da SEAL to win. Don't let dat happen." He made his exit. Chis looked after him.

"So Chris, what made you betray our country, hmm? Woohoo? Hello?" Karson struck up a conversation with his former comrade as he slowly walked to the Captain to check his vitals. He had a pulse. *"Thank goodness, Vic; I was worried."* Karson thought as Chris said:

"Money. Freedom. We" he pointed at Karson, himself, and Victor, "were bound by 'petty rules of engagement.' I am free and rich now, as well as Ojore's third in command. You should've learned which man to follow Karson. You could have been allowed to live. This your new whore?"

"Well, I'll leave all that to you. I wouldn't be good at it. I've immersed myself in this. When you immerse yourself in one thing, you get pretty good at it. I guess that is why I'd call your life the life of crime. You've always been a less than upstanding citizen. And if being another man's slave floats your boat-" Karson knew Chris was quick to anger. He pointed the gun at Karson, but Karson screamed, "WAIT!" Chris's eyebrows widened. "Wait... Wouldn't you rather gut me like a fish instead? I mean seal... That is my specialty."

"I'm listening..."

"Come on... Old time's sake. American service men, one last time. You don't think I can beat you do you? By the way, you're second. I killed Hatyara."

"Oh, I won't have any problem beating you, then dissecting your boyfriend... The only thing you can beat is that dead Beret's cock..." Chris smiled and holstered his gun and pulled out his long knife. Chris kissed the blade and hissed, "I should thank you, by the way, for making this more assured that I kill you. You understand. Second in command, that is a big responsibility. Let's play, pussy cat." Chris lunged at Karson as Karson pulled out his utility knife barely in time to block the strike.

Karson blocked the enemy blade and slashed through Chris's lip to his teeth as Karson ducked away from the following blow.

"Man! WHAT THE-OW!" Chris realized how damaged his face really was.

"We've come a long way from when you were my subordinate. I'm the greatest SEAL ever to join the ranks... Don't you forget it. And for the few seconds you still have left in this world before I send you to The Maker, you won't!" Karson threw a book at Chris, causing him to duck, as Karson closed the distance, crouched low. Karson parried a close slash to his throat from Chris's blade. Chris screamed and cursed at the Sailor and kept trying to slash, but Karson blocked it as best he could. However, he missed one swipe and felt the knife scratch into his side.

"Ahh, you see... High ground always works. Besides... You're far smaller than I remember." Chris said.

"Yup. You got fat. And stupid." Karson saw it coming.

Chris's head lurched forward as a computer fell onto his head.

He whined, rubbing his bleeding skull.

Karson kicked the knife from Chris's hand. "High ground also makes you a target. What's the matter? You didn't expect not to get beat up as a military man, did you? Certainly, my leading you taught you something…" Karson saw his opening in the extremely low pain tolerance man. Chris slashed at Karson's throat, again and again, wilder and wilder, each too close for Karson's likeness, but he remained calm and positioned himself to strike with all the force of a tiger striking down his prey.

"Chris, you have about ten seconds to surrender before I end your life. You best take it."

"DIE, AMERICAN! DIE!" Chris shouted, also disarming Karson with a flick of his leg, ignoring Karson's warning and chance for life.

"Seven. Six. Five. Four." Karson counted down out loud. *You're still a human. I don't want to kill you, man… Please, just stop!*

"SHUT UP!" Chris pulled his pistol, aimed at Karson, who ducked down and swept feet out from under Chris, revealing his hands' hidden weapon, and slashed up to cut Chris's throat.

"Zero." Karson spun on his heel, flicking the blood from his 'paws' as he cut his close friend free with his regained knife.

A horrible gurgling sound came from the multiple gashes as blood squirted out all over the place. Karson looked back to see Chris's hand up at his throat, the realization of what had happened and the horror of his death now plastering on his face. He looked at Karson in shock.

"I warned you," Karson said, matter of factly waving the clawed gloves at Chris. "I did not want, nor need to kill you, bro."

Chris's final move on earth was to throw the knife. It hit Karson in his bad arm as he stood up. The shock of the blade made Karson stumble and hit the wall and bend over. He sighed as pain overtook his body for a second.

"Son of a bitch!" Karson mumbled, still not used to taking a hit. He looked at it, then decided to pull it out of his already damaged arm and stood straight up again. Karson slowly walked to Chris who was ebbing into wherever his Creator would send him. Karson kicked Chris in the face. "I gave you a chance, man. I gave you a chance."

Karson crouched down and looked into the eyes of the psychopath. Karson, as he was trained, stared into Chris's soul and watched as his life flashed before his eyes. *Judgement day.* He watched as Chris's eternal sentencing, either good or bad was decreed. Karson not knowing which, saw Chris's soul start to leave. The eyes of evil staring back at him stayed evil however, with no pity, sorrow, regret.... Karson watched as Chris died, Chris trying to insult the victorious Navy SEAL, as Karson heard a yell from his buddy drawing him back into the present. Karson ran to Victor who yelled, "GO GET OJORE, MORON! What are you doing?"

"Right, sir." Karson nodded vigorously, the thrill of the hunt back on.

"Karson!" Victor called after him. Karson poked his head around the corner.

"I have to go, Vic, what?" Karson was eager to get to it.

"Kill him quick. If he gets a hold of you, he'll kill you over and over and over again. It will be worse than anything you've ever experienced."

Gulp

****

CHAPTER 51 - Realigned

Karson turned tail and opened the door towards the roof climbing the double staircase. Running up the first flight, turning, and running up the second, and so on as he made his way up. Karson was far too focused to hear other footsteps descending onto his position and Karson ran into a SEAL who also wasn't expecting someone to appear as he turned down the next flight of stairs. Karson's reaction time was off from the pain in his arm and the focus on Ojore. The SEAL grabbed Karson and slammed him into the wall, pulling his pistol and putting it into Karson's stomach.

"Wait, wait! Please!" Karson stared into the man's eyes, his eyes and voice pleading. He swallowed hard.

The Sailor stopped, pulling away fast. "Brother."

"Aye, sir. Two down in that room; Captain Paul is tied up and alive. Help him. I'm still engaged."

He nodded raising his primary weapon to enter the room. Karson turned and took the stairs three at a time to make it up to the roof, hoping the enemy wasn't gone yet. Otherwise, this war was going to continue and more dead would pile up.

Karson could hear rotors of a helicopter and broke through the door. Ojore, watching the door, standing, saw the SEAL.

"Ah!" Ojore growled in pure demonic rage. "Kill him. Now! Or it will be your head I mount over my mantel!" He stepped into the chopper as a guard moved to the door, crouched, and started shooting at Karson.

Karson wasn't fazed; the man couldn't seem to hit his target from his shaky stance, the way the helicopter rocked, and the downwash from the blades-bullets whizzed past Karson's head, struck other parts of the roof, or hit the ground before Karson's feet. Karson was too honed in on his target, too focused on ending this war to care that if this enemy got a better grip on his weapon, or if Ojore used his side arm, Karson's life could end in a flash. Karson, still moving forward, launched his in air foot up as his other foot pushed off the ground still running, and grabbed his throwing knife from his boot and threw it into the man's eye as the chopper started to lift from the ground. Ojore grabbed for the gun as the man fell, nearly being pulled from the helicopter. Karson watched as his enemy started to escape and tore as hard as he could towards the fleeing devil. Time seemed to freeze as he pushed himself harder and faster. Karson could feel each beat of his heart, became aware of the heat and the sweat running down his brow, and could feel his boots gripping into the ground.

I'll never make the jump! I need more speed and less weight!

Karson started unhooking his vest pockets as he ran, finally throwing the last of his gear off of him as he kicked off the roof and glided through the air like a cat pouncing on a bird that had taken off. Karson had to trust his body to do the right things at the right moments. As he barreled through the air, his knees pulled up to his chest and his hands pulled back, ready to grip at the first touch of metal or flesh, like a serval springing for a bird in the air to prey on, Serval sprung to catch hold of his prey, the enemy bird!

Ojore's boot was half on and half off the edge of the helicopter, and he had finally wrestled the weapon from the injured, still conscious Death Nation soldier, dropping him, causing him to plummet to his death.

Suddenly, Karson felt Ojore's boot and dug his fingers and glove claws into it as he wobbled through the air. Bullets still were fired at Karson, but none hit him as he swung in and out of view too fast to become an easy target.

Still, this is a bad spot to be. One lucky shot and I'm toast.

They turned to fly out over the city, finally, Ojore running out of rounds. Instead, he threw the gun and started grabbing for Karson's fingers, which led Karson to launch himself up and grab onto the enemy wrist. Karson leaned back, and he and Ojore fell from the chopper onto the building that happened to be below. Karson and Ojore hit the ground hard, Ojore landing and crumpling to the ground, Karson hitting, landed too hard on his heels, crumpling and slamming his back into concrete. Karson had the wind gone from his body and had felt his ribs crack under his skin as a searing pain shot to his head through his spine. The pain receptors throughout his entire body were going off the charts. Karson's body couldn't take much more. Ojore laying on his face, rolled to the side, looking at Karson. First with fear and caution as a Navy SEAL in his complete and total prime was a 'Soldier' that couldn't be beaten. A warrior that any and all feared, even the most powerful military personnel in the world. However, seeing Karson writhing on the ground in pain had Ojore reaching his feet first and moving towards Karson like he was easy prey. Karson had nothing he could do.

Karson was in agonizing pain yet again as Ojore lifted Karson up by his hair, which had grown longer since his torture in Pakistan. Karson tried to fight, but Ojore blocked all Karson's puny attacks and punched Karson in the temple, after removing Karson's cracked helmet that had saved his brain from becoming mush in the fall. Karson was lifted over Ojore's head, and Ojore limped towards the edge of the building. Blood dripped onto him as Karson bled, and drifted in and out of consciousness.

Karson, knowing that all fighting was useless and that his life was about to end, tried pleading.

"Hey! I know you understand me. Wouldn't you rather fight me like a man, Ojore? Like a real man, rather than pushing me off of a building like a coward?"

"Your stupid insults don't bother me, American. I'm not like your American 'friend' Christopher. I have fought you Americans too long. I assume you are one of many, but I have you, so I will make you suffer."

He dropped Karson onto his knee, cracking Karson's back. He let out a groan of agony. Suddenly, he was lifted above Ojore's head again. And...

He fell, striking his head on the right side as he slipped past the first roof onto the next, knocked unconscious before he hit the roof ten feet lower.

Karson jolted awake as a loud sound rang in his ears.

What was that? Ow! What is this... it doesn't feel good... This pain! How'd it happen? Who is that? OW!

"You should have stayed asleep. Your next drop will make that happen."

I'm paralyzed on my left side.

"Where am I? Who are you? Put me down!" Karson's left side of his mouth wouldn't move.

Ojore started laughing. "Americans... Always sissy out when the time comes."

Karson started panicking at the fright. All of his thoughts were forming, but fuzzy.

American. I'm a SEAL. Ojore! Training. Fight.

Karson started squirming and wriggling. Ojore looked up, anger building. He was at the edge of the building. Karson shut his eyes tight.

Ojore growled, "I hate the United States. Rot six feet under you-"

BZZ

WISP

PELT

PFFT

Karson's eyes flew open as something whizzed past his head. Ojore dropped Karson as rounds barraged the rooftop they were on. Karson looked beside him to see the SEAL and Victor firing at the two men. They couldn't kill Ojore for risk of dropping Karson.

Ojore s chopper returned, providing a block. Ojore stood Karson up as he entered the helicopter. "Drag him along. I want to finish him myself!"

The pilot nodded as Karson tried to reach for the air vehicle. As he did, the chopper disappeared, and Karson nearly lost his balance over the edge of the building. He regained his balance and looked up as a shadow engulfed his body. Victor was yelling something, the SEAL from the hallway was shooting still.

Suddenly, Karson felt a force knock him forward over the edge of the roof as a tread hooked the back of Karson's vest, causing the vest to slide up and choke him. His real panic came through in waves again from his feet losing touch of the roof he was trying desperately to cling onto with his boots. Rooftop gave way to air. "NO! NO PLEASE! I'M GOING TO FALL!

Karson screamed desperately, still unable to maneuver one side of his body, when the most painful jolt of turbulence as the chopper turned towards the sea snapped his back into place, sending full mobility, still through vast waves of pain, throughout his body. He could feel more injuries sustained in the fall now that his spine was realigned, the pain with a clear shot to the body's control center. This warm feeling of something oozing inside of him. Not like a female after 'the money shot' but a painful stream in vital places, like his lungs, where he was sure a bone had pierced, and his belly, where something must have torn. Karson was bleeding internally, and air was becoming harder to gain as his vest was still choking him. He started thrashing around to get ahold of the chopper, gasping for breath, resorting to hoisting himself up by placing both hands on the vest under his throat so he could breathe, still hooked by the helicopter. His eyes throbbed as his heartbeat picked up and fluid wreathed around the muscle and flowed through his blood. His ears rang from the blades beating above and the sound as the wind pelted past him.

I have to keep fighting!

****

CHAPTER 52 - The Heart of the Sea - Slit

The helicopter dropped altitude substantially and quickly as the sea came into view. Flying a half a football field into the water, Ojore reached down and cut Karson from his vest dropping him in the water, forcing Karson to swim to shore where Ojore awaited.

"Ya know…" Ojore began as Karson paddled up and lay panting on the sand. "You have been a thorn in my side since I started dis war in Europe. Always killing my people, dat's my job by de way, and getting closer and closer to my plots every time. I mean, most of it was done by sheer number, but a couple of occasions I had operations you thwarted or tried to. De only one you didn't get to was Poland. I know you get de purposes… You have to kill a lot of people to make them realize der own government can't save dem and should submit to someone who will kill de non-followers and still condemn dee followers, while still giving chance to live. Even you have to see brilliance in that." Ojore landed a kick into Karson's side.

He groaned as the air left his body.

"When I speak, I want answer."

Karson nodded, panting harder.

"What should I do with you? I could kill you. Save me a lot of trouble. I mean, you're one young boy. And yet you cause me issues. It's because you're smart. Dat is why. Educated. Strategic. Someone I could have used. I have Hatyara, so der is no issue-"

"Had." Karson croaked, his breathing slowing.

"Excuse me?" Ojore growled at being interrupted.

"I killed Hatyara. Even he couldn't stop me." Karson looked up defiant. "Chris," Karson laughed. "Chris wa-Chris was simple."

"Oh I knew you'd kill Chris, I just had de hope you'd choke. Hatyara, dis is saddening. It makes my second option not option anymore. I was going to make you mine. Replace Chris. But now, I tink I'll hang you, torture you, sometink. I tought of hem as son." He walked up to Karson and sat beside him on the beach looking out at the setting sun engulfed by the vast expanse of liquid. "At least de view is bootiful!"

Karson rolled onto his back and looked up at the man, panting, squinting in the sunlight.

"Oh my God, what have you done to your precious teeth? Are dese for me? Dat is actually a not bad idea." Ojore grabbed Karson by the cheeks and lifted his lips like vets do to dogs, revealing sharpened canines and incisors. "You'd pack a punch with dose. I tink my whores would be quite hot with teeth like yours… Except I don't want to get scratched on my downstairs area, if you know what I mean!" He winked and slapped Karson aside.

He walked towards the ocean, unzipped his pants, and pissed away his discomfort. As he did, he gave one final statement. "Captain Kadin Karson 'Serval' Hunter of De United States Navy. You now have a choice. You are a Soldier of de sea; you may have your throat slit in de water, drowned and fed to sharks. Or I can behead you." He turned around and walked up to Karson grabbing his hair, staring down into the soul of the young American's eyes. "And then feed you to the sharks. I'm sure you've got someone back at home who cares for you... Gotta affect dem too. Hell, maybe I'll go and rape, plunder, and torture your family after dis. Too bad you won't be around to see it. Your decision."

"I-I don't want to die... Please. PLEASE!" Karson looked up into the devil's eyes, oddly enough that had yellow and red specks of fire in them.

"What did you say..." Ojore laughed.

"Please. Please don't kill me." Karson begged.

"Like de child you are. Anyways, your fate is decided. I can decide for you if you'd like? ONE."

I don't know...

*If I am slit, **keep reading the story.***

"TWO!" Ojore continued.

If I'm beheaded, skip to Chapter 52 – The Heart of the Sea – Beheading, a few pages further along on page 426.

"THREE."

"Okay. Okay..." Karson gasped as Ojore raised the knife. "Water. Please, I want to die in the water... It'll be like being held by my mother in the womb. Safe, warm. Protected. My ocean mother. Please... Please."

Ojore giggled. As queer as that sounds, it was very menacing as the man dragged the young SEAL to the waterfront, his last moments drawing near. "Captain. Any final words?"

Karson's mind drifted. He stared into the sea. "Baby... I wish I could have held you one more time. I wish I could have done better. Been better. Not disappointed mom and dad. Boyfriends and girlfriends. Teachers and leadership. I wish I'd have worked at the zoo, complete school. Gone to Hollywood. Traveled the world. Made love one more time, had a child. Learned more than just death. Not killed a man. I wish I'd have done drugs. Played sports. Slept longer. Drank more. Ate fancy.

Spent money. I wish I'd published the book I wrote; the song I sang. Made that social media platform. Supreme Leader, I wish we could have been friends, sir. Maybe we could have brought the world together, not torn her apart. You and I. We could be unstoppable. After all, I proved myself above your second-hand man. Against all your guys. The little boy from Texas. I hope you have everything you truly want on earth. And I hope you make it to heaven… We'll both see very soon who was right, religion wise. May I ask you something?"

"Oh my word dat was a horrendously long, annoying monologue, Hunter. But sure, ask your question. Not like I have an udder nation, correction, hemisphere slash continent to conquer."

"Hah! Udder. Anywho, um, was this worth it?" Karson asked, the strength of his warrior might returning.

"Wha-"

Karson lunged forward with the last of his might and kicked Ojore with all of his might deeper into the ocean and pounced, fighting for control of the sharp metal. Both men struggled for grip, Ojore being taller, found the bottom of the ocean and had an advantage, Karson wrapping his legs around the terrorist leader's waist, like a woman riding a cowboy.

"YEE HAW!" Karson shouted as he gained control of the weapon, slashing through Ojore's ear. Ojore knocked Karson loose and swam slowly to the shore. Karson was faster, gaining on the man, who shoved his boot into Karson's face, flattening his nose, sending blood into the water. *Bring on the sharks!* The man turned in Karson's stunned moment and removed the knife. Karson knew the moment was now. He lunged forward and sank his teeth into the man's throat, ripping through vital arteries and tendons, ripping out and spitting out the hunk of meat that was Ojore's Adam's apple.

However, with the good deed, he felt the full length of blade penetrate through his stomach, slicing through the arteries and veins in Karson's belly, a fatal blow. *Humph. I am mortal. And so are you!* Karson smiled at the man who grabbed at his throat in fear. Attempting to move, but falling on his back as Karson did too, letting the tide draw them both into the water. The pain, as intense as it was, the worst Karson had ever felt, ebbed as the sunlight filled his sensitive blue eyes and the water filled the wound, as if preparing him like an embalmer.

"You know Ojore…" Karson started. "It's a good thing you didn't make a run for it just now. You wouldn't have gotten that far. You see… I have four fangs in replacement of canines. They are covered in a venom packet." He spit green syrup into the water. "I had to ensure you were killed. And I've accomplished my mission." He sighed, looking up at the stars appearing in the dusk light. *Just like my childhood!*

Ojore grunted as he tried to speak. "YOU ACCOMPLISHED NOTHING!" He looked at Karson who looked back at the hoarse man. "De... pawns are in motion. This world is lost by-"

"Oh don't you ever shut up?" Karson looked back up. "I beat you. I know there is still work to do, but my job is done. I'm done. It's time to sleep. Sleep forever!" After a few moments of silence, just the soothing lullaby of the sea, Karson looked back over. "Am I a warrior? A lover? A forgiver? I'm all of those things. Except for you. I'm your worst nightmare, Ojore. I took you to the valley of death. I am your reaper!" Karson laughed looking back up. "Ojore? You dead old friend?" He looked back over one last time as the man exhaled his last breath, his body starting to sink. "Thank the universe! A moment of peace and relaxation!"

The stars are so beautiful. I wonder if we become the stars, watching over the universe... watching over our friends... I'm sorry Victor. I'm sorry baby. I'm sorry mom. I'm sorry dad. I'm sorry friends... I won't make it home for holiday. I've got a new mission assignment, and that's the journey to the next phase of existence. At least I know I'm held by the sea.

Karson drifted farther out into the water, his soul pumping through his wounds into the ocean, swallowed by a mother, replaced by Karson's beating heart.

Karson sighed as he started to fall asleep. *Hmmm. I've become the heart of the sea... The Heart of the Sea. That is a great promotion.*

Kadin Karson 'Serval' Hunter. The Heart of the Sea.

♥ ♥ ♥ ♥

EPILOGUE - Eulogy

Hello. My name is Admiral Vi-..." Victor looked out at the Sailors before him, locking eyes on the empty seat with his best friend's picture. Then down to the casket in front. His eyes rose to two civilians Victor never thought he'd have the privilege to meet, and one he had met before, a long time ago. In the front row. Karson's, as he put it, 'better half,' his mom-the only one to see her son graduate Navy boot camp-and his dad. Three people who truly had Karson in their hearts. His old high school class joined on the ship as well to see the American hero. Sending final goodbyes to someone they hadn't cared about and forgotten, the only man to put his life on the line, and achieve more than all of them put together.

However, all of the previously stated, with the looks on their faces and the fact they'd showed up, allowed instant forgiveness to Victor.

Karson wouldn't and didn't blame them, nor hate them for their opinions. He respected them no matter what. He respected his history no matter what. He was good like that. Wise like that. Just a good man.

Victor nodded to the only link to Karson left on earth. The people who flowed through him and had created him, his would have been parents-in-law, and the one person on the planet that had been connected to Karson in the most intimate of ways. The one that loved him no matter what, who protected him at home, gave him a reason to live. The person who gave their life to Karson. Who would live his legacy on! Victor looked back out over the crowd.

"Ehem." He wiped his tears. *Real men cry, Victor.* Karson's voice sang through his mind. "My name is Victor Paul. United States Navy. The United States Navy has been my family, my home, my life. But, even though I make my family with the Navy, I've never loved anyone more than I've loved our fallen comrade. Karson was… Karson is my best friend. I say 'is' because it is our duty to live on. Our obligation to live on Karson's legacy as well as our own. In my opinion, though I would have to say it is a fact, Karson was one of the greatest men to live and a pivotal part of the history of late. A crucial part of the United States Navy. He and I have been through thick and thin together. Survived battles in China and Africa. To hell and back in BUDs. I like to say he was my BUDs buddy!" Victor chuckled a little.

"Oh, thanks for the one laugh out there! Anyways, as I'm sure all of you who have served with Karson could say… I'm sorry, I can't help the tears…" He wiped his tears from his eyes. "As I'm sure all of you who have served with Karse could say, I thought he was invincible. And when I was with him, I too felt like I was invincible. Nothing ever seemed to hit him, or if it did, bullet, knife, blast, fist, whatever, it never seemed to wound him, or if it did, it was just a scratch. Same with me. Whenever I was with him, nothing seemed to go horribly wrong, except for some instances out of our control. Karson had this spark. He knew his stuff, man. He could shoot, fight, piss you off, but you knew he had your back. He was your friend, and he was true. And he was the best SEAL ever… I know you're not supposed to 'out' that someone was a SEAL but he deserves to be recognized. I don't see how he is gone. He was a superhero, man! Of all the things that bastard had gone through. Explosions on the side of a mountain knocking people to their deaths, taking bullet after bullet either into his body or aimed at his body, enduring my stubborness, a helicopter crash or two, casualties of war, lost loved ones, knife slashes, broken bones, PTSD, visual horror, torture, the list goes on. I don't know what I'm trying to do up here… I guess I'm hoping you'll pop out of that casket Karson. Without you, this world will inevitably be lost. We've already lost. There's no possible way we can get through this. Everybody is abandoning. Heading back to their families. Most of the world is dying off at this rate. One hundred and fifty billion people have walked the earth. Ten billion were alive last year. Its estimated to be less than a billion left. Earth's last great extinction. We're turning into an endangered species. You said this world was beautiful Karse, even in the horrors. But I don't see it…" Victor sighed.

Wow. That was atrocious, Vic! Victor looked out to the sea.

"We need you bad, Karson. Bad!   Corrupted officials, horrible leadership, terrible men and woman who fight in the military ranks. These are destroying our world, bro. The resolve of American power and pride, our morals; they are broken. The United States was supposed to be a beacon of hope. Freedom. Prosperity. An extremist ideology tested these principals, the worst creation and history has ever seen, and we, America, rose to meet the challenge. But now we lay broken at our enemys' feet, or dead in your case. But I digress I guess. Karson, you were and are my best friend. You always had this faith about you that you had something to look forward too after the life you lived. So, if it is true, then Karse, I'll see you on the other side! I'll miss you, man! I love you! For now, I'll take comfort in the fact you watch over us all… Your heart was the sea, and now you are it. The Heart of the Sea…"

-Admiral Victor Paul, out.

FINAL TRANSMISSION OF ADMIRAL VICTOR PAUL… UNITED STATES NAVY 1757 2 May 2037.

Victor stood straight and saluted the casket, as the SEALs in the crowd punched their SEAL Tridents into Karson's casket. Victor was last, stepping up to the body of his friend, the emotion taking over him as he slowly pushed his trident into the glossed wood covering his deceased friend. The wind picked up.

I'm still with you

He jolted in the jeep he was driving as he was punched back into reality, ending his daydream of standing in front of a company of people. He looked around the car, but no one was in the vehicle with him. He looked up at the sky and a tear rolled down his cheek. *I wish it were in the flesh, Karse…* He shut off the speech he'd recorded and took the archives of the audio/visual files of every SEAL and headed, armed, for the west from Texas where settlements were being established. Tribes. The world, the Nation, indeed had been defeated by the pawns set in place by the barbaric ideology of the devil Ojore who had begun Death Nation.

One day, someone will find these and remember what we did here. What Karson did in this world. They will know. Maybe we'll be free someday. After all, Death Nation did die with Ojore. If not, whatever. I'm tired. Tired of fighting. Tired of running. I'm ready to sleep. A long, deep, peaceful and pleasurable sleep!

****

CHAPTER 52 - The Heart of the Sea - Beheading

"Okay. Okay…" Karson gasped as Ojore raised the knife. "Just take my head."

"With pleasure!" The man placed the knife to Karson's throat. Karson flinched at the cold.

"Too bad you'll die with no one to witness it… I'm sure de world would have loved to see der last hope die, a cruel and painful death!" He tensed to slice through, but Karson channeled his last warrior might. He grabbed the knife, turned his head into the blade, sent an elbow behind into the balls of his enemy, spun through and flipped the man to the ground. He threw the knife into the water and sprinted up the rocky outcropping. Ojore, standing, gave chase.

"You are all typical Americans. All talk, but when it hits de fan, you all bug out!" He was gaining. "Iraq." His breath stinking down Karson's neck. "Vietnam." He grabbed Karson's belt and threw him back. "Dis moment. You run."

Karson swept his legs up and up, flipping himself back onto his feet. "I wasn't running. I was pulling you into my ring." Karson assumed his fighting stance.

Ojore smiled. "You want a dance, little boy? I'll give you one." The man lunged forward, his superior strength barraging Karson's body as he dodged, slipping on the rocks.

You never said this would be easy. Karson found his moment every once in a while to break a rib or two, but Karson's strength was ebbing as the man continued to tower above. With his strength ebbing away, he fell to his knees. Ojore stopped for breath.

"I don't have my knife anymore, so it looks like you'll be thrown over de edge." He grabbed Karson's shirt and dragged him up the rest of the way to the ledge, looking down at the happiness he'd soon see. He turned his face back to Karson, who slammed a rock into Ojore's temple, shattering his skull.

"Die, man! SERIOUSLY!" Didn't account for that grip on his shirt. Karson plummeted below to the rocks, landing on top of Ojore, still breaking more and more bones in his body. *Did someone shout my name?* Ojore stared up at Karson, who was definitely internally bleeding now. *I have to be sure.* He straddled the unconscious man. He held his head down in the water, his hands on Ojore's throat, and ensured the man wouldn't take another breath, crushing his throat with the rock as overkill. "Say hi to The Maker for me."

"KARSON?" Karson's head snapped up the rocks as he rolled onto his back. "HANG ON BUDDY! WE'RE COMING DOWN." Soon, a rope was lowered on top of Karson who sighed at the completion of his career. *I'm going to die, but I'm done with the Navy.*

Victor landed beside Karson as a fast boat drifted up to the shoreline. "Hey, buddy."

Karson's eyes started to close.

"Oh no you don't. You don't get to do that, Karse..." Victor cradled Karson's head and body and gently tapped Karson's face.

"Victor, tell them for me, will you... Tell them I love them."

"You get to tell them yourself, Karson."

"I'm scared, Vic..."

"You don't need to be. I'm right here. HURRY UP WITH THAT STRETCHER!"

"I love you, Victor." Karson's lifted his hand to rub Victor's face. "I love yo-" He drifted off to darkness.

"Karson, you need to stay awake. KARSON!" Victor helped lay Karson in the fast boat and sat with him as the boat took off for any Navy vessel. The medic began work on Karson, Victor watched every move, not leaving Karson's side the entire ride.

ZZZZ

EPILOGUE - Home

The smells of America. One you can't really smell; no two places are completely different. We are all one world, after all there is only one race and that is the human race. We eat, sleep, relieve ourselves, reproduce, breath the same air, drink the same water. Some are just luckier than others. But the smell of home wafted in my nose as I cleared customs.

"Here you are, sir. Welcome home. And thank you for your service."

I forgot I was wearing my dress uniform. "Oh, of course! Don't mention it! Thank you for yours, sir!"

Welcome home. Boy did that feel good. Turns out, being in a coma on a hospital ship for a month isn't something that sits well with you when you wake up. All that wasted time to recover.

I remember stepping off the ship... Nah. I sprinted off the ship. I love my service, my history, but now it's time to go. I'm done with the Navy. Once a SEAL always a SEAL, but I never want to fight again. At last, though, I'm free again. Free at last. To be who I want. To go and be where I want. To be with whom I want. And there they are. My family. The most intimate, beautiful love of my life. The people who raised me, who, oddly enough, are still the loves of my life. And my friends. The other loves of my life.

Hello. My name is Kadin Karson 'Serval' Hunter. United States Navy. Well, almost **former** United States Navy SEAL Team Six Commander... Captain, sorry. I survived an... apocalypse, per say. Much of the world's population has been killed off, but unlike other nations, the United States cannot be defeated. Even with corrupted officials, horrible leadership, terrible men and woman who fight in the military ranks, the principals, morals, and resolve of American power and pride cannot and will not ever be overtaken or overshadowed by what the world has to throw at it. The United States remained a beacon of hope. Freedom. Prosperity. These principals were tested by an extremist ideology, the worst mankind and history have ever seen. But we, America rose to meet the challenge. I will admit. We have still lost. But it's a victorious loss none the less.

People, my friends may wonder why I'm leaving this place... This, home that I defended so desperately. Why I would run away before we could rebuild. It's simple. Well, maybe not. But... It's because I've felt a calling. A calling to move. More like a love. I fell in love, and it's time for me to follow that love. It's time for me to think of myself, rather than what others think of me or need. It's time I put myself first. Ya know, look out for number one. Well, now there are two number ones. Me and my 'friend.' We make a beautiful couple, I must say. Like, seriously, we are hot. Smokin'! Yeah. I just wanted to clear that up. I'm not leaving because I'm a coward. Maybe I'm moving on because it hurts too much to stay here. Bringing back memories of my abusive childhood, my days in school, and the love that I've seemed to have forgotten from that time... That blow I took fighting Ojore was one that caused the most damage... One that I'm setting out to repair. To remember. To be free again.

Something that is stained to me, and is brought up every time I see our flag, is the memories of my brothers and sisters, the ones who fought and died for fifty stars and thirteen bars, as well as the world as a whole… their deaths. That's what hurts the most. Maybe I feel like down under, I can feel free from their loss. I'll remember from time to time, I'm sure, and as I am now, I will cry… But I am not leaving because I'm afraid. I'm going to start over. A new life. With someone I love, and someone who loves me, and someone who will keep me safe and sane, and someone I can keep safe and sane. Yeah… From the beginning, I knew I was special… And now I get to prove it! Again! Who knows where my life will go. Maybe I'll come back. We'll see!

LAST TRANSMISSION OF UNITED STATES NAVY SEAL: KADIN KARSON 'SERVAL' HUNTER… 1757 HOURS… 2 MAY 2037.

Karson Hunter. Out.

****

www.ingramcontent.com/pod-product-compliance
Lightning Source LLC
Chambersburg PA
CBHW030333120726
47901CB00007B/1779